A MOTHER'S NIGHTMARE

Melanie awoke with a start. She reached over and turned on the bedside lamp and blinked in the sudden light. Her pajama top was soaked with sweat and her hair hung in wet strings. She got up and went to check on Polly, then went into the baby's room.

She brought the blanket up over her shoulder and turned her onto her side. The child did not respond to being moved and Melanie thought that peculiar. She turned the baby onto her back and felt for a fever, but the child was cool, almost cold. She lifted the baby in her arms anxiously. "Baby?" She rocked the child. "Denise?" With dread, the rocking became more vigorous, more frantic.

As terror overwhelmed her, she ran to the kitchen and laid the baby on the table. She pressed her open lips to the tiny mouth and forced air into the immature lungs. No response. She rushed back to the child's room, laid her on her stomach in the crib, and pounded her bottom. Whining through her tears, she pleaded, "Please cry. Oh, God! Why don't you cry?" She slapped the baby, again and again, and pinched her with all her might. Finally, she raised her high in the air and shook her hysterically, as if she were a flimsy rag doll.

Then she called the police emergency number. "Help me," she whimpered into the phone. "Help me," she wept hopelessly. "My baby's dead."

BLOCKBUSTER FICTION FROM PINNACLE BOOKS!

SHATTERED LULLABIES

MORTON REED

ZEBRA BOOKS
KENSINGTON PUBLISHING CORP.

To Elliot Slutzky
for having the first faith

PINNACLE BOOKS

are published by

Windsor Publishing Corp.
475 Park Avenue South
New York, NY 10016

First printing: June, 1989

Printed in the United States of America

PART ONE

ONE

By the time Melanie Wyatt got home from work it was six P.M., and though it was a bright, sunny California afternoon, she felt as if it were midnight. A whole day in the office, the incessant, never-ending phone calls, the mountains of technical typing that replenished themselves as if by spontaneous regeneration, the pressure to get through more work than was humanly possible in any one given day, symptomatic of an insurance claims office, was bad enough. But fighting the Monday evening traffic, when San Fernando metamorphosed from a flat, slow, hot village to a belching, burping network of auto-clogged arteries and veins, was a chore akin to waging war. And, her damned Pinto was acting up again, stalling in the midst of traffic half a dozen times, so that she felt like an idiot driver and was insufferably late getting home.

Chris had taken the Pontiac when he left and had bequeathed her the Pinto, and she sure as hell knew why. Frankly, she would have done the same to him had she had the opportunity. But he had always been the smart one with the cars and she had just taken his word for it when he told her that the little Ford was a gem that would never let her down. Well, it seemed like the mechanical monster never let her up, what with being in the garage every two weeks and the cost of repairs being such a horrendous drain on her cash flow.

Damn him, she thought. He robbed me every day we were married and he ripped me off the day he left. True to form. Damn him.

She pulled into her narrow driveway and stopped some distance from the garage. She glanced up at the outside of her house, at the chipped, peeling, yellowing siding that had once been stark white, at the shabby, greying overhanging shingle roof, at the sadly discolored front door that cried out for a sanding and a coat of varnish, and, as usual, Melanie felt that old urge to cry. But she did not cry anymore. She had gotten over that wasteful habit some time ago. Still, the urge came upon her every once in a while, especially when she was overly tired, near exhaustion, like now.

The house could have been so beautiful, she thought again, if only they had put something into it. She wondered if by *something* she meant money or love or what. She did know that the house was in such disrepair that it stood out as an eyesore in this well-manicured middle-class neighborhood and embarrassed her neighbors, though they would never be so cruel and insensitive to say so to her face. And, it had been such a beauty once, really promising, much like a dream come true for a young bride.

"Oh, please, Chris," she had begged, looking up at him with her dancing childlike eyes. "We can do it. I know we can do it."

They were sitting in the front seat of his old Chevy, he facing front and she turned to him, her knees on the seat. They had stopped on this very spot in the driveway alongside the bright crimson "for sale" sign half buried in the overgrown, densely weeded lawn, gazing at the house

8

through the windshield like two children with their faces pressed to the window of a doughnut shop.

"It's awfully expensive," he complained.

"I'll get a better job," she promised excitedly, her eyes flashing with the thought of it. "I'll bring home more. I know we can do it."

"What about the down payment?"

She pouted coyly. "We could borrow from your dad."

"No." He was adamant.

"He'd loan it to us. I know he would. I just know it."

"No."

"It'll be such a perfect home for us, Chris. We'll have our children here, raise our family here. There's a school just three blocks away. It's so perfect. It couldn't be more perfect."

He started to soften. "How would we pay him back?"

"Oh," she squealed. "Oh, Chris. Thank you. Thank you." She jumped up and down on the seat and almost bumped her head on the roof. She would give anything to have that house, that wonderful little house with the flower garden in front and the red brick walkway leading to the short columned porch and the shingle roof and the Tudor-style windows with all those little panes of glass sparkling like diamonds in the slanted sunlight. She threw her arms around his neck and kissed him long and hard. And, at that moment, it did not matter that he failed to kiss her back. That was just his way.

"I didn't say for sure," he said and pushed her slightly to the side, easing her out of her elation. He must have felt sorry for her then because he suddenly smiled and said, "I'll talk to my dad."

Melanie climbed out of the Pinto, wincing as the door hinges squeaked loudly, convinced the sound could be heard all over the neighborhood. She waved to Mark Lowell, the

9

sour old man who was her next-door neighbor and who pushed a dilapidated lawn mower over his front grass nearly every day at this time.

The smells that greeted her once she was inside started her mouth watering immediately. She identified a chicken roasting in the oven with whole potatoes and carrots—her absolute favorite—and heavy creamed spinach on the side. What an educated nose. She laughed to herself as she remembered preparing the chicken before going to work and telling Gladys when to shove it into the oven, seeing, in her mind's eye, the frozen spinach waiting to be microwaved.

She dumped her purse on the semi-circular walnut hall table, which wobbled on that one short leg Chris had promised to repair every day for at least six years, and glanced at her reflection in the oval antiqued mirror hanging on the wall over it. She quickly inspected herself—the prominent cheekbones, the deep-set brown eyes, almost black in their intensity, the full, sensual lips, the delicate face of fragile grace framed by waves of darkly glistening hair—and thought she was doing pretty well if she could look this good while feeling this bad, then lifted the short stack of mail from the table and went into the kitchen.

"Hi, Mom," Polly said, looking up from the kitchen table where she was grappling with a join-the-numbers picture puzzle. Tall and slender, large for her age, and already revealing the genesis of a beauty to match her mother's, the child brushed a strand of long blond hair back from her innocent blue eyes and smiled cheerfully at Melanie.

"Hi, sweetie," Melanie said. "Hello, Gladys." She nodded to the olive-skinned woman at the sink who had her hands buried in soap suds.

"Hello, Senora," she spoke, twisting her head over her shoulder. "Senor Joe, he call."

"When?" she asked absently.

10

"Fi' minutes, Senora." She held up five wet, soapy fingers.

"The baby cried," Polly said without raising her eyes from her puzzle.

"Oh, yeah?" Melanie turned to Gladys. "What happened?"

The woman shrugged. "Wet. Dirty."

"The baby cries all the time." Polly said matter-of-factly, seeming to be intensely concentrating on her work.

"That's not true," Melanie said. She leaned over and touched Polly's hair affectionately. "She cries when she's uncomfortable, honey. She can't talk like we do. So she cries when she wants to tell us something."

Polly thought for a long moment. "She must want to tell us something all the time." She nodded knowingly.

Melanie gazed at Polly, searching for some hidden meaning in her insistence but finding none. The little girl, the tip of her tongue protruding from the side of her mouth, was engrossed in drawing a straight line.

She dropped the unopened mail on the table. "Bills. I don't know why I check the mail. Nobody ever writes to me." She straightened up. "I'm going to check on Denise."

"Get ready," Polly said without looking up from her puzzle.

"For what?"

"She'll cry the minute you walk in there."

Melanie threw her an exasperated look and headed for the little bedroom off the hall where the baby slept. She peeked over the edge of the crib's headboard and watched little Denise kicking her tiny feet in the air and cooing to herself in her own special language.

"Hello, baby," she said softly. She gazed down at her child and smiled warmly. To hell with the house, she thought. To hell with Chris, too. The kids made it all worthwhile. She

11

reached both hands into the crib and lifted the baby out and laid her on her shoulder.

"How are you this evening?" she asked, walking about the room and patting the infant's diapered bottom. She held her up and the child laughed. "Are you glad to see me? Of course, you are. You're glad to see your mommy. Of course, you are." She buried her face in the baby's neck and kissed her loudly, wetly, and the baby giggled. Nothing was better than her two children, she told herself. Even the ten bad years with Chris, miserable as they were, could not change that.

She wanted to have dinner with Polly, but when she had finished setting the kitchen table and started to put out the food, she remembered the message from Joe. She excused herself and went to the phone.

"Melanie? How you doing?" He sounded truly happy to hear from her.

"Fine, Joe," Melanie said. "How are you?"

"I just got back from Denver."

"Oh?" She had not known he had been gone.

"You didn't miss me," he scolded. "It's been two weeks, Melanie. Didn't you wonder where I was?"

She felt badly. "I'm sorry, Joe."

Joe laughed. "First you won't marry me. Then you don't even know I'm gone. My stock must be going down on your exchange."

"That's not so," she said. "It's just that I've been so busy. I don't know where the time flies."

"Well, you should unbusy yourself a little. All work and no play. You know how that goes."

Perhaps that was why she had not missed him, she thought. He lectured so damn much. She had always liked Joe Hennessy, but she had to admit there was a little bit of the pompous ass about him.

12

"You're probably right," she said.

"How are the kids?"

"Good, thanks."

"The job's okay?"

"Absolutely."

"Well, then. How about a pizza tonight?"

Melanie hesitated. "Oh. Can't tonight, Joe. I promised Polly I'd have dinner with her and I don't like to break my word."

"Just tell her you're going out with Uncle Joe. She'll understand."

"No, she won't. She may agree, but she won't understand."

"You're right," he said apologetically. "I'm sorry. Look, have dinner with her and come out with me for a drink after."

"I can't leave them alone, Joe."

"Get the girl to stay," he whined.

"She's been here all day. She wants to go home, too."

"For an hour," he said. "What's another hour. One drink. Come on. Melanie. I need to see you. And you need to get out as much as I do."

She relented. "All right. I'll ask Gladys to stay, but you'll have to take her home."

"It's a deal," Joe said happily. "I'll see you at eight. Okay?"

"Okay," she said with some misgiving, although she did look forward to the attention he would spill over her. "Goodbye."

"Good-bye, honey."

With a new lightness in her step, she went back to the kitchen table. She was feeling quite good about Joe and looking forward to spending some time with him.

She had dinner with Polly and told her funny stories about

her day, just like she did whenever they dined together. After dinner, she let Polly hang out in her bedroom while she showered and dressed in a pair of tight black slacks and the bright red turtleneck sweater Joe had bought her on her last birthday. It was the casual outfit she liked the most because of how it flattered her figure, accentuating her breasts, pulling tight around her small behind, lying flat against her stomach so that no one could tell she had gone through two difficult pregnancies and deliveries.

While Polly lay on her stomach, stretched across her mother's bed, they pretended they were sisters and asked each other's advice about how to dress and how to behave on a date and when to come home. When Joe came for her she took Polly in her arms and kissed her and hugged her just as though she were a grown-up, and not an eight-year-old girl. The baby was fast asleep when she left so she did not disturb her.

They went to the Queen's Arms on Ventura and sat in a tight booth in the back of the quietly dark bar, where serious after-work drinking was done. Joe ordered a couple of martinis.

"No, no," she corrected. The waitress turned back. "One martini," Melanie said. "And one small glass of white wine." She smiled at Joe. "I'm going home perfectly in control."

Joe laughed. "You think I'd take advantage of you?"

"Yes." She smiled warmly.

"You're right. But I'd do it with class."

"I know." She put her hand over his and he entwined their fingers together. "I did miss you," she said.

He grew serious. "I tried to forget you. I left without saying good-bye and I hoped I wouldn't think of you. But, of course, that was a total failure. I kicked myself for not saying good-bye and I thought of you constantly."

"That's nice to hear."

"It's true. I was miserable all the time without you."

"Good!" she said, pretending petulance. "If you suffered, you won't do it that way again."

"If you really cared about my suffering, you'd marry me."

"Uh, uh." She wagged a finger at him. "You promised. I'm not bringing a man into my house until Polly can deal with it, and you know it. That's the deal. And, you've already agreed."

"Okay. Okay." He put his hands up in surrender and they settled down to enjoy the drinks the waitress set on the table before them. He did not mention marriage again and they spent the next hour together telling each other bits of workplace gossip and laughing at their outrageousness.

Melanie was home at nine-thirty. She bundled Gladys into Joe's car and waved them off. Polly listened to her mother lock up the house and then called her when she walked past her bedroom.

She went in and sat on the edge of the bed. Polly's little face, embedded in the big pillow, was framed by her long, flowing blond hair. Her eyes were half closed and she spoke softly and slowly, as if almost asleep.

"Good time, Mommy?"

"Yes, dear." Melanie leaned over and kissed her forehead.

"Uncle Joe?"

"Yes, with Uncle Joe."

"That's good."

Melanie smiled as the little girl's eyes closed. She pulled the covers up under her tiny chin and tucked her in warmly, then kissed her again and left the room.

A night lamp, shaded by a Donald Duck parade, burned in the corner of the baby's room, throwing odd, silly shadows on all the walls. In the crib, the infant slept on her stomach

15

with her face on the side, pressed into a lopsided little ball. She lay so still that Melanie became afraid for an instant.

She reached down and turned the small, warm body so that it faced upward, and she watched the tiny life yawn, smack her lips, then grimace as little rubber faces often do. The baby stretched her pudgy arms above her head and flexed the immaculate fingers, jerked once or twice, and pulled her hands back under her chin. Melanie was amazed at how overwhelmed with love she could become just watching her new child sleep.

She was out of her clothes and into her pajamas long before Joe called to say good night and tell her that he had gotten Gladys home safely. He whispered some very suggestive ideas to her, and when she was feeling sexy and half wishing she had let him talk her into something more exciting, he threw her a noisy kiss and hung up. She turned out her bedside lamp, rolled over onto her side, and pulled her knees up to her chest. She grabbed a pillow and hugged it tightly, in a sort of adolescent pretense, but in no way could she successfully imagine it as something other than what it was. And, soon, she was asleep.

She was not clutching a pillow. She was clutching a halter, leather straps stretched over her shoulders and attached to the line of covered wagons behind her. Across her chest, the wooden bar she held onto with both hands cut into her breasts and pressed her nipples flat.

Behind her, the wagon master cracked his whip and shouted for her to get going. She heard him moving up and down the line of wagons, apologizing for her weakness. He was telling the pilgrims that he had bought an expensive beast to pull the train but had been cheated when she turned out to be lazy and weak and obstinate.

"I'll never get this beast to pull her load," he shouted.

16

"She needs to be prodded. Who's going to come up here and beat on her?"

"I will," a familiar voice said.

She turned her head and looked back to see Joe climbing down from one of the wagons and heading toward her with a big, thick black switch in his hand. She shuddered in anticipation of the cutting edge of that whip.

"You going to move before this here man lays into you?" the wagon master demanded of her.

She wanted to tell him that there was a river directly in front of them and that she could not swim and that they would have to float across if they wanted to get across at all. But she was unable to speak. She opened her mouth but no sound came out except for a low, sad whimper.

First she heard, then felt, the crack of the lash and she stepped forward in a sort of reflex motion. She strained against the bar and pushed at it with her hands and her body. She heard the crack of the whip again and saw the river drawing nearer. She moved more quickly now, to avoid the touch of the lash. She ran toward the river. The wagon train became less of a burden; it became lighter and she knew it was flying along behind her.

Now she could not stop. There was the river right up ahead and she could not stop running toward it. She dug her heels into the ground but her momentum was too great. She plunged over the bank and into the boiling rapids.

Twirling end over end, she gasped for air, sucking great mouthfuls when she popped up above the surface and compressing them in her lungs when the bubbling water swirled over her. She went under once, twice, and then about ready for the third dive, she thrashed about wildly and reached for the smiling faces of the spectators watching her die.

Joe was there, cracking his whip high in the air and whooping with laughter. Mark Lowell was there, wearing a farmer's hat and Bermuda shorts. And the wagon master was directing her to go under, motioning with his hands for her to sink beneath the turmoil. He was her husband Chris, wishing her gone, willing her gone, and she drifted below the surface.

She awoke with a start and sat up quickly. She reached over and turned on the bedside lamp and blinked in the sudden light. Her pajama top was soaked with sweat and her hair hung in wet strings. Bad wine, she thought, running her tongue along the roof of her mouth and discovering an unpleasant aftertaste.

She got up and went to the bathroom to examine herself in the mirror. Other than being sweaty, she thought she looked pretty good, considering that her watch told her it was three o'clock in the morning.

She checked on Polly, something she always did whenever she awoke in the middle of the night, and rearranged the blankets under her chin again. Polly turned on her side and curled up like a ball.

She did the same for the baby, bringing the blanket up over her shoulder, flattening it out, and turning her onto her side. The child did not respond to being moved and Melanie thought that peculiar.

"Don't get sick on me now, baby," she whispered. "I can't afford to lose another day at work."

She turned the baby onto her back and felt for a fever, but the child, if anything, was cool, almost cold.

"Come on, baby," she said, lifting the child in her arms anxiously and rocking her, refusing to admit that she felt no response. "Baby?" She rocked a little harder, a little more rapidly. "Denise?" With dread, the rocking became more vigorous, furious, frantic. Where were those ugly grimaces? Let me see them! she begged silently. Where were those irregular reflexes? The perfect little fingers stretching in im-

18

perfect gestures? Show them to me! Do it! her mind screamed the demands.

As terror overwhelmed her, she pressed the little face to her cheek as if she could breathe for it. "Oh, my God!" she cried out. "Help me. Oh, God. Help me."

She ran to the kitchen and laid the baby on the table. She pressed her open lips to the tiny mouth and forced air into the immature lungs. No response. She rushed back to the child's room, laid her on her stomach in the crib, and pounded on her bottom. "Cry, baby!" she shouted, she ordered. Whining through her tears, she pleaded, "Please, cry. Oh, God! Why don't you cry?" She slapped the baby, again and again, and pinched her with all her might, twisting the flesh between her clawed fingers, raising welts on the delicate porcelain skin. Finally, she raised her high in the air and shook her hysterically, as if she were a flimsy rag doll, the small, silent, still head bouncing forward and back as if only loosely connected to the slender neck.

A short time later, she called the police emergency number.

"Emergency," a gruff male voice answered.

"Help me," she whimpered.

"Hello!" the voice said. "Hello. Speak up. I can't hear you."

"Help me," she moaned hopelessly.

"Lady," the policeman demanded, "where are you? Give me your address, please."

"Help me," she wept. "My baby's dead."

TWO

Phyllis Morley came over immediately and brought a suitcase filled with clothing along with her. She intended to camp at the Wyatt home for as long as Melanie needed her, and she was wise enough to realize that that could be some time.

Melanie, who had been heavily sedated by Dr. Miller, Polly and Denise's pediatrician—the only physician they could think of to call for her—was devastated and in deep shock. She was certainly unable to care for herself, much less another person, and someone had to keep the household functioning. Phyllis elected herself to that job, and it was a good thing, too; she happened to be the best person around for it.

The two had met in high school at the same time that Phyllis's father had died in the Goodbody factory fire—the only casualty of that fire and one of the few unskilled laborers the plant employed. Unfortunately for Phyllis's mother, the testimony of his fellow workers indicated that Jake Morley had been drunk at work that day and was probably unable to save himself when the alarm sounded. There was even some talk that Jake had started the fire himself, either

20

out of negligence or malice or both. Consequently, the insurance company adopted a dim view of rewarding his widow and her four children, of which Phyllis was the eldest, and denied the family's claim for compensation. One tough young lawyer for the insurance company even suggested the plant might sue Jake's estate for damages. As ludicrous as that suggestion sounded, it had the effect of convincing Jenny Morley that well enough was best left alone.

What Jenny did instead was to pick up where Jake had left off, and she continued his tradition of near-constant inebriation. With the aid of state food stamps and some monthly welfare cash, the family managed to survive without breaking up, albeit, just barely. However, one element of their life style did change radically. Whereas Jake had managed to fix the blame for their miserable existence squarely on Jenny and her ineptitude as a mother and wife, Jenny, on the other hand, was determined to put the blame precisely where she had always known it belonged—on her children . . . and, in particular, right on Phyllis who was, after all, the oldest, the firstborn, and the one who had surely started it all.

Phyllis objected to this new responsibility but that got her nowhere, other than being cuffed on the side of her head. The more she protested her innocence, the more Jenny pointed to her protestations as additional examples of how the child made her mother's life miserable. And, there were plenty of those examples, since everything that happened that displeased Jenny was attributed to the girl, no matter what it was or who was responsible.

At first, Phyllis convinced herself that she could live with the unreasonable state of persecution. After all, she told herself constantly, hearing that singsong rhythm in the back of her mind, sticks and stones will break my bones, but names will never harm me. But it was not very long before Jenny gave up being verbally abusive and started being physically offensive. In the beginning, she would only strike out at the girl when she was hopelessly drunk, but it was not long before it ceased to matter, drunk or sober, day or night. There was no time when Phyllis was safe from her mother and there were no adequate places to hide. That broomstick would find her back, her shoulders, the backs of her legs, even her head, at the strangest and least expected times.

Melanie was not the first girl at school to notice the dark, rude bruises that covered so much of Phyllis's body.

"Oooh," Glynnis McElwain had cooed after gym class one day. "Look at the marks." She stood under the shower, water pouring over her face like a fall, and pointed at Phyllis's back, where huge black and blue blemishes spread like a flattened-out map of the world.

"What happened to you?" Trudy Nelson piped and kind of shaded her eyes, as if the sight were too repulsive.

Phyllis turned under the water, her wet, dark hair clinging to her face. Ashamed and humiliated, she pressed her back up against the tiled wall. "Nothing," she said. "I fell down."

"You must've fallen off a mountain," Marcia Green said, looking around at the other girls and snickering.

Phyllis cringed as the girls filling the school shower joined in the laughter. She seemed to shrink into herself and crouched down, as if wishing to grow small and disappear.

"That happened to me once," Melanie Cunningham, on the very end of the long line of showerheads, spoke up. "The exact same thing. Had the same bruises and all."

The focus of attention turned immediately to Melanie. "Yeah?" Trudy queried. "What happened to you?"

Marcia Green giggled cynically. "Same mountain?"

"Fell off a race horse," Melanie said haughtily. She glanced around at the gaping mouths. "Since then, of course, I won't ride an untrained animal."

She shut off her showerhead and strode arrogantly into the locker room, leaving everyone staring after her, silent and wondering.

Walking home from school, Phyllis caught up with her. "Mind if I walk with you?" she asked awkwardly.

"No," Melanie said with a shrug of indifference.

"I wanted to thank you," Phyllis said, once again feeling awkward.

"What for?"

Phyllis smiled at Melanie's show of surprise. "Getting them off my back."

"Did I do that?"

"It was nice of you," Phyllis said with some difficulty. It was not easy for Phyllis to trust and she still suspected that the girl next to her might have been laughing at her all the while.

Melanie grinned at the memory. "They were really being mean and I hate it when girls are mean to each other. It's bad enough the boys are always mean to us. Girls should stick together."

It was almost spring and still chilly enough to wear woolen sweaters over their white cotton dickies. Soon it would be warm, even hot, in the afternoons, and they would be wearing tee shirts and shorts.

They walked a long way together, speaking little but enjoying the closeness of each other. Finally, the time came for them to separate, with Melanie moving off south of the boulevard where the slightly better homes were situated and Phyllis continuing on toward her mother's broomstick. They exchanged phone numbers, said it was fun having someone to walk with, and agreed to meet at the same spot the following morning.

As Melanie walked away, Phyllis, unable to contain her-

23

self, blurted out to her, "Could I go riding with you some time?"

"What?" Melanie, puzzled, turned and stared at the girl.

"When you ride," Phyllis said.

Suddenly understanding, Melanie laughed with a free and easy effort. "I've never been on a horse in my life."

After that, the girls became great friends, and soon they were seen everywhere together. Their classmates began to call them the Bobsy Twins and the Gold Dust Twins and the Siamese Girls and things like that. And, sometimes, when it got really bad at home, Phyllis would sleep over and Melanie's mom would pamper her a little bit to make up for all the deprivation she suffered in her own house. Melanie's dad began to call her Philip in a friendly, loving way, and that nickname meant she was accepted as one of the family.

One night, in their last year of high school, Phyllis came over about ten o'clock at night and stood on the lawn, throwing pebbles at Melanie's window for the longest time until her friend looked out, saw her, and rushed downstairs to let her in.

"What's going on?" Melanie asked breathlessly. "Why all the mystery?"

Phyllis was all bundled up in a big coat with a high collar and an old fedora hat pulled down low over her eyes. "I don't want your folks to see me," she mumbled.

She headed right up the stairs in front of Melanie and did not stop until she was in her friend's room with the door closed and locked.

Melanie came up behind her. "Now, what's this all about?"

Phyllis turned and removed her hat in one motion.

"Oh, my God!" Melanie gasped.

Phyllis's right eye was swollen the size of an egg and darkly discolored. Her lower lip was split in the middle and so large it could not be brought to close against the upper lip but hung loosely protruding from her face. "Don't ask me what happened this time." She could barely speak and sounded congested. "I don't want to talk about it. And it doesn't matter, anyway."

"Okay," Melanie said loyally. "Whatever you want. But I'm glad you came here. I hope you never go back there."

Melanie moved close to her, and they hugged and cried in each other's arms for a long time.

Later that night, in bed in the dark, Phyllis suddenly said, "Mel, I'm never going to have kids."

"Sure you will," Melanie reassured her.

"I swear I won't. It's cruel to bring kids into this kind of world."

"No, it isn't," Melanie said. "It's wonderful."

"I'll never do it."

"Don't say that."

"It's true. I'll never do it."

"Yes, you will!" Melanie turned over onto her side and faced her friend in the darkness. "You're so beautiful. And so good. God! All the men will want you. You'll probably get married right away—long before me—and have a bunch of kids right off. You'll see." She reached over and caressed her friend's cheek. "You just won't beat the hell out of them."

But Melanie had been wrong. It was she, not Phyllis, who got married and started a family immediately. It was Phyllis who went off to college, took lots of lovers, never married, and remained childless.

Phyllis tiptoed into Melanie's bedroom and stood over her friend, who slept fitfully. The medication Dr. Miller had administered to her had been only partially effective, and Melanie tossed and turned and cried quietly while half asleep. Phyllis leaned over and brushed back the strands of wet hair that clung to the tortured face; she stroked the hot cheeks with her cool fingers and sobbed to herself out of her own sense of pain and loss. She wondered if she would be able to help her friend while she hurt so deeply herself, while she was so immensely wounded by the terrible, tragic mishap. She questioned her own strength. And yet, she was enormously grateful that the doctor had reached out to her and not to someone else.

Dr. Miller had called her from the house after the paramedics and the police had cleared out. He did not know her personally, but Polly had insisted he call Aunt Phyllis to come over and stay. The doctor had been willing to call just about anybody in order to avoid having the little girl spend the night in a juvenile home.

"Hello!" Phyllis had answered sleepily, somewhat aggressively.

"Miss Morley?"

"Yes," she snapped. "Do you know what time it is, buster?"

"Look. You don't know me. My name is Miller and I'm Polly and Denise Wyatt's pediatrician."

She awoke quickly and sat up in bed. "What's wrong? What's happened to Polly?"

"Nothing's happened to Polly. But something terrible's happened to her sister."

"What is it?"

"Well," he said. "It's hard to explain. Certain things happen and we almost never know why."

A dark feeling of apprehension swept over her. "She's dead," Phyllis said.

Dr. Miller hesitated, then: "Yes." He breathed the word more than spoke it.

"Oh, my God! That poor baby. What happened?"

Dr. Miller cleared his throat. "Like I was telling you, it looks to me like crib death, although I'm sure that'll have to be verified by an autopsy."

"How's Melanie?"

"Obviously very upset. I've given her a sedative. She'll be out for about ten hours. But I can't leave Polly here alone and the police've suggested Juvenile Hall."

"No!" Phyllis screamed, causing him to pull the phone from his ear. "I'll be right over." She silently ran through a quick list of what she knew had to be done. "Listen, give me ten minutes. Just ten minutes. Don't leave till I get there. Okay? Dr. Miller? We can't let them do that to the kid."

Dr. Miller sounded uncomfortable. "Miss Morley. Please. Only ten minutes."

"Word of honor, Doc. Ten minutes." She slammed the phone down and was on her way.

Now, as she stood by the bed, she dried Melanie's sweaty brow and pulled the covers down below her shoulders. For an instant, the woman's eyes flicked open and peered up at Phyllis, who smiled down warmly at her.

"Phil," Melanie sobbed.

Phyllis sat on the bed beside her and took her hand in both of hers. "Shhh," she whispered. "Try to sleep. I'm here now. Try to sleep."

Melanie pressed her eyes shut, forcing lonely tears out of the corners of both of them, and in a moment was once again sleeping fitfully. Phyllis waited until she was confident that her friend was asleep again and then she quietly left the room.

She set herself up in Polly's gaily papered bedroom. Like roommates, like in college, she told Polly. She lugged the rollaway bed in from the garage, pushed the large wooden toy chest over beside Polly's bed, and unfolded the bed.

While the little girl watched through sad, confused eyes, Phyllis set the rollaway up in the corner near the closet, where the toy chest had always been, and hung her clothes alongside Polly's.

It was almost dawn before they finally got into bed. She could hear Polly sniffling from across the room, although the little girl had buried her head under the covers.

"Polly?" Phyllis whispered.

The sniffling stopped abruptly. "Yes?"

"Please don't be frightened."

"I'm not," the child said bravely.

"You'll be safe," Phyllis said. "Your mommy is very strong and she'll take good care of you. I promise."

"I miss my mommy."

"I know." Phyllis raised up on one elbow. "She needs to sleep now, but tomorrow she'll be better and you'll be with her."

After a long silence, "Aunt Phyllis?"

"Yes, dear?"

"Can I lay with you?"

Phyllis reached her arms out from the bed. "Of course, honey."

Polly jumped from her bed and ran across the room to the rollaway. She leaped into Phyllis's arms and wriggled under the covers, and they clung to each other desperately. They slept like that till the outdoor sounds of a busy day woke them.

Melanie slept till about one in the afternoon. She woke up worried about having overslept and not gotten Polly off to school with a good breakfast. And, the baby, she worried. Who had fed the baby? Gladys always refused to feed the baby on the grounds that it was a mother's job, not a housekeeper's. And Melanie agreed with her. No one ever fed the baby but her.

She jumped out of bed and almost fell over. She caught herself and leaned on the headboard for a moment, until the dizziness passed and she felt clearheaded again. It was then that she recalled the events of the night before. She cried out in anguish, fell back on the bed, and wept like an infant.

Phyllis rushed into the room and caught her friend up in her arms. She rocked her and comforted her.

"Oh, Phil," she wailed. "My poor baby. They took my poor baby." Tears flowed down her cheeks. "Oh, why? My poor baby."

"Go ahead," Phyllis whispered. "Cry. Get it out. Get it all out." She hugged her friend tightly to her breast. "Go ahead and cry." And Melanie wept tears that emanated from someplace deep inside of her, from the depths of a pain she had never imagined she could experience.

Later, after Phyllis had called both their places of employment to alert them that neither woman would be in for a few days, and had informed Polly's school that the child would be staying home that day, they sat in the kitchen and drank cup after cup of strong black coffee. They sat in silence while Polly watched them and waited for some signal from either one of them that she could speak. Her little hands were folded on the table in front of her and her seriously worried face kept moving from Melanie to Phyllis and back again.

Melanie avoided her daughter's eyes, staring self-consciously first up at the ceiling and then down at the floor. The child seemed to be accusing her. Of what? she pondered. What had she done wrong? Where had she failed? What should she have done differently. Her thoughts left an empty ache in the pit of her stomach.

"Tomorrow you'll go back to school," Phyllis finally spoke to the child.

"Okay," Polly said flatly. "If you say so, Aunt Phyllis."

"She should've gone today," Melanie said, sobbing. "It's no good missing school."

Phyllis gazed at her sadly. "It's okay, Mel. One day won't ki—I mean—"

"I didn't want to go today." They both looked at Polly and she hesitated. "I want to be here when Denny comes home."

Melanie began to cry softly, uncontrollably.

"Denny's not coming home," Phyllis said nervously.

Polly stared at them both, first one and then the other. Then she turned to Phyllis and, with total confidence, said, "Yes, she is."

"No, Polly," Phyllis said gently. "Denny's not coming home anymore. She's gone away for good."

"Where to?"

"Denny's gone to heaven," Phyllis said.

Polly thought for a moment, then pursed her lips. "That's silly," she finally said. "You only go to heaven when you die."

"That's right, honey. And Denny died last night." Phyllis chewed on her lower lip.

"No," the child said. "She wasn't even sick. She went away but she's coming back. I know it."

Melanie, unable to contain herself any longer, leaped up from her chair and walked quickly to the wall next to the refrigerator. She pressed her face into the corner and sobbed deeply and heavily.

Polly looked after her. "What's the matter, Mommy?"

"Your mommy's sad about Denny," Phyllis said quietly.

Polly jumped from her chair, ran to her mother, and clutched her around the legs. "Don't be sad, Mommy," she shouted. "Denny'll come home. I promise. She'll come home soon." She clung despairingly to her mother and sobbed with her.

Phyllis gently pulled the little girl's arms free, picked her up, and carried her to her crowded bedroom. She laid her down and sat on the edge of the bed next to her. With the tail of her blouse, she blotted the tears from her small round cheeks.

"We should leave your mommy for a while, honey. She's very sad and she's not herself."

"But she needs me," the child said. "Doesn't she love me anymore?"

"Of course, she does. Oh, please don't think things like that. Your mother loves you very much. And she does need you. Just like you need her. It's just that, right now, she has to be alone because she has a lot of crying to do."

Polly nodded her understanding. "I can help her cry."

"If you really want to help her"—at this Polly nodded her head eagerly—"you'll stay in your room and play by yourself for a little while. Until dinner time. That's just a couple of hours. And let your mommy get rid of all her sadness."

Polly remained thoughtful for a moment. She squinted her eyes as she thought and her little brow wrinkled like a wise old woman. "All right," she said. "I'll stay in here."

"Thank you, sweetie," Phyllis said. She leaned over and kissed the child, "I'll make it up to you. I promise."

By the time Phyllis got back to the kitchen, Melanie had regained her composure and was back at the table, sitting with her legs crossed and her hands folded in her lap. The deep black shadows beneath her eyes accentuated her gaunt, cadaverous appearance.

"I can't handle it," she said.

"Yes, you can," Phyllis insisted. "You can handle anything that comes down the pike. You're the tough one, remember?"

"I don't feel very tough."

31

"If you weren't tough, you wouldn't be feeling anything. You'd be out of it. In a straight jacket somewhere. Sucking on pills. Letting other people run your life for you."

"That sounds so good." She smiled weakly.

"Bullshit!" Phyllis exclaimed. "That's what Chris wanted. Remember him? Big Daddy? The parent you married and suffered with for ten years?"

Melanie's eyes pleaded. "Come on, Phil. Ease up. Give me a break."

Phyllis softened. "I'm sorry, Mel. I just don't want to see you give up."

Melanie began to weep again. "Why shouldn't I? I don't deserve anything better." Tears again flowed down her face. "Look what I've done to my baby." She started to rock back and forth in her chair.

"What did you do?"

"I killed my baby. I killed my baby."

"What are you talking about?" Phyllis screamed. "Shut up. And don't be stupid."

"It's true. I shouldn't've gone out. I shouldn't've had that wine. She needed me and I slept right through." She rocked more vigorously. "What kind of mother am I? My baby needed me and I slept right through."

"Stop it!" Phyllis commanded.

She gazed around her wildly, insanely. "You know what I think about, Phil? I think about Denny waking up in the middle of the night. She can't breathe. She's choking. She can't even cry. Her face turns red. Then purple. She thrashes round, struggling to get some air in her lungs. Finally, she chokes and I don't hear her, because I'm fast asleep. And I'm thinking, was she wondering where I was when she died? What went through her little mind? Did she hate me at that last instant? Oh, God. How can I live with this?"

"Please, stop it," Phyllis begged.

But Melanie could not hear her because she was deep into her weeping again and lost in God-knows-what fantasy. "Everything Chris ever said about me was true. This is the proof. I'm really no good."

Phyllis watched her helplessly. She thought of the dozens of times she had said similar things to Melanie about herself and how her friend had never failed to support her, to prop up her failing self-esteem. She wanted so badly to do the same for Melanie now, but she suddenly realized that it took a special skill to be that supportive, a skill that she, Phyllis, lacked. After all, there had never been a need for it. Not in their relationship. Melanie had always been the giver and Phyllis had always been the receiver. Now that the situation needed to be reversed, Phyllis was not quite sure how to do it.

At three o'clock, while they were still in the kitchen, two plainclothes policemen came to visit. When Phyllis opened the front door, they identified themselves to her as detectives from the Van Nuys Division and asked if they could come in. They explained that their visit was just routine and was mandatory for any unexplained death. A routine investigation, they apologized. In this case, the tall one said, it was imperative that they interview the mother.

Phyllis took them into the kitchen and introduced them to Melanie. The tall fair-haired one was named Collins, and the other shorter Hispanic-looking one called himself Ruiz.

"Please, sit down," Melanie said.

"I'll get you some coffee," Phyllis said.

"Thanks," Collins nodded.

They pulled out chairs for themselves and sat at the kitchen table. Ruiz drew a notebook from his inside pocket, crossed his legs, and sat poised with a ballpoint pen ready to take notes.

Phyllis put two mugs of coffee on the table, one in front of each of the detectives, and stood leaning against the sink.

Detective Collins cleared his throat. "Mrs. Wyatt, when was the last time you saw your husband?"

"What?" Melanie's head snapped up.

"Hey," Phyllis said. "That's not a very routine question."

"I'm sorry. Look, I just want to know how long he's been gone."

"He's not *gone*," Phyllis said. "They're getting a divorce."

Ruiz looked up from his notebook. "Could you let Mrs. Wyatt answer, please."

"How did you know he's not living here?" Melanie asked.

Collins tilted his head apologetically and said, "We checked with the neighbors first."

"I'll be damned," Phyllis said. "You have a lot of nerve."

Collins raised the coffee mug to his lips and took a long sip. "It's routine procedure."

"Like hell!" Phyllis said, her anger getting the best of her. "What you've got here is a woman alone in a man's world."

"Please." Collins held up his hand, as if directing traffic. "Don't waste everybody's time. There's nothing political about this, lady. We've got an unexplained infant death here and all I want is to get my few questions answered. Then, I promise, I'll get out of here and leave you all alone. I'm not totally insensitive to the occasion."

"Okay," Melanie nodded. "You're right."

"Thank you, ma'am," Collins nodded to her in gratitude. "When did you last see your husband?"

"About two weeks ago," Melanie spoke softly.

"What was the purpose of that meeting?"

"He came to see the children." Melanie glanced at Phyllis in wonder.

"How did he seem to you? I mean, was he his usual self? Did you notice anything different about him?"

Melanie hesitated and thought. "No. He was like always."

"How's that?" the policeman asked.

Phyllis laughed cynically. "Angry."

"Is that right?" He studied Melanie.

"Yes," Melanie said. "I guess he's angry about us."

Collins nodded and looked over at Ruiz. "You told the officer last night that you woke up from a bad dream and that's when you found the—"

"Yes," she answered quickly.

"You didn't hear anything? I mean, maybe a sound woke you."

"I don't know what you mean."

Collins stared at her before speaking, then said, "Was there anyone here with you last night?"

"Polly was here. My eight-year-old. And the baby."

"He means, a man," Ruiz said.

Melanie sat up suddenly. "Of course not."

Collins spoke softly, but there was a sharp edge to his voice. "If there was, we'll find out, Mrs. Wyatt."

"Hold it," Phyllis said. "What's going on here? What the hell is this all about?"

"I told you," the cop said. "I want a few questions answered. That's all."

Phyllis pushed away from the sink. "Well, I don't like your questions. They don't seem to have anything to do with last night. And, I think you're invading my friend's privacy."

Collins turned back to Melanie. "Look, Mrs. Wyatt, I'm sorry. I know this is a bad time. But I don't have any choice.

35

Your baby died in a very strange way, and we have to investigate."

"I know that, officer," Melanie said. "I've read about crib death. I understand."

"No, you don't," he said. He looked over at Ruiz and nodded. Ruiz closed his notebook and slipped it into his pocket. "There's something really strange about your baby's death, Mrs. Wyatt."

"What?" Phyllis asked.

Collins's eyes remained fixed on Melanie's face. "Well, the baby's lungs were filled with water."

"Pneumonia," Phyllis breathed.

"That's not possible," Melanie said defensively. "She didn't have a fever. She wasn't even warm. If she'd been sick like that, I would have known it."

"No," Detective Collins said. He shook his head, turned to Phyllis, then back to Melanie. "Tap water, ma'am. Drinking water. Your baby drowned."

THREE

Initially, she sat quietly, barely breathing, disbelieving, stunned by Collins's announcement. And then, before Phyllis could react and move to help her, she broke down. She slid from the chair to the kitchen floor, screaming and crying hysterically. By the time Phyllis got to her she was flailing, pounding her head on the floor. She had bitten her tongue and was spitting blood onto the linoleum.

Phyllis needed both of the officers' help to get Melanie calmed down and into bed. She stuffed two of the barbiturates Dr. Miller had left into Melanie and wrestled her down into a reclining position. Collins and Ruiz held her arms and legs while Phyllis stroked her face and her hair, whispering to her, comforting her, occupying Melanie's mind long enough for the drug to take effect. Finally, she surrendered to sleep, and they all released their holds on her and withdrew to the kitchen.

Collins, flushed and agitated, was apologetic. "I'm sorry," he said worriedly.

Phyllis displayed her anger. "How the hell could you do that? How goddamned insensitive can you get?"

"Just my job," he said sheepishly.

Phyllis turned from him and leaned on the edge of the sink. "It's not your job to dump things like that on people."

"Yes, it is!" Ruiz said, coldly eyeing her.

Phyllis turned her head and stared at him. She frowned and narrowed her eyes. The smaller of the two policemen infuriated her. She thought him arrogant and offensive. She was not surprised that he reminded her of Chris Wyatt.

"I'm sorry, miss," Collins said. "I needed to see her reaction."

"What?"

"You know," Ruiz said. "Just in case—"

Phyllis's eyes opened wide. "You don't think she—" She set her jaw hard. "That's the dumbest thing I ever heard. How could you think that?"

Collins interrupted her. "It's not important what I think. I collect all the information I can get and other people make the determinations. Of course, if you think she's got something to hide and you'd rather not talk to us, I would understand. We don't want to violate anybody's rights here."

Phyllis moved to the small table and sat down. She looked up at the two of them standing over her and suddenly became frightened for her friend.

"You want to help us now, miss?" Ruiz asked.

She nodded and dropped her eyes to the floor. "Sure," she looked up quickly, "—if you'll tell me what you're looking for."

"Fair enough," Collins said as he sat down across from her. "I'm looking for any kind of reasonable explanation as to how that death occurred. I'll listen to anything you want to tell me. I don't care how farfetched it is. I'm open. Whatever you know, or think you know, or suspect. Anything. Reach as far as you want. I don't care."

Ruiz added, "Tell us about the husband. Did they fight a lot? Did he hit her? Did she whack him? Did he cheat on

38

her? Did she sneak around behind his back? The boyfriends, the one-nighters. Does she like them big? You know, tough. Does she like to get slapped around? Does she like low lifes? Does she turn tricks on the side? Anything like that. Who had a key to the place? You know what I mean? Who'd she drink with? Did she do dope? With who and where'd she get it?"

Phyllis was shocked and angry. She stared at Ruiz with disbelief and disgust. "She doesn't do dope, as you say. And she doesn't go out drinking. As far as I know, nobody has a key to this place other than Gladys, the housekeeper. And I've never known Melanie to give a key to a man, if that's what you mean."

"That's what we mean," Collins said.

"Well, she's very careful about men. Polly's been a problem since her father left. Anyway, Melanie doesn't bring any strange men into the house. She isn't interested in men and doesn't go looking for them. I don't think she's ever been in a singles bar. And I sure can't get her interested in meeting any of the men I know."

Ruiz flipped open his notebook, touched his thumb to his tongue, and turned several pages. "What about the boyfriend with the blue Porsche?"

"I don't know what your talking about," Phyllis said. She glanced back and forth at their faces, hating their complete male arrogance and smugness.

"The neighbors said there's this guy who comes over. Parks his blue Porsche in the driveway." Ruiz grinned at her as if he had caught her in a lie and was about to enjoy watching her squirm.

"Then ask the neighbors about him," she snapped.

"We did," Collins said. "They told us she's got a boyfriend who comes to visit sometimes. Just tell us. You know him or not?"

Phyllis hesitated for a long moment. She truly did not want to respond. She hated the way they made her feel, like a snitch. She finally spoke. "That must be Joe. He's a friend. She sees him once in a while. But it's not serious. He's just someone to talk to. Someone who's willing to listen. He helps her get her mind off her troubles. You can't really call him a boyfriend."

"What troubles?" Ruiz asked.

Phyllis snapped at him. "You don't think being a single parent with two kids, one of them a baby, and a husband who won't help out is troubles? Let me tell you, she's got trouble just keeping it all together."

"Okay, okay," Ruiz said. "What's his name?" His pencil was poised over his notebook.

"Joe Hennessy. I don't want to get him in any trouble."

"No trouble," Collins said. "We'll just want to talk to him. Where can we find him? Do you know?"

Phyllis began to chew on her lip. "He's a real nice guy. He doesn't have anything to do with this."

"How do you know?" Ruiz asked.

"I know," Phyllis said angrily. "He's a gentleman. He's no scuz."

"Okay," Collins said. "Can you tell us where he lives or works?"

"I don't know. I know he travels a lot. But I don't know where he works."

"How about a home address?" Ruiz asked.

"I don't know," she replied. "I don't know anything else."

"Okay," Collins said, changing his position on the chair. "How about the husband? Any idea where we can find him?"

"No," Phyllis lied, without understanding why.

Ruiz was incredulous. "You don't know where he hangs out?"

"No," she continued to lie, without comprehending why she was protecting a man she so despised.

"Where he works?" Ruiz continued. "Come on!"

"Yeah," she said. "I know where he works. Listen," she said angrily. She sat up straight and flashed a defiant look at Ruiz. "What do you need to know all this stuff for? You're treating me like I'm a criminal. You're talking about my friend like she's a criminal. And all these questions about men, like she's been a bad girl or something. Why do you have to pry into her private life?"

Collins sighed deeply and sat back. He looked up at his partner and shook his head slowly. "Lady," he said. He raised his left hand and counted off his fingers. "One, if your friend brings home one-nighters, then maybe she brought some freak home. Maybe not last night, but once. And this freak's got something going for kids. Maybe. Maybe he goes crazy one night and remembers the chick he took home a month ago and her babies. Maybe. Just maybe. Two, if there's a boyfriend, maybe he don't like too many kids. Maybe he's jealous of them. Maybe he thinks he gets her all to himself if the kids are gone. Maybe he thinks she wants to get rid of the kids and he does it for her. Maybe he's just a crazy. They're out there all over the place. Three, an angry husband. Maybe he's pissed off that she's seeing somebody else. Maybe he blames the kid for the breakup of the marriage. Maybe he's off his nut. Maybe he wants to punish his old lady so bad that he does the kid. And on and on." He smiled grimly at Phyllis. "You see why we've got to know?"

"Well, none of that's possible here," Phyllis said. She crossed her arms over her chest and sat back in her chair. She could not believe they were talking about her friend Melanie's life.

"Yeah?" Ruiz said. "Well, let us be the judges of that."

"I'd appreciate it," Collins interrupted, "if you'd tell us

41

where to find Mr. Wyatt. Would that be okay with you? We've been very patient with you, miss. I think you could cooperate with us that much."

"Look," Ruiz said, trying to sound tough, "you hold back on us and you could be considered an accessory. Why would you want to protect the guy, anyway? He may be the one we're looking for."

"Okay," she said, finally agreeing with the short detective. "I'll tell you where to find Chris Wyatt." A look of determination crossed her face. "Try the police department. Central Division. He's a cop."

Melanie lay in her darkened bedroom, drifting in and out of sleep. She heard Collins speaking from down the hall, heard his enumeration of possibilities and shuddered at the thoughts and feelings they provoked in her. How often had she thought of doing some of those very things? How often had she contemplated revenge in the form of a strange bed, a strange man to give herself to?

She reached down and pressed both her palms against her abdomen the way she used to when she had been pregnant with Denny. She could almost feel the tiny heart beating under her flesh, the sudden kickings and thrashings that used to delight her so when she felt them and saw the little bumps and ripples rise up out of her. She shuddered with the memory of it. Those memories so close to her now, pressing on her from every dark shadow in her bedroom, in this room where she lay nursing her grief.

She could hear Chris scolding her again. His angry voice rang loudly in her ears.

"Son of a bitch!" he screamed. "What did you go and do that for? Like we don't have enough troubles."

"This isn't trouble, Chris," she said. How could he not understand how important this baby was to her?

"The hell it isn't." He was sitting on the edge of his side of the bed, undressing. She had finally gotten up enough courage to tell him she was pregnant, something she had avoided doing since she learned of it herself, somehow knowing what his reaction would be.

She had not been that happy herself with the news, initially. The thought of another baby overwhelmed her. She felt trapped most of the time now, as it were, trapped in a much less than perfect marriage, and a new baby seemed like another link in the weighty chain that bound her to her slavish existence. But, as time passed and she began to feel the minuscule biological changes taking place in her body, she grew more comfortable with her secret and finally arrived at the point where she truly wanted and longed for the child.

He pulled off a shoe and flung it across the room. Bang. "I can't afford to feed this family now. What's it going to be like with another brat to feed?" Bang. The second shoe followed and bounced off the far wall.

"It won't cost that much more," she said, mustering some defiance. "Baby food doesn't cost that much."

He looked at her and sneered. "It's not just the food, is it? There's doctors and—"

"We have insurance," she said.

"Shut up and don't interrupt me. And there's clothes and shoes and vitamins. Oh, Christ. The list's a mile long. I'm going to have to take a second job. Damn it. I didn't want to do that." He stood up and, with his hands planted on his hips, glared down at her. "Goddamn it! Can't you ever keep your legs closed?"

She started to tremble and struggled to conceal it from him.

43

"Oh, oh," he said. "Here come the tears."

"No," she whispered.

"Don't tell me no. I can see you trembling. And every time you tremble, the tears aren't far behind."

"Not this time," she said softly. But she knew she was lying. She could feel the tears behind her eyelids pressing to be released, about to burst out and flood down her cheeks.

"I don't want this baby," he said. "I want you to get rid of it."

She sobered. "I can't," she whined. "It's too late."

"It's never too late."

"I'm in my fourth month. No doctor's going to take a chance."

"Let's go to Mexico. We'll find somebody. They don't give a shit about those stupid rules down there."

He took off his shirt and draped it over the back of a chair. He gazed at himself in the dresser mirror, flexed his muscles, turned sideways, and enlarged his biceps, posing like a body builder. "I wish to hell you'd learn to be careful," he said to her through the mirror. "Goddamn it. Getting pregnant was a real dumb thing to do."

"I didn't do it alone," she said, feeling stupid and wimpy for saying it.

"The hell you didn't. I don't remember hearing you ask my permission. You sure as hell did it alone."

"I mean, you had to help."

"Like hell. If it was up to me, you'd always be protected. Goddamn it. You irresponsible bitch. You tell me you don't have the diaphragm in, I don't get near you with a ten-foot pole."

"You didn't give me a chance."

"Shut up!" he screamed. "It's your damned job to stay safe. It's not my job to have to worry about that. I've got

44

enough to worry about. I don't have to worry about your plumbing."

She fought back the tears and said, "I don't see how you can blame me like this. When it comes to sex, we always do what you want. I try so hard to be a good wife to you."

"How are you going to be a good wife with a belly out to here?" he said. He held his arms out as far as they could reach. "God! And you're so ugly when you're pregnant. You get fat and sweaty and your skin gets all blotchy. I can't stand to touch you."

She cried then. He had hurt her so many times that she had begun to believe she had become desensitized and could maintain control no matter what he said. But each time she felt strong and in control, he found new and unexpected ways to humiliate her. It had become a game with him, she was convinced. A game he loved to play. A game he played so very, very well.

He walked over to her and put one leg up on the bed. "We can get rid of it," he said conspiratorially. "I know how to do it."

"How?" She was suspicious of him and moved several inches away from his leg.

"We get you started bleeding," he said. "Once you're bleeding, it's a miscarriage and any emergency room doctor will finish it for you." He smiled at her and nodded. "What do you think? Huh?"

She was unable to respond. She sobbed and turned her face from him. Speaking to the headboard, she said, "I want this baby."

"Come on," he cajoled. "You don't mean that. You don't want another squealing brat. Listen, I can understand if you're scared. So, we won't stick anything up you. We'll start the bleeding some other way."

He pulled his leg from the bed and began to pace the

floor, thinking and talking as he walked. "We got to fake an injury. Somehow get you banged up without really hurting you. An auto accident might really do it, but I don't want to bust up the car. Every little dent costs a fortune to fix."

"Oh, God," she said. "You're crazy."

He laughed. "Crazy like a fox. I know how we'll do it. I'll borrow Larry's dirt bike and we'll go riding Sunday." He clapped his hands joyfully. "I'll hit every goddamned bump between here and Bakersfield. If that don't do it, nothing will."

"I won't go," she said.

He turned to her and spoke softly but menacingly. "You'll go. You'll go or else."

"No, I won't. And, if you try to make me, I'll call your captain."

He covered the distance between them in two strides and slapped her hard, knocking her back on the bed. "You better not call anybody." He glared at her. "You're threatening me? Who the hell gave you the right to interfere in my life? You'd do it, too. I know you would. That's just the kind of thing you would do." He paused. "You've already shown how much you can fuck up our life together. All right! You want it!" He shouted. "You can have it." He turned and walked away from her. "You know what? I hope you carry it for the whole nine months and when it's born, I hope it's dead. Yeah, that's what I hope."

He pulled the blanket from the bed and shoved his pillow under his arm.

"Where are you going?" she asked meekly.

He opened the door and looked back at her. "You know. The fucking kid isn't even born yet, and I hate him already."

She jerked her hands from her abdomen as if they had

been burned, seared by the memory of his fierce words. She hated him then more than she had ever hated him. Even more than she hated him now, if that were possible. And, she could not help thinking that, somehow, their hate for each other was deeply involved with Denny's death.

Collins pushed Ruiz out the door and hung back to whisper something to Phyllis. He held the door partially closed so that his partner could not hear what he was saying and leaned closer to her so that his whisper could be heard. "If I were you, I'd advise your friend to get a lawyer."

"Why are you telling me this?" she asked suspiciously.

"Because you're a nice lady. I don't know your friend, but I think if you picked her, she's probably all right."

She felt herself blush slightly. "I'll tell her," she said. "You think she's going to need help?"

"I think somebody gave that baby a real deep bath, and whether it was her or not, she's got to have something to do with it. You know what I'm saying?"

"No," she said innocently.

He looked at her and thought for a long moment. A flash of admiration passed through his thoughts. He felt a stirring of desire for her, for her perfectly proportioned body, the small, tight breasts, long, muscular legs, a runner's legs, the curved buttocks stretching against her fitted jeans. Those blue eyes!

He shrugged. "No stranger walked in here and gave that baby a bath in the middle of the night," he said sadly. "I don't know exactly what did happen, but I'll bet dollars to doughnuts that she's involved. If she didn't actually do it, then, at least, she's guilty of letting it happen."

FOUR

Phyllis felt so disloyal, so deceitful, like a sneak, but she forced herself to make the call anyway, even though Melanie had made her promise not to when she had told her about the detective's suggestion. Phyllis knew instinctively that someone had to take the necessary measures to protect against what she feared, but could not believe, might happen next.

It might not have been seen as a clear possibility to Melanie, but it certainly was clear to Phyllis that someone other than God had been responsible for little Denny's death and that someone, rightfully or not, was going to be accused of the crime.

Melanie argued against the idea. She mounted a tearful battle, complaining about the expense and bother and the implication of guilt that accompanied the engaging of an attorney. "I haven't done anything wrong," she insisted. "If I haven't done anything, why should I need a lawyer?" To Melanie's mind, hiring an attorney would be the same as admitting to the world her responsibility for her daughter's death.

But Phyllis was just as adamant, contending that everyone

had the right to seek help and advice and that not everybody who went to a lawyer was automatically guilty. Innocent people were accused of terrible things all the time, she persisted, and it was foolish and dangerous to be as naive as Melanie was pretending to be. But Melanie finally resorted to stubborn pouting.

"I won't talk to him," she said, hardening her face like an obstinate child. "No matter what."

"You've got to protect yourself," Phyllis argued, striving to retain her patience. "No one's going to come running to your rescue voluntarily. There aren't any white knights out there. You have to take care of yourself."

"I haven't done anything," Melanie declared. "And I won't behave like I have." She grew very angry then. "Damn, I'm a victim, too. I've lost my baby."

"I know," Phyllis said sympathetically, suddenly realizing that her sense of expediency had caused her to forget Melanie's tragedy. Perhaps, she thought, she had welcomed the new urgency to assist Melanie in pushing the memory of the poor dead infant from her mind. She felt ashamed and disloyal. She moved to her friend, put her arms around her, and embraced her tenderly. "I know, honey." And they cried together.

Phyllis agreed then not to interfere and swore not to mention seeking out a lawyer again. Melanie grew calm, seemed to relax, and thanked her. But Phyllis was not comfortable with that, telling herself the ill-advised promise had been elicited under duress and since there existed a greater priority, she was justified in doing what she believed was right.

So, she called the only lawyer she knew. She had been seeing Roger Gillespie on and off for a couple of years, and though he was far from her favorite date, he was one of her favorite friends. He was one of the few men she could make love with and laugh with at the same time. She admired that quality in him, his unwillingness to take himself too seriously. In her mind, lawyers were supposed to be stuffy, pompous, self indulgent, uptight people, but Roger Gillespie dispelled that idea by being a relaxed, easygoing guy with a great sense of humor.

However, he grew quite serious when she told him of the situation in which she found her friend.

"What do you think happened?" he asked Phyllis when she was done.

"I don't think Melanie did this terrible thing," she said "I won't say anything about anybody else, but I know that Melanie's not capable of such a thing. Unfortunately, the police don't know her as well as I do."

"Well, whether she is or isn't capable doesn't change the fact that she's entitled to counsel. And, judging from what you tell me about her, she needs someone desperately. It's plain naive to think that our system has anything to do with guilt or innocence. It has to do with what they call justice, and I always try to remember and keep reminding myself all the time that justice is blind as hell, as well as being deceptive and looking different to everybody who sets eyes on her."

"What can I do?"

"Get her to a lawyer as soon as you can."

"She refuses to go," she said.

"Then invite him over to the house," he said. "You've got to get her together with somebody. You don't have lots of time. You're very lucky that the cop warned you. They don't always do that, you know."

She was silent for a moment. "Okay," she said. "When will you come?"

"Whoa!" he objected. "This isn't my kind of case."

"You're a lawyer, aren't you?"

"Yes. Of course."

"Then what do you mean, not your kind of case?"

She heard him clear his throat, and when he spoke, he sounded tentative. "The law has become very specialized. I mean, I do civil law. You know, contracts and things. Business law." He hurried to add, "What you need is a criminal lawyer. A guy who knows his way around the courts and the system. You know, someone who's down there at court every day, knows the judges, who's comfortable in a courtroom."

"But I don't know anybody like that," she said, sounding helpless.

"They're all over the place," he said. "I can get you a couple of names."

She worried abut his apparent reluctance to get involved. Was that because he believed Melanie was guilty she wondered. Is that the impression her innocent telling of the circumstances had created? Had she unwittingly turned him against Melanie?

"I'm afraid of a stranger," she said. "I need to find her a friend."

There was a long silence on the phone. Maybe he is not such a good friend, she thought. Maybe he wishes I had called someone else. Maybe he feels put out over my burdening him.

"Is it because you think she's guilty?" she asked him finally.

"What?"

"Your not wanting to get involved."

"Hell, no!" he said. "Listen, Phil. Even if I was convinced she'd done it, which I'm not, I'd still want to protect her right to proper representation."

She released a sigh of relief.

"I'm not reluctant because of her," he said. "I'm reluctant because of me. When I say proper representation, I mean just that. She needs somebody who knows the ins and

51

outs of criminal law. I don't. I'd be a fumbler. I'd be afraid to run with the ball, afraid I'd drop it. That's all I mean."

"I want you," she said adamantly.

"I'm very flattered," he said with a slight laugh, his way of showing his discomfort with compliments. "But that would be a mistake."

"I don't care," she insisted. "I want you to help us."

He hesitated as he thought. She could hear his slow breathing over the phone. "Okay," he said. "On one condition."

"What's that?"

"If it gets sticky, I can yell uncle and we call in an expert? Fair?"

"Fair enough. When can you come over?"

"How about this evening?"

"That's great." She said happily. "Six o'clock? For dinner."

"Okay. Six o'clock."

"For dinner."

"Okay. For dinner. Good-bye, Phil."

"Wait!" She caught him before he could hang up.

"Yes?"

"Just what do you mean by *getting sticky?*" she asked.

He paused and was silent for a moment, while crisp static crackled on the line, then he spoke in a very soft voice. "Like if she gets indicted and charged with first-degree murder, Phil. That would be sticky as hell."

At three-forty-five Detective Collins phoned Central to speak with Officer Christopher Wyatt. He fully expected the man to be out on the day after the death of his child and was surprised to learn that he had not requested any time off.

Collins waited a long time for the desk sergeant to locate Wyatt, but he finally came on the phone.

"Hello?" a gentle voice said.

"Hello," Collins said. "Officer Wyatt?"

"Yes?"

"This is Detective Collins over at Van Nuys."

"Yes?"

"My condolences, Officer Wyatt," Collins said uncomfortably.

"Thank you."

"Listen, I don't feel good about bothering you at a time like this, but could we speak? I mean, if you feel up to it."

"I'm fine, Detective," Chris Wyatt said. "I'm not going to fall apart."

"Frankly," Collins said, "I'm surprised you're at work today."

There was sadness in Chris's voice when he spoke. "Well, that's when I would fall apart. If I let it affect my life like that. It's much better for me to keep busy than to sit around and brood."

"Yeah. I guess." Collins could understand that.

"I'm off at six. Want to get together for a beer?" Chris asked.

"Not this time," Collins said. "This'll be official. You know. Maybe it's better if we come to you."

"Okay."

"Fine. We'll be there at six. Oh, Officer Wyatt?"

"Yes?"

"Who told you about the—you know? Was it your wife? She call you?"

"No. Dr. Miller called me."

"Oh," Collins said thoughtfully. "Have you spoken to your wife yet?"

"No," Chris said. "My wife won't speak to me."

"But, under these circumstances—"

"My wife doesn't want to hear from me—ever. She has a new man in her life now. There's no place for me."

They agreed to share setting up the interviews, to split the difference, as Ruiz called it. Collins had taken Wyatt and Ruiz had taken Joe Hennessy. The dozens of Hennessys in the phonebook were whittled down to less than ten with the first name Joe, but that was only in the central book and did not include any of the outlying areas. Altogether, there must have been a couple of hundred Hennessys and a few dozen Joes, with an additional dozen or two of just the initial J.

Ruiz tried to get Mary Pettriccio to help him with the phone calling, but she was in traffic and there did not seem to be any lull in the killing on the freeway that day, which kept her too busy to get away. Too bad, he thought. He would not have minded one bit spending a few hours with her sitting on the corner of his desk, with her skirt all hiked up, dialing on his second phone.

He had Xeroxed the list of numbers for her, which he had stuffed in a drawer and now started plowing through himself. For the first two hours of dialing, most of his calls got no response and had to be left for a call back. One Joe Hennessy was nineteen, had just relocated from Toledo, Ohio, and had never heard of Melanie Wyatt. Another Joe Hennessy was seventy-two and wished he had heard of Melanie Wyatt.

On his ninth call, he reached an answering service where a young-sounding operator, responding nervously to Ruiz's declaration of a police investigation but being as cagey as she knew how, informed him that Mr. Hennessy might be the same Mr. Hennessy who, perhaps, drove a new blue

Porsche, which he might have just purchased. What was this all about and was Mr. Hennessy in trouble? she asked. She hoped not, for Mr. Hennessy was such a very nice man. And, yes, she knew him personally. And, yes, he might have received calls from a Melanie Wyatt; the name sounded a little familiar. The young voice developed a twinge of anger at that point. Or was it jealousy? Ruiz wondered. And, yes, he was indeed in town and she referred him, in turn, to the phone number of a downtown office in the midst of the diamond district. And, no, she would never be giving out that information to anyone other than the police, although she could not know for sure that she was truly talking to the police.

The receptionist who answered the phone at Apex Diamond failed to question him as to who he was or what he wanted, but put him through without any hesitation.

When Joe came on the line, Ruiz offered his name and asked for an appointment that very day. Joe, assuming that the call had something to do with the purchase of diamonds, did not bother to question him further but agreed to meet with him within the hour. And, when Ruiz and Collins walked into Joe Hennessy's small utilitarian office, with the huge antiquated iron safe against the far wall and the black felt-covered display table under the bright fluorescent hanging light, he was still unaware that they were policemen.

They were seated across a walnut-colored formica-covered desk perched on shiny chrome legs, staring at a stocky, good-looking, well-dressed man. Joe Hennessy's hair was expensively styled and his fingernails impeccably manicured. He wore a pale blue shirt and a dark maroon knitted tie with a very small knot. He was the picture of the successful businessman, but for the abundance of gold on his fingers, around his neck, and linking his cuffs closed.

Ruiz, in his most clipped, official voice, started, "Mr.

Hennessy, we're police officers. This is Detective Collins and I'm Detective Ruiz."

Joe stared at them in surprise as they each withdrew wallets from their pockets and displayed their identification.

"We want to talk to you about your relationship with Melanie Wyatt." Ruiz watched him carefully while the nonchalant Collins gazed past him toward the window behind him.

"I don't understand," Joe said, puzzled.

Collins said, "You do know her, don't you?"

"Yes. Certainly," he nodded. "But what's that got to do with you?"

Joe's puzzled gaze moved back and forth from Ruiz to Collins. His thoughts seemed to be racing, as if he were trying to recall what indiscretion he might have committed while with Melanie.

"We just need some general information," Collins said. "And we're talking to all the people who know her."

Joe grew serious. "What's she done?" His voice trembled slightly.

Ruiz jumped in. "Mr. Hennessy, how long have you known Mrs. Wyatt?" He whipped out his notebook and turned to a blank page.

Collins sat back and smiled to himself. I can smell the fear on the guy, he thought. This one will be easy. He'll cop without any prodding at all.

"Uh, not all that long," Joe said.

"How long?" Ruiz insisted.

"Maybe a year, more or less."

Collins said, "Did you know her before she split up with her husband?"

He hesitated and seemed to be calculating which of several answers would be best to offer. "Yes. I knew her slightly. I got to know her better after she filed for her divorce."

"Did you date her while she was with her husband?" Ruiz did not emphasize the question. The tone of his voice did not alter at all.

"No! Of course not."

"Just friends?"

"Just friends!"

Ruiz stared at Joe Hennessy and waited, as if he expected more. Finally, he looked down at his notebook and scribbled an entry. "What kind of mother is she?" Ruiz asked. "I mean, how would you rate her?"

Hennessy hesitated. "I don't know what you mean."

Ruiz chewed on his pen and smiled at Joe Hennessy. Collins asked, "Is she a good mother? Does she take good care of the kids—I mean, with working, and all? Or does she neglect them? Does she beat them up? Come on, you know what I mean."

Joe raised his eyes to the ceiling and seemed to be taxing his memory. He had to drag his gaze back to the two officers. "I would say she's a good mother."

They waited for him to continue. "Go on," Collins said.

"Oh, oh," he stammered. "Well, the kid's always dressed well and everything. I've only seen the baby once, but the older girl's always well-behaved and polite and she seems happy, I guess. What's this all about?"

"Are you her steady boyfriend, Mr. Hennessy?" Collins asked.

"Well, no. I don't think so. Don't get me wrong. I'd sure like to be. She's a terrific girl. And she's a knockout. But I'm positive she sees other guys."

"How do you know that?" Ruiz asked. "Do you know that for sure?"

Hennessy turned to him. "Well, I've called her for a date sometimes and she's told me she had a previous engagement."

"Maybe it was a P.T.A. meeting," Collins said.

"Could've been," Hennessy hurried to say. "I just assumed at the time that it was a date."

"Tell me," Ruiz said, "is she in the habit of leaving her children alone and unattended?"

A sudden look of understanding crossed Joe Hennessy's face. "I see," he said. "No, she's not. To the best of my knowledge, she never leaves them alone. She has a girl who comes in to care for them while she's at work, and when the girl's not there, Melanie stays home."

"What about discipline?" Ruiz looked up from his pad. "Any special ways she punishes the kids when they're bad?"

"No," Joe said. "Not that I know of. I've never seen her punish her kids. I mean, maybe she does it, but not when I'm around."

"You around much?" Collins asked.

Joe snapped his head back to Collins. "I guess. I don't know. I mean, how much is much? I guess I'm around a lot. Yeah."

"Sleep over much?" Ruiz asked.

Joe fell silent. The two policemen watched him lazily, very unconcerned, almost as if disinterested. Joe noted the small, wise smile that played along Collins's lips. "I don't think that's any of your business," he finally said angrily, caught between his sense of obligation and loyalty to Melanie and his need to be viewed as a successful cocksman. "Why are you asking me all these personal questions? If you think I've done anything, you better tell me what it is. That's my right, isn't it? You have to tell me what you're accusing me of?"

"We're not accusing you of anything, Mr. Hennessy," Collins said calmly. "We're just gathering information."

"For what?"

"For an investigation."

"What investigation?" Joe asked. "What the hell are you investigating?"

Collins watched him and that tiny smile played on his lips again. "The death of Mrs. Wyatt's baby," he answered.

"The what?"

"The baby's dead," Ruiz said.

"Oh," Joe said sadly. "That's too bad." He put his hand up to his head and ran his fingers through his hair. "How did that happen?"

"You don't know about it?" Ruiz asked. Collins watched closely for some significant reaction from Hennessy.

"How would I know?" Joe asked.

"No one called you?" Ruiz prodded.

"No."

Ruiz closed his notebook and put it away. "Mr. Hennessy," he said, "have you ever heard Mrs. Wyatt complain about her children?"

Indignant. "No!"

"Ever hear her gripe about the baby?"

"No!"

"You know, about keeping her up at night, crying a lot?"

"No. Never. She's not like that."

"How hard it is to raise kids alone?"

"I told you, no."

"About wishing she'd never had them?"

"No. Not ever," Joe said, enraged and frightened. "My God! What are you saying?"

Collins stood up. "Okay," he said. "We appreciate the time you've given us." He motioned Ruiz to rise as well. The two of them moved to the office door. "If we need anything else, we'll call you, Mr. Hennessy. That all right with you?"

"Yes," he said.

As Ruiz was about to step out the door, Collins turned

and said, "Did you lose the key she gave you, by any chance?"

Joe patted his pocket automatically. "No," he said. "I still have it."

"Oh, good," Collins said, appearing to be relieved. "As long as we know it's not in the hands of a stranger."

FIVE

A tormented Melanie sat alone at the kitchen window, pressed into the shadows, staring out into the deserted backyard where the thick, closely cropped lawn and the fragile, delicately cared-for flower garden awaited her loving attention. She focused sorrowfully on the pathetic white birdhouse, built by Chris so long ago under Polly's approving foremanship, which lay on its side, cracked and muddy, its pole having been fractured since the past summer when Chris had run into it with the gas-operated lawn mower after having had a few too many beers.

She had promised herself again and again that she would fix it, all the while knowing that she never would since carpentry was far from her long suit. However, she thought that as soon as Denny became big enough, old enough to run around in the yard, they would go out there together and do it. She could envision Denny squatting, her diapered bottom hanging down between her pudgy legs, poking her stubby fingers into the ground and learning all about the world of birds and bugs, while mother sawed away at the damaged dowel.

Now she remembered Chris building it, while Polly ran

about the yard exploring the wonders of the outside world. She remembered his laughter whenever Polly, perched on unsteady legs dimpled at the knees, fell over and landed on her rump and squealed in surprise and anger.

He was different then, at the beginning, before his disillusionment set in, before he somehow realized that she was not enough woman for him. She pictured him waving to her, and she saw him from this kitchen, through this window, and heard him call her name as he beckoned her to come on out.

"What do you want?" she asked when she stepped out onto the back porch.

He smiled broadly at her, his handsome face bright and shiny with perspiration, and wiped the sweat from his brow with the back of his strong brown hand. "Get a load of this crazy kid," he called to her. "Watch her do her dive bomber number." He laughed happily and pointed to Polly struggling to rise from one of her tumbles.

Melanie laughed with him. She went to him and slipped her arm around his waist while he laid a protective, proprietary arm across her shoulders. Together, they watched Polly's endeavors and laughed. The child stopped and looked at them and watched them for a moment, then she, too, laughed and ran to them and flung herself against their legs. Her daddy grabbed her under the arms and swung her way up in the air and then down to his chest, where he finally cradled her and hugged her to him, spreading kisses all over her little face.

They had been a fine family, way back then. It seemed like a hundred years ago to her, like another life in another world, when she devoted all of her time to making them a family. When she consigned all of her energies to maintaining a home, to caring for their child, to establishing a haven for him to escape to after his time in the streets. How did it crumble and fall apart? she wondered. She had asked herself that question so many times in the past year or so and she had usually been able to come up with the answer, an answer that invariably put the onus onto Chris. But today she was afraid to answer herself, afraid to think about the question. On this day, she might have been pressed into evaluating her own role in the destruction of their marriage. She dared not look too closely. Better not to look at all, she thought. But asking herself not to think about her past was like asking herself not to breathe. She had no control over her thoughts. She was helplessly and hopelessly at the mercy of her own history.

Two years after they were married, the birth of their first baby had coincided with Chris's decision to change careers. He arrived at that decision without consulting her and had kept it to himself for as long as he was able. He secretly gave notice at the print shop that he would be leaving shortly. Without informing her, he went downtown and sat for the police exam. But when the test results and his ultimate acceptance letter to the Police Academy arrived in the mail, he could no longer hide his deeds, and to Melanie's shock and dismay, he told her what he intended to do.

She was totally unprepared for the news. "Why in the world would you want to be a policeman?" she asked. In those days she cried much more easily and she was already on the edge of tears.

He attempted to be cheerful. "The money's good," he said. "And I get to wear a nice uniform." He laughed and his beautiful face shone with the joy he was feeling.

She could not laugh with him. She could not conceive of her gentle Christopher being armed and dangerous. "I don't understand it," she said. "You've never even so much as mentioned it to me."

"So what?" he said in surprise.

63

"So," she said, "I never knew you liked that kind of thing."

"What kind of thing?" he asked less cheerful suddenly.

"You know," she said. She groped for the right words. "Cops and robbers. That kind of thing."

"It's just a job, Melanie," he said. He watched her sideways, somewhat displeased with her reaction.

"No, it's not just a job, Chris." She was having trouble containing her tears. It was clear to her that he must have expected a negative reaction. Why else would he have kept it a secret for so long? "You don't carry a gun on just a job and people don't get shot and killed on just jobs. It's a dangerous job."

"Okay," he said. "It's a dangerous job. But that's why the pay's so good. We'll have all kinds of benefits we don't have now, Melanie. Cops get everything." He counted off on his fingers. "All kinds of allowances. Medical insurance. Hospitalization. Discounts. All kinds of things."

"Those things aren't important," she insisted. She was frustrated with his unwillingness to understand her fear for his safety.

"Sure they are, Melanie. Those are the things you're always worrying about. The things you always say we need and don't have."

"Don't put the blame on me," she said, softly crying now.

"No blame, honey," he said gently. "I'm telling you. This way you get what you want and I get what I want."

She looked up at him. "What do you want?"

He squirmed uncomfortably. "You know. A good job. Some security. Interesting work."

"You want to be tough," she said angrily. "You want to play gangbusters, like a kid." She pressed her lips together and spoke through tightly clenched teeth. "You actually want to walk around with a gun on your hip." Her voice rose in pitch, as if disbelieving of her own words.

"Somebody's got to do it," he snapped.

"But not you."

"Why not me, for Christ's sake? What makes me any better than the next guy? What've I got now? I'm a nobody, going nowhere."

She felt the argument getting away from her, taking a direction that frightened her. "Don't do it," she begged.

He turned from her with a shrug. "I'm sorry, Melanie." He walked away from her, leaving her feeling cold, unloved, insignificant. The room seemed to fill with his resolve and she shuddered with the sensation of apprehension that suddenly overwhelmed her.

Was that the beginning of the end? she now wondered. If it was, had it started because of his becoming a policeman or had it started due to her lack of support for his decision? He began to change immediately after that. He lost a certain softness, a gentle edge that he had always presented to her. He started to become easily impatient with her and slightly critical of her. He became demanding and finicky regarding her appearance at the end of the day. He complained that she was not keeping herself beautiful for him as she always had. He had always loved her smooth, shiny auburn hair, which she brushed so frequently in order to keep its sheen just to please him. He liked her body tight and firm and lithe and complained that she intentionally tried to appear dumpy simply to avoid lovemaking with him. He wanted her to be sexy and glamorous when he came home, no matter when that was. He dismissed her claim that it was impossible after twelve or fourteen hours of baby work and housekeeping chores.

She tried to remember a specific moment when he had changed in bed, but she could only recall realizing suddenly one day that all the gentleness had gone out of their infrequent lovemaking, that he had become rough with her, almost brutal, that he was taking her with a sense of vengeance, of violence, instead of seducing her the way he had always done in the past, the way he had done that first time in the back seat of his old Chevy.

But that was after the Academy. It had to be, she reminded herself. During his attendance at the Academy, they had seen so little of each other, and when they had been in bed they were both so exhausted, he from the almost inhuman training and she from the constant demands of an infant, that neither one of them had the energy or desire to start with the other.

She had not comprehended what was happening to him. She knew, however, that she did not enjoy the changes that were occurring. But she had had no understanding of them. She was suddenly shut out of his life outside the home. He spoke little to her, and at those times when they did speak, he refused to talk about his training or his work. Yes, she had become angry with him. Angry and jealous. But she had not yet grown to hate him. When had she started hating him? He had been her sweet, gentle boyfriend since her last year in high school. When had he started to appear grotesque to her? When had his touch begun to repulse her? When had he become a monster in her eyes? With the second pregnancy? No! She refused to believe that. Long before then. When?

Was it the night she was first introduced to the reality that he was not a policeman alone, that whether he included her in his professional life or not they were a police family? She recalled that night and shuddered with the vividness of the memory.

Chris had come home much later than usual and was dog tired. He snapped at her when she asked him why he was late. He had promised to take her out to dinner and a movie. Had he forgotten? Didn't he care about his promise to her? She heard herself sounding like a nag but could not help herself, could not shrug off the tiny, cloying desire to provoke him, to hurt him.

He could have simply told her he was late because he had to fill out an arrest report on a perpetrator he had brought in the hard way, taking his lumps as well as giving some. But he had snapped at her instead, and when she started to ask about the large bruise on the side of his neck, she thought twice about it and let it go.

Much later that night, when he felt like talking about it, he told her how he and his partner had cornered a mugger in a downtown alley. As they had moved in, the mugger had struck out with a short piece of lead pipe he had stashed up his sleeve, catching Chris on the neck and knocking him down and almost out. Chris's partner had drawn on the guy and was ready to put one into his gut when the jerk threw up his hands and lay on the ground, spread-eagled and face-down, and surrendered.

But by the time he was ready to tell her the story, she was no longer ready to listen, nursing her hurt and anger at him and wanting to punish him by seeming not to care.

She hated his street stories, anyway, and resented them being brought into her house almost as much as she resented not hearing them at all. She could not decide which she resented more, being included or being excluded.

But she knew she resented the police force. Out of a thousand careers he could have picked, studied for, been good at, she told herself, he had chosen the one that made him drag filth into their home. She hated everything around those stories. They were anecdotes that were invariably connected with an alcohol breath, glassy eyes, and a fumbling awkwardness, as if an abundance of beer was the key that unlocked the vault in which they were stored.

In the six months following graduation from the Academy, he learned to drink regularly and well. It seemed to her that every shift ended with a few brews with the guys, and weekends were barbecues and beer with the guys, and even Monday night bowling became suddenly a few beers with the guys. She learned to stop looking for the smell of beer on his breath and simply accepted that it would always be there. It became a sort of permanent fixture about him, much like the thick, dark mustache he suddenly grew, which she hated but which was worn by all of the guys. There were too many new permanent fixtures for her liking, and most of them were offensive to her, it seemed.

By the time he got out of the shower and started to dress, she was tapping her foot with impatience. She was fully dressed in the long, shaped low-cut black dress, which he always claimed made her look like the highest-priced hooker in the world and blew his mind, and the four-inch black heels that lifted her shapely legs and complimented her ankles the way he always said turned him on. Checking her watch every few minutes as if rushing time along, she secretly hoped he would fail to make it, secretly enjoyed the righteousness of her anger and wanted to feed it further.

"Damn it, Melanie," he said, throwing a grey V neck sweater over his head. "I hate when you stand over me. You're not going to make me move faster that way, you know." He peered into the mirror, smiled seductively at himself, and brushed back his hair. "There are certain things you just can't rush. One of them is a long hot shower after a day on the street. It takes thirty minutes to soak out the crud." He turned and patted her behind as he passed her, then sat on the edge of the bed to pull on his shoes.

"We'll be late and lose our reservations," she said testily.

"So call and tell them," he replied.

"That doesn't help."

He looked up at her, smiled, and shook his head. "Sure it does," he said, pulling on his second shoe and rising to his feet. "They'll hold it for you if you call."

"That's not the point," she said irrationally.

He slipped his wallet into his hip pocket, took his keys in his hand, and turned to her. "Okay," he said. "Have it your way."

He left the bedroom and went to say good night to his daughter. Melanie followed and waited for him in the living room.

When he joined her a few moments later, he carried a small black revolver in his hand. He held it down at his side as he came close to her.

"Here," he said. "Slip this in your purse."

She gazed at him in astonishment. "What?"

"It's my off-duty piece," he said, slapping his sides with his free hand to indicate the lack of space in his tight designer jeans to carry the weapon.

"Well, I'm not going to carry it," she said.

"Why the hell not?" he asked.

"I'm just not," she said stubbornly. The thought of the weapon lying beside her things—her lipstick, her keys, her wallet—was repulsive to her. "It's terrible that you'd think I would."

Without a word, he reached out calmly and took her purse from her hand. He held on tightly to the purse and examined her face carefully.

"I'm not going to carry it," she said. She was suddenly frightened by the strange look in his eyes. But he remained silent. "I hate guns," she added, almost as an afterthought.

He seethed. "I didn't ask you to fire it."

69

She touched her fingers to her throat. "I don't want it near me. It scares me."

"I'm asking you to be my holster," he said bitterly, "not my partner. All the girls do it."

"I don't," she said.

"Goddamn it, Melanie. You're a cop's wife. There are certain things you have to do for me."

"Maybe," she said stubbornly. "But not that. You don't need your gun to go to the movies and dinner."

Without taking his eyes from her face, he opened the purse and stuffed the revolver into it, then snapped it shut. "Carry it," he said. "And shut up about it."

"But I don't want to."

"You have no choice in the matter, baby. I don't go out into these streets unarmed." He tapped her on the chest with his outstretched finger. "If I witness a crime being perpetrated, I don't want to be unarmed when I do my job."

"You're off duty," she insisted.

"Enough!" he said. "No more discussion. I've heard your opinion and it doesn't mean a damn. Carry it, shut up about it, or stay home."

Tears welled up in her eyes. She took the purse from him and clutched it to her breast. The hard metal revolver pressed against her and she could feel its outline being burned into her flesh.

"And turn off the goddamned waterfalls, too. I'm sick of you bawling every time you don't get your way." He turned her by the shoulder and pushed her out the front door. "You just do as you're told," he said, "and we'll get along just fine from now on. You think you can remember that? You goddamn well better."

She carried that purse with its cargo all that night but promised herself she would never do it again. Another promise to herself that she would break many times over. And

70

she had known she would when she made it. But sometimes she had to say things to herself, even though she knew she could never live up to them, if only to preserve her self-esteem.

She not only carried the piece whenever she was told to, but she learned how to do everything she was told without a word of complaint. And, although she despised herself for her own display of weakness, she was able, with some effort, to convince herself that it was worth complying in order to maintain what was becoming a delicate peace in the family.

Phyllis returned from doing the marketing and wrestled the two large bags of groceries, one in each arm, into the kitchen, where she found Melanie sitting at the window staring into the backyard.

"How about some tea?" Phyllis asked.

"Okay," Melanie nodded. "Tea sounds fine."

Phyllis filled a kettle and put it on the stove. "One tea, coming right up." While she waited for the water to boil, she set out a cup and saucer and dropped a fresh tea bag into the cup.

Melanie, who had been watching her, turned back to the window and said, "I've been thinking. You know, remembering."

"Maybe you shouldn't, Mel."

"No. Let me talk. I've been trying to remember what happened to us. Me and Chris, I mean. How did we let such a good thing get so bad?" She turned on her chair and faced her friend. "I figured out why Denny died. I did it this morning sitting here thinking about my life. And I realized that I'm being punished. It's because I failed in my life. I failed as a wife and as a mother. I even failed myself."

"Melanie," Phyllis pleaded. "Don't—"

"Let me finish," Melanie said. "I just want to say this one thing. You know, just the one thing. That I don't feel so bad anymore because I really felt bad when I didn't know why. I was saying to myself all night last night why me, why my baby, and making myself crazy trying to understand it. But I don't feel so bad now 'cause I know why. It's because I've been bad. It's my punishment for being bad with my husband and my children."

"Stop it!" Phyllis snapped. "None of that's true. How did you ever get that garbage in your head? Cut it out. You haven't been bad, and even if you had, things don't work that way. You talk like the good guys always get rewarded and the bad guys always get punished. That's for movies and television. It doesn't work that way in real life." She pulled a chair close to her friend and sat facing her.

"Mel, believe me. You're a good guy if there ever was one. Nobody's punishing you. You've got to stop thinking that way."

Melanie stared at her and remained silent. Her love for Phyllis could not overcome the sorrow she felt for her friend. How terribly wrong she was, Melanie thought. How terribly out of touch with how the world works. It had all become so clear to her, as if the sun had suddenly broken through a cloud-filled sky and brightened her vision with beams of insight. Of course, she was being punished. Could there be any doubt? Her infant had been perfection and perfection is the reward for goodness. Clearly, God had tested her, given her another chance to earn her little perfect baby, and she had once again failed the test, as she had always failed such tests, as she had failed every important test in her life and every important person in her life.

After a moment, pitying Phyllis's ignorance, she nodded slowly, pretending to understand, and Phyllis happily nodded with her and began to smile. Soon Melanie smiled in return and Phyllis laughed joyfully, taking her friend in her arms and hugging her. They held onto each other for dear life and did not separate for some time.

Joe Hennessy called late that afternoon. Phyllis left Melanie sitting at the kitchen window and ran for the phone.

"Hello, Melanie?" he said hesitantly.

"No. This is Phyllis."

"Oh, hi, Phyllis." More relaxed now. "Joe Hennessy. How's Melanie?"

"How do you think?" Phyllis asked.

"Yeah. You're right. Sorry." He coughed and paused slightly, then said, "Can I speak to her?"

"Hold on." She cupped her hand over the mouthpiece and looked toward the kitchen at Melanie, who seemed puzzled. She mouthed Joe's name, and Melanie waved and shook her head.

"Joe? She's not up to it."

"Yeah," he said. "I guess she's in shock."

"She's grieving, Joe. It's not shock," Phyllis said.

"Yeah. Sure. I'm sorry."

"It's okay."

"Listen," Joe said. "Tell her that the cops were just here to see me and not to worry."

"What does that mean?"

"Tell her not to worry. I covered great for her."

"What the hell do you mean by that?" Phyllis spat.

"I mean, they asked me all kinds of personal questions about her and I gave them the right answers."

She looked over at Melanie and lowered her voice. "Are you saying you lied to the police?" she whispered.

"Well, not exactly," he said. "You know. I told them the truth and everything, but I told it in the right way."

"How?" Phyllis demanded.

Joe coughed. "Maybe I should call some other time. Maybe this isn't a good time."

"Like hell," Phyllis said. "If you told the cops some shit about her, you better tell me now. I don't want to get caught off guard."

"I swear," he said worriedly. She could imagine him twisting his neck in his tight collar, rotating the gold rings on his fingers, and she knew he was wishing he had not called. "It's nothing like that. I wouldn't do that to her. She's my girl, after all."

"Cut it," Phyllis said. "Plain and simple. What did you say?"

"They asked me if she was a good mother and I said the absolute best, I swear it. They asked me if she sees lots of men and I said absolutely not. They asked all that kind of stuff and I gave her the greatest buildup. I swear I didn't say anything bad."

"Okay, Joe. Good bye," Phyllis said shortly.

"Wait a minute," he shouted into the phone. "Hold on."

"What do you want?"

"Will you tell her what I said?" he asked hopefully. "That I did all right with the cops?"

"Yes, Joe," Phyllis said wearily. "I'll tell her."

"You know, another guy might've cleaned himself up by throwing dirt on her, but I wouldn't do that. You'll tell her, won't you?"

"Good bye, Joe." Phyllis dropped the receiver into its cradle.

"What did he say?" Melanie asked from her seat at the window.

Phyllis smiled warmly at her. "He sent his condolences, that's all."

74

"I heard you say something about the police. What was it?" Melanie chewed on her lip worriedly.

"Nothing, honey."

"What?"

"The police went to see him," Phyllis said reluctantly. "And they asked him how long he knows you, and he told them and they said thank you and good bye. Now, will you stop worrying?"

Melanie smiled. "He's a good guy," she said.

She gazed at her friend and thought that once again Melanie had proven how little she knew about men, how defective her judgment truly was. After ten years of physical and mental abuse at the hands of her husband, she had finally dragged herself to the conclusion that she could no longer tolerate being subservient to a man, and yet the first male friend she could find in whom to invest her trust was no better, no different, no less a self-centered, egotistical manipulator than her husband ever was.

Phyllis started to shake her head in despair, but she caught herself being judgmental and stopped. This was not the time, she told herself, to be instructing Melanie in how to defend against the vultures in the world who wanted nothing more than to use her.

"The best," Phyllis said, choking on the lie. "The absolute best."

SIX

Central Division, a squat, square grey-stoned police fortress, stood out prominently amidst the wooden frame dilapidated houses that surrounded it. A washed haven in a sea of refuse and waste. Its walls, strangely devoid of graffiti in this cartoon jungle, were darkly somber, staring down over the dim neighborhood that resented its existence.

Inside, Chris Wyatt, in civilian clothes, knowing he should feel at home here in his own division but feeling very much out of it, sat on the long wooden bench against the far wall, the bench that butted up against the candy machine on one side and the soft drink machine on the other, and watched the types, as he referred to them, come and go. They all looked different from each other and yet similar at the same time: a tall blond scabby guy holding hands with a short brunette lady easily twice his age but dressed like a teen punker; later, a round, fat guy in a dirty, torn tee shirt holding his side while blood oozed through his fingers; still later, a tall, skinny geek with a hook nose and bulging, popping eyes led in by two disheveled officers, one with a split lip and the other with a tear in his shirt that would send it for sure to the rag pile. But they all sounded alike; even the ones speaking English sounded like they spoke Spanish. And they all had that special high-pitched, scared quality to their voices that made them sound as if they were squeaking rather than speaking.

It was simply a big square room with a high built-in scarred and chipped desk and counter at one end, where the desk sergeant sat, and benches and machines around the other walls. Where he sat, everybody coming in and going out had to pass him. They all looked at him as they went by. Every one of them looked down at him, some smiling like he was one of them and some throwing him dirty looks like they knew he was a cop.

He had quit early, at four, figuring to wait around for his appointment with the detectives. But by four-thirty the thought of waiting there another hour and a half, with those filthy stiffs and flakes passing back and forth, really unnerved him.

He crossed the street and went into McGinty's. The bistro, as Dave the bartender liked to refer to it while the cops who frequented it called it the ginmill, was deserted at this hour but would be hopping very soon when the men from the six o'clock shift came across for their daily watering. It was clearly a place that catered to policemen: extremely masculine, decorated—if you could call it that—all in dark wood, cigarette burned and scarred, with saw dust on the floor, framed photos of regular customers in uniform all along the walls, and the perennial dank odor of stale beer that hung like a light mist in the very air.

He entered and waved at Dave, who hardly acknowledged him. A glass of soda water only, Chris told himself. Interviewing with a detective, he warned himself. Keep it clean, make a good impression, he thought as he climbed up on one of the many deserted stools. Dave the bartender, clad in his usual badly stained apron moved over toward him from his position, foot up on a low ice chest, sports page spread out on the bar, down at the other end. "Hiya." Dave nodded. "What'll you have?"

Chris stared at the bartender while he thought about it, smelling the comfortable atmosphere, rubbing his hands along the glossy wooden bar. Fuck it, he thought, then shrugged and said, "Make it a brew, Dave."

"A brew it is," Dave answered and moved away.

He looked around and saw Charlie Morris sitting at a back table, in the semi-darkness, with a tall blond girl he had never seen before. Above the table, they were fine, but from where he was sitting he could see underneath, to where she had kicked off one shoe and had her bare leg stretched out between his legs and her bare foot pressing into his crotch. He waved and Charlie waved back shortly. No invitation to join them in that wave.

"What's happening, Dave?" he asked as the bartender set the beer down in front of him.

"Same old shit," Dave said, wiping his hands across the front of his shirt.

"Anybody been in?"

"Too early."

Chris glanced at his watch. "Yeah," he said. Dave drifted back to his newspaper and Chris stared into his untouched glass of beer. He raised it to his lips and put down half of it in a couple of swallows.

He was not looking forward to this afternoon's interview. It did not promise to be much fun. He was not going to end up on the short end of the stick, if he could help it.

Too bad about the baby. Too bad about all of them. He wondered why the detectives wanted to talk to him, but he was not worried. He just wondered. If it had been Polly and they wanted him, he would have worried. That is what they look for, a history of child abuse. They always try to make a case. Poor bastards, as if they don't have anything else to do. And Polly had just enough healed fractures in her little body to make him look bad.

Besides, if it had been Polly, he would be a basket case by now for sure. Polly was a totally different matter. He had all kinds of feelings for her. He had been there, after all, while she was growing up, and they had done things together and meant something to each other and been something to each other. The feelings he had for Polly could not be compared to the feelings he had for the other kid. Maybe he didn't see Polly enough, didn't spend much time with her. But that did not mean he did not love her.

The way he saw it, the feelings he had for Denny amounted to a hill of nothing. He had not tried for her. He had not wanted her. And, because he had been kicked out of the house the same time she was born, he had never loved her or even liked her. As far as he was concerned, she was just a little shit machine.

Tyler came in the front door, stood in the doorway for a moment, letting his eyes get used to the change of light, saw Chris at the bar, and moved to him.

"Hey," he said, lifting his leg over the bar stool next to Chris. "Heard about your kid. Sorry."

They had been friends in the Academy and had tried to keep it up as rookies, but somehow they had gotten separated and drifted farther and farther apart. "Thanks," Chris said and nodded his head. Tyler had made sergeant the year before and they had not spoken since.

"Tough luck," he said. He motioned to Dave, studiously pouring over a racing form, to bring him a beer. "How's your wife taking it?"

"We're divorced," Chris lied.

"I heard." Tyler accepted the beer from Dave and threw

79

a five dollar bill down on the bar. "Want another?" He pointed to Chris's empty glass.

Chris nodded. "Yeah. Thanks."

Dave got him a refill and drifted off again. Tyler touched his glass to Chris's and said cheers, and they drank together.

"It's probably the biggest club in the department," Tyler said, wiping his mouth with the back of his hairy hand.

"What's that?"

"The divorce club."

"I know what you mean," Chris said. "Depressing, ain't it?"

"I got mine a couple of years ago."

"Yeah. I remember. What a mess."

"You can say that again," Tyler said, chuckling. "It's funny when I think back on it, but it sure wasn't funny at the time. The fucking broad took me to the cleaners, all right. My kids don't even want to see me anymore. Can you believe that? They got a new father now with a new Mercedes. What the hell they need me for? Right?"

"Goddamned women," Chris said.

Tyler turned and looked at him. "They're not all that bad," he said.

"No," Chris said. "Just the ones we married."

"That ain't bad at all," Tyler said, poking his thumb toward the back of the room, where Morris sat with the blond girl. They could hear her high-pitched giggle way up front.

"Till you marry it," Chris said. "Then it goes from being a great piece of ass to an unavailable piece of ass."

"Ain't it the truth," Tyler said, swigging down the last of his beer. "Got to go." He pushed a tip along the bar, put the rest of his change in his pocket, and rose from his stool. "Too bad about your kid."

"Yeah."

"You sure are taking it great. I'm proud of you."

"Yeah. Thanks."

He watched Tyler leave, watched the door close behind him and shut out the daylight he had let in. He turned back and stared at himself in the mirror behind the bar. His mustache needed trimming and his hair was too long and shaggy in the back, sticking out over his collar a little too much. But he was still ruggedly handsome, still reminded himself of the cowboy in the magazine cigarette ads.

He began to think of another time in another bar after a shift, sitting with Malone and Grier and Radcliff, drinking beer. Malone was telling some of his famous cook stories, and all of them were getting horny and wanting to hear more. He had gotten the horniest and threatened to pull it out and whack off right there in the joint. Radcliff had said no wonder, with a pregnant old lady at home. They laughed at that. They had all been there. Grier said that she wasn't just pregnant. He had seen her and could testify that she was very, very pregnant.

That was the price you paid, according to Malone. When you blasted off you took the chance of loading the oven, and then, while the loaf was baking, you couldn't get back in for a while. Grier had agreed and said what the hell, you could always turn a free trick just by flashing your shield. He had done it and found there was something real special about a hooker being with a cop, like she really put her heart into it.

Chris owned that the worst part was being stuck with the product for the rest of your life. Malone had laughed and said shit, it was easy to make a cake fall when it was baking; you just slammed the oven door real hard. They all howled over that one, slapping each other on the back and making obscene gestures with their fists and forearms.

When he got home that night she was either asleep or

faking, to avoid a row over the late hour. The lamp was on next to the bed and she was spread out on top of the covers, as if she had fallen asleep waiting for him. He looked down at her lying there on her side, with that huge melon of a stomach spilling out to the edge of the bed, and he wanted to slam her oven door real hard. He wanted to slam her so bad he could feel it down to his toes.

He made a lot of noise getting ready for his shower, walking around and slamming doors as he went. He knew she was faking, then. He made enough noise to wake the dead. He did not even dry off when he came out. He shut off the light and threw himself on the bed next to her, naked and wet.

He laid on his back, staring up into the darkness, listening to her measured breathing and trying to get into step with it, like falling into a cadence. After a while, he rolled onto his side and let his arm fall across her body, as if of its own will.

"Don't!" she said.

"Oh, you're awake," he said. "I thought you were dead to the world."

"I'm not," she said angrily. "But I'd like to be."

"I could accommodate you," he threatened.

"I'll bet."

"Don't give me any shit, lady," he said drunkenly. "I'm not in the mood to take any shit from you." He dug his fingers into her shoulder and pulled her to him.

"Don't, I said!"

"You don't tell me what to do in my own bed. I do what I want."

"Not this time," she said. "And not with me."

He slipped his arm under her and got her in a choke hold. With one arm squeezing her neck and the other hand holding her face in his pincer-like fingers, he said, "How would you like me to slam your oven door?"

"What?" she croaked.

"How about some hard rock on your tummy. You like that?" He shook her. "You like that? Speak up."

"Oh, God," she whispered.

"You bet your ass, oh, God."

He pulled her to him and wrapped himself around her from the back. He shoved his knees into the backs of her knees and bent her body forward like a spoon. He jammed his swollen penis up against her behind and wriggled it in between her legs.

He heard her softly begging him not to hurt her and he became even more enraged. He cupped his hands over her breasts and squeezed as though he were kneading bread, digging his fingers deeply into her flesh, first one and then the other, squeezing and prodding and poking, accompanied by her desperate gasps of pain.

She cried out when he penetrated her, slamming into her mercilessly. With both hands he grasped her hips and pulled her back vigorously while plunging into her like a pile driver. She wept as he brutally drove in and out of her, banging against her body with each downward thrust, again and again and again, until he finally expired in a burst of mixed wetness and grunting.

He rolled onto his back, exhausted but exhilarated. Next to him, she wept almost silently, her body moving only with the tiny sobs that escaped from deep in her throat.

He heard another sound and looked up quickly. Polly stood in the doorway, peeking in through the half-opened door, staring at him with eyes opened wide and an expression of confusion on her face. He started to speak, and she darted back and brought the door closed behind her.

Melanie sat up as well. She leaned back against the headboard and watched him like a wary animal. He saw clearly the hatred in her eyes, wet eyes that no longer wept. He looked back at the closed door and then back to her disgusted face.

Shit! he thought. The swirling fog behind his eyes was clearing. Shit! He could have come straight home after his shift. He could have passed by that fucking bar and come directly home. He could have passed up on another fucking fistful of brews with all the fucking guys. At least this one time, he fucking could have. He could have, sure as shit, but he had not.

Dave shook him out of his daydream when he passed in front of him. "More of the same?" the bartender asked, lifting Chris's empty glass.

He stared at Dave and hesitated for a moment. He had shoved the memory of that night out of his mind, but he could not rid himself of the profound feeling of disgust and self-hatred that clung to him like the odor of death. "No," he said. "Let me have some bourbon. Straight up. This beer ain't doing it for me."

Dave shrugged and poured him a hefty shot of booze. Chris lifted the glass unceremoniously and downed the hot liquid in one gulp, and that did not do it for him, either. He knew it would never do it for him. The stain of what he had become was indelible. It would be with him forever. He would carry it wherever he would go. Fuck, he thought. He had to meet with two detectives and he was six sheets to the wind. Fuck! How had he managed to do that again?

Collins forgave him the boozy breath, writing it off as the guy's way of coping with the loss of his kid. Ruiz, on the other hand, was less generous and thought that the guy was an asshole. He figured that only an asshole would get ready

84

for an interview with two detectives by downing a load of booze. He is a cop. He ought to know better, Ruiz told himself.

They were using an empty interrogation room at Central, a spare room devoid of all superfluous furniture, lighted dismally, and looking out onto a grey alley through heavily barred windows. The three of them sat around the only table, Ruiz and Collins on one side and Chris Wyatt across from them. His eyes were a little red and they burned him when he rubbed them. From the bourbon, Chris thought. Collins figured it was on account of him being broken up about his kid and all and doing such a good job of staying in control. Ruiz, the cynic, knew better.

"Officer Wyatt," Collins started.

"Call me Chris," he said.

Collins and Ruiz looked at each other. Ruiz nodded. "Okay," Collins said. "Chris."

He smiled at them. Collins said, "We know this is hard for you and it's not the best time. So, one apology at the beginning, okay? And then we can get it over with."

"Okay," Chris said.

"When's the last time you were at your house? I mean, your wife's house?"

"Couple of weeks ago."

"You didn't go there last night?"

He registered surprise. "No."

Collins hesitated. "Where were you last night?"

"What?" Chris leaned back in his chair. "What are you asking me?"

Collins remained deadpanned. "I'm asking you to disclose your whereabouts at the time of your child's death."

"What the hell for?" Chris asked.

"Just do it," Ruiz said.

He watched them working him over. What did they think,

that he was some jerk from the country? "No," he said. "First, you tell me what's going on. I mean it. I'm not going to say another word to you until you explain."

"We're from homicide, Chris," Collins said. The two detectives watched the transformation in Chris Wyatt. They watched him shrink down in his chair, watched his shoulders drop, his mouth fall open, the friendly, good-natured cop's arrogance melting away from his exterior.

"I didn't know," he said. He put his hands to his face. His cheeks felt like they were burning.

"Take it easy," Collins said. "I don't want you to jump to any conclusions."

"No conclusions," Chris said. "I promise."

He waited for Chris to settle down, to become less agitated, then said, "You okay?"

"Listen," Chris said. "Miller called me and said the baby died in her sleep. He said it was crib death. What the hell's going on?"

"As far as he's concerned, it was crib death," Collins said. He was searching his mind for a way of telling this that would be less painful, but there was none. "Look. There's no easy way to do this. Your daughter died by drowning."

"Aw, shit!" Chris looked as though he had received a blow to his solar plexus. "How can that be?"

"It is," Collins said. "And this is a formal homicide investigation. I have to tell you, in cases like these, we usually don't have to look too far from home. You know what I mean?"

Chris nodded dazedly. Collins continued. "We figure somebody—we don't know who yet—was giving the kid a bath, and maybe the kid got to be too much to handle and that somebody lost control and maybe didn't mean to kill, maybe just to punish, you know, or to shut her up. Maybe that somebody overdid it. You know what I mean? It happens."

"You think I could do something like that?" Chris asked. "To my own kid? I loved that baby. How could I kill somebody I loved like that? It's crazy." He dropped his head and sobbed.

"Look. It happens," Ruiz said.

"Give him a minute," Collins said to his partner, and Ruiz nodded.

Chris pulled himself together. When he looked up he was angry. "Yeah. Sure. But not to me. I didn't blow my cool and kill my kid, so get that idea right out of your heads. First, I wasn't near the place, and second of all, I don't blow like that. Shit, I'm on the street all day. If I blew like that, you know where I'd be by now?"

"Okay," Collins said. "Let's say you're out of it. Tell us about your wife."

"What do you want to know?"

"Why are you getting a divorce?"

He looked at them and wet his lips with the tip of his tongue. "I got sick of her," he said. "I got tired of her carousing. Out every night. Never wanted to stay home. I wanted a wife, not a playmate."

"She see other men?"

"You mean now, or then?" Chris asked.

"Take your pick."

Chris thought. "Well, I didn't think so then. But from the way she's been since we divorced, I wouldn't be surprised."

"How's that?"

"Well, you know, I've only heard."

"Okay. That's okay. Tell us what you've heard."

Chris looked away and a sadness crossed his face. "I've

been told that she makes it in the singles bars. They say that's her scene."

"Who says?"

He shrugged. "People see her. You know, guys I work with. They're out a lot and they bump into her."

"Give us a name," Ruiz said.

Chris stared at Ruiz and wet his lips with the tip of his tongue. "There's Grier. He's over at Westside. He told me about it once."

Ruize wrote something in his notebook. Collins said, "What else?"

"She's got a boyfriend."

"You know who that is?"

"No. I don't know his name. He drives a blue Porsche."

Ruiz said, "How do you know what he drives?"

Chris looked embarrassed. "I seen him bring her home once. I was across the street, watching, from the shadows."

"When was that?"

"Couple of months ago."

"What time?"

"About midnight."

Collins leaned forward and rested his arms on the table-top. "Did he go in with her?"

"Yes," Chris said.

"How long did he stay?"

"I don't know," Chris said. "I left right away."

Collins leaned back and stared at the wall over Chris's head. Ruiz seemed to study his notes. Chris squirmed in his chair and gazed from one detective to the other.

Collins finally said, "You think your wife could do that?"

"No! Well, I don't know." Chris seemed to be thinking and nodding at the same time. "She sure knows how to be bitchy. You know, when she doesn't get what she wants. She's like a kid herself. But she's a mother. I don't know."

"You never heard of a mother killing her kid?" Ruiz asked.

"I guess," Chris said.

"You never heard of child abuse, Officer? Who you shitting?" Ruiz demanded.

"Okay," Collins said. "Did you ever beat the kids?"

"No."

"Did she ever beat the kids?"

Chris hesitated. "Well, I've seen her hit Polly."

"Beat, not hit."

Chris shrugged. "She gets carried away. Sometimes she doesn't mean to, but she gets carried away. You know." He cleared his throat. "Look, I can't believe that my kid's mother would do that. Other people, maybe. But not my wife."

"Well, you just keep not believing," Ruiz said, "and we'll find out."

Collins stood up. "You know something, Chris?"

"What?" he asked meekly.

Collins said, "On television, they show the father always beating on the kids. It's always a good little girl and a real bad Daddy." He looked down at Chris. "I'm going to tell you something. In these cases—and I've been on a few, I'll tell you—nine times out of ten, it's the mother. Nobody knows the kind of pressure these women are under." He shook his head. "Fathers may hit a lot, but it seems like it's always the mother who kills."

SEVEN

Roger Gillespie had left his office at five and walked down the hall to the offices of Doyle and Crutchman. He had hesitated turning to Doyle for help, but not because of any failing on Doyle's part. On the contrary, he was perfectly willing to admit that Doyle was the absolute best criminal trial lawyer he had ever seen in action. What gave him cause to reflect and pause and think again were the obvious objections he feared the client might raise about the unusual litigator. However, Melanie's possible biases notwithstanding, Roger was well aware that he needed someone like Doyle and there was nothing about the lawyer to which he objected.

Harriet Doyle was waiting for him with her feet up on her desk, trim ankles lightly crossed and exposed from under the cuffless hems of her beige pant legs, a long, thin brown cigarette, matching her dark, creamy skin, clutched in her teeth. A pillow of light blue smoke danced around her head.

Roger had called earlier that day and asked for some time from Doyle—sort of a consultation he had said—and they had arranged to meet at five for a half hour or so.

"I have to pick your brains," Roger had told her. "On a criminal matter."

"That's perfectly all right," Harriet had said expansively. "Wait till tax time and see what I do to you." They had laughed together and agreed that it sounded like a good bargain.

Now Roger joined Harriet Doyle in her private office, a soft, warm place calculated to put a nervous client at ease, decorated in various shades of green and brown, designed to resemble a location out of the distant past, with its emphasis on polished wood and easy antiqued comfortableness, much more like a turn-of-the-century living room than an attorney's office. Roger sat across from her, watching her, through the screen of cigarette smoke, sip brandy from a snifter, the double of which had been set out for Roger with a finger of good brandy in it as well.

"I suppose," Harriet started, "you've got one of your filthy rich clients whose son's been a little bit bad and gotten himself in trouble with the law, and they want you to get him out." She flashed him a brilliant smile.

"Not quite." Roger laughed.

"That's usually it, isn't it?" Harriet quipped. "You never call me with a great stock market tip, do you?"

Roger smiled at her and nodded. "I promise I will the very next time I get one."

"No, thank you," she said, and grinned at him with her sparkling brown eyes. "I hear your tips always backfire anyway."

Roger studied her. She presented the perfect picture of relaxation. Harriet Doyle was tall and just a bit too thin for Roger's liking, but still attractive. More than attractive. Sexy. What she lacked in natural beauty she made up for with a magnetic charm that emanated from her happily intelligent face. And, even though he knew she was pushing forty, he would swear she could pass for twenty-seven. Her hair was full and wavy and parted slightly on one side. She wore a perpetual grin that seemed to say, "Come on, let's have fun together." She had loosened the top few buttons of her blouse and, in her brightly smiling fashion, like a cynical streetwise kid, waited patiently for Roger to start.

"It's a matter," he said, "that I've agreed to handle for a friend."

"Oh! One of those."

"What do you mean?"

"For a friend," Harriet said. "That usually means the money's short. Am I right?"

Roger grinned at her a bit sheepishly. "Well, it's for a friend, but the friend isn't the client. In a way, that makes it worse. I mean, yes, the money's short, and I'll be representing a stranger, not my friend."

"Pain in the ass," Harriet said.

Roger raised the snifter to his face in order to cover his blushing cheeks, and he inhaled the brandy fumes. They made him gag slightly and he thought how much he hated brandy. She always embarrassed him when she talked dirty.

"Harriet. I don't really know what I've gotten myself into here. I feel like a duck out of water, but I'm stuck."

Harriet pulled the cigarette from her mouth. "Why'd you take the case? You ought to know better, Roger."

Roger nodded. "It's hard when a friend asks. And she was begging."

Harriet pointed her cigarette across the desk at Roger. "You better learn to say no, buddy." She leaned back in her chair. "Anyway, tell me about it."

"I don't know too much. I'm meeting the client for the first time tonight."

She smiled and shook her head. "There's nothing like an early commitment. Oh, well, tell me what you do know."

"You see," Roger started, "there may not even be a case here. My friend's worried about her friend because she thinks there might be a case brought against her and she wants her friend advised and protected until that time, if that time ever comes."

Harriet steepled her fingers, just touching her long dark red fingernails together.

"And I don't know what the chances are. I mean, I know damned little, and what I do know comes secondhand." Roger leaned forward and set the snifter down on the desk top. "I know there's been a death. A baby. They originally thought it was a case of crib death, but there seems to be some question about that now."

"The child's been abused," Harriet nodded knowingly.

"I don't think so. My friend said that the child had drowned somehow."

"Aha," Harriet said. "In the tub. During her bath."

"No." Roger hesitated. "The child was in the crib, but her lungs were filled with water. And the crib was perfectly dry."

Harriet whistled through her teeth. "You're not talking negligent parenting now, Roger. Sounds like somebody killed that baby, cleaned her up, and put her back to bed. Probably killed her accidentally—I hope so, anyway—then panicked and tried to cover it up."

"I don't know," Roger said. "Strange time of death, you know."

"What do you mean?"

"I mean, who gives a baby a bath at one o'clock in the morning?"

Harriet closed her eyes and pursed her lips. "Doesn't sound good, Rog. Doesn't sound good at all."

"The mother says she didn't. And, if somebody else did, she didn't hear it. She didn't hear a thing. Says she had a glass of wine after dinner and slept like a log until about two o'clock, when a bad dream woke her up. She went to check on the children like she always does when she wakes in the middle of the night and found the baby dead."

"Who else is living in the house?"

Roger nodded thoughtfully. "The parents are getting a divorce. Father lives outside in an apartment. So, it's an older daughter of eight and the baby. There's a full-time housekeeper, but she doesn't sleep in."

"Any history of abuse?" Harriet asked.

"According to my friend, the sun rises and sets on this mother. She's supposed to be the perfect parent. Very attentive. Always available and accessible to her kids. Doesn't run around. Won't bring men into the house, etcetera, etcetera."

Harriet chuckled. "Sounds too good to be true."

"My friend says if there's a bad guy, it's the father," Roger said. "He's hot-tempered and quick to hit with his hands. According to my friend, he's pushed his wife around more than a little."

"She ever file a police report?" Harriet asked.

Roger shook his head. "The father's a cop, Harriet. She's supposed to be scared to death of him."

"So, even if he's the abuser in the family, there's no record of it anywhere?"

"You got it," Roger nodded.

"Well, you've got a problem, Rog." Harriet dropped her feet to the floor and, swinging her chair around, leaned forward over her desk. "In the majority of the cases of infanticide that I've heard about, it's almost always been the mother who did the deed, so to speak. That's a problem because, I'm guessing now, but I think it's the mother who's your client, and unless the police find some heavy evidence that some other party was there and available and was capable of such an act and had a motive, your client is going to be it."

"That's what I was thinking," Roger said.

Harriet held her forefinger up in the air. "But, before you go off half cocked looking for an outside perpetrator, let me warn you about something else." Roger sat up straight as Harriet spoke with emphasis. "If the mother didn't do it, the overwhelming odds are that whoever did do it, did it with the mother's permission—whether implicit or explicit doesn't matter—if not her direct participation." She sat back. "You've got a tough one here, Rog. I don't envy you one bit. I think your client's going to be indicted and she's probably guilty as hell, anyway, which means you're going to have one tough fucking job getting her off." She gazed at him quizzically. "What the hell are you smiling at?"

Roger sat back, arms across his chest, with the most contented of grins cutting his face in half. "Well, I'll tell you. My deal is that if she's indicted, I get to call in a heavy hitter of my choice."

Harriet stared at him silently for a moment. "You devil, you!" She nodded and grinned at him. "Oh, yeah? You think your client would be receptive to some black chick lawyer who talks dirty and smokes too much?"

Roger returned her grin with an equally mischievous one of his own. "If what you've told me today is correct, you can figure on being knee-deep in this mess any day now.

At two minutes before six, Roger rang the bell to Melanie Wyatt's front door. He heard a child's voice from inside the house scream, "He's here, he's here, then footsteps running toward the back of the house and diminishing as they drew further away.

The door opened and Phyllis—beautiful, sexy Phyllis—

was there, dressed in a plain blue dress that clung to her like skin, revealing every remarkable bump and curve on her body. Her dark red lips parted in a warm, affectionate smile.

"Right on time," she said. "Come on in." She met him as he stepped into the house and put her cheek out for him to kiss.

He put both hands on her trim waist and squeezed just a trifle. Just touching her did warm things to him. Over her shoulder, he saw a young girl dressed in a pink chiffon dress watching him shyly from the corner.

"This must be Polly," he said.

"Yes. Let me introduce you," Phyllis said, pulling out of his grasp. She took his hand and led him to the girl. "Polly, this is Mr. Gillespie. Mr. Gillespie, sir, this is Polly Wyatt."

"Hello," he said. He leaned forward, put his hand out, and she took it. "I want you to call me Roger. Okay?"

Polly nodded, dropped her eyes to the ground, and quickly walked off toward the kitchen. "I'll check on the chicken," she shouted back over her shoulder.

"I'm glad you're here," Phyllis said to him, and slipped her arm through his. She propelled him to the living room. "Come on. I want you to meet Melanie."

Melanie rose from the couch when they entered the room. "Hello," she said, and held her hand out to him.

"Hello, Melanie," he said sympathetically. "My deepest regrets."

"Thank you," she answered as they touched hands.

"Look, I have a good idea," Phyllis said. "Why don't you two get acquainted while I get dinner on the table." She turned to Roger. "Would you like something to drink?"

He hesitated. "No, thanks." He noticed, as she left, that she had not made the same offer to Melanie.

"Would you like something?" he asked as he sat down across from her.

"I almost never drink," she said. She smiled a bit sadly at him, and he thought that, perhaps, a drink might do her some good at this point.

"Good," he said. He looked around the room nervously, noting the inexpensive but tasteful furnishings. Melanie sat on a patterned couch with large, brightly colored flowers spreading across it, bordered on both sides by small maple end tables, each with a tall, heavily shaded ebony lamp on it. The chair he sat in matched the couch in color but was of a design and shape that contrasted with it. All the other pieces in the room—the low rosewood coffee table, the two wooden bookcases filled with contemporary novels, the tall surreal standing lamp over in the corner, looking like a couple of tall, twisted snakes rising straight up, the several rubber plants scattered about—combined to create a pleasant combination of shapes and forms, and the varying colors seemed to compliment their spatial relationships, all contributing to the rational, lived-in effect that the room possessed. Even the absence of a television set added to that effect. And everything appeared so clean and well cared for. Tidy.

"I'm very uncomfortable," she said suddenly, smiling anxiously. She was twisting a small handkerchief in her lap and her white knuckles testified to her nervousness.

He laughed nervously. "Me, too." She seemed so fragile to him, so dangerously vulnerable in her grief and yet, beneath the shadow of pain and suffering that blanketed her, she remained a beautiful and exciting woman, and she caused stirrings in Roger that embarrassed him.

"Why don't we just begin?" she asked, averting her eyes from his.

"That's a good idea," he nodded.

Her eyes down, staring at her feet, she waited for him to

97

continue, but when he remained silent, she finally said, "Okay. I'll start. How long have you known Phyllis?"

"About two years."

"You like her?"

"Oh, yes."

She looked up then and he noticed a slight tick to her right eyelid. "Then what are your intentions?"

He laughed in an attempt to relax her. "Hold on!" he said. "You sound like somebody's potential mother-in-law."

She grinned at him and did visibly relax. "I'm teasing you," she said. Then she grew serious once again. "Don't you think I know why Phyllis invited you over?" She shook her head sadly. "She thinks she can manipulate me so easily. She doesn't know that I let her get away with it when I want to be manipulated and I stop her when I don't."

"Does that mean that you really wanted to talk to me today?" Roger asked.

"I guess," she said. Her eyes took on a worried expression. "I hate the thought of needing a lawyer, but I suppose if I do and I don't do anything about it, I'll get myself into worse trouble." She turned from him and gazed off into space.

"Are you in trouble?" he prodded gently.

"I don't know, Roger." She turned back to him. "Maybe you should tell me. What do you think? Am I in trouble?"

He thought for a moment, not taking his eyes from her sad face. How far should he go at this time? he asked himself. What were this lady's limits? he wondered. How much could she take? "I think we should have dinner and get your little girl off to sleep, then settle down and have a nice talk. I think it can't hurt to talk. And, I'm a very good listener." He smiled at her warmly, having made up his mind. "And, I promise you, after we talk, I'll tell you exactly what I think."

There were tears in her tormented eyes when she looked up at him, and the handkerchief in her incessantly working hands was twisted into a series of tiny tight knots. "I'm afraid to hear," she said, a sob catching in her throat.

During dinner, Phyllis was careful to see that the conversation remained light and breezy, avoiding any of the subjects that might have unwittingly turned it in a more serious direction. She placed Melanie at the head of the table, with Polly sitting at her right hand, close to her mother, while she and Roger sat along the left, side by side. She made sure to touch his leg with hers as often as was possible. He did not know if she was coming on to him or thanking him for being there.

Polly began to warm up and feel more comfortable with him, and by the time they finished with the delicately baked chicken, which had been smothered in mushrooms and green peppers, and Phyllis was clearing the dishes away to make room for dessert, the child had told him all about her school, most of her friends, most of her teachers, and especially Miss Thurgood, the mean math teacher who was hated by all, boys and girls alike.

He was thoroughly charmed by the little girl and very impressed by the relationship between mother and child. They touched each other frequently without embarrassment and spoke to each other with the kind of respect and dignity one expected from two adults. Melanie, though clearly pre-occupied with her grief, showed genuine interest in Polly's stories and pretended that they represented the most important elements in her life at that moment.

Polly, at the same time, seemed sincerely concerned with her mother's feelings and condition. He could discern no fear of an abusing parent in Polly, one of the elements for which Doyle had cautioned him to watch. On the contrary, there were moments when the child appeared to be possessed of much greater composure than her mother and seemed to adopt the roll of parent to her mother's ailing child. There were moments when Roger sensed that the two could have been interchangeable, that if it had not been for the great disparity in their physical appearance, he could not have told them apart.

The dinner was wonderful. Melanie joked about what a catch Phyllis was with her great cooking skill and how some lucky man was eventually going to wake up about her and snatch her off the market. She grinned at Roger at that, while Phyllis pouted exaggeratedly and pretended to be put off by Melanie's interfering.

They finished with a chocolate mousse that they all raved about and for which Phyllis refused to accept credit, since she had bought it ready-made at a French shop on Third Street, which specialized in making inept housewives seem like great chefs. They had their coffee at the table, and Melanie forced a glass of milk down Polly's throat. And then they all helped in cleaning up, including Roger, even though both women were resolutely against it and only gave in because he insisted so vehemently.

Polly said good night and trudged off, with Melanie leading the way, and Roger and Phyllis settled down in the living room. It was only a moment before Melanie was back with them, and as if on cue, the lightness of the mood filtered away and the three of them found themselves sitting silently, solemnly, almost brooding, confronted with the real purpose for his being there.

"Dinner was fun," Melanie finally said. "Thank you, Phil."

"Yes, it was," Roger agreed. He turned to Melanie. "Your daughter is delightful. I really like her."

"Thank you."

"She's quite a kid," Phyllis said. "She sure is tough. I think she's holding up the best of all of us."

"Does she know what's happened to her sister?" Roger asked with some surprise.

"We've told her," Melanie answered. "It was hard, but I don't believe in lying to my children . . . child." She dropped her eyes and folded her hands in her lap once again.

"She may not grasp it fully," Phyllis said. "You know how kids turn things around to make them more understandable. Maybe she's done something like that. But she knows the baby is gone and won't be coming back."

He nodded. "Poor kid."

"She misses Denny desperately," Melanie said. "She cared for the baby like a little mother." She touched the twisted handkerchief to her eyes.

"But our problem now isn't Polly," Phyllis said.

"No, it isn't, is it?" Melanie asked dejectedly.

He looked at the two women and waited for either one of them to continue. When neither spoke, he said, "Why don't you tell me what happened."

Phyllis turned to her friend. "I told him generally, Mel. I think he wants to hear it from you."

Melanie hesitated, then nodded. "I went out with a friend and got home about nine-thirty. I really didn't want to go but my friend was insistent, so I got Gladys, the girl who helps me here, to stay longer, and we went for a drink. I don't usually drink, but I was tired and not too happy about being there. Well, I had a glass of wine."

"Just one?" he asked.

"Yes," she nodded.

He stared at her and waited.

"Then he brought me right home and he took Gladys home. That was our deal."

"Okay."

"I looked in on the children. I always do that, no matter what. It's automatic with me. If I'm up, I look in on them. Polly woke up, so we talked for a couple of minutes. Then I went into the baby's room and she was fine. They were both fine." She started chewing on her lower lip and a hint of renewed crying appeared in her eyes. "I locked up the house and went to sleep."

"Then what happened?" he asked gently.

"I had a terrible dream. I don't remember it now, but I remember that it was horrible and I woke up with a start. I don't usually dream. At least, I don't remember if I do. When I do remember, my dreams are pleasant and sometimes romantic. But this one scared me." She rubbed her eyes as if she were still trying to rid herself of that nightmare.

"I got up and I think I went to the bathroom, and then I looked in on Polly and she was fast asleep and so I went to the baby." She closed her eyes and her lips trembled slightly. "She was sleeping in a funny position, you know, all scrunched up. I turned her over and it was strange. She didn't respond. I mean, she was like a doll, not like a person. She didn't jerk or tremble or anything, you know, like babies do. I picked her up and then I knew. I just knew." A line of tears trickled down one cheek. "I don't remember what happened next, and then I called the police."

"Why'd you call the police? I mean, instead of your doctor, or your friend, or someone?" Roger asked.

She thought for a moment. "I don't know. It was automatic. I always tell Polly in case of emergency, dial nine-one-one. I tell her that all the time. I guess, I just did it without thinking."

"Did you look around the house?" he asked. "You know, to see if anyone had broken in?"

"No." She registered surprise at his question.

"Why not?"

"It didn't even enter my mind," she said. She looked around the room, biting her lip and trying to stay composed. "I thought God had just taken her. I didn't think—"

"Besides you," he asked, "who else has a key to the house?"

"Gladys does."

"Anyone else?"

"No."

"Are you sure?"

"She said no, Roger," Phyllis interjected.

He looked at Phyllis and grimaced. Then he turned back to Melanie. "Have you ever lost a key?"

"No."

He leaned forward. "Think very carefully. Did you ever lend anyone a key? Did anyone ever make a delivery when you weren't home and you lent them a key? Could anyone have made a copy without you knowing it?

Melanie looked at him blankly and shook her head.

"Do you leave your car with parking attendants?" he asked. "Could one of them have made a copy of your key?"

"No," Melanie said. "I always park on the street. It's a waste of money to use a valet."

He sat back and glanced over at Phyllis. He motioned with his eyes for her not to interfere. "Tell me about the men in your life."

"I don't know what you mean by men. I had a husband for ten years. That's the only man in my life."

"Okay. Did you have a boyfriend while you were married?"

She became indignant. "That's insulting."

"It wasn't meant to be. It's merely a question that will

103

be asked of you many, many times before this incident is over with.''

"I'm sorry.'' She looked away. "No, I never cheated on Chris. As a matter of fact, there's only one man I've been even a little close to since I filed for divorce."

"Who's that?''

"Joe Hennessy," she said. "He's the friend I went out with that night."

"Well, how about him?'' Roger asked. "Does he have a key?"

"She already told you, Roger,'' Phyllis said angrily.

Melanie sat quietly, her knuckles pressed to her teeth.

"What is it?'' he inquired, concern etched on his face.

Melanie nodded dazedly. "He does have a key. Oh, my God. I gave him a key months ago. But he wouldn't—not Joe."

"That's not the point, Melanie,'' he answered. "Maybe he lost it or someone made a duplicate from his key. We just want to know if anyone other than yourself had accessibility. That's all. It's not our job to find out who did this. It's our job to learn what the possibilities are. Do you understand that?"

"Yes," she spoke absently, as if she had not really heard him.

"I want you to think in those terms from now on. You have to help me with this. Okay?"

"Yes."

"All right. This is going to get delicate. Just keep in mind what we're doing it for and don't get angry." He turned to Phyllis. "You too, Phil. I'm the lawyer here. She doesn't need you representing her."

"I'm sorry, Roger,'' Phyllis said contritely.

He turned back to Melanie. "Other men in your life."

"There aren't any."

"Think about it."

"I don't have to."

"One-night stands?"

"What?"

He spelled it out. "Did you ever meet a man in a bar and bring him home with you?"

She was indignant. "Absolutely not!"

"Not in a bar. Somewhere else? A class? A lecture? A concert? A museum?"

"I've never picked up a man in my life. And I've never brought a man into this house—other than Joe, that is."

"Never?"

"Not ever."

"Okay. What about Joe?"

"I don't know what you mean."

"Does he sleep over when you bring him home?"

"Of course not," she said indignantly. "I don't sleep with Joe."

"Not ever?" He was incredulous. "You have a boyfriend and you don't sleep with him?"

She glanced furtively over at Phyllis. "Once," she said hoarsely.

"Melanie! Talk to me. No one's ever going to believe that you have a non-sexual relationship with your boyfriend. No one's going to buy that." Roger was adamant.

"It's true," Melanie insisted.

"Why?"

"For the children."

"What have the children got to do with it?"

Melanie chewed at her bottom lip. "I don't know. I didn't want Polly to think I was being unfaithful to her father. I didn't want her to think badly of me."

Roger nodded as if he understood. "You said you slept with him once. . . ."

105

Melanie gestured shyly and put her hand over her eyes as if about to cry.

"Where was that?" Roger asked.

"Well, it wasn't here, if that's what you mean."

"Where was it?"

"In his apartment." Her face grew flushed. "It was terrible."

"Why? Do you have a sexual problem?"

She looked up at him, not understanding at first. "No. That's not what I mean. There was a terrible scene. We hardly got to make love. The phone rang all night long. Every five minutes."

Phyllis began to chuckle. Melanie turned to her and soon was laughing with her.

"Let me in on it," he said.

"Joe'd been sleeping with an operator from his answering service," Phyllis said. "She must be very jealous. Whenever she thinks he's got another woman in his place, she rings him up every five minutes."

"Eventually," Melanie said, "he told me what was going on and took me home. Of course, he called the service first and left word that he'd be in transit." She laughed softly. "So, you see, it's really difficult for me to take Joe very seriously."

"All right." Roger nodded his understanding. "No one else?"

"No one."

"Absolutely sure."

"One hundred percent," she replied.

He sat back and got smug. "How does a good-looking woman like you get by without any sex? You want me to believe that you're celibate?"

She was instantly enraged. "Goddamn you!" she said, her teeth clenched. "I don't need any of this."

106

Phyllis sat forward, as if about to slug him.

He relaxed. "You're going to be asked that question a lot," he said, then softened. "I'm sorry I had to be the first."

She was crying now, and Phyllis moved to her, put her arm around her, and pulled her close. She threw an angry, unforgiving glance at Roger.

"Would you like to stop?" he asked after a few minutes of watching her cry.

"No," she sobbed. She wiped her eyes and pulled herself away from Phyllis. "Let's do the whole thing."

"Are you sure?"

She nodded and straightened her shoulders in a show of strength.

"Okay!" His face hardened. "Have you ever abused your children?"

"You mean, molested them?"

"Well, not sexually," he said. "Do you hit them, beat them?"

She hesitated. "No."

"Why did you hesitate? Don't you understand the question?"

"I don't know. Maybe I don't," she answered.

He stared at her intently. "Do you punish them physically? Do you beat them with broom handles or rolling pins or skillets? Do you tie them up when you're angry and lock them in closets? Do you burn them with cigarettes? With hot irons? Do you push their hands down on hot stoves? Do you—?"

"Stop!" she screamed. "My God! Are you crazy?" She looked worriedly over toward Phyllis, remembering, remembering, knowing that Phyllis remembered as well.

"Roger," Phyllis cried. "What are you saying? How dare you!"

"I'm naming off some of the methods of child abuse that have been documented in our city in the last couple of years. I'm not a ghoul. I'm explaining my question."

"That's horrible," Melanie sobbed.

"Yes, it is," he agreed. "Have you ever done any of those things?"

"No."

"Ever?"

"No."

"How about your husband?"

"No."

"Not ever?"

"He's not like that."

"No?" he asked.

"I mean, he believes in discipline and he's pretty rigid, but he wouldn't do any of those things. He's not like that." She gazed about her in desperation, first at Phyllis, then back to him. "Jesus Christ, he's a cop. He wouldn't do anything like that to his own kid. What do you think of us?"

"Are you telling me," he said, "that if I checked the hospitals in town, I wouldn't find a record of any treatment of physical injury to either of your children? Are you telling me that? You better be. Because you can be sure that the police will inquire at every hospital within a hundred miles of this house."

Melanie grew pale and her trembling increased until she was literally shaking. "I—I think—"

"What?" he demanded.

"Well, Polly had a broken arm once."

"Oh, yeah?" he smirked. "Fall down the stairs, did she?"

"Yes. She fell," Melanie hurried to explain, missing the sarcasm.

He softened. "Is that the truth?"

"Yes."

"You must never lie to your lawyer, Melanie," Roger cautioned.

"I know that." She sounded childlike. "I wouldn't lie to you. Never!"

He remained silent and watched her as she nervously twisted the tortured handkerchief in her hands. Her lovely face, puffed and discolored now from incessant weeping, appeared so innocent, so guileless, that he wanted desperately to believe in her. She sat before him not as a woman but rather as a frightened child, lost and forgotten, terrified of the possible consequences of her behavior—her supposed behavior—and feeling very much at his mercy.

Yet, he suffered a nagging disbelief in what she was telling him. He certainly wanted to believe her, but he could not make himself trust her. Somehow, her words had an untruthful ring to them. Perhaps he had been a lawyer too long, he thought. He had learned very well to distrust everybody. He sighed and felt depleted. The sad fact for a lawyer, he knew, was that clients always lie. They always lie and they always start lying with the overly sincere pronouncement that they would never lie to their lawyer.

"Melanie," he said quietly. "Did you kill your baby?"

"Oh, God, no!" she pleaded.

"Melanie, listen to me. I'm trying to be your friend. In order to do that, I might have to hurt you. Do you understand?"

She nodded sadly, sat up straight, and pulled herself together.

"Someone," he went on, "either filled the bathtub or carried water from the bathroom to the baby's bath, making several trips, and undressed the baby and stuck the baby into the water and held that baby under the water until she'd stopped breathing." He watched her stiffen as a wave of anguish rolled across her body.

109

"Then that person dried the dead baby off, put her back into her sleeping garment, and returned her to her crib, making sure that the crib and the clothing remained dry, and then left. That's at least ten minutes of noisy activity. Baby crying, water running, footsteps back and forth, water being emptied, coming in and going out. I mean, lots of things going on." He noted her face, far from lovely now, twisted and distorted into ugliness from the agony created by the images he was planting in her mind.

Was she hurting because he had been so accurate? He wondered. Did he bring it all back to her? Had she seen it or heard it all before?

"I'm going to ask you once again, Melanie. Did you kill your baby?"

"No!" she shouted, and her eyes were raging. "And I don't know anyone who's monster enough to do what you just said. There may be people in the world capable of that, but I don't know them."

She tossed and turned for hours before finally falling asleep. Roger Gillespie's questions assaulted her consciousness repeatedly. The sound of his voice echoed in her ears, pounding on her, pummeling her with the interminable implication of a foul and brutal murder that she might have perpetrated upon her own flesh and blood during some state of derangement, lunacy, madness. The memory of the description of the calculated, prolonged act worked on her like a series of electric shocks. Envisioning that tiny person pressed under a layer of bath water, battling to suck some air into her flimsy lungs, was like receiving a succession of blows to her abdomen, which drove the air out of her lungs as well.

She did not fear for herself. She did not dread punishment. After all, she was undergoing a severe punishment

110

wrought by her own thoughts. Surely, she was angered by the insinuations of her promiscuity, of her deviant behavior. But, though she was shocked by it, she was equipped to accept the suspicion, the distrust, the accusation of culpability. Perceptions of her held by the world around her meant very little to Melanie at this moment. Even Phyllis's efforts to reassure her, to persuade her that no one who knew her could ever believe her responsible for such a terrible deed, had no impact upon her. It didn't matter, she told herself, whether people around her believed her guilty or innocent. Neither attitude held any consequence for her. It all meant nothing to her.

It could never be what the world thought of her behavior with her child that would damage her. It could only be what she believed—or suspected—about herself that could prick so deeply. And, as she lay there, unable to shut it all out with sleep, tossing restlessly in a cold and foreboding bed, she agonized over the possibility that some part of her, some part deeply hidden within her, down in the very bottom of her ugly being, had risen up during the night to slay that for which she had sacrificed so much.

When she finally slept, she did so fitfully, like a fevered infant, dreaming of horrible colors and shapes pouring over her in a deluge of destruction, breathing very rapidly and quite unsatisfactorily.

She was almost relieved when the phone woke her with a jolt. She sat up quickly and fumbled with the lamp next to her bed. She found the phone and lifted it to her ear.

"Hello," she said sleepily.

"You murdering bitch," the voice croaked.

She recognized the drunken voice immediately. "Chris? Chris, what do you want?"

"You murdered my baby," he slurred.

"You're drunk, you idiot," she said.

111

"Yeah. I've had a couple of beers. So what? That's not anywhere near as bad as what you've done."

"I haven't done anything," she said, fearful that somehow he had plugged into her dreams.

"You killed the baby. I know all about it. I've talked to homicide. They know you did it and they're going to get you, you bitch."

"Since when did you care about the baby? You've hardly ever seen her."

"I loved her," he mumbled drunkenly.

"You wouldn't know how."

"They're going to put you away where you belong, you frigid bitch. Lock you up for the rest of your life."

She realized suddenly that her eyes were dry, that she had no desire to cry. Good old Chris had once again driven the tears from her life.

"Listen to me, goddamn you!" she seethed. "You shut your drunken mouth and go home and sleep it off. Because, if you don't, I may tell the police about a certain small hospital in Nevada that's seen you and your injured daughter more than once. Do you get my drift, big shot?"

She listened to the humming silence on the phone for a long time and wondered what was going through his alcohol-infected mind at that moment. Then she heard the click of a disconnection and the phone went dead. Just for an instant, she felt sorry for him. She had lost her baby, but he had lost all of them. Everyone.

She tried to get back to sleep but it was impossible. The hatred in Chris's voice had been too similar to her own, his words too comparable to her own thoughts and fears. She wondered if that was why she had failed to tell Roger about Chris's brutality. Was she so much like Chris, so much a conspirator by having allowed the torture to continue that she could not bear to hear the words even coming from her own lips? She had thought she was protecting him, hiding the truth of his persecution out of the last vestiges of loyalty she believed she was supposed to possess, but she thought again now. It was not loyalty she felt for him, it was fear. Though she knew she was safe from him, she feared him so deeply, so desperately, that she could not, no matter how much she wanted to, invoke his wrath.

She lay awake for the rest of the night and watched the sun come up through the curtained windows across from her bed.

EIGHT

Ruiz almost spilled his coffee when Collins hit a hard U-turn in the middle of Ventura Blvd and swung to a stop in front of the Jolly Tyme. He glanced over at his partner slumped behind the wheel and shook his head wearily. Thank God the day was almost over, he thought, before Collins got them both killed. They were both too exhausted to keep going much longer.

They had been to a dozen singles bars already that evening, walking into those dismally empty caverns, stripped of all the usual tinsel and looking naked and aged like an old, over-the-hill stripper after too long in the shower, armed with the wallet-sized photo of Melanie they had begged from Chris Wyatt. The picture was several years old and she looked a lot younger in it, but in places like these, with the kindness of indirect lighting, she might have looked as young in the flesh as she did in the photo.

A young guy in a black tee shirt was behind the long bar with his back to the room, counting bottles and making notations on a clipboard clutched in his hand. The rows of glass shelving before him were lined with unopened bottles of various liquors, and upside-down glasses hung from runners mounted on the low ceiling just above his head. The deserted room, tables pushed back, chairs stacked upon them, echoed hollowly with the detectives' footsteps, like an empty train station long after the last train has gone.

"Hiya," the kid in the black tee shirt said into the mirror when Collins stepped up to the bar.

"You the owner?" Collins asked.

"Bartender," he said to Collins's reflection.

Ruiz stepped up beside Collins and held up the shield pinned to his wallet so that it shone in the mirror. The young man glanced at it, put the clipboard down, and turned around. "Yes, sir?" he asked. He put both hands on the edge of the bar and leaned forward so that they could more closely examine the acne scars that marred his face. "What can I do for you?"

"I want to show you the picture of a girl. You tell me if you know her. Okay?" Collins asked.

"Sure."

Collins handed him the snapshot. He turned it in his hands, this way and that, to find the best angle. He moved to his side a couple of steps, seeking better light, and finally looked up.

"Yeah. I think so."

Bingo, Collins thought, and said a silent prayer of gratitude to the patron saint of searchers. He took the photo back and slipped it into his inside pocket. "Tell me about her," he said.

The young man shrugged. "I've seen her around. That's all."

"In here?" Ruiz asked.

He nodded. "I think so. I don't go nowhere else."

"When was the last time you saw her?" Collins asked.

The man scratched his head and sucked his lower lip while he thought. "Last week?" He looked up at them for confirmation. "No," he said. "The other night. Yeah. Just the other night. I'm trying to remember."

"Take your time," Ruiz said, climbing up onto a bar stool and waiting.

"Yeah," he said, suddenly remembering. "She sat at the end of the bar. Over there." He pointed in the general direction of the end of the bar toward the back of the room. "She drinks vodka tonic, heavy on the tonic and lots of ice. Yeah. Not much of a drinker. From the soda pop set. Nursed one drink all the time she was here." He smiled at them, proud of his miraculous memory. "Come to think of it, she always has just one drink. Nice lady, though." He nodded toward the photo stashed in Collins's inside jacket pocket. "And a real looker."

"She come here often?" Ruiz asked.

The young man shrugged his shoulders, stuck his hand out, and flipped it from side to side like an airplane dipping its wings. "Now and then."

"I'll tell you what I want to know," Collins said. "Does she come alone and does she go home alone? That's what I want to know."

He smiled at the two detectives. "I don't watch that close."

"Aw, come on," Ruiz said. "Cut the shit!"

"No, really," he insisted. "I never even see her come in. I just look up all of a sudden and she's sitting at the bar. It's like that with everybody. You know, I don't watch the door. I just look up and they're sitting there."

"What about when they leave?" Collins asked.

"That's different," he said, and smiled wickedly. "You know, if there's some action at the bar, I see it happening. You know, we're never that busy."

Collins nodded knowingly while Ruiz snickered. The young guy pursed his lips as if he were offended. "Then, like if

116

I'm interested, I notice who they leave with or who they don't leave with, if you know what I mean?"

"What about this girl?" Collins asked. "You ever see her pick anybody up here?"

"Well, I don't know." He lowered his eyes. "You know, I don't want to get nobody in trouble."

"You've been doing fine. Don't start getting coy with us now. It's been a long, hard day," Ruiz said.

He looked toward Ruiz and stared at the short cop for a moment. "Yeah," he said. "I've seen her leave with different people. You know. That's the way they do it, you know."

"The other night," Collins said, "who'd you see her leave with?"

"I don't remember."

"Do I gotta tell you again to cut the shit!" Ruiz threatened.

"Honest. I don't remember."

Ruiz squinted at him. "What's your name?"

The kid swallowed hard. "Rodriguez," he mumbled. "Alvin."

"That's what they call you? Alvin?" Ruiz was contemptuous.

The kid spoke softly. He could feel that Ruiz had a hard-on for him. Wasn't it always that way? he thought. A spick cop loved to lean on a Chicano homeboy. "Around here, they call me Slick."

Ruiz snickered. "I'll bet."

"Did you ever see her leave with somebody?" Collins asked impatiently.

"Yeah. Couple of weeks ago I seen her."

Ruiz got up from the stool. "Who'd she go with?"

"Let me tell you what we're looking for," Collins interrupted. "You know a lot of the people who hang around here. Did she ever get it on with—I don't know—let's say a

117

crazy or a hitter? You know the kind of guy I mean. Likes to do pain."

"Or," Ruiz added, "you can give us a general idea of the kind of guy she likes. Does she like beards and leather? Does she like button-down collars and suits? Tee shirts? Body builders? You know what I mean, Alvin?"

The young guy had started out smiling smugly but he was laughing now, and he was trying to hold it in and to control it, not to offend.

"What's your fucking problem?" Ruiz asked angrily.

"Shit," the kid in the black tee shirt called Slick said. "You're pissing up the wrong tree. Shit. No guys come in here. We went lesbian years ago."

Collins had promised Ruiz a ride home at the end of their shift because Ruiz had told him that his Plymouth needed a brake job.

"Take it in," he told him, grinning like an old bear. "I'll bring you home tonight."

"You don't," Ruiz said, "Maria'll cut your Irish nose off."

On the way, about twenty minutes onto the Hollywood Freeway, they pulled off and stopped at Saint Anne's so that Ruiz could jump in for a couple of minutes. "I don't want to do no confession or nothing, I just want a couple of minutes with my Lord," he said.

Collins sat in the car outside and waited for him. Ruiz could go pray if he wanted, but not him. He resented talking to himself. It was weird, and it made him think of the freaks on the street who walk around needing a shave and a bath and a good meal and talk to themselves all the time. But, he thought, maybe he should have gone into the church just to be with his partner. It had been a long time. So long, he could not remember when he had been in a church last, any kind of church, not just Catholic.

He turned on the radio and got the news on all the four stations he had buttons set for. He listened to the usual depressing reports that he always said, filled the air waves. He listened to the stories about a defecting Russian sailor who was not really defecting; a decapitated hooker, half of her found in the hills the other half found in the flats, both halves packed in hot ice and stuffed into green plastic garbage bags; a big drug bust in the south end of the city, once again the biggest drug bust in history; and some little country somewhere, he could not care less about, which was having another revolution, the fifteenth in the last ten years. It's a sorry world, he thought, but no headlines about the Wyatt case.

He wondered what the scribes would write about her if they had the chance to get their hands on her. Would they have a field day punching away at that broad? How many different ways could they describe a baby killer? He was sure they could come up with dozens and dozens. If not, they would find one good gruesome label for her, one good catchy nickname, stick her with it, and ride her all the way up to the gas chamber on it. Well, good for them, he thought. He had seen the body of that baby, and as far as he was concerned, no one deserved all the shit she could get more than that broad, with her sexy, big-titted come-on girlfriend sticking up for her all the time. "Goddamned dykes!" he swore under his breath. "Goddamned lezzies." They could all rot in hell as far as he was concerned.

He got Ruiz home a lot later than usual, but they sat talking for a while before they parted. Collins, at least, was in no great hurry to get home. They congratulated themselves on the good work they had done that day, agreeing that it would not be long before they could collar that Wyatt

119

bitch and stick her where she belonged. Finally, reluctantly, Collins said good night.

At home, Kathy was waiting for him. She had kept his dinner warm and he could smell the ripe odor of lamb stew the moment he stuck his head inside the door. She was sitting in the near dark on the overstuffed couch in the living room, thinking about him, waiting for him. She chewed slowly on one fingernail.

"Sorry I'm late, love." He stiffened when he saw her. "What're you doing sitting in the dark?"

"You're two hours late, Mickey," she said. "And not a phone call. Not a word. So I'm doing what you think I'm supposed to do when you're late and I don't hear. I'm sitting in the dark, waiting and worrying." She was seething and she spoke through tightly clenched teeth.

He took his jacket off and threw it over the back of a chair. "I'm really sorry, Kath. I just lost track of the time. I got so caught up." He snapped on a lamp, revealing her wrapped in her usual unwashed rust terry-cloth robe. She sat near the window, from where she could watch the street and see him coming long before he could see her.

"Save it, Mickey." She turned away from him. "I've heard it before."

"It's my job."

"The hell with your job," she spat. "To hell with your goddamned job."

He stood in the middle of the room and stared at her. Debris littered the floor and a glass lay on its side at her feet, its contents spilled out onto the worn carpeting. In her lap, she clutched a large glass ashtray, filled to the top with crushed cigarette butts and peanut shells. The couch was cluttered with old newspapers, some laid flat, some crushed into unsymmetrical balls. He pitied her then.

He wanted to explain to her, to help her understand how important this was to him. Cops were not like other people. And he was not like other cops. He did not stop to be with the boys, to rub up against them in that locker-room way they had, in that old schoolboylike comradery they tried to simulate. He did not hang out in bars and get sloppy drunk just to forget his family. Sure, he came home late. But if he was always late, it was because the work demanded it of him, because the work dominated him. That was the reason, he swore to himself, and he was almost convinced of it.

The difficulty with explaining all that to her was that it was not really true and he knew it very well. But the truth was something he was not prepared to disclose, not to her, anyway. The fact was he dreaded coming home. Sometimes, he wished he could have stopped with the boys. Sometimes, he wished there were somebody to hang out with other than the trash on the street. Even the trash on the street beckoned to him invitingly, at certain times, at those times when the shift was over and he knew that by the time he walked into his front door she would have consumed enough alcohol to lay him low.

It was her drinking, he told himself, had been telling himself for so very long now, that drove him away from his own home. But, no matter how many times he told himself that lie, he could not manage to believe it. He knew that her drinking was equivalent to his distancing. He could not deny that there was only a little difference between him staying out in the streets till all hours and her putting herself into a permanent liquid fog.

It was their distressed, disillusioned reality that sent them both off in opposite directions, the reality that they had nothing in common other than their own dislike of each other. Any semblance of loving intimacy in their lives had long ago passed into oblivion in order to be replaced with dislike and distaste. Truly, the only intimacy they could claim was found in those moments when they were at each other's throats. During her consistent, nagging pulling at him. In her unfailing drive to control him in a million little ways. In her need to be above him, criticizing him, belittling him, turning her pitiable little existence away from her own attention by glomming onto his and scrutinizing it as if under a microscope.

She had graduated from the shy, passive little Catholic girl he had married because she would have made the perfect policeman's wife, into the specter of a grey, unhealthy, shapeless, misanthropic calamity who thrived on the lifeline of pain and despondency she had stretched between herself and him.

He contemplated apologizing to her, begging her forgiveness, but it was no use, he knew, trying to smooth her over again. Not when she was in her present state of mind. She would not hear him or understand him. What she wanted most desperately out of their relationship was to be miserable, and it appeared as though he supplied her with more than ample cause.

He shrugged off his gloom. "Let's have dinner," he said in a weak attempt at cheerfulness. He turned and started for the kitchen. "You coming?"

"Yes." She pushed herself wearily up from the chair. "Don't worry. I'll get your dinner for you. Don't I always? I'll do my job."

The lamb she fed him was hot and good. She certainly could cook, he admitted. No matter what else was wrong with her, she certainly could cook. That much he would give her. She poured him a cold beer and herself a cup of coffee and sat with him, her red, chapped hands folded on the table in front of her, while he ate.

"Aren't you eating?" he asked. He tore off a piece of bread and dipped it into the dark brown gravy.

"No. I've eaten," she snapped.

"Oh!"

"I've decided not to wait for you anymore," she sneered. "I've decided to eat at the proper time whether you're here or not. I'm not going to wait for you anymore."

"Oh, yeah?" he chuckled. "How'd you make that decision?"

"That's what that lady doctor on the radio says. She says to take care of yourself. It's no good for a marriage for one to cater to the other. You have to keep your dignity, she says."

He swallowed a mouthful of stew. "That quack again."

"She said if you don't show me any attention, I should go out and get someone who will."

"She did, did she?" he laughed, and contained his anger.

"And she said the home is not a hotel and the wife is not a servant. If you're not home on time, you can get your own damned dinner from now on." She glared at him.

He put his fork down on the table and grinned across at her. "You going out to get a new job, Kath?"

"What?" She was genuinely surprised.

"If you're quitting the job of taking care of me and the house, I guess you're going looking for a new one."

"Don't get wise, Mickey."

"What's the radio doc say about that? You supposed to sit around on your ass and do nothing because I come home late sometimes when I'm working on a tight case?" He got up and went to the refrigerator, where he took another beer. "You want one?" he asked her before closing the door. She shook her head and lifted her coffee cup to show him.

"I just want some consideration," she said.

He walked back to the table. "You want that kind of

consideration, you marry an accountant. I don't have a nine-to-five and you know it." He sat down and poured the beer into his glass. "Why you doing this tonight?"

She started to cry. "I'm not doing anything, you dumb bastard," she sobbed. "I'm sick of being alone. I'm sick of being unimportant." She threw the coffee cup at the sink, where it shattered into dozens of pieces. "I'm sick of my empty life."

He stared at her in silence for several moments. He was momentarily tempted to go search the house, dig out all her hidden bottles, and pour them down the toilet bowl. Instead, he threw his beer can into the sink with the coffee cup shards and walked past her and out of the room. At the doorway, he stopped and, with his back to her, said, "When you want to hear what I'm sick of, you let me know."

She watched him leave and wished she owned a whole set of coffee cups, a whole expensive set. She would have relished smashing them all.

Much later that night, when they were in bed, each lying on the side near the edge as far from the other as possible, he listened to her sobbing and gurgling and burping in the dark, and he despised her. He shut her out of his ears, out of his thoughts, and he made his mind turn to other things.

Soon his thoughts were on Melanie Wyatt, and he swore to himself that she would not escape punishment for her despicable crime. He rededicated himself to bringing her in. By hook or crook, come hell or high water, he was going to nail her to the cross. He was going to crucify her if it was the last goddamned thing he ever did. He glanced over at his pitiable wife on the other side of the bed and saw Melanie Wyatt, saw all the Melanie Wyatts of this world rolled up on his bed. And he longed for revenge. Vengeance on the spoilers, he thought, on those who tip-toe into your life and pick at the edges with their tiny beaks, trying to shatter the borders, the boundaries which hold it all together, which hold it all so delicately together. When Melanie Wyatt had touched his fragile life, Mickey Collins told himself, she had brought pain into it, and he wanted so very badly to return some of that pain to her.

Well, I'll get you, Melanie Wyatt, by God! he said to himself silently. Damn your eyes! I'll get you, all of you, and I'll stuff you right into that elusive old gas chamber up north.

Dr. Ralph Nussbaum was also late getting home and he would be even later, since he was still at his desk on the sixth floor of the County Medical Examiner's building, resolved to complete the final report of his findings on the Wyatt baby before closing up. Any sense of urgency to complete was purely self-imposed. Certainly, he felt no pressure from the department to burn the midnight oil. On the contrary, staying late was his idea and, as was evidenced by his isolation, none of his colleagues agreed with him. But he maintained that sense of urgency, even if no one else shared it with him.

For him, this was one of those rare moments in the life of a forensic pathologist, the moment when a victim's remains yielded up that tiny bit of evidence that would solve a mystery. True, death was always a mystery. However, at times it was more mysterious than at others. The Wyatt case was one of those peculiar cases, more mysterious than it needed to be. And it truly fascinated him.

When he had been assigned the case, he had viewed it as a conventional autopsy, even less significant than conventional. There was no valid reason to perform an autopsy. A rudimentary perusal of the corpse had indicated no suspicion of child abuse, no bruises, contusions, sores, bleeding, burns, scars, nothing like that.

The police report offered no evidence of foul play, no domestic drama taking place around the dead child.

And yet the physician, a Dr. Miller, had requested an autopsy. Certainly not a mandatory act. Nussbaum would perform the autopsy as he had been ordered to, he knew, but first he would speak to this Dr. Miller.

He had called him that morning, and Miller had gotten right on the phone as soon as he learned who was calling. "Yes, Dr. Nussbaum?"

"Doctor, I'm calling you about the Wyatt baby."

"Yes?"

"I wanted to know," Ralph said, "if there was any special reason you requested an autopsy. Do you know or suspect something that I should know, doctor?"

There was a long silence on the line as Dr. Miller hesitated. "I was just thinking," he finally said, "that we should try for a differential diagnosis. You know, just to be safe. What I saw looked like crib death to me, but I wanted to definitely rule out ... oh, congenital malformations, or an infection, or even a tumor."

"I see," Ralph said. "Well, I appreciate your position. As you know, I'm sure, our department has lobbied for years for mandatory autopsy in this county. So I certainly agree with your caution. I wish more private physicians were as conscientious as you."

"Thank you," Miller said.

"The reason I called you, the reason I was so curious, was that there's no evidence of battered child syndrome here and it surprised me that you'd ask for an autopsy. But now I understand where you're coming from and I respect it."

"Thank you, Dr. Nussbaum."

"Listen, I don't expect to find anything, although one

never knows. Still, this one looks really clean. Anyway, I'll do it in the next couple of days, and if I find anything infectious, I'll call you. How's that? Doctor? Hello? Dr. Miller?" Ralph had thought Miller had hung up.

"Dr. Nussbaum?" Miller said.

"Yes?"

Miller cleared his throat. "I've been less than candid with you and I apologize for that. I didn't want to deceive you, but at the same time I didn't want to create possible difficulties for the parents, you know, unnecessary difficulties."

"What is it, Doctor?" Ralph asked.

"Okay," Miller said. "You said your name was Ralph?"

"Yes."

"Well, Ralph, I am concerned about this episode. I'm afraid the child might've been battered. Now, I don't have any evidence. I haven't treated her for any injuries or anything like that. But I have seen the older child frequently, and she certainly shows signs of having been battered. Unfortunately, I don't get to treat her. I always see her long afterwards. She's obviously being treated somewhere else, by someone who's not reporting the incidents. Anyway, that's why I asked for the autopsy."

"Wow," Ralph said. "I'm glad I called you.

"And," Miller continued, "there are times when I've seen the mother, when she's brought her child in with facial contusions. Not very serious ones. I don't want to give the wrong impression. But she's looked pretty bad and she's been really short with the child on those occasions. I don't know. I thought maybe she's having difficulties and taking it out on the child."

"What about the father?" Ralph asked.

"Well, the father's not in the house, so I guess I automatically thought of the mother."

"Divorced?"

"In the process. Frankly, I'm hoping you don't find anything, Ralph."

"I know you are," Ralph said. "You and me both. I'd much rather be stuck with the frustration of an unexplained crib death than be involved in a murder investigation. Let's pray we're just a couple of suspicious, overcautious busybodies. What do you say?"

"Here, here," Dr. Miller said and rang off.

Plagued by Dr. Miller's suspicions and his own concern, Nussbaum had started the autopsy immediately, and it was just three minutes into the procedure that he discovered the infant's water-filled lungs. One hour after that he was filing a cause of death report with the police.

But the sense of urgency that drove him now was somewhat unrelated to the cause of death. He worked furiously and angrily over his final report, not because he was so dedicated to his work but because he had found, at the last instant, the final and very necessary clue that led toward an explanation of what had happened to the Wyatt infant in that home.

They had all hypothesized an accidental drowning followed by an attempted cover-up. They had reconstructed the scene, placing a colic-plagued baby in the hands of a lonely, rejected, frustrated mother who had reached the edge of her endurance and could not hope to cope with her inadequacies any longer, could not tolerate the demands of an uncomfortable infant any longer. They saw her plunging the child into a bath, to soothe perhaps, to quiet it, to play with it, to punish it. . . . Who would ever know? They saw her lose control, the baby slip from her grasp, slide under the water. They saw her grope for the drowning child, miss it, perhaps touch it, perhaps back away from it, perhaps hold it under. Who would ever know? They saw her lift the dead child from the water and wrap it in a bath towel. They saw her towel it down, wipe it dry, warm it, fondle it, hold it lovingly, quiet now, not a bit troublesome. They saw her dress it carefully and replace the body in the crib, to be discovered later. When? Ten minutes later? Half an hour later? One hour later? Who would ever know? They had constructed a scenario of a sadly unfortunate woman attempting to hide her failure from the eyes of the world. But, now he knew, they had been hopelessly wrong.

He sat at his desk and recalled the elevator ride down to the basement, to the refrigerated room, the aluminum-shelved room where the children were kept. He chewed on his pencil as he remembered pulling on the drawer that held the Wyatt infant, remembered examining, once again, for the last time, the tiny buttocks, the puffy doll-like thighs, the backs of the legs, and confirming, once and for all, that he had truly found what he knew he had found, that he had found that which so easily could have gone unnoticed, indeed, had gone unnoticed until the very last minute when, by accident, pure and simple, his poor eyes had wandered over the same territory again and registered what they had not seen during a dozen journeys before.

He bent over his desk and wrote the last line of his conclusion. He sat back and stretched. His back ached and his eyes burned and he longed for some sleep. He could go home now. He had finished. In the morning he would have it typed, sign it, and have it delivered to the homicide detective in charge of the investigation.

He felt a deep sense of satisfaction. He knew this was a job well done and his chief would be proud of him. He had managed to do that for which the pathologist believes he exists. He had solved a mystery. He knew now that their scenario was poppycock, a fiction of their desires to maintain the belief that mothers do not do that sort of thing, that contemporary human beings are not really capable of such foul deeds.

Because of him, they had passed beyond accidental drowning. Because of his perseverance, they had found the evidence needed to complete the more accurate scenario of murder.

NINE

Wednesday morning, Melanie got out of bed early, woke Phyllis quietly, and insisted that her friend return to work and get back into the swing of her life. Phyllis was reluctant to do that. Concerned about Melanie's haggard appearance, she was reluctant to leave her friend alone.

"I'm fine," Melanie insisted. "I just couldn't sleep last night," she said apologetically, as if she had done something wrong.

"You've got to sleep, Mel," Phyllis pressed. "You'll make yourself crazy this way. You've got to start taking better care of yourself."

Melanie considered telling Phyllis about her late night phone call from Chris, about how the viciousness in his intoxicated voice, the loathing in his words, had shattered any possibility of rest or escape from her torment for a few hours. But she decided not to at the very last instant, when she recalled that Phyllis was just angry enough with her ex-husband to make real trouble for Chris, which would bring his wrath down on her head, and she, Melanie, could not handle any further confrontations for a while.

She promised to be good, to nap during the day, and got

Phyllis out of the house before Polly rose for school. By the time Polly wandered in, still in her pajamas, Melanie was ensconced in the kitchen, deeply involved in preparing breakfast. The child rubbed her eyes with the backs of her fists and beamed happily when she saw that it was her mother who was making all the racket.

The bacon had been fried and the coffee had been perked, and the delicious smells of toast and bacon and eggs were wafting through the house like invisible magnetic beams, drawing hunger victims to their source.

"What'll you have this morning?" she asked Polly as the child released her hold on Melanie's legs and moved to the kitchen table.

Polly looked up and grinned at her mother. "Pancakes," she said.

Melanie laughed, truly laughed for the first time in several days. "I have everything in the world except pancakes, you little devil. You'll have bacon and eggs and like it."

"Okay, Mommy," Polly said delightedly.

"Go on. Brush your teeth and get dressed, and I'll even brush your hair this morning. Then we'll have breakfast together."

The little girl turned and ran from the room giggling loudly, and Melanie felt cheered. She knew she was recovering from her initial trauma, and though the loss of Denny still weighed heavily on her, in the light of day she felt more herself. Most of the good feeling she was experiencing she attributed to Polly and the love she felt radiating from the child.

As far as Phyllis and her predictions of doom were concerned, well, she refused to worry about them. She was of the belief that you do not cross bridges until you get to them, even though there seemed to be a wise voice in her head urging her to be prepared.

132

She put two breakfasts together and set two places at the table, and by the time she had done that, Polly was back, dressed for school and ready to be groomed. She climbed up on a kitchen chair and turned her back to Melanie while holding out her favorite mother-of-pearl hairbrush. Melanie stepped in behind her and hugged her quickly, then took the brush and started pulling at the long blond hair.

"We're going to be short on time," Melanie said. "I'll do this, then we'll eat quickly and it's off to school for you."

"Do I have to?" Polly asked, pouting.

"What kind of question is that? Of course, you have to. For you, going to school is like me going to work. School's your job." She pulled hard at the long hair and the child was almost pulled off the chair. "Sorry."

"I wish I didn't have to go," Polly said.

"Why do you say that? You love school, Polly."

Polly grimaced. "Nobody loves school, Mommy. Don't you know that?"

Melanie smiled to herself. "I know that you love school. Don't kid me."

Polly waited and then said, "I'm afraid."

Melanie stopped brushing, put her hands on her daughter's shoulders, and turned her around. "What are you afraid of? Are you having trouble with the kids at school?"

"No," the third-grader said.

"What then?"

The happy little face seemed to crumble in on itself and some tears fell down the smooth cheeks. "You won't be here when I get back," she answered. "I'm afraid."

"Oh, Polly," Melanie said. She knelt and took the child into her arms. She held her closely and stroked her hair with the palm of her hand. She chastised herself for not realizing sooner that Polly would be just as affected by Denny's death as she had been. "I promise you I'll be here," she reassured

133

her child. "I would never leave you. I love you so very much. Please believe me. I'll never leave you."

Polly sobbed loudly. "Everybody leaves me. Everybody, Mommy. I know you're going to leave me, too. I'm afraid to come home and you'll be gone. Don't make me go. Let me stay here with you."

"Polly," she said, "if I let you do that, you'll never believe me. You'll always think that I was here because you stayed with me. And that's not true, my love. No. You go to school, and I swear to God I'll be here when you come home."

Polly pulled away slightly and looked at her mother. She was encouraged by the tears on her mother's cheeks, which matched her own. She touched a tear with the tip of her finger and carried it away with her. "Okay." She nodded and threw her arms around Melanie's neck, squeezing her and kissing her hard.

At eleven-thirty, while she was going through her closet and pulling out sweaters she wanted to give away because she knew she would never wear them again, because she needed something to do to keep herself busy, to avoid thinking, the telephone rang.

"Melanie. I was hoping I'd catch you. How are you?" Joe Hennessy asked.

"Better," she said. She was annoyed that he was calling, disturbed by his interruption. She felt invaded. She did not want to speak to anyone who could remind her of her failure that night.

"I was shocked when I heard," Joe said sympathetically. "You should've called me, Melanie. I would've come right over."

"I didn't think of it," she said.

"You know I'd do anything for you."

She stared out the bedroom window at the quiet, uninteresting street outside. "I know, Joe."

She wondered how he could reason her thinking of him at a time like that. She thought how his self-preoccupation had never bothered her before, how it had always seemed entertaining. But then, it had never counted before.

"The police came to see me," he said. "Did Phyllis tell you?"

She sighed. "Yes. Phyllis told me."

"Did she tell you how I stuck up for you?"

"Yes," she lied. "But I don't think it was necessary."

"Well," he chuckled, "you never know with cops. You don't know what's going on in their tiny little heads. How's Polly?"

"She's fine," Melanie answered, wishing he would hang up.

"Tough on the kid, huh?" he continued.

"Yes," she said.

"Listen, if you want me to take her somewhere—you know, like to the zoo or someplace like that, just to get her out—you know I'd love to help you out."

"That's very nice of you, Joe. But it won't be necessary. She's going to school and then Phyllis is here and Gladys has been terrific. So we're pretty well-set."

She heard him breathing on the line. "I wish you'd let me do something for you, Melanie. I feel so useless. What I want to do is come over there and pick you up and kiss you and make it all better."

She almost laughed at him. "I don't think that'd work too well, Joe. It's been a long time since I believed you could kiss wounds and make them go away."

"Well, how about getting out of the house?"

"Not yet," she said. She thought that before she got out

135

of the house she would have to fix what was wrong inside of her, and she did not know how to begin doing that. Just the mere thought of making funeral arrangements incapacitated her. Though she believed she had put her initial grief behind her, she dreaded the thought of watching a miniature coffin being lowered into the ground, dreaded the finality of that procedure. She did not look forward to closing that part of her life irrevocably.

"That's a mistake, Melanie," he said. "You'd be surprised what good medicine that is. To get out and have a drink, a little dinner, come over to my place, listen to some good music. Have some fun. To take your mind off . . . you know, your troubles."

"No thanks, Joe," she said, amazed at his insensitivity.

"How about me coming over there? We could all have dinner together. I'll bring a game for Polly. Come on, we'll have some laughs."

"I'm not much for company," she replied, surprised at how impatient she was beginning to sound. "I think I'll pass."

"Listen, Melanie. I want to see you. Don't cut me off. I think very seriously about you, about our relationship. I know you're hurting now, and I think that's the time you need me and I should be there for you. You shouldn't be alone at a time like this."

"I'm not alone," she insisted. "I've got Polly and Phyllis and Gladys."

"You know what I mean, Melanie."

"No! I don't know what you mean," she snapped.

"I mean, a man. You need a man with you now."

His arrogance offended her. "Like hell, I do." She felt her face flush with anger. Had he always been so terribly self-centered? Had she seen it? Had she only pretended he was someone who could care? Had she just refused to recognize who he was and what he truly wanted from her?

"Sure, you do," he insisted. "You need someone to take care of you. I'm willing to do that. You know, I'd love to take care of you. If you'd just put yourself in my hands, your troubles would be over."

Her voice grew cold. "Look, Joe, I've got to go. Call me later."

"You know I will. Melanie?"

"Good-bye!" she said quickly.

"Wait!" He stopped her. "Are you absolutely sure?"

"Absolutely! Good-bye, Joe."

"Well, if you—"

"Good-bye, Joe."

"Good-bye, Melanie."

On her way back to the closet, she passed the small pile of sweaters on the floor. She stopped and looked down at it. Suddenly, she kicked it with all that was in her and sweaters flew all over the room.

She was enraged at Joe Hennessy, at his selfish denial of any of her needs, at his greedy hunger for his own gratification. She wondered how she could ever have cared for him at all and resolved that she would end their relationship very soon. But, as she dwelled on that thought, she softened toward him. Her anger was not legitimately directed toward him. It was she who had allowed Joe to consider her one of his playthings. It was she who had given him the permission to believe that she was willing to put away her own malaise in order to cater to his wants. It was she who was the villain here, not Joe Hennessy, and it was she who deserved to be the object of her own wrath.

Well, she thought, she would put it all right once and for all, as soon as she could get her head together, as soon as she could finish with the feeling of emptiness that Denny's death had left in her life. But she had no idea how long that would take.

An hour later, Detective Collins telephoned and very respectfully asked if he could impose on her for another interview for later that day. She told him it would be fine, but that she had engaged an attorney and was sure he would want to be present. She noted an instant change in the policeman's tone after that, and in his attitude as well. He sounded much less sympathetic, much more professional.

She gave him Roger Gillespie's phone number and suggested he call him to arrange a meeting. Collins thanked her coldly and hung up. In ten minutes the phone rang again and Roger informed her that they had agreed they would all be at her home in an hour.

She thought of brewing a pot of coffee for them but then thought better of it. After all, she told herself, the police are not making a social call. They would be here on very serious business, and she had better keep that in mind. The police were not her friends and the impending meeting promised to be anything but cordial. That knowledge, of course, would explain why she was so anxious, so terrified of its outcome.

Collins started right in with little introduction. "I only have a few questions, Mrs. Wyatt. Just a few things that need clearing up. Things that we don't understand exactly."

She was sitting in the corner of the couch with Roger Gillespie beside her, while Ruiz sat across from her, writing into a pad balanced on his knee, and Collins stood in the center of the room facing her. He turned to Roger. "I assume, Counselor, you'll be advising your client whether or not to respond to any of these questions."

Roger shrugged. "I don't see any reason not to respond, Detective Collins. We're here in a spirit of cooperation. The same spirit that Mrs. Wyatt has always presented to you. Isn't that so, Detective?"

Collins was polite. "It most certainly is, Counselor. And I appreciate your client's cooperation very much. Let's hope that after today we can put this matter behind us."

"I certainly agree with that." Roger smiled broadly.

Collins turned back to Melanie then. Ruiz held his pen poised over his notebook. "Mrs. Wyatt," Collins said, "last time we saw you, we were led to believe that you had given no keys to any parties other than your housekeeper and the lady who is staying here with you now. Is that correct?"

"Yes," Melanie said. "But—"

"Would you like to change that statement at this time, Mrs. Wyatt?"

Melanie looked over at Roger, who nodded to her. "Yes. I'd forgotten that I'd given a key some time ago to a male friend of mine."

"Who is that friend, Mrs. Wyatt?" Collins asked.

"Joe Hennessy," she said. She put her thumbnail between her teeth and bit down on it. She felt foolish and ashamed, as if she had been caught in a schoolgirl lie.

Collins nodded. "That's the Mr. Hennessy who drives a blue Porsche."

"Yes."

Ruiz scribbled furiously in his pad. "Mrs. Wyatt," Collins continued, "last time we spoke, you led us to believe that you did not bring men to this home. Is that correct?"

"Yes."

"Would you like to change that statement at this time?"

"No." She sounded puzzled.

"Have you brought Mr. Hennessy to this home, Mrs. Wyatt?"

"Well, yes. But I thought you meant overnight. He's been here for dinner and to visit, but—"

139

"He's never stayed overnight?" Collins interrupted.

"No. Never." She was firm.

"Are you positive of that, Mrs. Wyatt?"

"Yes."

"Suppose I were to tell you that Mr. Hennessy claims you and he are lovers and that he has stayed here overnight?"

"That's a lie," she snapped. "If Joe said that, he's a goddamned liar."

"Why would he lie, Mrs. Wyatt?" Collins asked calmly.

"I don't know." She looked around desperately. "Maybe he wants to brag about his conquests. Maybe it's wishful thinking. How do I know?"

"Thank you, Mrs. Wyatt," Collins said smugly.

Roger reached over and took Melanie's hand. He leaned over and whispered to her. "Don't get scared. He's acting tough, but that's just posturing. Just remember that I'm here."

"Mrs. Wyatt," Collins continued, "last time we spoke, you led us to believe that you did not drink nor did you frequent the bar scene. Is that correct?"

"Yes."

"Would you like to change that statement at this time?"

She glanced at Roger. He leaned close to her her. "What should I do?" she asked.

He stared at her and said, "Tell the truth."

"Well, yes and no."

"Which is it, Mrs. Wyatt?" Collins prodded.

"I don't frequent bars, but I do go once in a while. Not very often. Just to get out. Just to see some people."

"We usually drink in bars, Mrs. Wyatt."

"Maybe a glass of white wine," she said. "I don't like hard liquor."

"Is that the best of your recollection, Mrs. Wyatt?"

"Yes."

"Perhaps you've forgotten?"

She became indignant. "No. I don't think so."

"Does vodka tonic jar your memory, Mrs. Wyatt? Tall, light on the vodka?"

"No," she answered.

He smiled at her. "Does the name Jolly Tyme, with a Y, mean anything to you?"

"No."

"A seat at the end of the bar in the back?"

"No."

"A tall vodka tonic?"

"No."

"A bartender named Alvin? Slick?"

"No. No."

"Mrs. Wyatt," Collins said, all pretense at decency gone now, "it seems you've lied to us on several matters."

"Hold it!" Roger snapped. "I haven't heard any lies. I've heard some clarifications and some misunderstandings. Please be careful, Detective."

Collins stared at Roger and his right eye began to twitch. "I apologize, Counselor. I apologize, Mrs. Wyatt."

"It's okay," Melanie said. But it certainly was not okay, she thought. She was beginning to realize to what extent this detective was her enemy and she shuddered with the thought.

Collins resumed. "You told us, Mrs. Wyatt, that you never brought male sex partners home from the bars. Do you remember that?"

"Yes." She was frightened. "And I don't want to change it."

"No," he said. "I shouldn't think so." He reached into his pocket and retrieved a notebook of his own. He flipped the pages and stopped halfway through. Seeming to be reading, he spoke without looking up. "How about women?"

"What?"

"Women sex partners, Mrs. Wyatt. Did you ever bring any of them home with you? Did you pick up women at the Jolly Tyme and bring them home to have sex with you?"

Melanie grew pale. "I—I—" She was staggered by the accusation.

"You only need to answer yes or no, Mrs. Wyatt. Which is it?"

"Hold it," Roger said. "I don't want you to answer that, Melanie." He turned to Collins. "Are you fishing, or making some kind of accusation, or what Detective?"

"I'll let it go, Counselor," Collins backed down. "She doesn't have to answer that." He turned back to Melanie. "I only have one other question, Mrs. Wyatt. I also asked you this before, and I'm giving you an opportunity now to alter your response."

"Go on." She nodded. Her entire body trembled and she chewed desperately at her lower lip.

"Mrs. Wyatt, did you kill your baby?"

She bit down hard on her lip and all the color drained from her face. She twisted away from the impact of his words, his voice, his penetrating eyes. "No!"

Collins leaned forward and fastened his eyes onto hers. "Did you stuff your baby in the bathtub and hold her under the—"

"Come on. Come on." Roger was on his feet. "What the hell are you doing?"

Melanie crumbled and burst into tears. "No!" she screamed. "No! No! No!"

Collins straightened and turned to Roger. "I'm questioning your client, Counselor."

"The hell you are. You're trying to terrify her. You've already asked her that question and she's answered it. How many times do you want to ask it?"

"Until she tells the truth," Collins said. "Until she tells

142

us what happened and who helped her. Until she owns up that she murdered her baby."

"That's it," Roger snapped. "Interview's over. No more."

"We'll get a warrant," Collins shrugged.

"Get one! I'm advising my client not to answer any further questions. And you, get the hell out of here." He pointed at Ruiz. "And take your damned secretary with you."

Roger found an old bottle of brandy in the cupboard, which Gladys assured him was for medicinal purposes, and got some of it into Melanie. After a while, she stopped crying and caught her breath. He propped her up on the couch and fed her the brandy in little swallows.

"Listen," he said. "Just hear me out. None of that amounted to a hill of beans. All that stuff is circumstantial. None of it has anything to do with the death of your child. They can try to disparage your character, and that's obviously what they're trying to do. But that doesn't link you to any criminal behavior." He saw her eyes drift off and he knew she was fading from him. "Stay with me, Melanie. You have the right to live any kind of life you want. It makes no difference. You could eat poppy seeds standing upside down on Broadway in a bikini and it wouldn't mean that you did anything wrong to your child." He straightened her up as she started to fall over. "Melanie! I want you to listen to me."

"I hear you, Roger," she whispered, but she was not listening to him. She was much too preoccupied with hearing Collins's accusations all over again. His words were like steel bands tied around her, squeezing the breath from her.

He lowered his voice and spoke less frantically. "I don't know what this was all about. It was pretty sloppy police procedure. But we're not going to let it get to us. It's all nonsense. Can you see that?''

She nodded, but she saw nothing of the kind. She knew that Collins could not be shrugged off as nonsense. After all, was he not the bearer of the ultimate punishment she had been waiting for? Was he not the messenger from her vengeful God? Was it not time to pay for her dreadful sins?

Roger went on. ''They don't know what happened here. They're groping at anything that comes along. I want you to remember that. You have rights and they'll be protected. But you've got to stay strong. Okay? Okay, Melanie?''

She wet her lips with the tip of her tongue. ''Roger,'' she said softly. He leaned closer to hear her. ''I didn't do any of those things, those horrible things. I swear to God, I didn't do anything.'' She reached out and placed her weary hand on his arm. ''You believe me, don't you?''

''I believe you.''

''The other things''—she shook her head slowly—''they're not true. It's not true.'' She began to cry again. ''Oh, God, it's not true.''

Collins was mad as hell. He had been so sure he could break her. He had been positive she would own up to it. He had taken one hell of a risk questioning her like that, but he had been convinced it would be worth it. He had been positive he would get a confession out of her today. Shit! Without a goddamned confession, she could go scot-free. Shit!

By the time he got back to his desk, he had cooled off. The ride back to the station and Ruiz's calming stability had helped, and he was feeling a little better. But when he sat down at his desk, he instantly began to feel wonderful.

Lying in front of him, neatly typed and duly signed, was Dr. Ralph Nussbaum's final autopsy report. He looked at it and grunted. Who wanted to read six pages of medical mumbo jumbo? Hell, he sure didn't. He turned to the last page and read the final paragraph, which enumerated succinctly Ralph Nussbaum's conclusions.

He sprang up from his chair like a shot, a huge grin breaking his glum face in half. Ruiz was startled and watched him warily.

"Don't tell me she didn't do it!" he shouted to Ruiz. "I got the goddamned autopsy report right here in my hand. And she did it, my man. She did it!"

Half an hour before Polly was due home from school, Detectives Collins and Ruiz, accompanied by two uniformed police officers from the Van Nuys Division, served Melanie with an arrest warrant. Gladys, the housekeeper, stood by nervously, wringing her hands while Collins went through the reading of her rights. Ruiz stood off to one side, leaning against the wall, a sly smile on his face. A stunned Melanie stood limply before him, only half hearing his memorized speech.

"You want to change your clothes, it's okay," Collins said when he had finished with the official part.

Melanie looked down at herself, running her hands down the front of her T-shirt and jeans, as if seeking to comprehend what he meant.

"Go on, Mrs. Wyatt," he said. "Go change your clothes."

She staggered into the bedroom and Gladys followed her, standing just inside the closed door and watching. "You want some help?" she asked.

Melanie stared at nothing, then started and turned to the housekeeper. "No, thank you, Gladys," she said. Her reactions were slowed. She responded after some delay, as if her answers were being monitored by some outside source.

She bent over and picked up one of the sweaters she had intended to give away, a solid dark blue one with a crew neck and a faint white stitch trim at the cuffs. From the closet, she pulled a pair of blue slacks and a pair of brown loafers. She slid out of her jeans, letting them fall to the floor around her feet, and pulled off her T-shirt, standing before her full-length mirror in nothing but her undergarments. She had never felt more naked than she did at that moment, nor more helpless. She looked around her and believed that she would never see this room again. She looked around her and believed that nothing and no one could save her now. She looked around her and knew that her life, as she knew it, was over, gone, and would never be the same.

She pitied herself, wanted to shed tears for herself, to mourn for herself, but could not. Part of her felt satisfied at this turn of events. Part of her was pleased that she was finally being thoroughly and righteously punished as she always knew she should be, as she had always been told she should be. That part of her anticipated her finish with anxious excitement, could barely wait for it. That part of her was feeling strangely satisfied.

As she pulled her clothing on, she thought of Polly, that the girl would be arriving home from school shortly, and shuddered at the realization that she would find her mother gone, just as she had feared that morning, just as she had confessed that morning in tears. Melanie had promised Polly she would be there for her. She had promised that she would never desert the child and, yet, that is exactly what she was doing. Oh, God, she thought, I am failing them both.

She felt a profound sorrow rising up from within her. She had never lied to the child. Polly believed her, believed in her. She was the child's rock. Her foundation. The only thing left that was solid in her life. The only person she could truly count on to love her, care for her, be available to her, be dedicated to her. And now, the last thing Polly would ever remember about her mother was that she had been abandoned by her.

"Be here when she comes home," Melanie said, as if to herself.

"Of course," Gladys replied. "I'll wait for her. I'll take care of her."

Melanie nodded. Yes, she thought, someone will have to take care of her, because from now on she will be motherless.

Gladys helped her dress then and led her out into the living room, where the police officers were all waiting for her. Ruiz held a pair of handcuffs dangling from his fingers. He moved toward her, extending the cuffs, but Collins waved him away. "We don't need those," he said.

She stared at him and he nodded at her, as if he expected her to be grateful. "Let's go," he said.

One of the uniformed officers kept hold of her arm and led her down the driveway toward the waiting black and white. The other went ahead and opened the door for her. Ruiz and Collins walked behind her. At the car, she turned and looked back at her house. She saw Gladys standing in the doorway. The woman waved to her joylessly.

Tears clouded her vision as she whispered a silent goodbye to her home, her life, her world. She bent over and, with the police officer still clutching her arm, climbed into the back seat of the black and white. It felt to her as though she were dead and she were being inserted into her final resting place, into her coffin.

TEN

By ten-thirty the next morning, when she walked into the County Jail to visit with her client, Harriet Doyle had been on the case for twelve hours, ever since Roger Gillespie had reached her at home after learning from Phyllis of Melanie's arrest. She had already read all of Roger's notes, which had been messengered to her home that night, had had a lengthy conference with him in her office early in the morning, and had learned which assistant D.A. would be trying the case. She had accomplished most of her discovery, knew precisely the nature of the case against her client, and had plotted out, in her mind, the appropriate course of attack. The best defense is an attack, she told anyone who would listen. You cannot win cases by being passive. "To the aggressors go the worms" was her favorite mixed metaphor.

She relieved Roger of any responsibility for the client, although she had criticized his handling of the police interview.

"Why?" Roger asked. "What did I do wrong?"

"You let it happen," Harriet told him, lighting up one of her long, thin brown cigarettes. "It should never have taken place."

"I don't understand," Roger said.

Harriet chuckled, shook her head slowly, and exhaled a cloud of blue smoke. "This isn't some tax audit we're talking about, Roger. This is stick ball, hard ball, and there are different rules to this game. Like, for instance, charge her or leave her alone."

Roger was silent. He thought for a moment, then nodded his understanding.

"No popularity contests in this business. I don't cooperate with the police. The police are the enemy. I don't want to give them anything, even accidentally. Whatever they're going to get, I want them to work damned hard for it. You see what I mean? We're dealing with this woman's life, and the system is geared to protect that for her. But if we start being good guys with the opposition, the system gets all fucked up and doesn't know what the hell it's doing. We're adversaries and we don't even talk to each other without snarling." She growled and bared her teeth, then laughed and slapped Roger on the back. "Once the trial is over, we can go out and get smashed together if we want. It's different then."

They agreed that Roger would stay close and be available to Harriet for any help she might need. The budget was so tight that they both knew they would be clerking for themselves and they expected to be doing most of their own leg work.

She waited for Melanie in a private conference room reserved for attorneys and their clients. It had thick iron mesh grillwork outside its windows, which threw crisscross shadows down on the floor. There was a long metal conference table in the center that, along with the matching metal chairs, was painted a dull grey, battleship grey, lifeless and depressing. The walls were bare and dull, as if having gone unwashed for an eternity, and reflected the overhead light with a yellow, dirty cast.

She sat at one end of the long table and, while she fingered the soft leather handle of her attaché case, stared out through the metal mesh at the bright blue sky. She wondered if her client would ever again see that sky without the design of barred windows appearing branded on it. She wondered what Melanie was thinking at that moment, if she were having those same thoughts.

Melanie, led in by a stern, heavyset matron, looked angry and aggressive, although at the arraignment just an hour before she had appeared calm and subdued, cautiously aware of what was going on, and Doyle had felt sad for her, wondering how such a pathetic little thing could be suspected of such a heinous crime. Now, she pulled her arm from the matron's grasp, jerked a chair out from under the table, and slammed herself into it, and Doyle was introduced to another side of her new client.

In court, Melanie had worn her own blue slacks and sweater and shoes. Here, she had been returned to jailhouse clothes—the dull grey prison dress and the brown rubber-soled lace-up shoes. Her hair was tied back in a bun and looked dry and strawlike.

She sat across from Doyle, hands folded in her lap, and glared down at the scarred tabletop. Doyle, not knowing what to make of this girl, wanted to remain objective, unattached, yet she was drawn to her empathetically, liking her almost against her will and hoping that Melanie was not merely acting, was truly a fighter, and that she could remain so under the pressure of what was about to befall her. She prayed that the degree of rage Melanie was exhibiting would continue to relate to the amount of dignity the system would strip from her, because her situation was going to get a lot worse before it got better.

"Melanie?" She queried softly.

Melanie raised her head and gazed at Doyle. "Get me out of here," she said.

"I wish I could do that, honey. If it was up to me, you'd be home with your family right now."

"Get me bail," she demanded belligerently.

Doyle shook her head. "There is no bail, Melanie. You're accused of a capital offense. It's not bailable."

Melanie bit her lip and the knuckles on her clenched hands turned white. "I can't stay in here."

"I'm afraid you'll have to. For a while, anyway," Doyle said. "Is there anything you need? I can't get you out, but I can see to it that you're comfortable."

She laughed sadly. "How can I be comfortable in here? This place is worse than I could have ever imagined."

"I know," Doyle nodded.

"No, you don't!" Melanie said sharply and, at that instant, began to distrust Doyle, began to worry about being represented by a black woman, felt again that instant of shock she had experienced in the courtroom upon first meeting the lawyer. Why had Roger failed to tell her, to warn her? She might not have agreed if she had known in advance. How could she have agreed? What could this brown-skinned woman know about her or the way she lived her life? They were miles apart in their perceptions, oceans apart, and they could not possibly work together. Melanie felt lost and helpless. "You don't know anything!"

Doyle stared at her in amazement. Here was this white cop's Waspy, arrogant wife telling a black street woman about jail. Didn't she know that black women compete with jails all their lives? "Melanie," she said forcefully, "I'm not your enemy. I'm your soldier. I'm going to be doing the frontline fighting for you and I'm going to win this war, too, but I don't need you sniping at me from the rear. I don't care what you think about black people. I don't care what you think about white people. I don't care what you think about anybody. I do know that you're going to assist me to the best of your ability. You're going to tell me everything, not hold anything back, level with me from top to bottom. And I'm going to go out there, into that angry courtroom where everybody is gunning for you, and beat the living shit out of the opposition. Is that clear?"

The two women stared at each other for a long moment, and when Doyle finally relented and relaxed and smiled at her, Melanie's feelings of insecurity were gone and she knew that Roger had been right in picking this lawyer, who was not afraid of anything.

"We have lots to talk about and very little time to do it in."

"Okay," Melanie said. She straightened up and appeared attentive.

Doyle nodded gratefully. "I've gone over all of Roger's notes and I've also seen the evidence the state intends to present at your trial."

"What evidence, for God's sake? I didn't do anything."

"I know that, Melanie. And the evidence is truly all circumstantial. However, it could, in combination, sway a jury. First of all, the occurrence itself is highly emotional. It will be difficult to get a jury free of people who won't be prejudiced against you. Some jurors will really believe you're innocent. They'll want you to be innocent. But others will secretly start out believing you're guilty because it was your infant and you're the mother and they'll think that the mother is always responsible."

Doyle stopped and waited for Melanie's understanding to catch up. "Some others will come in really open-minded, and the prosecution will weigh them down with character assassination, with dates and times and acquaintances and relationships. You're getting a divorce and they'll make the most of that. And they'll drag all kinds of rumors of sexual deviation and aberrant behavior into the courtroom."

Melanie shuddered. "You make it sound so hopeless."

"I want you to know your situation," Doyle said, wondering if she were making it sound more hopeless than was necessary, wondering if she were deriving some perverse pleasure from shattering the naivete of this over-protected housewife. She steepled her long, slender fingers and paused for a moment.

"Then there's the fact that you're a woman," she added. "Some of the male jurors will want to punish you for all the ill will they bear against the primary woman in their lives. You'll get the brunt of all their pent-up hostility. You'll be their scapegoat."

Melanie laid her bare arms on the table and leaned slightly forward. "Let's get some women on the jury. We can do that, can't we?"

"Yes," Doyle said. She peered at Melanie thoughtfully and then, seeming to make her decision, proceeded. "But there's another problem with women. Some women will rally to your defense. They will identify with you. You know, woman alone. A single parent. Making it by herself. That kind of stuff. And they'll want to free you." Melanie smiled, suddenly encouraged. "But," Doyle continued, "on a given jury of twelve, we might be able to get one like that. Maybe two, if we're lucky." The smile faded from Melanie's face.

Doyle reached over and put her hand over Melanie's. "On the other hand, there'll be women who will be very harsh with you because you're one of them. If you haven't noticed, let me inform you that today, in our new society, women are far more critical of other women than men are. They'll have, in the quiet of their own envious opinions, options by the dozens for you, things you could've done instead, things they'd have done in your stead, things other women are doing in your situation, etcetera, etcetera."

"But I haven't done anything," she pleaded.

"These women will lose sight of that, I'm afraid. They'll theorize and hypothecate and lose sight of you, the person." She waited another moment. "And then there are women who will judge you harshly because you're so pretty. They may suffer from unconscious envy. They may have developed a system back in childhood which allows them to diminish pretty women by writing them off as silly and foolish, or empty-headed. Or lets them attribute to pretty women evil motives, loose morals, selfishness, a lack of conscience, a self-centeredness that would allow them to turn away from their children. They may want to punish you for that."

"You make it sound really hopeless," Melanie said in despair.

Doyle smiled warmly at her. "It's not hopeless," she said. "But it is sticky. I'm very confident that this can end well for you. But we must be aware of what we're up against and we must make plans. Because, you see, it's really a matter of planning the appropriate strategy." She waved her hands slowly in front of her like a stage magician. "It's all done with mirrors, Melanie. Now you're here, now you're not."

"What kind of strategy?" she asked.

Doyle glanced at her sideways in that very special, mischievous manner that she had developed over her years of learning how to survive in a white, male-dominated world. "The strategy is what's called the defense. We have to get a handle on the right defense. Let me ask you a few questions. Maybe you'll get the idea."

Melanie interrupted her. "Isn't the best defense that I didn't do it?"

Doyle smiled again. "Of course," she said. "The opposition has to prove, beyond the faintest doubt, that you did it.

That's the theory. The problem is that the theory doesn't always work. And mostly because it's twelve people on that jury, not twelve machines.''

Doyle shrugged and pursed her lips. ''Even though they're not supposed to, the jurors will be looking to us for acceptable explanations for all of the opposition's allegations.''

''Okay,'' Melanie said. She looked up expectantly at the black lawyer. ''Tell me the allegations you're talking about.''

Doyle leaned back and sighed. ''Well,'' she said, ''first of all, they've got a death by violent means that's unexplained. That's probably the toughest one of all, because they can put you and the victim at the scene at the same time. And there's no one else around but you who could do what was done. There's an old rule, Melanie. Things that we look for when a crime's been committed. Availability, ability, and motive.'' She let that sink in for a moment. She watched Melanie's impassive face for some spark of understanding, some give-away gesture that might offer a clue into what made this lady tick.

Doyle continued. ''One, you certainly were available and so was the victim. No question there. Two, you're big enough and strong enough to do what you're being accused of.'' She paused and took a deep breath. ''It's on three that it gets a little better for us, because motive is not so cut and dry.''

''What will they say about that?'' Melanie asked. She had turned pale and her lips were dry.

''Oh, probably the old saw about a divorced woman being lonely. Being tied down by an unwanted infant. They'll say you wanted to live a wild life and the infant restricted you. They'll probably hint at a lover somewhere who'd be your accomplice. But, mostly, they'll hint that all your frustrations, your discontent, your helplessness and anger, got focused onto the child, and when you finally couldn't take it

155

anymore, you acted out your fantasy of being free by being rid of her."

"Oh, God!" she cried out in despair. "That's all so untrue. I can't believe this is happening to me." She grew agitated and shifted in her chair.

"So, you see," Doyle continued, "we need a defense."

Melanie nodded. "All right." She seemed to steel herself. She sat up straight and took a deep breath. "Let's do it."

Doyle relaxed and smiled at her. "Okay," she said. "Let's go back to that night."

"All right!" Her voice trembled slightly.

"Are there things you don't remember about that night?"

"What do you mean?" Melanie seemed puzzled. "I don't remember my dream."

"No. I mean, are there blocks of time that you can't remember?" Doyle asked softly.

Melanie considered her answer. "No."

"Think about it," Doyle urged. "Think carefully."

Melanie tried to remember. She wanted to remember. She closed her eyes tightly and strained to recall all of the details of that night. Had she forgotten something? Had her dream been real and therefore forgotten? Had she walked through that watery night, eyes closed, cut off, performing hideous acts while she slept? Had she done the unthinkable while in a blind, comatose stupor?

"What if I asked you to tell me exactly what happened between, say, two o'clock and two-fifteen? I mean, exactly. Every tiny detail," she suggested.

"I couldn't remember that."

"See what I mean," Doyle said quickly, excitedly, encouraged. "Right there, you have a little loss of memory. Right there."

Melanie stared at her quizzically. She grew afraid and

distrustful suddenly. "What are you trying to get me to say?"

Doyle's face showed her disappointment. "I'm not trying to get you to say anything, Melanie. I'm merely asking questions to get at the facts." For an instant, she wished that Melanie were black, that she could possess that instinct for survival that grows out of continuous and undiminishing struggle.

"No," Melanie said. "you want me to say that I don't remember what happened that night."

"Do you?"

"Of course, I do," she snapped angrily.

"I wonder," Doyle said thoughtfully. "I wonder if you do."

"Harriet," Melanie said with resolve, "I'm not going to lie about this."

"I wouldn't want you to, dear. We all want to get to the truth." She hesitated, frustrated, then tried another approach. "Tell me, when you got up did you go to the bathroom?"

"Yes."

"Are you sure?"

"Of course, I am."

"What makes you so sure?"

"Well . . ." Melanie paused to think. "I always do."

Doyle nodded. "So you must've?"

"Yes."

"Then you went to Polly's room?"

"Yes."

Doyle smiled. "Did the door squeak when you opened it?"

"The door doesn't squeak and it was already open."

"Are you sure?"

"I always leave it open."

Doyle nodded. "I see. Did Polly wake up?"

"Yes."

"Speak to you?"

"Yes."

"What did she say?"

Melanie hesitated. "I don't remember."

"But you're sure it happened?"

"Yes, of course." She looked away from the lawyer. She wore a puzzled expression. She was growing tired and wanted to stop but would not say so. She could not remember anything anymore. She did not know anything.

"What's the matter, Melanie?"

"I don't know," she said. "Did I go to the bathroom? Was Polly's door open? Why do I see it closed in my mind? Maybe you're right. There's so much about that night that I really don't remember. I remember getting up. I remember going to Polly. Then I remember holding the baby and she was dead. And the next thing the police were there."

"That's what I've been trying to show you. So often we think we remember things that didn't happen at that time at all but happened some other time altogether. Or we're sure that certain things took place because they always do. Well, maybe that's because we expect them to take place. They always have, why shouldn't they now? But most important is that if you don't remember what happened that night, if there are some blank spots, is it because you're confused now, mixed up, mistaken"—Doyle leaned forward and punctuated her next words—"or did you . . . black out?"

"What?"

Doyle noted the look of shocked surprise on Melanie's face. She nodded and smiled at her client. "That's right! That's right! Are you beginning to see what I mean?"

"No!" Melanie said angrily. "I don't like what you mean."

Doyle suspected she had gone too far too fast. "Listen, you don't have to think about that right now. Just push it onto a back burner in your mind. We'll talk about it again some other time." She tried to be reassuring.

Melanie turned away, somewhat subdued now. "Okay."

"Let's talk about some of the other allegations of the prosecution, shall we? They will contend that you travelled in a fast circle. That you frequented less than respectable singles bars and that you picked up strangers and had one-nighters with them."

"What?"

"Do you know an Officer Greer?"

"Yes. Of course," Melanie said. "He's a friend of my husband's."

"He claims to have seen you partying in half a dozen sleazy places. With his testimony, they'll try to prove that you neglected your children frequently in order to go out drinking. . . ."

Doyle raised her hand and stopped Melanie as she started to speak. "They will also contend that you are gay and that your sex partners were frequently women."

"It's a lie," Melanie answered. That same terrible lie again, she thought.

"They have a witness."

"I don't care what they've got. It's a lie!" She shouted. She put her hands up to her face and pressed her burning cheeks. "Who's their witness?" she asked through her fingers.

"A bartender in a gay bar called Jolly Tyme swears he's seen you there and watched you leave with other patrons."

"I've never even heard of the place."

"Melanie," Doyle sighed. "Please don't set me up. If you tell me you don't know the place, I'll believe you and I'll

159

investigate. But if you're hiding something from me, you'll only cost us precious time."

"I swear it," she said. She dropped her hands and her eyes bore into Doyle's.

"Okay." Doyle reached into her attaché and came out with a shorthand notebook. She flipped it open and scribbled a note to herself on the left side of the page. "That takes care of Jolly Tyme. What about this Joe Hennessy? He says he's stayed over with you at your house."

She laughed. "How can I be gay and sleeping with Joe at the same time?"

Doyle did not laugh. "It's been known to happen," she said very seriously. "You tell me!"

"Listen, Harriet," she said wearily. "I'm not gay and I never brought Joe Hennessy home to sleep with me. He's never stayed over and he never will. And that's the God's honest truth."

"All right." Doyle skipped a line and made additional notes down the left side of the page. "Interview Mr. Hennessy," she mumbled to herself.

"What else?"

Doyle looked up at her and studied her for a moment. "Did you know that your husband intends to testify against you?"

"It doesn't surprise me. That bastard. But I thought a husband can't testify against his wife."

"No," Doyle said, "a husband can't be made to testify against his wife. First, you're in the process of divorcing him. Second, he's a cop with lots of credibility. And, third, he's a willing, voluntary witness who seems to be just aching to testify against you. That's something which may work against him when I get him under oath."

"Good," Melanie spat. "The bastard deserves whatever you give him."

Doyle liked Melanie's anger. "Do you know what he's going to say?"

"No. How could I? I mean, he's drunk so much of the time, who knows what he's dreamed up."

"Would you like to know?"

"You bet I would."

"He's going to testify that during your marriage, you displayed erratic behavior. That you have a violent temper. That you suffer from chronic loss of control. That you've struck your children and you've struck him. That you didn't want that baby and because he did, you punished him continually until he couldn't stand it any longer and left you."

She flushed a deep red. "That lying son of a bitch."

Yeah, Doyle thought, now we're cooking. "There's more," she said. "He's claimed that you've seriously injured your oldest daughter on several occasions, to the extent that she's needed hospitalization as a result and that he's taken her to the hospital himself and covered up for you. Is that true?"

"No!" she shouted, jumping to her feet and glowering down at the lawyer, her face contorted with rage.

Doyle shouted back. "Melanie, if there are hospital records, the prosecution will find them." She needed Melanie's anger and she goaded the woman for more.

"That bastard!" she screamed.

"Melanie!" Doyle's voice was firm. "Has Polly been abused?"

Melanie avoided the lawyer's eyes. She glanced down at her hands, knuckles white, clamped onto the back of her chair. Finally, she sighed deeply, released her grip, and turned away.

"That's your answer?" Doyle asked. Melanie nodded without turning back. "Tell me. How about the infant?"

"No. Never," she said. Her head popped up and she swung back to face Doyle. "I wouldn't let him near her."

Doyle shouted. "Are you telling me that it was your husband who hurt Polly?" She used an intentional tone of disbelief.

"Yes! Goddamn you!"

"If that's so, why didn't you tell that to the police?"

"He's a cop. Who's going to believe me?"

Still shouting. "And he was the one who took her for treatment after he hurt her? Not you?"

"Yes!"

"And he's done this more than once?"

"Yes!"

"But you protected the little one?" Doyle said ironically. "Is that what you want me to believe?"

"Yes! Goddamn you!" The expression on her face was madness and Doyle was sure of it.

"How did you do that?"

"I threw him out!" she screamed. "Wasn't that enough?" Then she dropped her eyes and grew sad. "He's only seen the baby twice and both times I stayed in the room watching him. I couldn't trust him, so I stayed and watched. He never touched the baby. He never got near her." Melanie sobbed and slid back into her chair.

Doyle leaned back and shook her head sadly. "Then who abused the baby, Melanie?"

"What are you talking about?" She put her hands to her face.

"Someone abused the baby, Melanie. Who did it?"

"You're insane. What the hell are you talking about?"

"I'm talking about the Medical Examiner's report, which states that the autopsy on Denise Wyatt indicated that she'd been physically abused—and more than once."

She looked up. Her eyes had grown wild. "That's crazy. That's crazy, Harriet. Never. It's impossible."

Doyle pulled a copy of a typewritten report from her case

and glanced through it. "According to this report, they found bite marks—old, faint bite marks—on the backs of the baby's legs and buttocks."

"Bite marks?" she asked puzzled. "Bedbugs?"

"No, Melanie. Human bite marks. Human teeth." She watched Melanie carefully. The prisoner suddenly grew quite pale. Her expression became dazed and she seemed to lose the connection with her lawyer, seemed to drift off and tune her out. Her breathing became shallow and rapid, and her eyelids fluttered as if she were about to pass out.

Doyle jumped up and moved around the table to her. She put her hand on Melanie's shoulder and leaned over her. "Are you all right?"

Melanie turned to her and pushed her hand away. She slid her chair back, stood up, and walked to the wired window. She leaned her shoulder and her head against the cool glass and stared outside into the busy street below.

Doyle spoke to her from across the room. "Melanie, do you remember doing that to your baby?"

"No," she whispered.

"Did you ever see those marks?"

"No."

"Is there anyone else who would've done that?"

"No." She had not moved from her position at the window. "No one."

"How do you explain it?"

She did not respond. Doyle thought she had not heard her. "How do you explain that, Melanie?" she asked again.

"I heard you," Melanie sighed.

"Help me with this," Doyle pleaded.

Melanie turned a little, just enough so that she could see Doyle and still remain pressed up against the glass. Her face was wet with tears and she chewed on her lower lip slowly.

"Harriet," she said, "I can't help you."

"Why not?" Doyle pleaded.

"Because I did it, Harriet." Melanie shrugged in surrender. "I killed her, Harriet." She smiled weakly at her lawyer. "I know there's no hope for me to lie my way out of it now."

PART TWO

ONE

Paul Murphy closed the door behind his last patient, locking and bolting it. The coded wall clock he glanced at periodically during his work with patients, the one with the weird surrealistic lines and circles that no one could recognize as a timepiece but all thought of as a work of modern art, told him that it was eleven-fifty-five and he would be pressed to make his lunch date by twelve-thirty. He pulled the patient chart from the top of his desk, made a quick notation in it, filed it in his deep right-hand drawer, and locked his desk.

He stripped off the dark blue shirt he had worn to work and flung it onto the couch, thinking he would get it later. From the closet behind his desk he retrieved a clean white shirt, which he struggled into, then tied a maroon paisley tie around the collar. In the washroom, he brushed his straight, boyish brown hair back out of his eyes and splashed some cool water onto his face. He was forty years old but looked thirty. His body was lean and well-toned, thanks to a daily morning run and a low fat, low calorie diet. He was somewhat fanatical about health and fitness, something many of his fellow psychologists scoffed at. But it was Murphy's belief that a healthy mind necessitated a healthy body, and he was resigned to live by that concept.

He was pleased that it was the third Friday of the month, and as usual on that day, he could look forward to a long lunch downtown in the judge's dining room at the County Courthouse. It was one of the traditions he had personally helped create and the one that he most enjoyed taking advantage of. Not only did he get to rub elbows with the people who sent him most of his business, but he got to eat a free meal as well. It was traditional that the judges paid the check. And, as he had often said, the best thing—if not the only good thing—about City Hall was the quality of the food in the judges' cafeteria.

When he arrived at the entrance, he found the seating chart posted on a portable bulletin board and noted that he was assigned to the table presided over by Judge William Barret, an old friend with whom he had not lunched in at least a year and who always made for an interesting and spark-filled meal. Barret was notorious for putting psychologists on the spot with direct questions, which could not possibly be answered directly, and for enjoying watching them try to squirm their way out.

He found the table toward the back of the large, clublike wood-paneled room after dodging his way around a dozen others just like it, each with a presiding judge or two and several lawyer and/or doctor guests, and saw Judge Barret rise when he spotted Paul approaching.

"Ah. Here's our missing lunch companion now," the judge said as Paul arrived at the table. "Dr. Murphy, so glad to see you." He extended his hand and Paul shook it.

"Sorry if I'm late," Paul apologized.

The judge smiled. "Not at all. As a matter of fact, we're all early." He indicated the two others at the table with a short sweep of his left hand.

The judge was a tall, grey-haired man, very thin and wiry, with a long, slender, intelligent face permanently lined by years of deep thought and contemplation. He loved to present himself as a crusty old jurist who no longer took life very seriously but, instead, had tuned into the humor in the world around him. He seemed to toy with people as he conversed with them.

Paul pulled out one of the two vacant chairs and sat across from Judge Barret. "At least I'm not the last to arrive," he said.

"That chair," Barret said, "is for a guest of mine who can't join us until later. Knowing her, she'll be here in time for coffee and dessert." He smiled slyly. "You know Mr. Winston and Ms. Rayfield, I'm sure."

"Yes, of course. Hello, Mary Anne." Murphy smiled at the heavyset social worker. He reached over and shook hands with Harvey Winston, an attorney he had worked for several times in the past.

"I'm glad you're here, Paul," Judge Barret said while buttering a small piece of French roll. "You can help settle a disagreement."

The waiter hovered over Paul, who quickly ordered a small seafood salad without dressing and black coffee, silently commending himself for eating right. "What's that, Your Honor?" he inquired when the waiter had left.

The judge pursed his lips and adopted a serious tone. "Harvey and Mary Anne are split on a question that I posed. I was looking for a concrete answer and what I got was . . . well, less than that. Perhaps you can clarify for me."

Murphy grinned at him. "I'm sure, Judge, there's nothing I could say that you haven't already thought of."

The judge smiled broadly. "A diplomat as well as a shrink, eh?"

Paul laughed, flashing his straight white teeth. They had

liked each other for a long time and it showed in the gentle way they played with each other. "Diplomacy is the better part of valor for a shrink. We're already vulnerable, just by the nature of what we try to do, and if we aren't clever about it, how can we convince all of you that we know what we're doing?"

"You'll never do that," the judge chided. "I already know better."

The waiter poured coffee from a silver server into Paul's cup and moved a small crystal tray of sugar substitute in front of him.

"The question is this," the judge continued. "In a custody matter I'm reading about, the contention on the mother's side is that the father should not be allowed to have the children alone at any time because he is of the habit of showering nude, of course, in their presence. Actually, he takes them into the shower with him. These are two little, impressionable children, both girls, of course—if they were boys there'd be less of a question—aged seven and five."

Paul nodded as he listened and sipped his coffee. He watched Winston sit back and smile. Mary Anne took the matter much more seriously.

"Now, then," the judge went on, "Mary Anne says that nothing dire could come of such a practice, while Winston here says it's a sick activity and will damage the girls psychologically." He held his hands out in a gesture of puzzlement. "You see? Which is it, Paul?"

Paul looked into the old man's eyes and caught the sparkle of mischief dancing there. "Well, Your Honor, that's a tricky question."

"I thought so, too." The judge laughed. "Would you rather pass on it?"

"Oh, no," Paul answered quickly. "Just give me a second to think about it."

"Take as much time as you'd like. I don't like to rush you scientists," the judge said.

Winston snorted mirthfully.

Paul caught the barb and fielded it well. "Inasmuch as we're inexact scientists, we need all the time we can get."

The judge nodded appreciatively and bowed to Paul.

"First of all," Paul said, "I think that if the husband had showered more often with his wife, there might not have been a divorce and this whole question would be moot."

Winston chuckled and Mary Anne laughed openly. "Bravo," the judge said. "My sentiments exactly. Don't you detect a little bit of jealousy behind the wife's accusation?"

"Perhaps," Paul said.

The judge waited. "Well, what's the answer?"

Paul smiled. "Judge, to my view, the behavior is neither good nor bad. It's simply behavior, and for some it may be pleasurable and for others it may be harmful."

"You are cagey, Dr. Murphy. Is that how you got so successful, by not taking a stand?"

Paul stared at the judge. "I take stands, Your Honor, only on individual matters when I know the parties thoroughly."

The judge nodded slowly and smiled. "No general rule, eh? That's reasonable."

"But, I'll say this about it," Paul concluded. "If that's the most dangerous behavior that father manifests, I'd say those little girls are lucky. Hell, skinny-dipping never hurt anybody. Not half as much as being beaten up." They all laughed and agreed.

The waiter brought their food and placed it in front of them. Paul looked at his healthy salad and wished it were a bloody rare porterhouse steak and a baked potato drenched in melted butter. He advocated eating carefully, but he never claimed to be free of temptation. And his cholesterol count

171

went up just thinking about it, he was sure. He bit into a shrimp wrapped in a piece of lettuce.

Winston received a breaded veal cutlet with mashed potatoes drowned in brown gravy, and Mary Anne nibbled at a spare carrot and raisin salad—a ball of shredded carrot laying exposed on a huge lettuce leaf. They ate in silence for a while.

When the judge had eaten half the rare roast beef on his plate, he put his utensils down and pushed the dish away from him. "What do you know about the Wyatt case, Paul?"

Paul looked up from his plate and thought for a moment. "Don't know the name."

"That's the mother who killed her baby, isn't it?" Mary Anne said.

"Allegedly," the judge answered.

"Tough case," Harvey Winston said, cutting into his breaded veal cutlet. "I heard the D.A. has a lock on it."

"Well," Judge Barret said, "I don't want to discuss the case or its merits. I'll be sitting for it and I don't think it proper for me to gossip about it over lunch." He turned back to Paul. "Can it be that you truly haven't heard anything about it?"

"There are lots of things, Judge Barret, that I'm not aware of. I guess I'm not a news hound," Paul apologized.

"In a way, I'm glad. That may suit me just fine. It'll be easier for you to be objective. There's been far too much notoriety in the press already on this case." The judge rolled the end of a cigar around his lips but didn't light it. "Tell me if this is going to bother you, Mary Anne." The woman shook her head and smiled. "Good!" The judge revealed a thin gold lighter and lit the cigar, puffing out a sizeable billow of blue smoke. "I don't have to be polite with you fellows," he said. "I don't care if it bothers you."

Paul waited for him to continue. The judge leaned back

172

and sighed contentedly. "I'm going to ask you, Paul, to see the accused woman." He held his hand up before Paul could respond. "It's simple. All I want to know is is she able to stand trial. Will she know what's going on? Will she understand the significance of the proceedings? That's all. I don't want to know if you think she's guilty or not. I don't care what you think about that." He pointed the cigar at Paul. "And, we've had trouble like that before. Right?" The judge grinned at him then. "Just a simple determination of competency."

Paul nodded, remembering the feeling of being reprimanded in open court. How many times had he sworn to himself that he would never play detective again?

"Competency to stand trial. That's all I want. What do you think? You think you can do that?"

Paul nodded and stared at the judge, who was looking beyond him toward the entrance to the room. "Ah," he said. "Here's my last guest. What a timely entrance." He stood up and welcomed Harriet Doyle.

"Hello, Harriet," he said. "This is Paul Murphy."

Paul stood up and shook her hand. He had heard of the famous Harriet Doyle. The male lawyers he knew, in their locker room fashion, kidded about her magnificent, perfectly proportioned body, draped now in a tailored powder-blue suit, which appeared molded to her, and about the hauntingly exotic beauty of the classic face, which masked a cutthroat courtroom killer instinct. He was surprised at the firmness of her grip and a little disappointed when she pulled her hand away.

"And, Harvey Winston," the judge continued. They shook. "And, Mary Anne Rayfield."

Doyle reached across the table and touched the other woman's fingers.

Judge Barret motioned her to a chair. "Sit down, Harriet.

Have anything you want. It's all on me today." Doyle sat but the judge remained standing. He rolled up his napkin and dropped it on the table. "I'll be leaving now."

Paul rose. "When do you want to see me, Your Honor? To finish about that matter?"

"I'm finished, Paul," the judge said, glancing at Doyle. "Harriet'll take over now." He gave them all a short wave and walked away from the table.

"What was that mystery all about?" Paul asked.

"Well," Doyle said, smiling brightly, "I guess we're going to talk about the Wyatt case and he shouldn't be here when that happens. Actually, he shouldn't be anywhere near me right now, since I'm representing Melanie Wyatt." She winked at him and pursed her lips mockingly. "How's the shrimp? I'm a meat and potato person myself."

After lunch, Doyle walked Paul to his car, which was parked in the subterranean garage under the courthouse, and used the time to register a vigorous appeal on behalf of her client. She briefed Paul on the details of the case, as much as she could, confessing that most of her information came from the prosecution and implying that she would be looking to Paul for a greater understanding of what had happened that night. She told him that no one truly knew what had happened that night; only the perpetrator knew the truth, even if that truth were buried somewhere deep in an unconscious mind.

"You could get at it," Doyle said. "That would be something. Don't you guys have some kind of truth serum? I've heard about it."

"You're referring to sodium pentothal," Paul said.

"Yes."

"I can't use that stuff," Paul answered. "Only psychiatrists can administer drugs. But, even if I could, I wouldn't."

174

He felt an old sensation tug at him. God, he wanted to play detective!

Doyle was surprised. "Why not?"

"On whom, Ms. Doyle? Are you suggesting I use it on your own client?"

"Sure."

"She'd have no control under it. Aren't you afraid of what she might say?" He studied her lovely face. "Hold on! You think she did it?"

Doyle did not hesitate. "Of course. She just doesn't remember it. And that means she might not be held responsible."

"I see." Paul smiled at the lawyer. He felt her pulling at him, tempting him. He needed to be strong. "I'm afraid I'm not going to be able to help you, Ms. Doyle."

"Call me Harriet, will you! And why not?"

"First of all, it's not my job to accumulate evidence for the defense, and second of all and much more important, Judge Barret's already warned me not to have any opinions about guilt or innocence. He hates when I play amateur detective and has told me so on many occasions. I've made the mistake of crossing him before. And, believe me, I have no intention of doing it again."

Doyle shrugged. "What the judge doesn't know won't hurt him," she said. "And, whatever you think your job is, you're wrong. It's the job of everybody involved with this case, no matter what they're doing, to help get to the truth. That's all that counts, Doc. The truth!"

Doyle stood in front of him and poked her forefinger into the psychologist's chest. "You may tell yourself all you're going to do is find out if she can stand trial. But you're lying to yourself, Doc. Because every time you unearth a little tiny particle of truth, you're going to feel overjoyed and you're not going to be able to keep it to yourself. you're going to need to tell someone about it, and the judge has warned you not to have opinions or else, and he means it, we both know that. So, I figure you're going to do the next best thing. You're going to call me and tell me about it. you know why you're going to do that, Doc?" She did not wait for a reply. "Because you believe in justice, that's why. You and me, Doc. We're going to save that woman's life."

Paul was fascinated by this woman. If she only knew, he thought, how much I want to comply. But instead, he touched Doyle's shoulder and gently pushed her back. "You may be a very persuasive lawyer, Ms. Doyle, but you're very wrong about me. I'm sure I'm not going to discover any truths. I don't even know what kind of truths you're imagining."

"You know damn well what I'm talking about. She'll answer your questions and she'll sound lucid as hell, so there's no way you're going to find her incompetent. But, Doc, she killed her own kid—in a gruesome way—and that's crazy. I don't care what anybody says. That's crazy. And, if I have to go to trial with her, I'm going to need all the help I can get."

Paul studied the lawyer's face. "Whether I find anything or not, I'm not going to call you, Counselor. I don't work for the defense. I work for the judge, the trier of fact."

Doyle grimaced. "Come on, doc. Don't be naive. Who the hell cares who you officially work for?"

"I care, Doyle!"

"Jesus, Doc," Doyle said, turning away in exasperation. "Don't give me a hard time. Come on, use your head. What do you think he invited me to lunch for? That man doesn't do a thing without a damned good reason."

Paul squinted at the fiery lawyer. "You're saying he wants me to do this for you?"

"No!" she snapped. "I'm saying he wants you to do this for the sake of justice." She drew in close again. "Look, you think he wants to put somebody away if they're innocent? Christ, don't you hear all the bitching from the cops going on all the time about lenient judges? Think about it. How many times have you heard some cop complain that he collars them and the judges let them out? Any judge who's worth his salt would much rather make a mistake of letting someone guilty go out than letting someone innocent go in. You know what I mean? They bend over backward to protect the accused. That's the great part of the system. That's what makes it work." She poked him again. "You don't go to Siberia because someone doesn't like you."

Paul sighed deeply. "What you're not seeing, Doyle, is that even if I did learn something—purely by accident, because I'm not going to be looking—I wouldn't be able to disclose it, anyway. I'm bound by the same rules of privilege as you. I can't reveal anything. Only the patient can reveal."

Doyle gazed at him and smiled broadly. The smile split her angelic face in half. "I once had a colleague—a guy I don't deal with anymore, I might add—who used to say that a shrink would swear to anything under oath if you paid him enough. . . ."

"Hold on!" Paul interrupted angrily.

"I was going to say, he should've known you."

Paul relaxed. Doyle tapped him lightly on the side of the arm and he responded with a smile. They stared at each other for a long time. Finally, she said, "What do you say, Doc?"

Paul turned and unlocked his car. He climbed in and rolled his electric window down. He accused himself of being hopelessly romantic. "I'll give you this much"—he paused and pursed his lips—"I'll think about it."

"That's good enough for me, Doc," Doyle said, and she threw him a kiss as he pulled out of the parking space and drove away.

Doyle whistled happily as she walked back to the elevator. She had not done her best piece of work, she knew, but she was happy with it as a beginning. Suddenly, she heard the squeal of tires braking and the rush of a speeding car coming at her. She turned and saw Paul's car returning in reverse. It pulled up beside her and stopped.

"Look," Paul said out the open window. "Why don't I start tomorrow?" Doyle was silent. "I'll see her in jail. For the first time only. Why don't you set it up for me." Doyle grinned from ear to ear. "And get me a private room for the interview, will you? And get me at least two hours, three if you can." He shook his head. "Okay, Harriet?"

Harriet Doyle smiled at Paul Murphy and there was no mischief in her eyes. "You'll see her Saturday, Doc? You're something else."

"I know." Paul reached a hand out the window and they shook warmly, like old and very dear friends.

TWO

Melanie was conscious of the soft whooshing sound the door made when it closed behind her but not of much else. She operated on instinct and followed direction. She did not want to think, had chosen not to think, for all her thoughts, no matter what they were, caused her extreme pain and suffering. She waited for the thudding metallic sound that her cell door made when it grinded closed and was startled by the insignificance of the small lock when it clicked home. Amazing, she thought against her will, how in just three days the sights and sounds and smells of the place had become so much a part of her. She smiled at that thought, at the realization that she was rapidly succumbing to what she had promised herself she would resist.

The room was the same in which she had met with her attorney. It was so familiar that she actually felt comfortable there. It was a better place to be than her cell. Any place was better than that stiff metal box, if only that it allowed her to believe, for a short time anyway, that she was not caged and could roam about freely like everyone else. Another sign, she guessed, of her speedy adjustment to the institution—the ease with which she slipped into those infantile fantasies for the minimal comfort they offered her.

She had grown haggard almost overnight. She had aged years and no longer even faintly resembled the woman who had been arrested only three days ago. She had difficulty even remembering being arrested. The memory seemed so ancient to her, so far in the distant past. She could remember nothing with clarity other than the diminutive coffin being slowly lowered into the small, shallow grave the day before. The small group of black-clad mourners gathered around in a thin semicircle. The guard beside her, handcuffed to her, uncomfortable at being bound to a mother burying her child. Phyllis had come to her and had wept on her shoulder and had clung to her, deep sobs driving wedges between their bodies. She knew that Phyllis had made the funeral arrangements, but she had not been grateful. Even if she could not have cared properly for Denny in life, the least she could have done was care for her death. Was she such a total failure then? And, when she recalled those events, the visions appeared to her in miniature, greatly reduced, as if being viewed through a long telescope in reverse, as if being observed from an enormous distance.

Her life, at least this phase of it, seemed to commence, in her memory, with the gentle revelation of Harriet Doyle trying to comfort her. She could remember Doyle reaching out to her as she sensed herself slipping down into some strange, dark place. She recalled reaching out to the lawyer, straining to touch her extended fingers, to enter into her grasp, but then she heard her own voice announcing her guilt and shame, and the hands slipped away from each other and drew farther and farther apart, until she could no longer see either one of them. Melanie had wanted to connect with Doyle. She truly trusted the lawyer, and she was disappointed that she had missed that opportunity.

Had she abandoned Doyle as well? she wondered. She touched her parched lips and winced at the instant flash of pain. As she had abandoned Polly? She ruminated about Polly, wondered where she was, who was caring for her, suspecting that she had doomed her child by going off and leaving her. A sense of self-loathing overcame her and she remembered why she had committed to give up all thinking. She yearned for purification, to be cleansed, to be expunged. She longed for punishment.

She stood by the closed door and examined the man sitting at the table, in the same chair Harriet Doyle always used. He had risen when she came in. She liked that about him instantly. She was impressed with his tall good looks, with his informal but neat manner of dressing, with the warm smile he offered her without knowing her. He seemed friendly to her, as if he were on her side, as if he were there to help her out of this situation. She suddenly felt embarrassed, knowing that she was smiling at him coquettishly like a flirting teenager.

Paul Murphy had stood up when the door swung open and the matron pushed Melanie into the room. He was surprised when he first saw her, not by her depressed demeanor, which he had expected and not by the flat, discouraged, demoralized look of the unprepared first timer hopelessly lost in the process of prison dehumanization, but by her general appearance, which was anything but what he had expected.

He had been told that she was an attractive young woman, quite beautiful, if you will, but he discovered her to be anything but. She looked mousy, ferretlike, tight and shrunken and unkempt. And it wasn't because she was in jail, he thought. He had interviewed many people in jail and very few degenerated this far so quickly. She even appeared unwashed, unclean. Her hair, unbrushed and uncombed, fell about her face like matted straw. Her lips were dry and chapped, and her skin appeared blotchy and unhealthy. Her shoulders and her breasts sagged in the same degree, and her body looked like that of a sixty-year-old rather than that of the twenty-nine-year-old he knew she was.

He observed her eyes swing around the room and bring it all into focus, watched her recognize the place and visibly seem to soften to it. The door swung closed and locked behind her, and she jumped at the tiny sound as if it had shattered the silence her tingling nerves sought.

Her eyes rested on him finally and a look of distaste, of disgust, crossed her face. She gazed at him, he thought, as if he were some obscene object that was offensive to her. He recognized the hate in that expression. Was it hate he was seeing? Could he read her correctly from this distance? He noted that her attitude might make this first interview more difficult than he had anticipated.

Melanie, however, watched him motion her over to him and point to a chair across the table. She knew instantly, in the distortions of her mind, that this handsome man was obsessed with her, longed for her body, wanted and needed so desperately to seduce her that he was putty in her hands. She was aware of her intense beauty, thinking willfully, wait until he sees me made up and out of here, and tingling with the anticipation of their tryst. She thought she straightened herself up, made herself tall and proud, threw her head back so that her lovely long hair would fly from her face the way she knew men liked, and wet her lips with the tip of her tongue.

Leaning her weight on one hip seductively, she believed she stepped out with her long career-girl stride. She was sure she walked to the chair eagerly. She knew that she swayed her hips as she did when she walked along a downtown street. She assumed she bowed her head slightly to him,

182

thought she gave him an appreciative grin in recognition, and sat down carefully, wanting to cross her knees in just the right way to display what she knew was one of her most attractive features—her sexy long legs.

But, when Paul had motioned toward the empty chair across from him and indicated to her that she was to sit in it, she stared at him and did not move for a long moment. It occurred to him that she was resisting coming near him; her distrust and dislike of him were holding her back. Perhaps she feared him as well, he thought. Was it the doctor in him she feared and distrusted, or was it the man he wondered.

Suddenly, she seemed to him to have made a decision. She dropped her eyes and focused on the spot of floor before her. She sighed and forced her body into action, shuffling slowly toward him. The soles of her feet did not leave the ground but slid along, were pushed along like two blocks of wood, first one and then the other, in many small, easy steps, like an aged person who had lost the ability to bend a knee or raise a leg.

It took a long time before she reached the chair and grabbed for the back of it, as if about to fall over. Sighing deeply, she leaned her weight on the chair and eased herself into it, slowly and cautiously, settling finally, like a slinky toy that settles in sections. She sat staring at the wall behind him, looking through him as if he were not present in the room.

The dull, distasteful expression on her face remained unchanged. She looked emotionless and unfeeling.

"Hello, Melanie," he said. "I'm Dr. Murphy."

She raised her eyes to his face slowly. "Hello," she answered flatly.

"How are you feeling?"

"Fine," she said dully.

"Are you nervous?"

She looked off to the side of the room. "Yes."

"That's understandable," he said. "Have you ever been to see a psychologist before?"

"No."

"Do you know what we do?"

"Yes," she said, and then seemed to think about her answer. "Uh, no."

"Okay," he said. "Well, we're going to talk for a while. I'll ask you some questions and make notes of your answers. And then I'm going to administer some tests." Her eyes became wary. She tensed as though preparing to leap from the chair. "These are written tests. Lots of multiple-choice questions. You'll mark the appropriate answers and I'll feed them into the computer, and it will tell us something about how you think and how you feel. Okay?"

She relaxed somewhat after his explanation. "Yes."

He nodded and pulled his long yellow pad closer to him. "How old are you, Melanie?"

She hesitated. "Twenty-nine."

He wrote. "Where were you born?"

"Here."

He looked up. "Where is that?"

She looked around her in confusion. "Here. In Mercy Hospital, I guess."

He nodded and returned to his pad. "Are you married?"

"Getting divorced," she said sadly.

"Any children?"

She brightened and raised her voice slightly. "Two."

"You have two children?" He watched her closely.

"Yes. Two girls."

Paul waited and watched for Melanie's expression to alter, but it did not change. She gave him no indication that she was aware of any discrepancy. "What are their names?"

"Polly and Denise."

"How old are they?" He laid his pencil down on the table.

She put her finger to her lower lip. "Hmmm. Let me see. Polly's eight and Denny's nine months."

"Where are they now?"

"Polly's in school."

"And Denny?"

"Denny?" she repeated. She became somewhat agitated and squirmed for a moment on her seat. "Denny's home." She stared at Murphy with wide-open, glassy eyes. "That's why I have to get home to her."

"How long have you been here, Melanie?"

She moved her lips silently as she counted. "Three days, I think. I'm not sure...."

"Do you know why you're here?"

"No." Again, she seemed confused. "Well, maybe."

"What brought you here?"

She scowled like a child. "They say I did something bad."

"Who's they?"

"Them," she said. She pointed off toward the building they were in. "The police."

"What do they say you did?"

She grew sad. "They say I did something bad to Denny."

"What did you do?"

"I didn't do anything," she said with consternation.

"I'm sorry," he said. "What do they say you did?"

"They say I hurt her." She became very agitated. "They say I killed her. But I didn't do that."

"Are you sure?"

"Yes. I didn't do that."

"Why would they say that if it weren't true, Melanie?"

"They're wrong!" she tried to explain.

"Who do you think did it?"

"Nobody. She's home. She's waiting for me."

185

"Denny isn't hurt?" he asked. "She's all right?"

"Yes." Melanie was emphatic. "Except that she's frightened being home alone."

"Surely there's somebody with her."

"Oh, yes," Melanie nodded her head vigorously. "My mother is with her."

"Then she's in good hands, isn't she?"

"Yes. Very good."

"You're not really worried?"

"No."

"Your mother is a good friend?"

"Yes."

"She's not a problem for you?"

"Oh, no," Melanie answered. "She's wonderful. We get along very well. We get along best in the family."

"Who else are you close to in your family?"

Melanie pondered the question for a moment. "No one."

"Do you see your husband?"

"No," she said.

"How long were you married?"

"Ten years."

"Why did he leave?"

She was surprised. "He had to. I told him."

"What did you tell him?"

"What?"

"You said you told him," he said to her patiently. She stared at him and then nodded abruptly.

"Yes," she said.

"What did you tell him?"

She avoided Murphy's gaze and looked up at the ceiling. "To get out."

"Why did you tell him that?"

She snapped her head back to face him. "I hate him," she said viciously.

186

"So you wanted him out?"

"Yes."

"He didn't want to leave?"

"No."

"Why would he want to stay if you wanted him to go?"

She laughed a flat, dull laugh, which sounded like sobbing. "To torture me," she said matter-of-factly.

Paul hesitated. He watched her for some sign of emotion, some indication that she was feeling something, but found none. "Who else is in your family?" he finally asked.

"No one."

"Do you have any brothers or sisters?"

"No."

"How about your father?"

"Oh, no." Her lips twisted slightly, for the first time, as if she were about to cry. He became excited at cracking through her protective wall of flatness.

"What about your father, Melanie?" he urged her on.

"He's gone." She sobbed softly.

"Gone where?"

She wept but no tears appeared. "To heaven."

"He's dead."

"Yes."

"How long ago, Melanie?"

"What?" She seemed puzzled again.

"When did he die?" he asked.

She looked away and thought for a long moment. "Oh, two years ago."

"Was he very sick?"

"No." She shook her head. "He was never sick in his life."

"He died suddenly?"

"Yes." She stopped weeping.

"What did he die of?"

187

She picked a piece of lint off her dress. "In an auto accident."

"That's too bad," he said.

"Mother was driving," she continued without a pause.

"But your mother survived," he said.

"No," she replied.

"You said your mother was home with Denny?"

She looked up at him suddenly with that same puzzled expression of confusion on her face. "Did I? I meant Denny's with my mother, in heaven."

She smiled at him weakly and adopted an expression that seemed to imply he was not very bright and had failed to listen to her carefully.

"I'm sorry," he said. "I must have misunderstood."

She relaxed and nodded shortly. "Of course," she said. "If you want to understand, you have to listen very carefully."

Half an hour later, Paul Murphy held an open book on the table in front of him and pretended to be reading, when in truth he was watching Melanie surreptitiously. He had handed her the questionnaire and answer sheet for the Minneapolis Multiphasic Inventory and four sharpened pencils almost half an hour before, and he had been watching and waiting since. He would watch her alternate between chewing on the eraser end of her pencil and scratching very small marks onto her answer sheet. She studied each question carefully and slowly and labored over each answer.

He noted the various contortions she put her face through, the pink tip of her tiny tongue protruding from the side of her mouth, her eyes squinted nearly to closing, her brow furrowed deeply, the many distortions that emanated from her deep concentration.

She was like a young child desperately trying to please and wanting so much to be correct. She mumbled to herself under her breath as she worked at the test, as if discussing each answer with a stranger. And after each scribble of an answer she looked up at him to see if he had noticed her and if he was pleased by what she had done.

Paul noted her infantile posture and wondered if he could trust his impressions. Melanie moved in and out of lucidity as if she were two people, as if she could do it at will, and something about that flexibility bothered him. He wondered if he could trust it. Was it real? Was it pretense?

Finally, she finished. She laid her pencil down and lined it up with the other three so that they all lay together like a group of logs. With the fingers of both hands, she pushed the completed form to the center of the table and sat back, pleased with herself and waiting for him to react.

"You're finished," he said.

"Yes." She nodded.

"Was it difficult?"

"No." She shook her head.

"You were frightened before you started."

She nodded. "Yes."

"Afraid of me?"

"Not you," she said. "The test."

"Are you always afraid of things before you try them?"

"I never was before," she said.

"Before what?"

"Before I came here," she said.

He studied her for a moment. "You've changed in here? You're different?"

"Oh, yes," she said.

"In what way?"

Her eyes cleared for an instant. "Mostly, I'm confused," she said. "And I can't remember things."

"What things?"

"I can't remember," she said.

"Do you know who you are?"

"Yes. I'm Melanie Wyatt."

"Do you know what day this is?"

"Thursday?" She strained. "Tuesday?"

"Who's the President of the United States?"

She stared at him stupidly. "I . . . don't . . ."

"Are those the things you don't remember?"

She thought, turned on the chair, then turned back to him and folded her hands in her lap. "I don't know," she said calmly, her eyes glassing over once again. "I don't remember." She drifted off and sat back relaxed, as if he were not there with her. Suddenly, she began to hum a soft lullaby and rocked her body forward and back in small, gentle motions.

"Melanie?"

But she no longer heard him, or she chose to ignore him.

"Melanie?" he repeated, "I'm talking to you."

She stopped, turned to him and grimaced. "Who the hell are you? Shut up and let me rest!" And she went back to her rocking.

After that, having grown tired and unwilling to respond to his questions, unable to concentrate on the task at hand, he suggested that they had done enough and that they should stop. He gathered up his papers from the table and stuffed them into his briefcase.

"I want to thank you for being so cooperative," he said.

"Thank you," she said politely.

"I would like to see you again Monday. Would that be okay with you?"

She almost smiled at him and her eyes brightened for an instant. "Yes," she said.

"Good," he said. "I thought it went very well today."

He stood up and she stood on the other side of the table. He walked to the door and rapped on it. He turned and watched her as he waited for the matron. She stood with her hands clasped behind her and swayed back and forth, averting her eyes like a shy schoolgirl.

The door opened and the matron stood in the entrance and called to her. Paul stepped to the side to let Melanie pass, but she stopped directly in front of him. She turned and looked up at him and suddenly, without any warning, planted a juvenile kiss on his cheek and ran past the matron into the hallway. The matron glanced at Paul and smirked; he scowled and shrugged back at her.

In his office again, Paul leaned back in the chair behind his desk and sat for a long time before deciding to call. Even then, he reached for the phone reluctantly and then replaced it in its cradle several times before actually punching in the number he wanted.

"Hello?" Harriet Doyle replied.

"Hello, Harriet. It's Paul Murphy."

She chuckled. "I knew it was you. How many people you think I give my private number to?" There was silence on the phone. "You want to tell me something, Doc?"

"Yeah," he said. "I guess I do."

"You sound tired, Paul."

He laughed. "In case you didn't notice. It's been a long day."

"I noticed," Doyle said. "I noticed. I'm here, too."

"Harriet, I can't make a habit of these calls. So, short and sweet, okay?"

"It's your nickel, Doc. Go!"

"She seems delusional. I'm not sure what it all means yet and she may even be faking in order to cop a plea."

"No," Doyle interrupted. "She wouldn't do that. She's not that kind of person."

"Stuff it, Harriet," Paul said. "I know you already." He laughed in spite of himself. "But I'll see her a few more times and I gave her a test. I need the results before I can be sure of anything. Then I'll let you know what you've got."

"Doc," Doyle said quietly and softly and with affection, "I love you. I really do."

"Sure you do, Harriet," he said. Something in him tingled at her words despite himself. "That's because I'm all charm."

"Well, you remember what I said."

"Sure!" he answered. "I'll bet you say that to everybody you want something from."

Her soft, throaty voice grew serious. "You don't know what you're missing."

He closed his eyes and saw her wonderful, lithe body in his mind's eye. He sighed. "The hell I don't!"

Fifteen minutes later, he made another call. "Judge?" he asked when the phone was picked up.

"Good evening, Dr. Murphy. To what do I owe this honor?"

"You wanted to know fast."

He heard the judge chuckle mischievously. "Don't you dare tell me she's not guilty. I'm not interested in your opinions about that."

"No, Your Honor. No opinions about that."

There was a long silence finally broken by Judge Barret as he coughed and spoke gently. "Okay, Paul. Let's have it."

"She may be delusional. She may even be hallucinating. She's certainly diffuse and flattened out and a little too concrete. All of which means she may be mentally ill. But her behavior is so inconsistent that I don't know whether or not to trust what I'm seeing."

"Come on, Paul. Is she competent or isn't she?" the judge asked impatiently.

"Judge, I honestly don't know. She may be a great actress for all I know. I think you may have to try this one."

"Paul, it doesn't work that way. You have to know. If you mental people don't know, then who does? I'm counting on you. I don't want to put that woman on trial if she's not responsible. That would be irresponsible of me." The judge paused, and Paul heard his deep and measured breathing over the phone. "You'll have to find out. The court is blind in this matter and is relying on you, Paul." Paul started to speak, to make excuses, to alibi himself, but the judge continued. "And, Paul, you don't have a lot of time. So hurry."

THREE

Phyllis let Gladys go home early. Actually, she was taking pity on the girl, who had worked like a slave for the past few days getting Phyllis fully moved in and literally rearranging the house, the bedrooms, the closets, the bathrooms, and all.

Phyllis's decision to move in and keep the household intact had not been made hastily. She had thought about it at great length. Other than causing an upheaval in her own life, her greatest concern was for Polly fearing that the attempt to take Melanie's place as mother in the home would backfire and cause a negative reaction in the little girl, would cause her to withdraw even more than she had.

But she had worried needlessly. Polly, who had taken to isolating herself by locking herself in her room since her mother had been taken away, who had refused to go to school and had resisted all attempts to get some decent food into her, who had rejected any overtures of concern or affection, smiled for the first time that week when she observed Phyllis struggling up the driveway loaded down with overstuffed suitcases hanging from her hands, arms, and elbows.

The child had run to her, grabbed onto her legs, and

pressed her face against the rough cloth of her skirt, crying more from relief than anything else. They had shuffled into the house together that way, like a crab sliding sideways, with the child refusing to let go and Phyllis so pleased by the girl's display that she did not really want to be released.

Together, they had unpacked Phyllis's life onto Melanie's bed, her chairs, the floor of Melanie's room, and though Polly's face grew dark for a moment when she saw her mother's clothing being pushed aside in the closet, she was soon bouncing around happily putting things away. She climbed up on a chair to hang up dresses and she fondly caressed delicate things, things that went against Phyllis's body, as she folded them and put them away in one of the mahogany drawers in the chest across from the bed. But every few moments she ran back to Phyllis to hug her or touch her, as if to reassure herself that Phyllis's serious and complete entry into her world was truly happening and was not some luckless dream.

It was Roger Gillespie who had encouraged her to make the move once she told him about the idea. They agreed it was a solution that would solve several problems at the same time: the problem of Melanie's worry over Polly, of Polly's possible placement in a juvenile facility and the possibility of Chris gaining quick custody, something that Melanie refused to hear about, and the problem of what to do with the house. It was Roger who reasoned that the one simple move would reduce the pressure on all of them. And Phyllis was glad he had.

Therefore, it was logical that when Polly and Phyllis had decided today to celebrate the completion of the move, Roger should be included in their party plans. The two of them shopped together, unloaded the groceries in the kitchen together, and finally cooked the splendid feast together, Polly stuffing the turkey and Phyllis sewing it up. They chopped vegetables and made a huge salad and boiled and then whipped potatoes till they were fluffy smooth. They even made the gravy from scratch rather than popping open a can but compromised on the green beans by buying a frozen package. Roger's role was to be the guest of honor, and he heartily agreed that when it came to planning, cooking, and preparing dinners he was truly best at guesting.

He proved it that night by arriving at six-thirty, long after all the work was done, armed with a bottle of Verdiccio to go with the bird and some cherry soda to make Shirley Temples for Polly. "I told you I was the perfect guest," he said as they both squealed with delight when he presented the drinks he had brought.

It took the two of them three trips back and forth from the kitchen to carry out all the delights they had prepared, and when the dining room table was covered with dishes, they sat down to eat. Roger opened the bottle of wine and poured for Phyllis and himself, then fixed a Shirley Temple for Polly. They raised their glasses and clinked them together, making toasts to the completion of the move, to the new partnership of Phyllis and Polly, to success in school, to achievement at work, to the meal, to the friendship, and to dozens of other things, and especially to the speedy return of Polly's mommy.

After dinner, Phyllis washed and Polly dried, while Roger, sipping brandy from a light blue snifter, relaxed and supervised from a kitchen chair, leaning back precariously against the wall. They booed him and accused him of being lazy. He replied that it was not laziness that kept him from participating but gross ineptitude. He told them that he still held the all-time Michigan State record for most dishes dropped and broken by one person after one meal.

Later, they sat together on the couch and Roger read to them from *The Little Engine That Could.* They all laughed at the childish story, Phyllis sitting on one side of him, her head resting on his shoulder, and Polly sitting on the other side snuggled up close to him, clutching his hand with her little fingers.

Then Phyllis carried a sleepy Polly to her bedroom and tucked her into her bed, pulling the covers up snugly under her chin.

"Good night, sweetheart," she said. She kissed Polly's forehead and got up to leave.

"Thank you, Aunt Phyllis."

She turned back. "For what, honey?"

"For coming to live with me," the child said.

Phyllis smiled at her. "Oh, baby, you don't have to thank me. I consider myself lucky having a little girl like you to live with." She turned her face and wiped a tear away.

"And for loving me," the little girl said.

Roger poured himself another brandy and returned to the couch.

"That's something," she said. She had returned to the room quietly. "I've never seen you drink so much." She sat down beside him and hiked her legs up under herself Indian fashion.

"I need it tonight," he said gloomily.

"Oh?" She smiled. "I didn't think I was that bad looking."

He turned to her and smiled. "You're beautiful," he said. "My problem doesn't have anything to do with you."

"Oh?"

"No," he said. "It's just going to be hard to tell you about it."

"Melanie?"

"Yes." He took a long swallow of brandy. "Harriet's going to enter a new plea in the morning."

"What for?"

He squirmed a bit. "For a better defense. A better chance to get her off."

"I don't get it," she said.

"She's going to plead insanity."

She jumped. "What?"

He nodded. "It's the safest."

"What in the hell for?" she asked. "That's as good as admitting she's guilty."

"She is," Roger said miserably. "She did it."

She became angry. "What the hell are you talking about? Do you know who you're talking about? I know Melanie better than any human being in the whole world. I know her better than she knows herself, for Christ's sake. Don't you think I'd know if she'd done it? She's not capable of something like that. Killing her own kid?"

"Obviously, she is." He shrugged.

"Like hell. I've known her since we were kids. She's got more kindness in her little finger than most people have in their whole bodies." Her eyes pleaded with him. "I grew up with her, Roger."

Roger interrupted. "It doesn't matter, Phil. It's the only way."

"Jesus Christ," she snapped. "I thought you were a friend. You don't give a damn about her. Neither one of you do. Well, the hell with you two. I'll get a new lawyer. I'll borrow the money somewhere and I'll get a big shot lawyer who won't sell out his client when the going gets tough." She jumped up from the couch. "You two don't know what the hell you're talking about. I'll be goddamned if I'll let you convince her to cop a plea."

"She told us!" Roger shouted.

"Told you what?" she screamed. "What are you talking about?" she glanced over toward Polly's room and lowered her voice. "Told you what?"

"She told Harriet that she did it. She confessed."

"Oh, God!" Phyllis said. She chewed on her lip and fought back the tears that started to appear in her eyes. "How can that be?"

He patted the couch next to him and motioned her to come sit down. She moved to him and slid down onto the soft cushion. "How can that be?"

"You see why I need the booze?" he asked.

"I don't believe it," she murmured.

Harriet says she just turned to her and told her. Out of nowhere. Just looked up all of a sudden and said it," Roger offered.

"Why? How?"

"She says she doesn't know. She says she doesn't remember any of the details of that night."

Phyllis glanced about the room nervously. "I can't believe that about Melanie."

"Believe it," he said. "And stop thinking of Melanie the way you used to know her. She's not the same Melanie, Phil. Harriet says she's so changed she can hardly recognize her. Overnight she changed. Harriet says she doesn't even look the same. Since she confessed, she's become another person. Harriet's convinced that she's mentally ill."

"Oh, no," she moaned. Slowly, she began to cry.

"Wait," he said. "I want you to remember something else. I shouldn't be just blurting this stuff out. Everything I've told you so far is secondhand and it might be exaggerated. I haven't seen her myself. Only Harriet gets in to see her—Harriet and the doctor."

"What doctor?" she asked.

"There's a psychologist seeing her. He saw her today."

He reached over and took her hand in both of his. "I know it's tough, Phil. But at least everybody's on her side. Everybody's trying to help her."

Phyllis raised his hand and pressed it against her cheek. She closed her eyes and sighed deeply.

"The doctor was recommended by the presiding judge," he said. "Harriet called him and told him that her client's probably unstable and might not be able to stand trial. That's usually a defense expense. You know, the psychologist. But everybody knows there's no money in this case."

She nodded. "I could borrow at work," she said.

"No. This doctor does a lot of work for the court. He's seeing her now only to evaluate if she's capable of standing trial."

Phyllis trembled suddenly. She reached her hand up to her throat as if she needed help to breathe. "What will happen to her?"

He shrugged. "What Harriet wants is to avoid having the judge postpone the trial. But if the judge thinks that Melanie is incompetent, he will put off the trial and order her into psychiatric treatment. He's got to be convinced that she can understand what's happening to her during a trial. Otherwise, he'll force her into treatment until such time as he becomes convinced that she's no longer incompetent. And that's a big problem. Because, if she gets well—I mean, when she gets well, no matter when that is, she'll have to stand trial at that time." Roger shrugged and held his hands out in supplication. "But if we go ahead with the trial now and plead temporary insanity and she's acquitted, she'll still get psychiatric treatment. But the difference is, when she gets out, she'll be free to pick up her life again."

Phyllis nodded that she understood. "This is all so terrible. I can't handle it all at one time."

"Of course," he said. "But with the new plea, everything changes for her. It becomes so much easier."

She stared at him in wonder. "I don't understand you," she said. "How does any of it get easier?"

"At least, now," he said, "we don't have to refute all that evidence against her. Some of it is even going to help our case. It all takes on a new significance."

She shook her head. "I'm lost, Roger. I don't know what you're talking about."

"Look," he said. "All the negative things people were saying about her. Her husband's testimony, for example. Or the allegation that she's gay and makes the rounds of the bars. All that stuff. We would've had to fight that stuff. Disprove it. Refute it. That's damaging stuff."

"You bet it is," Phyllis said. "And it also isn't true. Those lies hurt so much because anybody who know Melanie knows they're not true."

Roger waved her statement away. "That's unimportant now," he said. "Whether they're true or not, I mean. What's important now is how to use that evidence to our own advantage."

"Even if it's all lies?"

He tilted his head and gazed at her crookedly. "We may never know, Phil." He looked at her sadness and wanted to say something encouraging, although he knew that what she wanted to hear and what was reality were not one and the same.

Finally, he said, "if we allow the prosecution to present its case and don't challenge their evidence at all—I mean, we don't have to say it's not true. We don't have to attack their witnesses, do we? We simply don't respond. Then all that evidence, which means she was living a double life, because you and all her other friends are going to testify as to what kind of person you knew her to be, which was very inconsis-

201

tent with what the prosecution is contending, all that evidence works for us as showing her mental instability. You see what I mean? It's like karate, Phil. Like judo. Where you use the other guy's weight to throw him."

"But she's not gay. She doesn't hang out in bars and bring weirdos home," Phyllis insisted.

"Who cares!" he shouted in exasperation. "You want to uphold your truth and have Melanie go to prison for the rest of her life? Is that what you want?" He was shocked at his own outburst. He reached out and took her into his arms and held her gently. "I'm so sorry, Phil," he said. "But you're worried about her goddamned reputation and we're trying to save her life."

She sobbed against his chest. "I know you're right," she said. "I just hate to see her accused of all those terrible things she never did."

He pulled her closer and held her more tightly. "Oh, Phil, you're so naive. What hurts me most in this is your innocence. I know you love Melanie, but you're going to have to be realistic about her." He paused and stroked her hair and kissed the top of her head. "She's guilty as hell, Phil. Of all of it. Of every last thing she's accused of."

Some hours later, Polly, who had been unable to sleep since she had been awakened by their screaming in the living room and who had listened to everything they had said about her mother, got out of bed and tiptoed to the bathroom. She looked at her face in the mirror, hating her red, puffy eyes and her tear-stained cheeks. She wiped her face with a dry towel and went to her mother's room to find comfort in bed with Phyllis.

She opened the door a crack and peeked in. She was about to run to the bed and jump in when she noticed that there were two bodies asleep under the covers. She tried to catch the gasp before it escaped from her mouth but she was not quite quick enough. Roger must have heard her exclamation of surprise because he suddenly sat up in the bed and looked over toward her. She hurriedly closed the door and dashed down the hallway to her own room.

In the bedroom, Roger cursed himself for falling asleep after making love. He had no business sleeping there, he told himself critically. He got up, found his pants on the floor, dug his shoes out from under the bed, and dressed quickly. Just before he left the bedroom, he leaned over and kissed Phyllis's sleeping eyes.

As he closed the front door of the house, he thought he heard sobbing coming from Polly's room. He was sure he had, and he carried some guilty feelings about it around with him for the next couple of hours.

Harriet Doyle almost gave up after six rings and was about to hang up, fix herself a drink, and go to bed when she heard the sound of the receiver being lifted and a sleepy voice saying, "Hello?"

"Hello," Doyle said. "Mr. Hennessy?"

"Yes."

"Harriet Doyle here. Mr. Hennessy, I've been calling you all day. Didn't you get any of my messages?"

There was a long pause. "Oh, Doyle. Yeah, I got your message. I was just so swamped today. One of those days. You know how it is. Jesus, what the hell time is it, anyway?"

"What's the difference? I'm calling on behalf of Melanie Wyatt, Mr. Hennessy. I would've thought she'd have some priority with you."

"Oh, she does. Sure, she does. But, you know," he whined, "it was just one of those days."

"Mrs. Wyatt's on trial for murder, Mr. Hennessy. You think she had one of those days today, too? Huh? What do you think?"

"Okay, okay," Joe said. "So I didn't call you back. Big deal. I don't even think I'm supposed to talk to you, am I? I'm a witness for the prosecution."

"Is that your understanding of our judicial system, Mr. Hennessy? One side keeps secrets from the other side and it all comes out in the wash, the very last second of the last day in court? Like Perry Mason? Is that what you think?"

"Well, no," Joe said. "I guess not."

Doyle lowered her voice to the lowest register she could reach. "Would you rather not talk to me, Mr. Hennessy? It's okay with me if that's what you want. I can serve you and bring you into my office and put you under oath, where I'd like to have you anyway, and take your deposition. Would you rather do it that way?"

"What are you getting so huffy for? Did I say I didn't want to talk to you? Did I say that? Of course, I'll talk to you. I'll do anything I can to help Melanie out—I mean, within reason. You know, I don't know too much. I mean, if I ever thought she could kill—I mean, she never was that kind of person. But I guess you never can tell. Anyway, I don't owe her anything, but she was okay with me, so I guess I can try to help. Ask away."

Doyle wondered about her client's taste in men. She had not questioned the husband as yet, but if this was the boyfriend, she thought, she couldn't wait to get to Mr. Wyatt. "That's mighty white of you, sir. I'm sure Melanie'll be pleased to learn how highly you regard her friendship."

"Well, all you have to tell her is that I'm rooting for her. You don't have to tell her things that will depress her."

Doyle chuckled bitterly. "I'm afraid, Mr. Hennessy, she's

beyond being depressed. However, I'd rather talk about you and Melanie before this terrible tragedy occurred."

"Okay," Joe said. "What do you want to know?"

"It's simple, Joe. Is it all right to call you Joe?"

"Sure," Joe grunted into the phone.

"It's simple. I just want to know how intimate you two had become. You know what I mean by intimate?"

"Certainly. You mean sexually."

"That's right, Joe. I want to know if you two were making it regularly. I want to know how often, when, and where. Can you help me with that information, Joe?"

There was a long pause and Joe coughed away from the phone. "I don't really keep score, you know. I mean, I don't like to talk about my women behind their backs."

Doyle laughed again. "We're not concerned with her honor, Joe. Her honor and reputation can wait till after the trial. Let's get her home first."

"Maybe she shouldn't come home, Ms. Doyle. I mean, if she killed her kid."

"Do you think she did that?" Doyle asked.

"Why would they arrest her? I don't know anything, but I figure the police don't arrest people unless they're pretty sure. Isn't that so?"

"That's generally true, Joe," Doyle said. "But they have been known to make mistakes now and then. Anyway, we're lucky because we don't have to decide if she's guilty or not. We'll let the jury do that. You didn't answer my question, Joe."

"You mean about where we went?"

"Yes."

"Different places."

"Where?"

"Oh, sometimes my place, sometimes hers."

"How often did you go to hers?"

"I don't remember. I don't keep score."

"Good," Doyle said. "Too many to remember is certainly more than one. That's fine, Joe. You're doing swell."

Joe was surprised. "I am?"

"Now, when did you meet, Joe? Was it like every Wednesday afternoon? Something like that?"

"Well, no. Not exactly."

"How about the weekends? Was it on the weekends?"

"Well, no. You know, she spent the weekends with the kids."

"Then it must have been nighttime, Joe. How'd you manage that?"

"What do you mean?"

"Wouldn't Polly know?" Doyle asked.

"Well, to tell you the truth," Joe said, "it wasn't all that often. I mean, it was hard finding good times when we were both free. You know, she worried about the kid a lot. She didn't want the kid to think she'd replaced her father. She was very worried about that."

"You know something, Joe?" Doyle said. "I don't think you really had much to do with Melanie Wyatt after all."

"Why would you say that?"

"I don't know, Joe. You sound awful cagey." She paused to let him stew for a moment, then said, "Come on, Joe. One hip guy to another. How was she? Does she swing? Like around the world? Is she crazy wild in the sack? Come on! Give a little. Does she scratch and bite? Moan and scream? Is she an animal? I mean, does she go out of her mind?"

"That's disgusting," Joe said. "You're a woman."

"Did she beg for it, Joe? Was she all over you every chance she got? Did she tear your clothes off? Oh, oh, yes. Does she really moan, Joe? Does she cry out your name? Does she love it when you slam it to her? Did you think she could bite it off?"

Joe sounded frightened. Doyle could imagine him growing pale. "What are you trying to do? We were good friends. We had a nice friendship. I even asked her to marry me. What the hell's the matter with you?"

"I want to know all the dirt, Joe. All the low-down stuff. I want to know what a great cocksman you are."

"Hey, knock it off!" Joe said.

"Come on, Joe. You told the police. Those horny cops? Why won't you tell me?"

"I didn't tell the police anything. I don't know how they got that idea. She's not that kind of girl."

"What kind of girl?"

"The kind you're talking about."

"What kind is that?"

"A nymph like that."

"What kind of girl is she, Joe?" Doyle asked softly.

"She's a good girl. A great girl. A good mother. A good friend."

"But she snuck around behind everybody's back fucking in hideaways with you."

"Never!" Joe shouted.

"What do you mean *never?* You have a key to her house. You took her to your apartment frequently. You had a serious love affair going."

"I— "

"Joe." Doyle called out his name to get his attention. "Listen to me carefully. I really don't care what you testify to in court." Joe sputtered. "No. Hear me out. I really don't care and I have no intention of giving you a hard time on the stand. Really. Trust me, Joe. I wouldn't lie to you. But you should only be very careful to tell the truth. Only the truth, Joe."

"I intend to, Ms. Doyle," Joe said softly.

"That's good. Joseph!" Her voice returned to its normal

volume. "Okay, I'm done. See, wasn't that easy?" She chuckled loudly, good-naturedly.

"Good-bye," Joe said.

"Oh, Joe!" she shouted. "Wait. I forgot something."

"What?"

"Joe, you should go to your doctor and get checked out for AIDS."

"What in the hell for? What's that smart-assed remark supposed to mean? You calling me a queer?"

"Oh, no," she said. "It's just that the prosecutor will present evidence to suggest that Melanie is a very active and promiscuous homosexual. Maybe worse. You know, Joe. Switching off. Men and women. So I just figured, you know. If you fucked her, you better watch out. You may have one of those days again."

FOUR

Melanie felt ready long before the matron came to get her. She knew she would be because she had planned to be from the day before and had started preparing the very moment she awoke, the very moment she had been told to. When she left the lovely doctor who she knew desired her, she promised herself that she would be ready for his passionate advances the very next time they met. She was reminded of that fact the moment she opened her eyes and heard for the first time her instructions being whispered to her, discovering the sound of a new companion, a formless companion who dwelled inside her ear.

She combed and brushed her hair scrupulously and slaved over her nails for hours with what little equipment they allowed her in her cell. She wanted to smell pretty for him, wanted to drown him in her sexual odors, but she had no perfume with her. They allowed none of those things in jail, none of those pretty things, so she collected the little yellow flowers they always brought with breakfast and crushed them and rubbed the pulp against the skin of her neck to capture as much of the oil onto herself as possible. She was amazed at her own ingenuity. She felt irresistible and knew he would not be able to keep his hands off her. She asked her secret companion and was assured that he would be her slave this day.

Even the matron was impressed when she came to get her. "My, aren't you pretty today," the matron commented. And Melanie knew that she was. She knew she was extra pretty this day because the tiny voice had told her. She even felt pretty, something she had not felt in some time.

She started down the long, narrow corridor and could see him, small and obscure, standing in the distance, at the far end, waiting to greet her in front of the door. Fool, she heard, get a move on! She picked up her pace and walked more rapidly toward him. She understood that the broad smile on her face was giving away the secret of her feelings, but she could no more control herself than the sun could keep from rising in the morning. Go, go, go, go, go! she was told. She rushed forward toward him.

He extended his hand to her as if showing her a beacon, a light to guide her in the storm of her incarceration. She reached him and slipped her fingers into his, and she instantly felt the silent, loving commitment he made to her, heard the whisper of his dedication to her. The pressure of his fingers on hers spoke to her louder than any language could. She tingled with his message as if an electric charge had bolted through her.

He guided her into the familiar and private room and led her to a chair. She half expected to find a luxurious bed moved in, surrounded by soft lights and gentle music, and was disappointed that none of those things were there. But she would make do with the chair. She must, she was told. He sat her in it and gazed down at her passionately. She observed the lust in his eyes and her body opened to him. She flung her arms and legs wide, and her parted wet lips encouraged him to enter her and to own her.

210

Dr. Murphy moved around the table and sat across from her. He watched her grinning at him like a well-stuffed, satisfied cat. He wondered what was going on in her injured mind. What kind of psychotic fantasies was she conjuring? He was quickly growing increasingly convinced that she might never let him in to find out. She had not only begun to look detached, but her behavior was clearly adopting a schizophrenic style.

She had behaved strangely from the first moment he observed her. Her demeanor was different than it had been at their last interview. When she stepped into the corridor leading from the square, empty reception room, she had been squinting, pressing her eyes shut, as though guarding them against bright sunlight, although there was none, or as if gazing down a long distance at an object far, far away.

She had stopped shuffling when she saw him and actually walked, lifting her feet off the ground, toward him. Granted, it was not much of a walk. She was wobbly and unrhythmic and stepped awkwardly, almost as if she had had too much to drink. But it was most definitely walking. She had almost fallen when she drew close to him, and he put out his hand to catch her and lend her himself as a balancing stick. She grabbed onto his hand and held tightly, as if desperate. He remembered the kiss she had planted on him when leaving the interview on Saturday and he warned himself to be careful. He allowed his fingers to remain limp in her grasp and returned none of the squeezing pressure that he felt from her. No gesture that could be misleading, he had told himself. No movement at all that could be read as being seductive. She would fantasize enough of that without him contributing, he told himself.

To be perfectly safe, he had pulled away and guided her into the interview room. He watched her flutter about, her head tilted to one side and cocked, as if listening, her hands bouncing about like little frightened birds. He noticed the torn and bleeding nails on both hands. She had made some attempt at fixing her hair, and it lay plastered down and wet on one side, dry and wild on the other.

He had led her to and placed her in the same chair as the last time. She had looked up at him as he did so and pouted her lips, as though throwing him a kiss. He could read the madness in her eyes. He could certainly feel it in his own uncomfortable reaction to her presence.

Now, seated across from her, he watched her and appreciated the fact that she was as unconnected to him, to reality, as any patient he had ever worked with. He concentrated on her insidious grin and read distrust there. He could feel the suspicion seeping from her toward him. She twisted her cracked and bleeding hands in her lap until, suddenly, she raised her right hand and slapped at her ear like a horse's tail slapping at flies. This woman is no actress, he told himself. As far as he was concerned, the person sitting before him was presenting a classic picture of paranoid schizophrenic behavior.

"Hello, Melanie," he said. He shifted his chair closer to the table and rested his clasped hands on top of it. "Remember me?"

She nodded and smiled grotesquely at him. He noted that she appeared to become more animated when he spoke to her.

"Remember we did a test together on Saturday?"

"Yes." She grinned at him.

"We're going to do another one today."

She stiffened and looked away from him. "Remember," he said, "we talked about being afraid of things before they happen? Do you remember that?"

"Yes," she said hesitantly.

"This is the same. It will be easy and you'll laugh about

being afraid of it." She chewed on her lower lip. "We won't do it now. In a little while, all right?" She nodded gratefully.

"You mentioned your father last time." She looked up at him. "Tell me about him, Melanie," he said. "What kind of guy was he?"

Her eyes brightened for an instant. "He was a wonderful man," she said, twisting her head about as if straining to hear better. "He was gentle and kind."

"Is that what you thought when you were a child?"

She pondered this for a moment. "No. I didn't think like that. I just loved him." She became slightly agitated and picked at the lint on her dress with two bloody fingernails. "He loved me most of all."

"What do you mean by most of all?"

She hesitated, as if catching her elusive thoughts. "More than anyone else. More than anyone."

"More than your mother?"

"Yes." She nodded.

"More than his wife?"

"Yes."

"That must have been a very special relationship."

"It was," she said. Her lips began to tremble and he waited for her to cry, but she regained control. "He was a good Daddy and I was his very good little girl." She laughed shortly. "He called me Nanny. Short for Nanny Goat. You knew he loved you when he made up a silly name for you."

Paul was impressed. She had made the longest speech he had heard from her as yet. He did not know why or what he was doing to elicit it, but he was grateful and intended to take advantage of the situation. "Did he have any other names for you?" he asked before she could drift off again.

"No," she said. "Just that. He called me that all my life." Her face clouded suddenly. "I mean, his life." She paused. "Except, he didn't."

"Didn't what?"

"Didn't call me that all his life." She chewed on her lip again. "For the last few years, he called me Melanie." She turned her face away and her voice became desolate. "And he didn't love me anymore."

"Why did he change?"

"Oh, I don't know. Maybe he got tired of me?" she asked him.

"How do you feel about that?"

She stared at Paul. "It's okay. You want to get along in this world, you accept whatever a man gives you. That's the way it is."

"I don't think that you feel okay about that," he said. He was leading her into dangerous territory, and he reminded himself to move slowly and cautiously.

Instantly suspicious. "You're saying I'm lying?"

"No," he said. "I don't think you're lying. Unless you're lying to yourself. I think you're hiding."

"From what?" she asked.

He paused for a moment. Dare he make the next move? "From how you really feel about your father," he said, taking the risk.

"Listen!" she said. Her tone became tough, hard. "It wasn't me. I didn't change. He did. It's not my feelings that's a problem. It's his. He changed about me. He stopped loving me. I never stopped loving him."

"Why did he stop loving you?"

"How should I know?" she said. "Maybe I didn't please him anymore. Maybe he found somebody else better than me. How do I know?"

"I think you know," Paul said, pushing a little harder.

She thought for a moment, looking around the room as if she had lost interest. "Because of Chris," she mumbled softly.

"I'm sorry," he said.

She raised her voice. "Because of Chris. Because I married Chris."

"Your father was opposed to the marriage?"

"Opposed!" She sat up rigidly. "He damn near disowned me." She relaxed and leaned back. "He never called me Nanny again, that's for sure." She stared at Murphy and a huge grin broke across her face. "You know the funny thing? You want to know what's really funny?"

"Yes," he said. She was on her own now. She had gotten into it and Paul knew he was going to learn.

"Everything he said about Chris was right." She laughed. "That's the funny part. I gave up my daddy to get my husband, and both sons of bitches deserted me." She glared at Paul as if daring him to contradict her. She nodded then and grinned at him, wetting her lips with the tip of her tongue. "And so will you." She laughed. "So will you!"

Later, he administered the Rorschach Inkblot Test, although he had learned to place limited faith in its validity as a diagnostic tool. What he did enjoy, however, was its ability to confirm the existence of the schizophrenic process and the ease with which he could get into anxiety-provoking subject matter with the use of the inkblots.

He made extensive notes while they talked, using a kind of shorthand system he had developed for himself over the years, unreadable, of course, by anyone else, but easily deciphered at a glance by him.

She responded to the early cards as most people would, seeing in their images common objects, which are usually seen by a large majority of people tested, and having little to say about them. She saw clouds and dancers and certain benign, harmless animals, generally non-threatening images.

It was on the first color card that she reacted violently. The muscles of her face grew rigid. She bit down hard on her back teeth and stiffened her body. The sudden burst of color threw her into a shocked silence. Her eyes narrowed and she pressed her lips tightly together till they formed a thin line across her face. Whereas before she had been speaking so freely to him, she now refused to verbalize any of her reaction.

He waited, then finally asked, "What do you see there?"

She shook her head and pressed her lips even tighter still. However, she would not move her gaze from the card. He turned it over and placed it facedown on the table, and she grunted angrily at him.

"You want to see it again?" he asked.

"Yes," she insisted.

He lifted the card and revealed its garish splash of color once again. "What do you see?"

She started slowly and then gained in momentum. "He's killing her," she said. Her fingers pulled at her dried-out hair. "He's cutting her up in pieces. There's blood all over the place. And pieces of her thrown around. See there, on the edge"—she pointed at a corner of the card—"there's her body. And down below there, her arms and a leg." She suddenly cringed and sat back. "See him grinning up there, on the top. See his face. His mouth is open. Teeth. He's going to eat her remains. His helpers are coming to the table to eat with him. They're all going to eat her. They'll eat every drop of her. There won't be any left. She'll be gone. Gone. She'll be gone."

She paused. Her breathing had become labored. "These are flames here," she said. She trembled as she put out a finger to point to the bottom of the page. "The world is blowing up. It's all burning up. What they don't eat is going to get burned up. See it. See it there!"

She turned in her chair and hid her face in her hands. He put the card down on the table. "You can look now," he said. "I put the card away."

She peeked out from behind her hands and checked to see that he was telling the truth. "See," he said, holding up his empty hands.

She sat up then and stared at him. "That's a terrible picture," she said. "What twisted person could draw a picture like that?"

When he had calmed her down, she resumed the interview as if nothing had happened.

"Do you miss your husband?" Paul asked her.

"No," she said. "I miss my children."

"How often do you see him?"

She had to think, to remember that they were talking about Chris. "I don't."

"Not ever?"

"I've seen him twice since he left."

"Don't you miss him a little?"

"I told you," she insisted, "I don't miss anybody."

Paul reflected on what was happening before him. He needed to test the concreteness of her thinking. In order to validate his new belief that she was truly psychotic, he needed to test her inability to comprehend abstract thinking. As he plunged ahead, he thought of the exciting news he might have for Doyle that evening.

"You said you miss your children," he began.

"Yes," she said. "That's right. You're right. I do. I miss my children." She paused and looked away.

"What's the matter?"

She shook her head. "Nothing," she said. "I was thinking about Chris."

"What were you thinking?"

"I was thinking why I don't miss him."

"Why is that?"

She wet her lips with the tip of her tongue. "I couldn't please him, either."

"What do you mean by *either?*"

"Like my father."

"You couldn't please your father?"

"You see I couldn't." She started to grow angry at him. She glared at him as if he were an annoyance. "I did something wrong, didn't I? And I couldn't please Chris, either."

Paul thought the color card had done the trick. It had broken through her barrier of silent denial, and she was about to open up and let him in. If only he did not blow it, he warned himself. "What did you do wrong?"

"I told you," she said impatiently. "I married Chris."

"What did you do wrong with Chris?"

She hesitated. Her eyes darted around the room again. She became agitated and squirmed in her chair. "Everything," she said to no one.

"Everything?"

"Everything." She nodded. "I never did anything right."

"He criticized everything you did? Is that what you're saying?"

"Yes! No. Not everything."

"What, then?"

She grew more uncomfortable and squirmed all the more. She rubbed her feet forward and back on the floor in a small shuffle. "Only the big things. The important things. On the big things I always screw up."

"I don't believe that."

"What the hell do you know?" she snapped. "You don't know anything about it."

"I don't believe you always screw up. I just don't believe that."

"Then you tell me why he punished me all the time. If it wasn't because I screwed up, you tell me. Go on, smart ass. You don't understand anything. God, you're dumb. Don't you understand anything?" She twisted around on her seat and faced the side wall. After a long pause, she spoke softly. "He had to punish me because I didn't know how to please him. That was the way to learn. He could teach me, I'm sure of it. He could teach me if he tried. He didn't try hard enough. That's what the problem was. He didn't try hard enough. And then, when I really screwed up, it was too late to learn."

"When did you really screw up?"

She turned to him. "Don't you know? Don't you listen? I already told you."

"No, you didn't," he insisted.

"I know I did. You didn't listen to me. Oh, well, that's to be expected. Why should you listen to me, anyway?"

"I want to listen to you. I'm listening now. Very carefully."

"All right!" she said, resigned to the fact that he could not understand what she was saying. "I'll tell you again. But I know it's no use. You won't remember."

"Try me."

She thought, pressing her fingertip to her chin like a petulant child. "I forgot. I don't remember now."

"You don't want to tell me," he said.

"What's the difference?" she asked. "I can't please you, either. See how you're begging me and I can't please you."

"I only meant it's okay if you don't want to tell me," Paul answered. He warned himself again about hooking in.

"You don't care?"

"I want to hear only what you want to tell me," Paul responded carefully.

She watched him as if waiting for more. "I screwed up with the baby, silly. I told you I ruin the big things. I got me pregnant when we couldn't afford it and when we didn't want it. Chris was right. He showed me how I fucked up. I got us pregnant against his will. That was a terrible thing for me to do. It was a bad mistake. I tried to correct it, but it was too late."

"How did you try to correct it?"

"You know! You're a doctor."

"I'm not a medical doctor."

"What kind of doctor are you?"

"How did you try to correct it?" he asked again, ignoring her attempt to shift the interview away from herself and onto him.

She smiled. "Oh, I tried to make a miscarriage. You know, to kill it," she added hurriedly. "But I didn't let him know. That's what he wanted, but I didn't want him to do it to me. I tried to do it myself, but it didn't work."

"What did you do?"

She looked at him and started to cry. She shook her head and cried softly and quietly. "No," she said. Suddenly her grief burst out of her. She dropped her face into her hands and sobbed deeply, weeping like an infant. Tears flowed from her eyes, and she moaned pathetically through them and the crying. She sat in the chair and wept uncontrollably, with no end in sight, weeping as if she were standing on the edge of the end of the world.

"Oh, God!" she wailed to heaven. "I killed my child."

FIVE

When Harriet Doyle got back to her office after a very unsatisfying Monday lunch with three of her least interesting colleagues, the first thing she did was accuse Mrs. Finch, who had been her personal secretary for almost seven years, of misplacing her phone messages. Mrs. Finch, having been made wise by experience, smiled and shrugged, denied having done any such thing, and went back to typing the brief she had been in the middle of when accosted.

Doyle was not quick to anger, but she was drawing close now. She checked her own record book and counted the times she had called the County Medical Examiner. She was not a woman who shrunk from confrontation. Therefore, she was a woman who made it a principle to return phone calls. She was also a woman who abominated those who failed to return phone calls.

She pounded the intercom button on the side of her telephone.

"Yes?" Mrs. Finch's voice, dripping with her hurt feelings, came across clearly.

"Get me the M.E."—Doyle rummaged about on her desk,

sliding papers about, lifting and dropping files—"whatever his name is."

"That's Dr. Nussbaum," Mrs Finch said with superiority.

"Right," Doyle snapped. "Get him for me. And don't take no for an answer. We've already called four times in the last three days with no reply."

"Yes, ma'am!" She clicked off.

Doyle opened the hidden bar behind her desk, the one she had had built in and finished off in dark panelling to match the rest of the wall, and fixed herself a shot of Scotch on some ice cubes. She justified the drink by recalling that she had suffered through a bad lunch with three boring lawyers. She loosened the bow around her neck and unbuttoned her collar, pulled her earrings off and dropped them into a clean ashtray, then sat back to regain her composure.

Actually, she told herself, it was the husband, Chris Wyatt, she wanted next. And that was an interview that could not be conducted on the telephone. That one had to be managed face to face. "This is one guy I want to see eyeball to eyeball," she mumbled to herself.

The intercom buzzer got her attention. "Yes!" she said, punching the button on her phone.

The calm voice of Mrs. Finch replied, "I've got his secretary on the phone. The man himself is not available. What message shall I leave?"

She thought for a moment. "None," she said. "I want to talk to her." She cut off the intercom and lifted the telephone to her ear. "Hello," she said sweetly. "This is Harriet Doyle. To whom am I speaking?"

"This is Patti," a young voice said. "Dr. Nussbaum is not available, Ms. Doyle."

"So I've been told," Doyle answered. "Do you have any idea where I might find him?"

"Oh, I know where he is, Ms. Doyle. But you can't reach him there."

"Why not?"

"He's in the O.R. doing an autopsy. He never takes outside calls when he's working."

"When will he be out of there?" Doyle asked her.

"I don't know that. It's impossible to predict how long an autopsy will take."

"Well," Doyle said, "this is a very important matter and I really have to speak with him. Is there some way you could make sure that he calls me back today?"

"I can give him the message, Ms. Doyle," she said coldly.

"Why do I have the feeling," Doyle said sweetly, "that he's avoiding me?"

"I'm sure I don't know," she answered.

"Well, you're not being very helpful, young lady."

"Look," she snapped, "I just work here. I do what I'm told, so don't give me a hard time, okay?"

Doyle felt her ire rise. "All right," she said. "Here's a new message for your boss. Got a pencil?"

"Go on," she said.

"If I don't hear from the busy doctor by the end of this day—I repeat, this day—I will go to Judge Barrett and tell him that a county employee is refusing to cooperate with the defense in a murder trial. And I will get a court order to make him talk to me. And, if that doesn't do it, I'll make damn sure that he gets brought up on contempt charges and then he'll talk to me, because he'll be in a cell and they don't do autopsies in jail cells." She took a deep breath. "Have you got all that?"

"Yes, ma'am," the girl said meekly.

"Good," Doyle said, and dropped the phone back into its cradle. She sat back and finished off her Scotch in one swallow. "I'll be goddamned," she said to herself, "if I'll let some shit-head corpse cutter give me the runaround."

Melanie folded her pillow double so that lying on it would raise her head higher. Lying flat had begun to bother her. Breathing in that position had suddenly become difficult and sleeping, though desirable, had become impossible. It seemed to her that she had not slept in days. She could not remember when she had last slept. The microscopic voice lodged inside her right ear would know exactly how long she had not slept, but she dared not ask it, dared not acknowledge its existence lest it take complete control of her.

A wide beam of late afternoon sunlight, entering through the high window in her cell, cut across her upper body and flooded into her eyes. It was the sunlight, she told herself, that prevented her from sleeping, although she knew that was untrue, for she had not been able to sleep during the night, either, when all the lights were out and the cell block was almost pitch-black.

She threw herself onto her stomach and buried her face in the doubled-over pillow. Perhaps it would help, she thought, if she could smother out the penetrating day. But it would take more than that, she knew. If she wanted some peace, she would have to smother out her memories, all of them, every last one of them.

She tried to force her mind blank. She focused her internal vision onto a spot on the inside of her skull. In the front. On the inside of her forehead. And, for a moment, she thought she was successful. Her thoughts disappeared and were replaced by blackness, darkness, emptiness. Everything was gone except for the laughter in her ears. The faint, childlike laughter that carried her back to the rear seat of Chris Wyatt's old Chevy, where she also had to labor to breathe as he pawed her, as he grappled with her girlish brassiere, his hooked fingers pulling her panties away and probing roughly into her, his wet lips covering her mouth, her nose, her eyes.

His animal grunts filled her awareness and terrified her once again, as they had done so many years before when she could imagine her father leaving the house, walking down the driveway, and peering into the car to view her naked thighs thrown up into the air, exposing her to Chris's pulsating hand. She could see the ancient nightmare again, could see the face peering in through the steamy glass, could see her father's leering face watching her hungrily as her hips leapt and jumped in rhythm with Chris's plunging fingers.

She sobbed loudly as she realized that she had been caught. She jumped up and sat on the edge of the bed, crossed her legs, and squeezed them tightly shut. She shuddered and wrapped her arms around herself as if she were chilled. The blackness behind her tightly shut eyelids exploded with condemnation and guilt, promising her images of even more frightening consequences. Of her children, torn and rendered, discarded in vacant alleys, lying among the tattered remnants of her marriage. Of the bloody corpse of her bludgeoned husband, riddled and punctured, mutilated by her insensitivity. Of the spirits of her parents, tormented by their daughter's filthy indiscretions. Oh, God! she thought. Her mind screamed out. I need the sunlight. I can't stand the darkness of my memories.

Molly Barnes, the day matron, dropped her *People* magazine when she heard the haunting screams coming from the cell block. Her first thought was that it was just some goof-off looking for a little extra attention. But, when it failed to stop after a couple of minutes, she began to think that maybe it wasn't a goof-off and that maybe somebody, some prisoner, was in serious trouble.

She left her station and went quickly down the metal stairs, prepared to warn whoever it was to shut it up or she would stuff it up. But, when she arrived at the cell block, she found Melanie Wyatt stumbling around in her cell, bumping into the walls, falling down, screaming in terror, and rubbing her bloody knees where she had fallen on the concrete floor.

Barnes unlocked the steel door and rushed into the cell. She grabbed Melanie, laid her down on her cot, and attempted to comfort her, to get her to relax, to stop sobbing and gasping, to breathe easy and to stop screaming her head off. But she could not accomplish that. On the contrary, the more she implored the prisoner, the more the woman screamed and bellowed. Barnes felt bad that she could not help her, could not make her feel better somehow, but all Melanie could do was scream in pain and weep.

"Calm down," Barnes pleaded. "Take it easy, lady." She rubbed her shoulders, her back. She tried to comfort her, tried to mother her, did not know what to do first. "Where does it hurt? What happened?" Barnes did not even know what questions to ask. She clutched the terrified woman to her and rocked her as if she were an infant. "Shhh," she whispered. "It'll be all right. You'll be okay. Just take it easy." She put her fingers over the terrified mouth and stifled the incessant screaming, bringing it down to a sobbing, a moaning. "There, there!" she whispered. "Nothing's that bad." She brushed the hair away from Melanie's face. "Tell matron what happened," she said. "Tell me what it is and I'll make it all better."

Melanie's pitiful fingers clutched at the matron's sleeve and her trembling lips could barely form the words. "I'm blind," she wailed. "I'm blind. I can't see."

At four o'clock, Harriet Doyle was at Central Division waiting for Officer Chris Wyatt to end his shift. She gave the desk sergeant her name and asked to have Chris made aware that she was there to see him. Then she stood over by the candy machine and observed the human traffic going by. To anyone else the characters playing out their sad tales in the police station might have been repulsive, might have appeared to be the lower layer of the city's sewer system, but to Doyle, who had spent her entire adult life practicing criminal law, they were her people, her clients, her livelihood. She had an affinity for them. She liked them—the poor, the unsophisticated, the disenfranchised.

As for Officer Chris Wyatt and his colleagues, that was another matter. Cops were another matter altogether. She watched a young man dressed in blue jeans, a tight black tee shirt, and a pale blue windbreaker enter the lobby through the steel reinforced door in the back, which was labelled "Private, for official use only," and recognized the enemy. As profoundly sympathetic as she was for the recipients of the law enforcement system, that was how unsympathetic she was toward the dispensers of law enforcement. Clearly, Doyle disliked cops.

She introduced herself to Chris, although there was no need to. The policeman recognized her the same way she had recognized him. They shook hands ritualistically and eyed each other like two boxers entering the ring together for the first time. But these two were old adversaries. The guy who put them into a cell and the woman who put them back on the street. Old and wary adversaries.

They walked across the street to McGinty's Bar and sat in the back at that same poorly washed table, which smelled faintly of ammonia and dishwater, where Charlie Morris had been sitting with that fantastic-looking blonde with the long, talented legs the last time Chris had been in. Chris noticed that Doyle's legs looked even better but they were black, and to Chris Wyatt black was far from beautiful.

"Want a beer?" he asked Doyle when they had sat down.

"That's fine," she said.

Chris waved to the front and shouted to Dave, the bartender, for two beers. Then he turned to examine Doyle more closely and smiled. She was sexy, he admitted to himself grudgingly. His eyes roamed all over her, settling on the tight breasts that pushed at her neatly cut jacket. "So you're my old lady's lawyer?"

"That's right," Doyle said. There was no lightness, no humor in her voice.

"What do you think of your client?" Chris asked, grinning maliciously.

"The reason I'm here, Officer Wyatt, is to find out what you think of your wife."

"Ex-wife," Chris said. "We're divorced."

"Oh? I didn't know it was final yet."

Chris nodded. "Not yet. But what's the difference? It's just a formality."

Doyle stared at him, and Chris continued. "I'll tell you what I think of her. But, if I'm going to talk about her, I better take some penicillin first." He laughed at his own derogatory joke.

Dave brought two tall glasses of beer and set them on the table between the two opponents. Chris reached for his wallet.

"No, let me," Doyle said. She threw a bill down next to the glasses.

Chris shrugged and nodded. "The new society. A few years ago I would never let a woman pay for me. Especially not a—" He stopped and shrugged, lifting his glass and tilting

228

it slightly toward her. "Here's to old ladies and clients who—" Again he paused and shrugged. "Never mind."

Doyle left her glass on the table and, with blazing eyes, stared at the man in front of her. She watched Chris swallow half his beer and waited for him to put the glass down. "Let's set some ground rules, Officer Wyatt. Okay with you?"

Chris leaned back arrogantly in his chair and hooked his thumbs inside the waistband of his jeans. "Sure, Counselor. Do your thing." He grinned at Doyle and threw her a suggestive wink.

She said, "I'm an attorney representing a defendant in a criminal action. You're a witness with information pertinent to the proceedings. I have the legal right to speak to you. I have the right to gather all the information I can pertaining to this case and my client. I'm in the process of doing that now by interviewing you. Do you follow me?"

He nodded, and she paused and took a deep breath. "Under no circumstances will I ever be one of your good old boys. The kind you can crack wise with about your old lady, your wife, your soon-to-be ex-wife, my client. I'm not a chick you can fuck with and I'm not impressed by any of your tight jock macho bullshit."

Her eyes burned into his as he grew pale. "Rest assured, I will always be on the look out to trap you, to catch you lying, to trip you up." She grinned then. "Do you dig?" And then she grew deadly serious once again. "I take Melanie Wyatt's plight very seriously. You, on the other hand, are not required to. Nor do I demand that you do. However, let it be understood between us that everything you say to me will be committed to my memory like an indelible photograph and that you will be on the witness stand one day, in court, under oath, in these black hands, and your wit and arrogance will come back to haunt you. On my soul, I swear it. Have I made myself perfectly clear?"

A tight-lipped, angry Chris Wyatt nodded his understanding. "Perfectly," he whispered.

"Okay," Doyle said lightly. "Here's mud in your eye." She lifted her glass and chugged her entire beer right through the foam at the top.

Paul Murphy, unable to locate Harriet Doyle, was forced to call Judge Barrett's clerk in order to get permission to see Melanie in the prison ward of County General Hospital. The clerk in turn had to interrupt the judge in chambers, in conference with opposing counsel, to get his signature on the order and to explain what had happened and why it was needed. The judge excused himself from his conference and got on the phone with Paul.

"How did that happen?" the judge demanded without any preliminaries.

"All I know is what the matron told me. She called me as soon as the paramedics moved Mrs. Wyatt to County. They confirmed that she apparently has lost her sight and required immediate hospitalization."

"How serious is it?" the judge asked.

"I don't know, Your Honor," Paul said. "I can't get any more information until you sign the release."

"I've already done that, Paul." He paused, and when he spoke, there was anger in his voice. "If she's done any injury to herself while in custody, you can bet your bottom dollar some heads are going to roll."

Paul remained significantly silent.

"Anyway," the judge said, "you get on over there and find out for me, will you?"

"Yes, sir."

"I guess her behavior has answered my original question, hasn't it?" the judge said. "There's certainly little question about her competency now."

Two hours later, Paul stood at the grilled entrance to the hospital prison ward, his signed court order clutched in his hand, and argued with the guard to be allowed in. He was respectfully referred to Dr. Gottlieb, Chief Resident in charge of the ward, whose office was just down the hall, on the free side of the bars, and who was in there now.

Gottlieb, a man in his early thirties, mustached, bespectacled, and possessed of a chronic bitter facial expression, looked up from his paperwork and grunted for Paul to have a seat.

"Thanks," Paul said. He sat down at Gottlieb's desk and, facing the resident across it, reached out and dropped the court order in front of him.

"What the hell is that?" the resident asked. He lifted it up and brought it close to his face to read.

"The court wants me to see Melanie Wyatt," Paul answered.

The resident looked up at him and grimaced. "Fuck the court."

Paul shook his head. "That's a hell of an attitude you've got there, Doctor."

"What do you expect, Buster?" Gottlieb challenged him. "You come busting in here with this piece of paper, expecting Hilton-quality service. Who the hell do you think you are?"

"That doesn't matter," Paul said. "The judge wants me to see Mrs. Wyatt."

"I don't care what the judge wants." Gottlieb stood up and pushed his chair back on its wheels. "I don't care what anyone wants. I only care about the needs of my patient."

"Me, too," Paul said.

"Oh, yeah?" He walked out from behind his desk. "Did you come in and ask about her? Did you ask if I thought she was up to seeing you? Does my medical opinion even matter to you? Who the fuck are you kidding, Buster?"

"You're right," Paul said contritely. "I apologize. You're absolutely right."

Gottlieb sat on the corner of his desk and crossed his arms over his chest. "That's better," he said, "Now we're more like colleagues and less like servant and master."

Paul grinned sheepishly. "I deserved that."

Gottlieb smiled at him. "You bet your ass you did."

Paul stood up and extended his hand. "Let's start all over from the beginning. Okay?"

Gottlieb hesitated for an instant, then reached out and took Paul's hand. "Okay."

Paul sat down again, and Gottlieb walked around and returned to his side of the desk. "Here's the situation," Paul said. "I was evaluating Mrs. Wyatt for the court when this—whatever it is—happened. I have no details. Nobody's told me anything. But the judge wants me to find out if this is a self-inflicted injury or what. He also wants me to see Mrs. Wyatt, if possible, and try to maintain the relationship that's been initiated."

Gottlieb grinned at him. "You said a mouthful. Now, I guess, you want answers?"

"Right."

"Okay," Gottlieb said. "Get ready. Here comes my speech. First of all, her condition at the moment is very stable. She's been sedated so there's no point in seeing her now, 'cause she isn't going to talk to anybody. She's out cold. And that's a blessing, because the lady was really hurting.

"As far as the injury being self-inflicted, I don't know

what to tell you except that there's no injury to her eyes, and since there's no injury, I guess it can't be self-inflicted."

Paul was surprised. "No injury?"

"That's right," Gottlieb said. He shrugged and shook his head slowly.

"So she's not blind," Paul said.

"She's blind, all right, but I just don't know why." He pulled open his top drawer and brought out a brown manila file folder. "Let me tell you what we've done so far." He rummaged through the documents in the file.

"Go easy on the medical terms," Paul said. "I'm a psychologist."

Gottlieb grinned at him. "Okay," he said, and lowered his eyes to the file. "Our ophthalmologist can't find anything in the eyes themselves. There could be some injury to the nerves leading to the eyes, even like a viral infection, but that's farfetched. That would mean that two separate nerves, each serving a different eye, were injured identically at the same time." He shook his head. "Weird, right?"

Paul nodded.

"We tested her blood for sugar. Sometimes severe diabetes causes blindness, but she has no history of diabetes and isn't diabetic now. Besides, her blood's as pure as creamery butter. We sent her down for a brain scan thinking maybe a tumor, but her pictures are as clear as a bell. The big test that's left is an angiogram and we're taking our time before doing that one."

"Why?" Paul asked.

"Do you know anything about angiograms?"

"No."

Gottlieb closed the file and laid it down on the desktop. "Well," he said, "it has some element of risk. It's a test in which we invade the body—you know, enter the arterial system and travel up to the ... well, take my word for it, it's

233

dangerous. We'll do it if we have to, but we've got some other things first."

"What's next?" Paul asked.

"Well, you should know. Sometimes these things just go away by themselves and we never know what caused them. And sometimes they're right down your alley."

Paul nodded. "I was thinking that. If this is a conversion reaction . . ."

Gottlieb said, "I was thinking hysteria."

Paul grew contemplative. "She might be the perfect candidate for it," he said. "Except that would mean I had her terribly misdiagnosed."

Gottlieb shrugged. "Frankly, that's my inclination. I have to keep on testing her just to be safe, but I believe it's psychological. I'm convinced of it"—he grinned and winked at Paul—"unless she's faking altogether."

Paul nodded thoughtfully. "When can I see her?"

Gottlieb squirmed a bit and looked away. "You might as well stick around and see her when she wakes up. The truth is, she's been asking for you since she got here."

"Jesus Christ," Paul said. "Then why did you give me such a hard time?"

Gottlieb hunched his shoulders up around his neck. "I don't know," he said. "I thought maybe you were one of those cocky shrinks who think they know it all."

"Have you changed your opinion?"

"Yeah, sure." He grinned broadly. "Now that I know you, I can see you don't know shit."

Harriet Doyle was nursing her second beer while Chris Wyatt was downing his fifth and motioning for Dave to bring him another. A full hour had gone by, during which time

Chris had gone on at great length about Melanie's complete failure as a wife and as a mother.

There was no sense of comradery between them and Chris avoided the use of sarcasm like the plague. Doyle was pleased to see that the policeman had taken her warning seriously and had decided to play it straight.

He told Doyle about Melanie's ambivalence regarding children, how he had always wanted a houseful and how she had balked at the idea of having any. He described the strain it had put on their marriage, telling Doyle of long battles that went on for days during which she would punish him unmercifully just for wanting to build a family. He recounted her screaming fits when she terrorized him with her violent behavior, demanding that her body was her own and not for him to use to produce offspring like some cow. Still, they had had a child, he told Doyle, against her wishes and even though she was demanding an abortion. Somehow, he had managed to win out.

However, once the child had been born, Melanie had exacted her revenge against him by punishing the little girl. He told of coming home nights to find a wailing infant wallowing in her own filth, unchanged for the entire day as well as unfed and uncomfortable, and Melanie in their bedroom, lying on top of the bed with a pillow over her head to shut out the infant's sounds.

As the years went by and the child got older and less manageable, he told of beatings, of isolation, of hosing down. He told of broken bones and of driving hundreds of miles to another state for treatment, to avoid detection. He told of begging Melanie to go for psychiatric help, of offering to go with her, of explaining to her that there was no stigma today, in this day and age, and that the best people went into therapy. It was the thing to do, he had told her. But she had always refused.

Then he told Doyle about her carousing, about her staying out late at night and leaving him to sit with the baby; he spoke about her excessive drinking, partying, sexual encounters with strange men, drug experimentation, and group orgies. He told Doyle that of all the unfit mothers he had ever encountered as a policeman, she was the worst and there was nothing he could do about it. Because, he told Doyle when she asked, she had brainwashed Polly, who would lie for her every time and make him look like a fool.

But none of it was as bad as it got when she became pregnant with Denny, he told Doyle. Then it got really bad. She had gotten pregnant because she had forgotten to take the pill, but she blamed him just the same. She had ranted and raved at him as if he had committed some terrible crime, he said, as though he had purposely tried to make her pregnant to punish her.

One time, he told Doyle, they had had the biggest fight in the history of the world. She had been calling him filthy names for about an hour, until finally he couldn't take it anymore and he sat her down on the couch and told her exactly what he thought of her, what he thought of mothers who hated their children and treated them like shit, who ruined them and twisted them and made them crazy with their own crazy ways. He even slapped her that time, he said, first and last time he had ever laid a hand on her. And then he had told her he was leaving her, that he could not live with a woman like her anymore, that he was going to take the child and disappear if he had to, but that he was going and to hell with her. And that was the time she had threatened to do it.

When Doyle asked him what it was she threatened to do, he sat back and looked at her for a long time. He did not answer immediately. He lifted his beer glass first and finished off what was left at the bottom, then he put the glass down in a very deliberate way and looked up at Doyle, shaking his head slowly and sadly. "That's when she did it," he said. "That's when she told me that if I left her, she'd kill my baby."

SIX

Melanie was fully aware that she was awake, but she was much too terrified to open her eyes. The rememberance of sightlessness horrified her, sending vibrations of panic through her body. She moved her hands down to her sides and felt about the bed she was lying on, felt the crisp, clean sheets, the silken texture so very different from that of the rough, brown soaped sheets she had slept on in jail. She turned her face and felt the similar crispness of the pillowcase against her cheek. Even the fragrance of the room was different, not the stale, urine/pine-sol mixture she remembered from the cell block. This aroma was medicinal, bitter and sharp and pungent as in a hospital.

She remembered then, as if in a dream state, being transported from place to place, tormented with the never-ending babble inside her head urging her to scream; being wheeled about on rolling stretchers, led, she feared, to her death; being punctured with hypodermic needles, prepared for her ultimate sacrifice, and restrained with leather belts and straps, her life offered up to the gods; and finally being deposited in a stationary bed and filled with a wonderful, dreamy, floating sleep.

She heard herself sigh deeply. Was it she, after all, who sighed, or was it her miniature constant companion, like a weary traveller, used up but with miles to go still? She felt like that, too. She felt exhausted, as though she had just completed a long journey that had taxed her energies to their limit, that had drained all the strength and will and desire from her like juice from an orange. She began to relive that journey, that long excursion to madness and back again. The scenery flashed before her sightless eyes—a tiny dead infant, confinement in a steel cage, accusing stares in a court of law, probing aliens testing her, testing her, testing her. Enough!

Her eyelids fluttered open, very slowly at first, opening a fraction and then pressing shut again so quickly, and though she could not see, she was not surrounded by infinite blackness as she had been when the blindness had arrived in her cell. She sat up and looked around her, but she could not see as she had always thought about seeing. The dull greyness about her was punctuated with shapes of various sizes and configurations, objects that stood about her but which were unidentifiable. Sight as she had always known it was denied her.

She laid back and let the tears flow freely. She wept gently, almost silently, letting the pain that seemed such a part of her slip away with the tears, as if crying were cleansing her, releasing all the poisons of despair that had been gathered up inside her. She examined herself with her mind's eye, sort of reviewed herself as if she were outside of herself watching herself operate, move about, react. She saw herself dwelling in a cage, eating slop from a tray, walking about shackled, down corridors, up stairs, in an exercise hall. She observed her madness, her appearance of insanity, her bizarre behavior, and she felt ashamed.

She remembered and explored her fingertips with the

thumbs of both hands, encountering the split and crusty ends and weeping all the more. She remembered Murphy and their time together and his gentle patience with her and she was grateful for having him, though she was ashamed at the recollection of the harlot she had played, of what she had been like with him.

Someone rummaged at her side, touched her, fixed her. "Who's there!" she asked tremulously through her gentle weeping.

Tender hands responded. Cool fingers brushed back the hair from her heated forehead, caressed her feverish cheek. The odor of alcohol stung her nostrils and a chilling coldness was rubbed onto her skin on the inside of her elbow. She wanted to pull her arm away but it was locked in a firm grasp.

"Take it easy," a sweet, gentle voice said.

Melanie was aware of the bite of a needle, a quick sting that came and went as quickly as a blink, and almost immediately following a similar wonderful drowsiness returned and subdued her, and she gratefully allowed herself to fall back into its bliss.

In there, she knew, in that deep, floating hole, she could easily forget who she was and what had happened to her.

Phyllis became more irate with each passing minute. The more adamant the police sergeant became at frustrating her, the more determined she became to beat him at his own game. She was unwilling to understand why she was not being allowed in to see her friend. This hour was, after all, the prescribed time for visitors, she insisted. And she was a legitimate visitor. Other prisoners were meeting with their visitors. The polite sergeant agreed with her but still would not permit her to visit with Melanie Wyatt and refused to offer any explanation whatsoever.

It was when she called Roger Gillespie to involve him in getting her in to see Melanie that she learned about her friend's illness. It was Roger who told her about Melanie's sudden transfer after he had gone to the sergeant's superior officer and solicited the full story.

He had called Phyllis back where she was waiting at the pay phone in the jail and explained the situation to her. While she listened to Roger's accounting of what had taken place, she threw despising looks at the unhappy sergeant who sat by, avoiding her stares, pretending innocently to ignore her.

"You could've told me that," she said to him as she hung up with Roger.

He looked at her guiltily and shrugged. "Sorry, lady," he said. He grinned foolishly.

"I'll bet you are, you jerk!" She stormed out of the police station and had no difficulty finding a taxi out in front. She directed the driver to County General Hospital, then sat back on the leather seat and closed her eyes.

All she could remember thinking of during that long ride was the fragility of their lives, hers and Melanie's. She perceived with amazement that less than two weeks before her entire world had been totally dissimilar, whole, unfragmented. The shattered pieces of the life she recalled lay at her feet all about her. Her friend was gone for who knew how long. She had taken on the responsibility of mother to Polly, perhaps forever. She had given up her home, her life style, in exchange for someone else's. And now this devastating illness that she knew nothing about had entered the picture. And, worst of all, she felt frighteningly alone. She felt unsatisfactorily alone in the knowledge that all of it, every minute detail of it, needed to be dealt with. Needed

241

to be dealt with immediately, for her new life had no patience with procrastination. And not by someone else, not by some other person who could step in and rescue her. But by her. Phyllis.

She wished, at that moment, ashamedly, that she had a man in her life upon whom she could rely to arrive and straighten it all out. She wished for someone like Roger— not Roger himself, of course, but someone like him—to marry her and take her under his protective wing. It would be so much more comfortable, she told herself, to know that at six o'clock, after offices around the city were closed, he would come home, kiss her warmly, roll up his shirtsleeves, and relieve her of all pressure by taking on the unsolvable dilemmas of the day. What a disgusting, wimpy dream, she thought.

Phyllis forced her eyes open. She caught herself before falling into that old trap of being weakly dependent upon another, ineffectually needy of rescue, reliant on a man.

"That's bullshit!" she said out loud. The driver looked up and glanced back at her through his rearview mirror.

She told herself, if what you want is a man to take care of you, what you will most assuredly get is a man for you to take care of.

At that moment, she could not even imagine dealing with all of this day's trials and then rushing home to cook his dinner, clean his house, pick up yesterday's dirty underwear, and end her day by comforting him because he had had such a hard time competing with the jerk in the office next door. Who the hell wanted two full time jobs, anyway? she thought. And one you don't even get paid for. "Too bad, Roger," she mumbled to herself. "You just lost out."

She laughed under her breath, causing the driver to gaze at her again. She wanted very much to kick herself. She had spent too many years protecting her independence to cancel

242

it out now because the going was getting a little rough. Hell! She was much too tough for that.

She suddenly noticed the driver watching her in his mirror. It's okay to be afraid, she thought, staring at the back of his head. But being afraid sure as hell doesn't mean I'm incompetent.

Paul heard the loud argument going on down the hall and stuck his head out the door of the doctor's lounge to see what was happening. He saw a beautiful young woman, about Melanie Wyatt's age but much prettier, raising a huge fuss about being admitted to see a patient. She was outside the bars doing battle with the uniformed guard who was on the other side. She insisted upon being let in and he insisted upon her staying out. By the time Paul, curious about this lovely girl, arrived at her side, her voice had escalated to a high-pitched screech.

"You've got her in there," she was screaming, "and I want to see her."

"You can't!" the guard insisted. "You need a special pass."

"How do I know she's all right if you don't let me in to see her?"

The guard shrugged. "Take my word for it."

"Fat chance!" she said.

"Listen!" the guard said. "Nobody sees Melanie Wyatt without a police permit."

"Damn!" Phyllis grew red in the face with anger.

Paul, realizing they had a common mission, stepped up beside her and whispered into her ear that she could not possibly get what she wanted the way she was going about it, then led her off down the hall with the promise of assistance. She stared at him incredulously but did not resist his leadership. He was too good-looking, she thought, to be anyone bad. Once they were at the entrance to the doctor's lounge, he guided her inside and closed the door behind them.

"Come on," he said with a friendly smile. "I'm going to pour you a cup of coffee and get you calmed down." He was fascinated by her large blue eyes.

"Who the hell are you?" She glared at him.

He extended his hand. "I'm Paul Murphy. I've been working with Melanie."

She relaxed immediately. "Oh, I'm sorry," she said. "You're the psychologist Roger told me about."

He was puzzled. "That's right."

She realized he did not know what she was talking about. She took his hand. "Roger Gillespie, the lawyer." She laughed. "I'm Phyllis Morley, Melanie's friend. I'm staying with her daughter."

"Hi." He smiled at her. "I knew someone was caring for Polly, but I didn't know who." He grinned. "I guess I can't say I'd know you anywhere?"

She laughed. "No! I guess you can't."

"Who's Roger Gillespie?" He lifted the half-filled coffee pot from the hot plate it rested on and poured her a cup. "Here," he said. "This'll bring you down a little."

She took the cup and held it in both hands. "He's a lawyer working with Harriet Doyle." She could have said, He is one of my boyfriends, she thought, but did not. "And you can't blame me for being mad," she said. "I've been getting the runaround all day."

"They won't let you see her, huh?"

"That's right."

"Don't feel bad," he said. "They won't let me see her, either. At least, not yet."

"I don't believe that," she said. "You're her doctor. How can they keep you out?"

"I'm not really her doctor. I've just been testing her for the court. But that doesn't even matter. She's got a medical doctor now and his orders take precedence." He shrugged. "He wants her to rest, and if that's what he wants, that's what he gets, and I wait just like you."

She smiled at him. She liked his easy manner. "Waiting with someone is a lot easier than waiting alone."

He liked her, too. He could not stop staring at her eyes. "Especially," he said, "if it's someone like you."

She was not offended by the easy compliment. She touched her coffee mug to his, lifted it to her lips, and watched him over the top with her magnificent blue eyes.

Later, when Melanie was almost fully awake, Paul let Phyllis go in with him to see her friend. He wanted to reassure her that her friend was not really very seriously ill. Melanie was seeing slightly brighter images by that time and was able to separate the two of them, although she could not distinguish between them.

Paul stood off against one wall and let the two women hug and hold onto each other and whisper to each other. They spent ten minutes like that and then Phyllis rose to go. Melanie cried and begged her to come back the next day, and Phyllis promised and looked over to him for reassurance that she could make that kind of promise.

Phyllis was reluctant to leave and lingered for as long as she could until Paul finally drew up a chair for himself next to the bed and literally pushed her out. As she left the room, he took her hand in his and squeezed her fingers gently. She looked up at him and nodded her understanding. They had found a common bond in Melanie's situation and clearly had agreed to join together in her defense.

As Phyllis left the hospital, she was feeling desolated for

Melanie, despondent and aggrieved, but still relatively good about herself, although somewhat guilty. Her personal interest in this kind, handsome doctor was a development upon which she had not counted. And there was no question that she was interested in him. She was more than a little attracted to him and wanted to pursue the possibilities, while at the same time holding back because of the feeling that, at the present time, with Melanie's future so unsure, pursuing her own interests was somehow an immoral and deceitful act of betrayal.

Her confusion troubled her and she pressed her shoulder bag against her side with her elbow. Though she questioned the appropriateness of it, she was comforted by the thought that in her purse she carried a slip of paper with Dr. Murphy's private number on it. To be used, he had said, only in case she was forced to cancel their dinner appointment for the next evening.

The first thing Paul did after Phyllis left the room and they were finally alone was to direct Melanie into some simple relaxation exercises, things he usually taught when preparing a subject of hypnosis. Melanie was an excellent candidate for hypnosis. She was highly suggestible and very trusting, and though she was still extremely overwrought about the condition of her eyesight, she was ready to follow his lead in any direction.

He took her through a whole battery of exercises, and when she was calm and fully relaxed and breathing very easily and rhythmically, he led her into a discussion of her blindness.

"Do you remember the moment when you first lost your sight?" he asked her.

"Yes," she said. "I think so."

"What happened at that moment?"

"You mean, before it went black, or after?"

"Which do you remember?"

"I don't know," she said.

"All right. Then, before?"

She tilted her head as if listening to a distant sound, a far-off voice. She remained that way for a long moment, thoughtful. "I'm not sure anything happened," she finally said.

"What were you doing? At that moment, I mean."

She screwed up her face as if the memory could cause pain. "I was sitting on the edge of the bed. I—I was crying. Yes. And all of a sudden, the tears stopped. I was sitting on the edge of the bed and I had my face covered with my hands. No. Not up. Down. I had my face in my hands and I was bent over so I was pointing downward, to the floor." She showed him.

"Then what?" he asked eagerly.

She looked up at him, unseeing. "The tears just stopped and I thought, How strange. I lifted my head and looked up and there was . . . nothing. I couldn't see." She shivered as if suddenly cold.

He reached out and touched her arm with his warm hand. "Did you feel any pain? Any strange sensations? Any discomfort at all?"

"No," she said hesitantly. "Nothing like that."

He shifted in his chair and she jumped at the soft sound, as if anticipating an attack.

"What were you thinking?" he asked.

"When?"

"Just before."

She became thoughtful again. "I don't think I remember. Afterwards, I was terrified. I remember thinking that I'd be in blackness for the rest of my life, that I'd never see anything again, not colors or shapes or people. Oh, yes, and I thought what a perfect punishment for me. I don't know why I thought that. It doesn't make a lot of sense. But it felt like I was glad it had happened. Like I was cleansed by it."

He was surprised and quite pleased by the clarity of her memories and perceptions. Though her thoughts were painful ones, they were clear and not diffuse. So much of her recent psychotic thinking and behavior was suddenly gone now, replaced by the devastating sadness of her affliction, that once again she had become, by her reversion to normalcy, almost unrecognizable.

"Try to remember what you were thinking before," he said kindly.

She was silent for a long time. "I can't," she said finally, shaking her head, weary and discouraged.

He reminded her. "You said you were crying."

Sadly. "Yes."

He urged her. "Why were you crying? What were you crying about?"

"I don't know," she said pitifully.

"Were you sad?"

"Yes." She nodded and her face twisted, as if she were about to cry. "I remember feeling heartbroken."

"Okay," he said, nodding sympathetically. "What else did you feel?"

Her fingers fluttered to her cheeks. She glanced about the room as if seeking some escape route. "I—Trapped? No, not trapped. Guilty. Yes. Guilty."

He leaned forward. He was no longer objective. He knew he was on the edge of a breakthrough and he was as excited as a neophyte. "Guilty of what?"

"I . . . don't know. Don't remember," she said helplessly.

"It was just a feeling. I didn't want to have it. It was just there."

"Try to put it together with a thought," he almost pleaded.

"I'm trying," she said. She grew angry and frustrated. "Don't you think I'm trying? I want to remember everything. I know my blindness is psychological. I want to remember everything."

"How do you know it's psychological?" he asked, suddenly wary.

"Dr. Gottlieb told me."

"When?"

"Just before," she said. "A little before you came in with Phyllis."

Damn! He had thought that Gottlieb had a big mouth. "Do you know what that means?"

She nodded. "Yes. I think so."

"Tell me."

"There's nothing wrong with me. I mean, physically," she said. "He said all the tests were negative. So it's in my mind. Isn't that what it means?"

Murphy agreed reluctantly. "Yes. In a way."

"Well, if it's in my mind, you can help me. That's what you do, isn't it?" She was slipping away from him. He felt her leaning toward her hostile, paranoid defense, in which he would become the enemy again, and he cursed Gottlieb for being an arrogant fool.

"Yes. Sometimes," he said.

She sounded suspicious. "Won't you help me?"

"That's what I'm trying to do, Melanie."

"Yes," she said, "but you're angry with me."

His face registered surprise. "Why do you say that?"

"Because you are." She had grown smug. "You're angry because I can't remember." She pouted like a child.

"I don't get angry when people can't remember," he said as sympathetically as he could. He stood up and walked to the window. He stood by it and looked back at her. "Truly, I don't."

"It's true," she said petulantly. "I can't remember. I really can't remember. It's not like I'm doing it on purpose. I can't remember."

"I believe you, Melanie," he said.

"Thank you," she said. "It's like on the tip of my tongue. But I can't quite catch it. Any instant it'll come to me. That's what it feels like."

"I know," he said. "Does it have to do with Denny?"

"Who?"

"Denise," he said. "Your baby."

She turned her face to the side. "Denise is dead."

"I know," he replied softly.

"I don't talk about her anymore."

"Why not?"

She shook her head from side to side. "I don't want to remember her."

He moved to his chair and stood leaning on its back. "You said you wanted to remember everything. What happened to that idea?"

She continued to shake her head. "I do. I do. Everything except for Denny."

Paul sensed he was getting her back. "How about your mother and father? You want to remember everything about them?"

"Yes," she said.

He pressed. "Then why not Denny?"

"Because she's dead," Melanie said matter-of-factly.

"I know that," he said. "But so are your mother and father."

She glared at him. "It's not the same."

"What's different?"

She turned her face half sideways, as if hearing a sudden voice, and waited. When she spoke she directed her words upwards, toward the ceiling. "I didn't kill them," she finally answered.

He straightened up tall to make the sound of his voice come from somewhere up there. "Maybe you didn't kill Denny, either."

She bared her teeth like a vicious animal. "I did," she growled. "I know I did."

"How?"

"What?"

"How'd you do it?" he asked.

"I—I—That's a stupid question." She sneered in his direction. She was having difficulty responding to the two separate directions, to Murphy's big voice and the other little voice.

"Why is it stupid?" Murphy asked. And it sounded to her like he was defending himself. She was disappointed in him.

"Everybody knows how," she said, thinking what a fool he was becoming.

"I don't."

To hell with him, she thought. "That's tough tacos for you."

"Go on, tell me," he challenged her.

She would be damned if she would give him anything. "No."

"If you can!" he continued to challenge.

She would be obstinate. "No!"

"If you can remember," he said.

Let him beg me, she thought. "No!"

"You don't remember!" he accused her.

She grew angry. "No!"

Again, he accused her. "You don't want to remember."

251

She grew angrier still. "No!"

"But it's there, isn't it?" He pressed on her, pushed against her. He would not let her breathe. She felt herself falling into the old abyss again. She wanted to struggle upwards, to flail her arms and catch a breath of air.

"The whole thing!" he shouted. "It's in your head. In your memory. Isn't it?"

"No!" she screamed, feeling like she was losing it again.

He insisted. "You could see it as clear as day if you wanted to."

"No!" she screamed, and flung her head from side to side.

He spat the words at her. "You're stopping the memory."

"No!" she screamed again.

Louder. "You're stopping the memory, aren't you?"

"No!" A long wail of wolflike pain.

Louder still. "You're fighting the memory, aren't you?"

"No!" she shrieked so loud that the word was almost indistinguishable.

"Aren't you?" he shouted at her in persistent response.

She arched her body off the bed "Yes!" she screamed.

He softened. "Why?"

She was weeping now. She sobbed deeply and gasped for breath. "I can't remember it."

"Why not?" he whispered.

She whimpered. "I can't remember it."

"Why not?" he murmured.

"I can't remember it," she moaned.

"Why not?" he muttered.

"I can't! I can't! I can't!" she shouted, as angry as he had ever seen her.

He shouted back, "Why not? Why not? Why not?"

She bared her teeth like a wild beast and screamed at him, "Because I'm blind, damn you to hell."

SEVEN

It was six-thirty when Harriet Doyle got back to her office. Mrs. Finch had already gone for the day but one of the other secretaries was still there, down the hall, typing away furiously on what must have been a last minute motion. She could hear the sound of raised voices emanating from the office behind her and deduced that a couple of her partners were having a rough time of it. Nothing like corporate law, she thought, to develop a flaming ulcer.

Finch, bless her heart, had spent her last moments in the office thinking of and caring for Doyle's needs. On her desk stood her bottle of Cutty Sark, accompanied by a tumbler and a small crystal ice bucket with half a dozen partially melted cubes of ice in it. Taped to the neck of the yellow labelled bottle was a pink telephone message slip. She tore it from the bottle and brought it close to her weary eyes.

"M.E. did not return your call," it said. It went on to say, "Called him at 5:45. Had gone for the day. Sorry." Hence, the Scotch, Doyle thought. Wise old bird, she chuckled to herself. It would be tough to get by without her.

She helped herself to a generous measure of the liquor which, in her present mood, could be viewed as medicine.

As it flamed going down, she wished she could burn out the bad taste Chris Wyatt had left in her. Tough as she was, his sexually seductive stare left her feeling filthy, unclean. She shuddered with the thought of the fantasies that must have passed through the demented mind of the racist bastard. She would have liked to purge herself of the man's venom. She shook her head wearily. It would be hard work, she thought, but once she got him on the witness stand, she would enjoy using him to her own ends.

She poured herself another, shorter drink and, filling the glass with ice, leaned back in her chair, kicked her high-heeled shoes off, and rested her feet up on her desk. She could hear her two partners screaming through the walls. Not a bad idea, she thought. If she had had a partner there at that moment, she was sure she would be screaming at him as well. What the hell were partners for, anyway?

She leaned over and dialed Paul Murphy's number. She heard it ring four times and then a recorded message came on telling her what to do in case she wanted to say something to the doctor. She listened to the whole message, waited for the beep, and then hung up without a word.

Her problem was, she told herself, that as much as she wanted to destroy Chris Wyatt's testimony, as much as she wanted to pummel the man, to chew him up and spit him out, she would not. On the contrary, she would draw out of him all the poison he had showed her today and more, if she could get at it.

Doyle knew exactly how she would do it. Like trout fishing, she would feed him line, more and more, give him lots of room, let him wriggle and dip and dive and resurface and slither all over the place, and then Doyle would reel him in. Make him admit how erratic Melanie had always been. Make him admit how unpredictable she had always been. Make him admit that he had always thought she was crazy. Doyle would not even object to Wyatt sticking in an opinion like that. She would not try to refute that. She would open it up for more, widen the hole, deepen the cave, and let Wyatt fall right into it. She would let Wyatt prove to the court that his wife Melanie had always been unstable and in no way could she be held responsible for the unfortunate death of her child. Hell, Chris Wyatt was so good at bad-mouthing her that he would end up being the defense's best witness.

When Phyllis got home from the hospital, she caught Gladys before she could leave. She told the girl that she would be going out to dinner the next night and asked her if she could stay with Polly. Gladys was willing, but after she had left for home, Polly started to pout and stamped around the house unhappily. Phyllis let it go for a while, but when the behavior escalated and Polly started slamming doors, she put a stop to it.

She marched into Polly's room, where the child was propped up on her bed pitching her many dolls at the blank wall across the room from her. Phyllis grabbed a battered Snoopy out of her hands.

"Hold it," she said. "That's enough destruction for a while."

Polly threw herself facedown on the bed and began to weep. Phyllis sat next to her. She was thinking, instant motherhood may not be such a good idea. She put her hand on Polly's back.

"Turn around, sweetie," she said. "Turn around and talk to me." Polly shook her head violently. "I can see that you're angry with me, Polly. But I don't know why and I can't do anything about it if you won't tell me."

The child stopped crying and lay still for a moment. "Come on, honey," Phyllis said softly. "Turn around and

255

let me look at you." She slipped one hand under the child and lifted her up. The little girl turned and threw her arms around Phyllis and clung to her tightly, burying her face in Phyllis's neck.

"Tell me what's the matter," Phyllis said. The child remained silent. "We're partners, aren't we? No secrets between partners. That's bad business."

"I don't want you to go," Polly said.

"I'm not going anywhere, sweetie," Phyllis said.

"Yes, you are. I heard you."

"What did you hear?" Phyllis was puzzled. She held Polly away from her and gazed into the little girl's face.

Polly sobbed. "I heard you tell Gladys. You told Gladys to stay with me."

Phyllis laughed. "But that's not going away, honey. That's called going out to dinner."

Polly hugged her tightly. "Please don't go, Aunt Phyllis," she cried.

"Polly, it's only a dinner date. Look, I'll come home even earlier tomorrow and we'll spend some time together. Then I'll stay with you while you and Gladys have your dinner. And then I'll go out. Okay? I'll be back two hours later, Polly. I promise I will."

"I know you won't," the child whimpered.

"I promise I will," Phyllis said. "I don't lie to you. Did I ever lie to you? Tell me. Did I ever?"

"That's what Daddy said." The little girl pouted.

"What?"

"That he wouldn't go away. That he didn't lie."

Phyllis wiped the tears from Polly's face with her fingers. "It's not the same," she said. "I'm not getting a divorce from your mommy. You know all about the divorce. Didn't we all explain that to you?" Polly nodded thoughtfully. "Well, it's not the same. I want to live here with you. I

256

wasn't forced to move in here. This is my choice. I haven't got any reason to leave."

Polly looked at her and thought for a moment. "Mommy went, too."

"Not because she wanted to," Phyllis said. "Your mommy didn't have any choice. She's sick and in the hospital and the doctors won't let her come home. I explained that to you."

The little girl nodded. "I'm afraid, Aunt Phyllis. I don't want to be all alone." Phyllis held her and rocked her gently. She stroked her hair as Polly looked up at her. "Everybody leaves me, Aunt Phyllis. Everybody goes away and doesn't come back. I don't want you to go. Please, don't go."

Harriet Doyle's sensitivities were offended by the Jolly Tyme, and though she was even willing to admit they should not have been, she could not deny that she was truly phobic and usually had a tough time being around homosexuals, especially in the bar scene.

So, she was not that enlightened, she thought. Her skull was too small for her to be that broad-minded. She was a product of her times, which apparently were long gone, and no matter how hard she tried, she could not keep up with this high-speed, crack-powered world.

She stood on the street out in front and gazed up at the garishly painted windows, the rainbow-colored front door, the obscenely flashing neon sign that projected the silly name in a rhythm reminiscent of a bossa nova beat. She hesitated going in. Pairs of heavily made-up, pretty women walked by her and looked at her hungrily as they passed, and giggled before entering the noisy place. One woman who walked with her arm around a beautiful blonde winked at her as she passed, then slipped her hand down inside the waistband of

257

her partner's jeans and suggestively caressed her ass. Doyle smiled self-consciously, thinking she would probably be bright red at that moment if she had not been black.

She had chosen to do this piece of legwork herself, although she had endeavored to get Roger to do it on his own. Of course, Roger was smart enough to claim a prior engagement immediately, grab his jacket and briefcase, and beat it out of the office in a split second. What the hell, Doyle thought, and she smiled to herself. Consider it an experience, she told herself. Not that she needed too much more experience, having been born in Montgomery, Alabama, kept there until she was six, then transported north and raised on the streets of Harlem. Hell, so she never got to Harvard. Brooklyn College and Columbia Law were good enough for her. After all, what were the alternatives? It was lawyering or hooking. No contest. Shit! She was also ready to admit that she, as much as the next person, if not more so, could use some goddamned consciousness expanding.

The heavy metal music hit her in the face the instant she passed through the rainbow door. The place was two-thirds empty but the sound was enormous, as if the room was stuffed with people three levels high. Multicolored light beams bounced off a ball made of tiny mirrors, which was suspended from the ceiling on a metal rod and rotated slowly and perpetually. A huge screen, upon which streaks and flashes of weird-colored light danced, had been erected and tilted at an upward angle, like a square satellite dish, in the back against the rear wall.

Scattered about at various tables throughout the place were couples drinking and smoking and laughing. Several couples danced under the turning ball and rubbed their bodies against one another and slipped their hands inside each other's clothing. They talked to each other by putting their lips up against the other's ear. Doyle could not imagine communicating in any other way with the music as loud as it was.

The bar was empty and the long line of unoccupied stools stood in a row like military reserves. Behind the bar, two people were working. The woman, who was as broad as she was tall and had biceps like a weight lifter, was busily mixing drinks while the man, skinny and scrawny, scratchy-faced, but trying to be sexy in his tight black tee shirt, sucked a toothpick and leaned on his hand, watching the dancers.

The muscular barmaid watched the very well-dressed Doyle, wearing a six-hundred-dollar suit from Saks, a white silk blouse from Bonwit's, and two-hundred-dollar Italian imports on her feet, suspiciously as she walked past her and climbed up on a stool in front of the kid with the black tee shirt.

"I'm looking for Mr. Rodriguez," Doyle said at the top of her voice.

The young guy looked her over appraisingly. Like most men, he liked what he saw. "What you want him for?" he screamed back.

"I'm a lawyer," Doyle said. "I want to ask him some questions."

The man leaned forward and strained to hear. He stared at Doyle for a moment, then shifted his eyes around past her and back to the dancers. "He ain't here," he shouted.

Doyle turned her head and gazed back to where the kid in the black shirt was looking. A couple of women were massaging each other in the middle of the dance floor. "He's supposed to work here," Doyle yelled over her shoulder.

"Ain't his shift."

A waitress dressed in a very tight black body suit and carrying a small round brown tray moved up to the bar. "Hey, Slick" she shouted. "Two white wines, huh."

The man slid down the bar to her, poured out two skinny

259

glasses of white wine from a gallon jug, threw a couple of white poker chips onto her tray, and slid back.

"Your name Slick?" Doyle asked, feeling the muscles in her neck strain. The young man smirked at her. "That what they call you?" He shifted the toothpick in his mouth and looked away. "Well, you aren't very, are you? Slick, I mean."

The music stopped and the sudden silence was like a shot of pain killer. "Get lost!" the young guy said.

"Okay," Doyle said. She could feel the eyes all around the room focused on her. She glanced over the small group of patrons who were all truly watching her at the bar. "Get smart!" she said to the young man. "You want me to subpoena you, Rodriguez? You want me to really fuck up one of your days? Drag your ass downtown into my office? Keep you answering questions for eight hours until your eyelids fall off? You really want that? I'll make mincemeat out of you, punk. You sure you want to make an enemy out of me?"

Rodriguez took the toothpick from his mouth and threw it to the floor behind the bar. "What do you want?"

Doyle smiled. "Now you're being slick, Slick. I want to talk. Five minutes. Maybe ten. But not here. That music starts again, I'm a dead woman."

Rodriguez nodded. He turned to his massive co-bartender and, using a special kind of sign language, motioned to her that he was taking a break. She nodded and threw him a salute. "Let's go," he said to Doyle.

They left the place through a back room, where Rodriguez pulled a scruffy brown leather jacket off a hook on the wall and threw it over his shoulders. They walked down the street in silence, Rodriguez leading the way, until they got to the Coffee Dan's on the corner. He entered, with Doyle right behind him, and sat down in a back booth.

"You want coffee?" he asked.

"Yeah," Doyle said. "Black."

Rodriguez pointed to the gang of jars and bottles stacked in one corner of their table. "You fix it yourself." He waved to a waitress and held up two fingers in the air once she had seen him and acknowledged him.

He drummed his fingers on the tabletop until the coffee got there. Then, he said, "Okay. What do you want?"

"Your name is Alvin Rodriguez. Is that correct?"

"Yes."

"I'm going to call you Alvin," she said. "I call you slick I feel like I'm in a bad movie. Okay?"

Alvin nodded. "Whatever you say." He looked at Doyle sullenly.

She pulled a copy of the police snapshot of Melanie out of her inside pocket. She palmed it, then reached over and showed it to Rodriguez. The young man looked at the picture and visibly relaxed. "Why didn't you tell me it was about this broad?" He smiled at Doyle. "I thought my fuckin' old lady found me. Shit, man. You scared the piss out of me."

"You didn't give me a chance, Alvin. You lied to me right off."

Alvin shook his head slowly. "What'd you expect? A black number like you dressed to the nines drags in and drops that lawyer shit on me. I thought you was from my old lady in Chicago. I thought you was going to drag me into court."

"Tell me about this girl," Doyle said.

"I already told the cops," Alvin said. He leaned back and sipped his coffee.

"Yeah," Doyle said. "But they're on the other side, Alvin. They're the bad guys. And I'm with the good guys. I don't want to know what you told them. I want to know what you forgot to tell them. You know what I mean?"

He was nodding thoughtfully. "I told them everything."

"Okay." She sighed and shook her head sadly. "The hard way. Tell me what you told them."

Alvin cocked his head to one side. He was thinking, remembering. "She comes into the place every once in a while. She has a drink. Usually a light one. You know, vodka and a lot of mix. She always sits at the bar." He wet his lips with the tip of his tongue. Doyle thought he was missing the toothpick. "Let's see . . ." He became thoughtful. "That's all I can remember."

Doyle threw some Sweet 'n Low into her coffee. "What about pickups?"

"Oh, yeah," Alvin said. "They asked me about . . . you know, who she leaves with, who she comes with. You know, things like that."

"What did you tell them, Alvin?"

He smiled at Doyle as if they were sharing a secret. "I told them, yeah." His head bobbed up and down while he grinned like a filthy-minded little kid.

"Yeah, what?"

"I told them she comes in alone and goes out with somebody. What did you think I told them? That's the truth. They all do it in there. That's what the place is for, for customers to like find each other. You know what I mean?"

"Alvin, listen to me." Doyle leaned forward and put her elbows on the table. "This girl is my client. I know her. I know her very well, Alvin. I can't believe what you're telling me about her."

"It's true," Alvin said. He touched his fingertips to his tongue and held them up in the air. "Swear to God."

Doyle sat back. "Okay," she said. "She comes in. She just wants to get away from it all. She has a light drink. She doesn't want to get drunk or anything like that. She sits at the bar by herself. Doesn't look to dance or anything. Doesn't do any of that groping that I saw inside." Alvin

Rodriguez laughed. "Minds her own business. Talks to a few people. Hell, you can't talk in there. It's the perfect place to just get away and hide."

"That's about the size of it," Alvin said.

"Then she gets up and goes home. She's refreshed. She's charged her batteries. Gets up and goes home—by herself. Think, Alvin. Doesn't that sound right? Can't you see her walking out of there by herself? Close your eyes and envision it, Alvin. Can't you see it?"

Alvin closed his eyes and screwed up his mouth. He pondered for a moment. "No," he said. "I can't see it like that. It never happened like that."

"You're sure?"

"Positive," Alvin swore. "She always left with someone. She always does. She likes them little, you know, petite. Small hands and small feet. She told me so. She won't leave until she finds one like that. Shit, Mobrey, the waitress, brings them over to her. All the time. And she gives her a big tip. She's a spender."

Doyle preferred her scenario. She wanted Melanie to go home alone. She wanted her to be straight. Okay, be curious. But when you get into bed with someone, make it a man. Damn! "Maybe they just walk outside together, Alvin? Is that possible? You never saw them drive off together, did you?"

Alvin laughed. "Okay. If you say so."

"Come on, Alvin. Help me on this. Isn't that possible? Isn't it?"

"Sure, it's possible," Alvin said. "But it ain't true. 'Cause the next time she comes in, she tells me how great the fucking was. And she's sitting at the bar stretching her neck, looking all around trying to find the same chick again. Sure. Anything's possible."

"Okay," Doyle said. "Try this. It really wasn't this girl."

263

She pointed to the picture held in her palm. "Looks almost exactly like her, but it isn't her. Take a good look, Alvin. Go ahead." Doyle held the picture up close to Alvin's face. "You can see, now that you look so close, that it really isn't the same girl. They look identical, but you can see it isn't her."

"That won't work," Alvin said. "I know it's her. It's her. I'm not going to lie about it."

"How do you know? What makes you so sure?"

"I know." Alvin shrugged.

"Come on, Alvin. This is a little picture. You can't be totally sure. Give me a break. Isn't it possible that you're wrong? Police ever take you downtown and show her to you?"

"No," he said.

"No lineup?"

"No."

"So how can you be so sure?"

"I just am," Alvin said. He dragged his eyes away from Doyle's face and stared over at the wall. He bit his lip nervously.

Doyle picked up on it. "What's the matter, Alvin? Tell me. You're holding out on me, aren't you." Doyle pointed an accusing finger at him. "Goddamn it, Alvin. If you're holding out on me, when I get you on the witness stand, I'll cut your—"

"Look," Alvin interrupted. "I promised I wouldn't tell. But you're not the cops, so—"

"Give," Doyle snapped.

"I know it's her because she told me so. I mean, she told me she was in trouble with the cops and she knew everything I was talking about. Everything I told her, she said yeah, yeah."

"I don't understand, Alvin. What kind of trouble? What did she tell you?"

Alvin squirmed in his seat. "I shouldn't've done it, I guess. But I don't give a shit about any cops and she's like a customer. You know what I mean? Like she tips me good all the time. She's a good lady." He looked away and did not speak for another minute, as if putting it all together in his head. "Next time I seen her, I told her the cops talked to me about her. I shouldn't've done that. But what the hell? She said she knew about it. Something about bad checks. She said she was blowing town."

Doyle stuck her hand up in front of Alvin's face like a traffic cop. "Hold it! When was this?"

Alvin thought with his mouth open. "Uh, night before last. Yeah. Wasn't last night." He nodded. "Night before last."

Doyle pulled her wallet from her purse and extracted a laminated calendar from one of its compartments. "Let's see," she said, searching the card. "That was the twenty-first, right?"

Alvin thought. "Yeah. Tonight's the twenty-third. That was the twenty-first." He continued counting on his fingers and nodding his head as his calculations worked out.

"Are you sure?" Doyle asked.

Alvin smiled at her and winked. "You trying to get me again?" he taunted. "I should call you slick. You lawyers slide all over the place."

"My client was in jail the night before last," Doyle said. "The night of the twenty-first she was in a cell without a paddle, Alvin."

Alvin stared at her, then looked away, then returned to stare again and cocked his head to one side. "What you trying to pull, lady? You trying to catch me up? I told you I'm not gonna lie for you." He pounded his fingertips on the tabletop. "She was here night before last. She sat at my bar. I had a conversation with her. I made her a drink. Her usual. She found an old friend. And, a little later, she went home with her. You tell me different and I'll tell you you're crazy. What do you want from me, anyway?"

Doyle smiled broadly, stood up, and threw a five-dollar bill down on the table. "Just tell it like that in court, Alvin. That's all I'll ever want from you."

EIGHT

The next morning, Paul Murphy called Judge Barret in his chambers before court was in session. He sensed that the judge was in a bad mood just from the way he said hello in that gruff, low-down voice that had none of the lilt it usually had when he was trying to charm someone.

Paul played it safe. "I'm sorry to disturb you, Your Honor."

"I'll bet you are," the judge said. "Especially since you were supposed to report to me last night."

"I'm sorry, Judge. It was just too late by the time I got home last night."

"Listen, Paul," the judge said. "I waited for your call. When I expect a call from you, I expect a call. Am I understood?"

"Yes, sir," Paul answered. The simple reprimand made him feel like a scolded child again.

"What can you tell me about Mrs. Wyatt?"

Paul was relieved to be talking about the patient instead of himself. "She seems to be suffering from a conversion reaction, Your Honor."

The judge interrupted him. "No time for technical stuff,

Paul. Tell me what that means in a way that I can understand."

Paul smiled to himself. He was back on familiar ground. "The blindness has been brought on by some internal stress the nature of which we can probably guess. All her tests indicate that there is no organic foundation for her loss of sight. The conclusion, then, is that it is what's commonly called a psychosomatic disorder."

"Can it be cured?" the judge asked.

"I certainly hope so."

"I mean," Judge Barret said, "without eight years of couch-bound psychoanalysis?"

"On the contrary, Judge," Paul said. "I think a very direct approach by a confrontational therapist could do the job relatively quickly. And, before you ask, no, I don't know how long and I can't predict."

The judge laughed. "You know my mind, son."

"I should by now," Paul retorted.

"Can you tell me anything encouraging?"

"I can tell you this. She's already partially regained some sight. She sees images, shadows, and shapes, and she can pick out movement around her. Those are all very good signs."

"Should we get someone to treat her?" the judge asked.

"I would think that's an excellent idea, Your Honor," Paul said.

The judge paused and Paul could imagine him, lips pouted and eyes lifted, pondering, as he would call it. "You wouldn't want to do it yourself?"

"Well, Your Honor," Paul said. "I wouldn't want to put a burden on the court, if you know what I mean."

"No, I don't," the judge said.

"I just think the court would be better off with someone who had different credentials than mine."

"What's that called, Murphy?" Judge Barret said. "Reverse bigotry? Who could I find with better credentials?"

"I didn't say *better,* Your Honor. I said *different.* I just thought it might sound better in court if treatment was put in the hands of a psychiatrist instead of a psychologist."

"Whether it might or mightn't," he said, "that's my business, not yours. And since when did you get involved in those silly mental health politickings? Quit playing it safe, Murphy. You've got to learn to take more of a stand, son. You get to work with her. And keep me posted."

"Okay, Judge," Paul said. "One more thing."

"What's that?"

"I want to interview some of the people who are close to her. I'd like to see her husband and her daughter, at least."

"Why are you telling me, Paul?" the judge asked.

Paul laughed. "I guess I'm asking permission, Your Honor."

"You do what you have to do. Is that clear? Just expedite it, Doctor. Let's get this matter cleared up."

When Harriet Doyle arrived at her office in the morning, she found Detective Collins reading a *Sports Illustrated* in the waiting room. Finch looked up from her typewriter and shrugged at her, shifting her eyes over to the policeman and then back to Doyle.

Collins closed the magazine, dropped it on the end table next to his chair, and stood up. "Ms. Doyle?" he said, and he extended his hand. "I'm Michael Collins, Detective . . ."

Harriet took his hand. "Yes. You're the investigating officer in the Wyatt matter." Collins nodded and Doyle led him into her private office.

When he was seated, Collins asked, "You wanted to see me?"

"Well, yes," Doyle said. "I mentioned that I wanted to talk to you, but I didn't mean for you to make a formal visit out of it. I could've come down to your office."

Collins waved it away. "That's okay," he said. "I have a day off."

Doyle nodded and they smiled at each other. "Coffee?"

"No, thanks," Collins said. "Had my breakfast."

"You're telling me you want to get right into it?"

"Yes, ma'am," Collins said. "I would appreciate that very much."

"Okay," Doyle said. She stuffed an unlit cigarette into her mouth and pulled an overstuffed file from her desk drawer. She laid the file on her desk and opened it, then she looked up at Collins.

"I've gone through this file with a fine-tooth comb. I mean, I've studied it. Pored over it. I've read every word of your reports at least a dozen times. Over and over again." She turned some pages. "I've read all your partner's reports. That's Ruiz?" She looked up at Collins and he nodded. "I've read all his reports a dozen times. I've talked to most of the witnesses you talked to. I've gone over the same territory you went over. And frankly, Detective, I'm puzzled."

"Why's that, ma'am?" Collins asked.

"Well," she said, "it's like going to a big banquet with lots of courses, and you eat and eat and they keep bringing dishes and you keep eating and they keep bringing and you lose track of what they brought and you lose track of what you ate. And then, afterwards, you realize you had lots of appetizers, lots of little things—cold fish, funny soups, pickled vegetables drowned in lettuce, tiny slivers of cheese—you know, but no main course. And you think, Where the hell is the meat and potatoes? I'm a meat and potatoes person. You?" Collins nodded and smiled.

"Well, sir," Doyle continued, "this file is just like that. It's got soup and salad and fish and bread and veggies and cheeses and even some little chocolate finger desserts, but, Detective Collins, where the hell's the meat and potatoes?"

"I don't know what you mean, Counselor," Collins said. "It's all right there in that report that you've got in your hands."

"No it's not," Doyle said. "There's no meat and potatoes here. There's no substance here. There's nothing here that sticks to the lining of your stomach. There's only fancy little foods. I want the meat. I want to know why you recommended indictment and where the evidence is that warrants that indictment."

Collins sat up straight. "If you read it objectively, Counselor," he said, "I'm sure you'll find everything you need."

"I've read it objectively, Detective. I've read it and I've read it and I've read it. And there's something missing."

"Well, I don't know what that could be," Collins said.

"For one, there's no physical evidence to tie my client to the act. Nothing."

"There wasn't any," Collins said. "By the time we got there, she'd cleaned everything up."

Doyle squinted at him. "How do you know that?"

"The place was too clean," Collins said. "The place was spotless. You couldn't drown that baby without making some kind of mess. And there wasn't any, not even a drop of water left in the tub, which means she cleaned it up."

"How do you know it was her?"

"Who else?" Collins countered. "The bogeyman? You want to go with that unknown assailant idea, go for it, Counselor. But we didn't find any evidence that someone had entered that home. Everything was locked from the inside and nothing was broken—no glass, no locks, no doorknobs, nothing."

"Is that enough for you?"

"Hell, no," Collins said. "But put it together with the fact that the lady is bad news, and that's enough for me. Okay, you're going to say, circumstantial. So what if it is? For lack of better evidence it's good enough."

"Maybe," Doyle said. "That's for a jury to decide."

"That's right," Collins said. "And I don't try to second-guess juries. I just collect the facts and turn them over. And that lady's bad news. She's got a history of child abuse, a history of barhopping, and she's a sexual pervert. Just talk to her husband."

Doyle snickered. "Her husband's a fool and a liar."

"He's a police officer," Collins said, taking offense.

"Okay. I'm sorry. He's a foolish, lying police officer. Is that more accurate? Don't tell me, Collins, that you believed what he told you?"

"The man's emotional," Collins said. "I'll give you that. But that don't mean he's a liar."

Doyle smiled. "How about the boyfriend? You going to tell me he's reliable?"

"It doesn't matter," Collins said. "He's not even important."

"Well, how about the bartender at the Jolly Tyme? What about him?" Doyle prodded.

"You can shake him," Collins said, smiling knowingly. "He's got a rap sheet as long as his tongue. So, I figure you'll bust him in court."

"I'll do more than bust him, Detective. He identified the wrong woman."

"Says who?"

"Says me—and him."

Collins shrugged. "We'll find somebody else to put her on the street. She's bad and we all know it."

272

Doyle leaned forward and squinted at the policeman. "How can you be so sure?"

"Because I know that kind of woman. I'm a cop. And I know the kind of women that do to cops what she did to her old man."

"That's not enough, Detective Collins," Doyle said. "Your personal opinion, your intuition, if you will, just isn't enough. I'm going to beat you on this. I don't think you've done your homework. I think this was a shitty investigation. There's holes in it I could drive a Mack truck through and I'm going to barrel my beat-up Plymouth right on through."

Collins nodded. "You do what you can, Counselor. That's what makes the system go round."

Doyle stood up, signalling the meeting was over. She put her hand out. "You're a good guy, Collins. I think you fucked up on this one, but I'll bet you're a hell of a good cop."

Collins blushed as he took her hand. "Thank you, Ms. Doyle. I do my best."

Doyle came around her desk and walked Collins to the door of her private office. "By the way," she said at the door, "can you think of any reason the Medical Examiner would be avoiding me?"

Collins stared at Doyle for a long moment. He became thoughtful. "No, I can't," he finally said.

"Well," she said, "he's probably just overloaded. I'll keep trying."

She watched Collins leave the office, then turned to Finch. "You want to try the M.E. again?"

"I already did," she said. "Twice this morning."

"What's up?"

The secretary shrugged. "He isn't in and he isn't expected."

"What the hell's going on down there?" Doyle said to herself.

"Maybe the good doctor doesn't like your bedside manner, Ms. Doyle," Finch offered. "You should try being more pleasant, more charming."

Doyle stuck her tongue out at her, produced an obscene noise to accompany her laughter, and walked into her private office, slamming the door behind her.

Paul Murphy guessed that the prison ward authorities had received some kind of message from Judge Barret's court suggesting that they cooperate with Dr. Murphy, because he was greeted like visiting royalty when he arrived later that morning.

Dr. Gottlieb was waiting for him, greeted him personally, and took him to a treatment room set aside for him to work with Melanie. "This is the room I use," Gottlieb said. "Consider it your own. Make yourself at home." He looked around the room. "Anything else you think you're going to need?"

He examined the place quickly and decided that it had everything he could want. He thanked Gottlieb and told him he would be fine just the way it was. Gottlieb reassured him that if he did decide he needed something else, the nurses were there to help him. "Just ask," he said to Paul. "Don't be shy. Ask and if we've got it, you'll have it."

Melanie was brought to him half an hour later. She was pushed in, seated in a wheelchair, by a male nurse who looked like a professional wrestler. Paul dismissed the nurse and helped Melanie move to the soft leather chair. He settled her in and sat in the duplicate chair, which he had shifted, directly in front of her. The low coffee table, which had been between the chairs, he tilted up lengthways and stuffed away in the clothes closet.

"How's your sight?" he asked while he was moving furniture.

"Better, thank you," she said.

"Can you see me?"

"I can make you out, just," she said. "I can't see your features, but I can see that you're there and I can see you move every time."

"Good," he said. "That's a steady improvement."

"I hope so." She pressed her lips together. "I worry that I'm going to get stuck like this. It's half blind, I know. But to me it's just as bad."

"I think there's a very good chance you'll get all your sight back."

"You think so?" she asked hopefully.

"Yes," he said.

In just the short time in the hospital, her appearance had changed drastically. Her hair had been shampooed and brushed and combed back. Someone had applied some light makeup to her face, and with lipstick and a bit of color on her cheeks she actually began to look pretty again. But the greatest change in her was her drastic return to reality. As quickly as what appeared to be a psychotic episode had come upon her, she had shrugged it off and now seemed as much connected to reality as he was.

"You know," she said, "of all the things I'm afraid I'll be unable to do, the one that scares me most is eating. Isn't that silly?"

"Why does that scare you so much?"

"I don't know. It's so silly. But when I think of not seeing the food on my plate or groping for my mouth with a forkful, I become terrified. I've always taken such pride in my table manners, you know. It's always been so important to me. Eating properly, I mean. You should see Polly, my daughter. She eats beautifully."

"Why is that so important to you?" he asked.

She pursed her lips and thought for a moment. "I guess my mother and father made it important."

"How?"

"They taught me. Just like I taught Polly. They taught me and when I did it right, they complimented me. They used to brag about me to their friends. And they said they could take me anywhere with them, I was so polite at the table. They used to say they wouldn't be ashamed to take me to Buckingham Palace." She thought a moment longer and then frowned. "God, how I loved to hear that from them. Especially Daddy. It was a big thrill coming from him. There just wasn't that much he complimented about me."

"So your father made it important?"

"Yes. Sometimes Mother would tease him that he was making me too prissy. But he was a stickler for manners. He knew what he wanted, all right. I'm grateful to him for that. I like being elegant in restaurants." She laughed. "It's one of my few good qualities. Of course, with Chris I didn't get much chance to show it. Getting Chris to take me out to dinner was like getting the Pope to go to a Bar Mitzvah. They were certainly different in that respect."

"Who?"

"Chris and my father. My father loved to go out to dinner. Chris wanted to bring in hamburgers from McDonald's. Two with everything, French fries, and a vanilla milk shake was a gourmet meal to Chris."

"They were very different, your husband and your father," Paul said.

"Oh, yes. They were nothing like each other." Her hands became agitated and she locked her fingers together. "It's me. I'm the same."

"What do you mean?"

"They're very different but I was the same with both of

them. I wanted so bad to please them. I tried so hard. At least with my daddy I could please him, once in a while. Now and then. Like with my table manners. But with Chris it was impossible. I could never please him, no matter what I did. It wasn't that bad at first, when we first got married. But later, after he became a policeman, then it got bad, really bad. If I breathed out loud, it was wrong and I got criticized for it. And the more he did it, the more I wanted to please him. It was like a trap I was in. Like a maze. I couldn't get out of it. He'd punish me and I'd try harder to give him what he wanted. The only problem was I never knew for sure what he wanted. Or he'd change it on me. He'd want one thing one day and the next he'd criticize me for doing what he'd wanted yesterday. You know what I mean?"

"Did you talk to him about that? Tell him how you felt?" Paul asked.

"Yes. But he'd laugh at me. Or he'd get angry at me. I used to tell him that I needed someone to listen to me and he told me to go call my mother if I was still a little baby. Once I suggested we go to a marriage counselor, because I was so unhappy, I told him. And he said I could go by myself. He said he didn't need a shrink telling him how to solve his problems. First, he said, he didn't have any problems. I had them all. But even if he did, he said, he'd know how to solve them by himself. He said one cry baby in the family was enough, too much, he said. I only asked him once more. About a month later. I said, 'We have to see somebody. We need help. The way we treat each other, it's no good,' I told him. He said no, that I could go anywhere I want as long as it didn't cost money, but not even to talk about him. If he found out that I'd talked about him, he'd bust me up. I was angry that time. I threatened to call his watch commander. That was a mistake. I told him there were professional people in the department to help people like us. And he exploded. He hit me and knocked me down. I thought he was going to kill me. 'Don't you ever call the department,' he said, and he had his fist stuck in my face. Believe me, I took him seriously."

Paul watched her as she talked to the empty room, away from him as if he were not there. "Is that when you left him?"

"Oh, no," she said. She turned toward the sound of his voice and laughed loudly. "That was when Polly was about two. I didn't leave him till almost six years later."

"If he was hitting you, why did you stay?"

"Well, you just don't pick up and leave a husband. It isn't done like that. You have to work at a marriage. I mean, so what if one of you loses his temper now and then? That's natural, isn't it? To lose your temper, I mean. You don't bust up a marriage for that. Besides, there were plenty of times he was good to me and I loved him."

"You said you wanted him to see a counselor with you?"

"Yes." She nodded.

"Was that because you had good times with him?"

"No." She laughed again. "That was because I couldn't please him. You know, I wanted to find out what it took to please him. I wanted to go to a counselor to make me a better wife. You know what I mean. I was sure something was wrong with me. I know something was wrong with me. If it wasn't, I would've been a good wife without looking for help. That's what my daddy told me. He said, 'You should know how to please a man without going to school for it. That's natural to a woman,' he said. 'Women know that stuff inside. They don't have to be told.' But I didn't know that stuff inside. I was afraid to tell him that I didn't know what to do. I knew that there was something wrong with me. I knew it."

Paul watched her silently for a long time. She had cocked her head—one of her old gestures—to hear her mystical voice maybe, or perhaps to see his foggy image better. She wore a small smile, a warm smile. Finally, he asked, "What did you think was wrong with you?"

She wet her lips. "Oh, I knew, I didn't *think*. It's because I'd been rebellious when I was little. They never got that badness out of me. My father failed me just like I failed him. I couldn't please him, but he didn't do his job, either."

"What was his job?" he asked gently.

"You know," she said, and raised her unseeing eyes to heaven. She shook her head and smiled sadly. "Spare the rod and spoil the child. He was much too permissive. He didn't hardly beat me when I was a kid. So, naturally, I stayed bad. That badness is still in me." She stopped and breathed deeply for several seconds. "Did you know that? That's what this is all about. If it wasn't for the badness in me, everything would be just fine."

NINE

Paul felt wrung out by the time he finally insisted on breaking for lunch, much to Melanie's chagrin. He started down to the hospital cafeteria, thought of the cardboard-textured and flavored fare offered there, turned around, and left the building. On the street, just outside the main entrance, he stopped at the pay phone mounted on a post and called over to Chris Wyatt's precinct to set up a meeting with him. The officer was not in, and Paul asked the desk officer to get word to him to call Dr. Paul Murphy at the prison ward at County General Hospital as soon as possible.

He went over to the Bob's Big Boy down the street. The appalling plastic decor was not at all conducive to a healthy appetite, but at least the food was more or less edible. He noted, as he entered, that the place was filled with white-jacketed hospital employees, crowded into booths in groups of five and six, which certainly validated his decision to avoid the hospital cafeteria. Paul sat at the long counter and picked at a dry chef's salad.

His thoughts were not on food, however, but remained with the patient he had just left, Melanie Wyatt, the enigma. Her sudden burst of disclosure had left him perturbed—

pleased, yet perturbed. Through all the hours he had spent with her, the one characteristic she had consistently displayed was her reticence, her unwillingness or inability to form complicated thoughts and verbalize them at any length whatsoever. Her responses had consistently been short—sometimes to the point, sometimes not—but rarely if ever did she volunteer information. What Paul had learned about the unfortunate woman had been pulled out of her, pried out of her like a dentist pulling a tooth.

But now she had suddenly become so cooperative that he had almost relaxed with her. And, once again, he was forced to warn himself to be on guard against being dragged into her malfunctioning system and becoming part of it, which would certainly render him ineffective. Ignore the content, he reminded himself again and again, and focus on the process. The clues to Melanie's turmoil were not buried in what she said, but in how she said it. It was her neurotic style he had to be interested in. Her stories could have no entertainment value for him if he expected to help her.

Melanie had not wanted this break; she had wanted to continue on, without stopping, into the afternoon. She was revelling in the attention, Paul knew, as well as enjoying the cathartic aspect of the outlet she had found for her suppressed feelings.

Paul explained to her that although she felt no need for a break, he felt the need. He needed time to digest all that had gone on, all the material she had given him, and he needed to put some fuel into his stomach so that he would have the strength to continue later, he joked. Melanie had not laughed; she did not want him to leave. He observed a sudden change come over her. She became childlike. She smiled sweetly and tilted her head slightly to one side, becoming compliant and overly cooperative. She said sweetly, "Whatever you say, Doctor."

281

He recognized the ploy and determined to point it out to her. "What are you doing, Melanie?"

"Nothing," she said with a pert smile. Her eyes opened wide in mock innocence.

"You're trying to please me, is that it?" he said. "You want to show me how it's done?"

"Don't you want me to?" She seemed genuinely surprised. "I'm trying to be a good girl."

"You don't have to do those things to be a good girl," he said flatly. "You are a good girl."

She pouted. "But I don't want you to be angry with me."

"What could you do that would make me angry, Melanie?" he asked.

She looked sad and he thought she was going to weep. "If I don't do as you say, if I pout, if I'm obstinate, that'll displease you and you'll get angry with me. If I'm cute and agreeable, you won't get angry at me. If I cry and make you stay, that'll get you angry at me."

"That's true," he said. "If you made me stay, I might be angry. But you can't make me stay, Melanie. If I want to go, I'll go. If I want to stay, then I'll stay."

"I can't make you stay?" Again, she was genuinely surprised.

"No," he said.

She looked up at the ceiling and pushed the tip of her tongue out the side of her mouth. She looked as though she was trying to put her thoughts together. Then she said, "If you stay, that means you like me. If you go, that means you don't like me."

"No, Melanie," he said. "That's not true. It doesn't work that way, either. My going or staying has nothing to do with liking you or not liking you. I'll go or I'll stay because of what I want. You can't make me do anything, Melanie. You don't control me. And you're not responsible for me."

She nodded thoughtfully. He was not sure she had heard him or, if she had, that she believed him. "Will you come back?" she asked.

"Of course," he said.

She did not believe him. "Even if you're angry at me."

"I'm not angry with you, Melanie," he answered patiently. "But even if I were, I would come back."

She thought for another moment, staring at him sideways, almost coyly. "Okay," she said. She nodded and pursed her lips in all seriousness. "But it doesn't really matter because I don't like you, anyway."

Chris Wyatt called back during his lunch break and spoke to Paul about what he wanted. Paul told him about his wish to interview some of the people who were close to Melanie, in order to better evaluate her condition. He asked Chris if he would be willing to help out. Chris was reluctant, but as Paul became more insistent, he finally agreed. They arranged to meet at four-thirty that afternoon at the prison ward in the hospital, after Paul's session with Melanie.

He sat in the same chair in which Paul had put Melanie earlier, and though it was a deep, soft chair, Chris sat rigidly straight in it, his head and shoulders held high and his hands folded neatly in his lap.

"If I asked you to tell me about your wife very briefly, in just a couple of sentences, what would you say?" Paul asked.

"That would be hard to do," Chris said, then chuckled. "I don't think I could do it briefly." He thought for another moment. "First of all, I would say you better disregard everything she's ever told you about me because she's a terrible liar."

"Do you know what she's told me?"

He shrugged. "I can imagine," Chris said with the briefest of smiles.

"Tell me what you think she's said," Paul said.

The policeman twisted slightly in the chair and rearranged his hands in his lap. He started to speak and then thought better of it. "No. That's okay," he said. "Let it pass." He pursed his lips and squinted at Murphy. "I would say she's like a spoiled kid. Always has to have her way. Insists on it. Very selfish. Never thinks of anybody but herself. Very inconsiderate wife. Very lazy mother. Hates housework. Hates cooking. Let's see. What else? No. That's it. That's what I'd say, briefly."

"Was she always like that?" Paul asked. "I mean, from the very beginning of your relationship?"

"Hell, no," Chris said. "If she'd been like that at the beginning, I would never have married her."

Paul nodded. "When did she start being those things you said?"

Chris stared directly at him. "I don't really remember exactly when."

"Was it before Polly was born?" Paul asked.

Chris thought. "I don't know."

"Was it just after Polly was born? Sometimes people change. Women change after giving birth, especially if the pregnancy was particularly hard."

"Yeah," Chris said thoughtfully. "It was just after Polly. We should never have had a kid. Big mistake. Melanie wasn't cut out to be a mother."

"Whose idea was it—to have a baby, I mean?"

"Well," Chris said, "I think we both agreed when it came to Polly. We both wanted to start a family. We didn't know what it was like to have a baby. It was tough. I know Melanie was sorry right away. She just couldn't cope with the demands the kid put on her. And I was away a lot. I'd just started on the force and I was working nights a lot. Here was this young woman stuck at home alone all the time with a little baby. It was just too much for her."

Paul leaned forward. "How did you know she wasn't coping? Did she tell you?"

"No," Chris said, shaking his head. "She'd never admit to that. But I could see it. She got short-tempered, screamed a lot. Screamed at the little kid a lot and shook her—shook her real hard like she wanted to really hurt her." He looked down at his hands and shook his head in despair. Finally, he looked up and smiled weakly at Murphy. "And then she got real lazy around the house. Never cleaned it. Never vacuumed it. The dust would get that thick on the carpet. Dishes would pile up in the sink for days on end. It was pretty miserable."

"Did you try to get her help?" Paul asked.

"Sure. I got her help," Chris said, as if it were obvious. "First, I got a girl to come in twice a week to do the housework, and then, when that wasn't enough, I got her for three times a week."

"I didn't mean that kind of help," Paul said. "I meant psychiatric help."

Chris grinned sheepishly. "Oh! I didn't understand you. Well, sure, I tried to get her to go, but she absolutely refused."

"You picked a therapist for her?"

"No. I tried to get her to go to the department shrink ... uh ... I mean, psychologist. I'm sorry about that."

"That's all right." Paul smiled. "I've been called a shrink before. I don't take offense." Paul waited a moment, then said, "She says she could never please you."

"I don't know how she can say that. I'm real easy to please. Hell, it doesn't take hardly anything to please me.

What do I need! A hot meal at night when I come home. A clean house. A warm bed. Hell, I don't need a lot."

"I don't think that's what she means," Paul said.

"What then?"

"I think she means that you criticized her a lot."

He laughed and shook his head. "Aw, she can't mean that. I never criticized her. Hell, I put up with almost anything. I couldn't care less. You don't understand. I'm easy."

"You have any idea why she would say that?"

"Sure," Chris answered. "She wants to make me out a bad guy. She wants to push the guilt for what she did off of her and onto me. That's easy to see. She does that all the time, you know. She'd break something and yell at me, 'Look what you made me do.' I mean, I'm just standing there talking to her and she drops this dish right out of nowhere and blames me like I made her do it. You ever hear anything like that? She blames me for everything. She blames me for the baby. I mean, Denise. She blames me like I forced it on her. She wanted an abortion, she could've had an abortion. Who the hell stopped her? She shouldn't have had that kid. She couldn't handle the first one. How was she going to handle two at the same time? Hell, we talked about it. We knew it wasn't going to work out. But, she's like a kid. I told you. She wants what she wants when she wants it. You know what I mean?

Chris was looking for a sympathetic comrade, but Paul could not oblige. "Wasn't it you who suggested an abortion?"

Chris hesitated for an instant and squinted suspiciously at Murphy. "No. I thought it might be too dangerous. I didn't want her to get hurt. But she talked about it a lot. She went back and forth. Couldn't make up her mind. Crying all the time. Asking me, 'Should I do it? Should I have it?' And me all the time saying, 'Do what you think is best, dear.' But she's like a child herself. She needs a grown-up to make decisions for her. That's from her father. What a guy he was. The king of all pains in the ass. He wouldn't let her shit without his permission. One tough cookie. I told her, 'Don't you go raising my kids the way that guy raised you. I don't want any kid of mine so feeble they can't decide to make or get off the pot.' You know what I mean?"

"Well," Paul said, "that sounds a lot like criticism."

"What does?"

"Don't raise my kids the way you were raised. Doesn't that sound like criticism to you?"

"Oh, yeah, sure," Chris said. "But I'm criticizing her dad, you know, not her."

"You think it might sound to her as if you were saying that she didn't turn out right because of the way she was raised?" Paul asked.

Chris's mouth was open. He thought for a moment. "Never thought of it like that," he said. "You have a good point there, Doctor."

"You were saying . . . about the abortion."

"Oh, yeah." Chris looked bewildered. "What was I saying?"

"You were saying that you thought an abortion might be too dangerous for her, but that Melanie was leaning toward getting one."

"Oh, yeah!" Chris nodded vigorously. "But she didn't get one. Obviously, you know that. She had the kid."

"Were you happy about that?"

"Sure," Chris said. "That baby was wonderful. I was very happy. Two girls? Daddy's little girls. It was terrific."

"Did she know that you were glad about the baby?"

"Sure. I told her. But that didn't change anything for her. She was just as miserable. She never cared what I wanted. It was always what she wanted that counted. She's like that. Whatever she feels at the moment. Real impulsive like that. That's probably how she did it to the kid."

"How's that?" Paul asked.

"You know," Chris said. "On impulse. All of a sudden she had an urge and she did it. God knows, she threatened to do it often enough. Hell, she threatened to do it to Polly half a dozen times. And she beat her often enough for me to be scared she meant it."

"That's something that's troubled me, Officer Wyatt."

"What's that?" Chris asked.

"You've made the statement before that she hurt your daughter and now you say she threatened her life. What bothers me is why you agreed to have another child if you feared for the safety of the one you had. Didn't you suspect that another child might be enough to send your wife over the edge?" Paul leaned forward, fixed his eyes on Wyatt's face, and waited.

Chris shrugged uncomfortably and smiled at Murphy. "I have to admit I'm guilty of that, Doctor. I should've put her away back then. You're right."

"Instead," Paul said, "you moved out of the house and left her there alone with both children. Wasn't that taking a big risk?"

"Right again, Doctor." Chris grinned at him. "It sure looks like I made some serious mistakes. Maybe if I'd've stayed in the house, the kid'd be alive now." He sobered, straightened up in the chair, and looked at Murphy. "The worst part of all this, Doctor, is that I really wanted that kid. I lost Melanie and I guess I really didn't care that much. But I'm going to miss the kid. That's a real loss."

Paul sat back and watched Wyatt sitting before him with his hands out in supplication. The policeman finally grinned as if he had just told a joke, crossed his legs, and sat back contentedly. "It's a real pain."

Phyllis waited for him at the bar in the Valley Hilton and had two piña coladas before he arrived. She had gotten Polly fed and settled down in pajamas, as she had promised she would, before she left, and at the last minute had to go through another ten minutes of reassurance before the little girl would let her go peacefully. Still, with all that, she arrived at the hotel early and decided to go in and have a drink rather than drive around to kill time.

Several times during the day she had determined to use Paul's private number to let him know that she just could not make dinner with him. Several other times during the day she had thought about being with him and grew so anxious and excited that she did not think she could wait until evening. She wondered if her attraction for him could be connected with the fact that he was treating Melanie. Did that somehow initiate him automatically into their inner secret circle? She wondered what Melanie had told him about her. What secrets had she divulged? How much intimate knowledge had he acquired about Phyllis?

She knew that her feelings for him bordered on those of a schoolgirl and that she was being carried away with her flights of fancy, but she could not stop. She hardly knew him and yet her fantasies about him were all structured around homes and families and permanency. Of all people, she told herself, she was the last one she would expect to believe in love at first sight. It was Phyllis who had consistently poohpoohed the entire concept of romantic love for as long as she could remember. It was Phyllis who insisted that she would never marry, that she liked being single, being free, having multiple lovers; that she could never see herself committed totally to one man. And now it was Phyllis who continually glanced over at the entrance to the Hilton Bar with immense anticipation, almost unable to wait for him to enter and walk toward her. She was feeling foolish, but she was loving it.

When Paul finally arrived, he declined to join her at the bar but instead had the waitress bring her drink to the table he had reserved in the dining room. He ordered a tall grapefruit juice on the rocks with which to keep her company while she finished her drink, and they both ordered swordfish steaks and salad for dinner.

With the ordering out of the way and the glass of cold juice in his hand, he pulled his tie loose at the collar and let his shoulders sag a bit with weariness.

"Tough day?" she asked. She wanted to move behind him and rub his neck, but she remained seated.

He shrugged. "More depressing than anything else." He touched his glass to hers and drank.

Phyllis looked worried. "Is Melanie worse?"

"No," he said. "If you're talking about her sight, she's recovering very quickly."

"What else is there?" She chewed her bottom lip and he recognized she had the same nervous habit as Melanie.

He stared at her lovely blue eyes and was amazed again at how large they were. "Actually," he said, "my mood isn't dreary because of her as much as it is because of her ex-husband."

She was puzzled. "What've you got to do with Chris?"

"I interviewed him today."

"I'll bet he had some wonderful things to say about Melanie." She grimaced. "He loves to let her have it. Does it at every opportunity. When they were married I used to call him Captain Punisher." She shuddered. "He hates me."

Paul wondered how anyone could hate this beautiful woman. "Well, he certainly painted a picture of a different Melanie from the one I know," he said. "According to him she's what we used to call an inadequate personality. The way he tells it, she's so dependent on others she can't tie her own ribbons without help.''

Phyllis laughed. ''You're kidding, of course. Melanie's the most independent person I know. If she were that weak, could she have thrown him out the way she did?''

''He says he's the one who left,''Paul said.

''That's a lie,'' Phyllis snapped. ''I was there. I stayed with her the night she threw his clothes out on the lawn. For weeks after that, he was begging her to take him back.''

Paul shook his head. ''That's not the way he tells it now. Now, he's saying that her father dominated her and she's never been able to make decisions.''

Phyllis lowered her eyes. She toyed with her drink, spinning the long, thin stem between her thumb and forefinger. ''The only real problem Mel had with her father, as far as I could tell, was that he showed more attention to her friends than he did to her. I remember how that used to kill her. She was so jealous of us girls when we came over and her dad would kid around with us and ignore her. He used to tell her it was because he didn't care that much about us but he cared a lot about her, so he treated her differently. I don't even understand that today, so you can imagine what I thought about it then.''

The waitress brought their swordfish, and Phyllis heaped butter on her baked potato while he watched enviously but ate his dry.

''I don't want to talk about Melanie and Chris all night,'' she said. ''So let me just say this one thing and then I promise I won't ask you another question about them. Deal?''

He chuckled. ''Deal.''

''I've known Melanie practically my whole life. This Melanie everyone's talking about is a person I don't know. She's their Melanie. The person I know is my Melanie. My Melanie is the best mother any kid could want. Any kid would be lucky to have her as a mother. My Melanie is the most loyal friend anybody could have. You can count on her no matter what. My Melanie works a full-time job, keeps a house, and raises two kids all by herself. I know my Melanie has problems and maybe you can help her with them. Maybe she's always had them. Maybe she's always been a little fragile underneath her tough exterior. But—and I know what I'm saying—my Melanie would rather die than hurt one of her kids. My Melanie would take on the pain herself before she'd let one of her kids suffer. My Melanie is an angel."

He watched her silently as she went through her pitch for her friend, and for a moment he forgot how beautiful she was. For a moment all he could see was a wonderful, desperate girl opening herself up, risking herself in order to help a friend. And his feelings for her deepened. He was pleased that his initial reaction to her, which had been originally based upon her appearance, her torrid sexiness, had been validated by her exposure as a warm, sensitive, and caring human being.

After dinner, he drove her home and they parked in front of the house. He turned the motor off and she moved over to him without shame, put her arms around his neck, and kissed him passionately. She clung to him, forced herself as close to him as she could get, plumbed him with her lips and tongue, and he returned her urgency with a pressing need of his own.

"Come inside and stay with me tonight," she whispered into his ear when she finally pulled her lips from his. Her hands were all over him, searching him, examining him.

He pulled away slightly, breathing heavily. "No," he said. "Not in that house. I can't. Not with the child in there."

She leaned away and touched her fingers to her mouth. "I forgot," she said apologetically.

In the darkness in the car he could not see her eyes, but he could imagine them focused on him. His body ached for her. He ran his hand along the inside of her thigh and she shivered up against him. He pulled her gently back to him and kissed her tenderly. "There will be other times and other places, I hope," he said. "When I finish with this assignment."

She nodded and smiled, then kissed him quickly. "I can't wait."

"Good," he said. "Do you know where my office is?" She shook her head. "Call me in the morning. I'll tell you how to get there. I want you to bring Polly to see me tomorrow afternoon after school. Will you do that?"

"Sure," she said. "When did you decide to see her?"

"After my interview with her father," he said. "And I think that after seeing her, this episode may be over. Then you and I can settle down to some serious getting-to-know-one-another."

She grinned in the darkness. "I like that idea," she said, and wrapped herself around him again.

Harriet Doyle took the slender silver flask, newly filled with twelve-year-old Cutty Sark, from her desk drawer and stashed it in her purse. Then she stormed over and parked herself outside the swinging doors leading to the pathology operating room. Nussbaum was inside cutting up a cadaver and there was no other way out but through Harriet Doyle.

She would be damned if the little bastard would get by her again. She had had enough of telephoning, enough of being put off, stalled, lied to. And when she got her hands on the M. E. she intended to teach him some manners.

Doyle's first lesson in common courtesy, she called it. And she intended for it to be quite painful.

However, when Nussbaum emerged it was already after ten at night, and Doyle could see the exhaustion written clearly all over the little doctor's face—in his tired shuffle, in the way his shoulders hunched forward, and in the deep lines under his eyes and along his mouth.

She approached him, flask in hand, and clutched his arm. "Dr. Nussbaum," she said. "I'm Doyle. I've been calling."

Ralph Nussbaum gazed at Doyle wearily, as if attempting to place her. "Doyle? You?"

"Yes. Melanie Wyatt's lawyer. Look, you're exhausted. Let's go somewhere and have a shot of this pick-me-up." Doyle showed him the flask. "And maybe we'll talk a little."

Dr. Nussbaum took her up to the sixth floor in a shiny chrome elevator and let them into his private office—a small, crowded, cluttered cubby of a room. He threw a pile of journals off the extra chair, motioned for Doyle to sit, pulled two paper cups out of the dispenser next to the ancient water cooler, and sat himself behind his mountainous desk. He stared at Doyle appreciatively for a moment, letting his eyes drift down to her knees, her slim stockinged brown legs, and sighed, shaking his head as if remembering better times, younger times. Then he held out the two little cups. "Pour!"

Doyle obliged gladly. "This is very fine stuff," she said. "Twelve years old. My stock of this is more important than my law clerks."

Nussbaum laughed. "That's how I feel about interns." They held the paper cups out to each other, toasted, and drank.

"I've been chasing you all over town," Doyle said.

"What's your name?" Nussbaum said.

"Doyle."

He held one finger up in the air. "First name?"

"Harriet." She smiled.

"Mine's Ralph," the little doctor said. "Hiya." He reached over his desk and shook her hand. He held her soft fingers much longer than she had expected.

"Yeah," Doyle said shyly and refilled their paper cups.

"Why you looking for me, Harriet? I got something you want?"

She nodded. "I wanted to talk to you about the Wyatt autopsy."

"Oh, yeah?" Nussbaum said. "Why's that?"

"I had a couple of questions—" she started, but he interrupted.

"Everybody's got questions, Harriet. On every case. That's probably why you couldn't get through to me. My people try to protect me. If I talked to everyone who had questions, I'd never get to do another autopsy. Who'd have the time?"

"But," Doyle said, "the Wyatt case is special."

"Why's that?"

"Well," she said, "you know."

The weary doctor laughed. "How would I know, Harriet? You give me a name out of the blue and I'm supposed to know what you're talking about. Are you kidding?"

She was surprised. "You don't know the case?"

Nussbaum shook his head.

"You did the autopsy," she said.

Nussbaum shook his head again.

"An infant? Drowned? In the crib? They're saying the mother did it?"

The doctor's eyes opened wider. "The baby I remember. Lungs filled with tap water."

"That's the one," Doyle said. "I represent the mother who's been accused—"

Nussbaum interrupted her. "I can't help you, Harriet."

"Sure you can."

"No," the doctor said. "You're looking for something to help the defense."

"Of course," she said.

"I don't have anything like that."

"How do you know?"

"First," the doctor said, "because I gave everything I have to the police and I'm sure you've already seen it. My report, I mean. And second, I don't ever concentrate on perpetrators. That's for movies and television."

"Look, Ralph," Doyle said. "A report is a dry piece of paper. It can't give you nuances. It can't deal in shades and grades. It tells it one way and that's it. I need something more. I know it's there, somewhere. Hell, I can feel it. There's a piece missing to this puzzle."

"Trust me, Harriet," Nussbaum said kindly. "I don't have your piece."

Doyle studied the doctor's face—his weary face—and felt sorry for him. Let the poor man go to bed, she told herself. Stop wasting his precious time. "Ralph," she said instead, "one favor, please."

The doctor thought for a moment, then nodded.

Doyle said, "Pull your file. Five minutes. That's all I'll take. I promise. Five minutes in the file."

Nussbaum smiled and shook his head. "I give up," he said. "Okay. Five minutes." He got up and left the room. Doyle poured a touch more Scotch into her cup and sipped it slowly. In a moment, Ralph Nussbaum was back with a manila file folder in his hand. He sat down and sighed wearily.

"I'm really sorry, Ralph," Doyle said.

"Listen," the doctor said, "you have the right to see these. I'm not complaining about you doing your job." He wagged his head happily. "Ten o'clock at night might not be the best time, but we do what we can. Don't we?" He held out his empty cup and Doyle obliged.

The doctor opened the file on his desk and rummaged through it. "I don't know what you want to see."

Doyle said, "Anything unusual."

Nussbaum looked up and laughed. "There's nothing unusual to a coroner. You get jaded very quickly in this job."

"Anything, then," Doyle said. "Anything at all."

"Well, let's see." He thumbed through the exhaustive report, turning pages rapidly. "You know about the water in the lungs and some in the stomach."

"Is that significant?" Doyle asked.

"It's hard to get into the lungs without going into the stomach as well, Harriet. That's just natural."

"Tell me about the bites," Doyle said.

"The bites," Nussbaum wondered. He turned a page. "Here." He read to himself, moving his lips as if he were praying. "Not terribly deep. Not very damaging. Painful, I'm sure, but not that serious."

"How do we know that the mother did them?"

Nussbaum looked up at her again and laughed. "I never said the mother did the biting."

Doyle was shocked. "The prosecution certainly has."

"But I'm not the prosecution." He turned the file around and passed it to Doyle. "Show me where I said the mother did it." He pushed the file to Doyle, who refused to take it.

"Look!" he said. "In this department we're not interested in whodunit. We're only interested in what did it. Can you understand that?" Doyle nodded. "Those bites never killed anyone. They didn't do any serious damage. Sure, they left faint bruises and impressions, but they certainly were not lethal. At best, they can show that someone played a little too hard with the baby. Sure, it sounds bizarre out of context. But think about it, Harriet. How many times have you seen parents bite their babies out of love? I've seen it dozens of times."

Doyle nodded thoughtfully. "However," she said, "I'm curious about something."

"What?" Nussbaum asked.

Doyle shrugged. "Can't you identify the biter from the impressions?"

"Well," the doctor said, "it depends on how much of the impression is available."

Doyle laughed. "Frankly, Ralph, it seems to me that in a case like this one, someone would try."

"I'm sure the police did."

"Well," Doyle said, "what did they find?"

"I don't know, Harriet. That's not my business."

"Well, Ralph, would you call them big bites or little bites? I mean, like a man's bite or a woman's bite?"

Nussbaum referred to the file. "I think they were small. I measured the bite size and it measured small."

"What does that mean, Ralph? Small like a bug, like a cat, like a dog, like a person, what?"

"Don't be silly, Harriet. It's in the report. They're human bites. And they're small. Made by a very small or dentally retarded adult, probably a woman. I mean, it's right in the report." He laughed. "I told the police not to look for a shark on this one. I told them to look for a minnow."

Doyle stood up. She held a page from the file in her hand and pushed it under his face. "These measurements show a woman's bite size?"

"Just read it," he insisted.

"How the hell should I know what's big and little in bite sizes, Ralph? Why do you assume that everybody speaks your language? Damn it, I can't read this stuff!"

Nussbaum hung his head sheepishly. "Sorry. You're quite right, of course." The tired man looked so contrite.

Doyle relaxed and smiled sympathetically at Nussbaum. "Right or wrong," she shook her head, "doesn't make any difference now, Ralph." She sat down dejectedly, poured some Scotch into her paper cup, and downed it in one swallow.

"If you're sure those were not man-sized bites, you just put my client on the hook as a chronic child abuser."

Nussbaum smiled, shrugged, and nodded sadly.

PART THREE

PART THREE

ONE

Images moved laterally. More than mere images, then. They appeared to rise and fall as well, almost as if they were bobbing on the ripples of a gentle sea. Finally, blurred faces appeared out of the grey milk fog. Featureless faces they were, comprised of simple outlines that might or might not have been properties, characteristics of human countenances. An unfamiliar visage grew more distinct, clearer, more dimensional as Melanie strained to behold more of the world about her.

"What?" she questioned the several animated creatures stirring around her.

A tender arm slid under her back and lifted her slowly to a sitting position. Another swung her legs off the bed and fitted furry-feeling slippers onto her feet.

"Can you stand, Melanie?" a kind female voice reached out to her.

"Yes," she said. Her voice echoed in her own ears as if coming from down a long, distant tunnel. She pushed herself up from the bed and stood with her arms held out slightly away from her body as if balancing on a tightrope.

"I'm going to help you dress," the gentle woman's voice

whispered to her. She felt her hospital gown being lifted over her head and shivered as the cool room air touched her bare skin.

She was held around the waist as her legs were lifted, one by one, into her blue slacks. Then her sweater was pulled down over her shoulders, the familiar odor of her own perfume wafting to her from the woolen garment, and her arms were shoved into the sleeves.

"My clothes?" she asked.

"Yes," the gentle voice said. "These are your very own clothes."

Delicately, she was directed several steps and then silently urged to sit. She found herself in a wheelchair, could feel the large wheels on either side of her, the leather padded armrests beside them.

"Where am I going?" she asked no one.

She could barely hear the whispering behind her. The gentle voice debated with a stronger, rougher voice. She twisted her head about and watched the two indistinct images face each other, arguing. She turned away quickly, in fear, distressed that she was hearing and seeing her private parties again, those parties she had not heard from or seen in some time. She listened. She tilted her head sideways and listened attentively, but heard nothing more than the insistent arguing behind her. And those whisperings were very different from her internal whisperings. She knew the difference. There was no doubt that she could tell the difference. She knew from where those interior voices came.

She bit down hard on her lip. She did not want to slip back into that place. She could almost remember herself— how she was, looked, felt when she had been there—and was petrified that she could easily return to that place. She knew that in that place there was no Melanie, no Polly, no Denny, dead or alive; there was nothing real. No! her entangled mind screamed as she bore down hard on herself to stay, to stay grounded, to stay awake, to stay real. No! she commanded. No more madness.

Judge Barret reread the final paragraph on the last page and closed the blue covered file on his desktop. He pushed himself back and rose. His fingertips danced pensively on the closed file while he stood and thought about what he had read. He should have been very well satisfied, he thought, but for some unknown reason was not. He was peculiarly troubled by the report, although he should have expected its inevitable conclusion.

He moved to the window, which looked down at a street filled with outrageous downtown traffic, never-ending lines of automobiles, buses, cars, trucks, and streams of pedestrians dashing through the traffic as if engaged in some child's game of catch me if you can. How close they all are, he thought, and yet so unaware. There but for the grace of God, he thought, and smiled to himself at his appreciation of human fragility.

He reflected on Paul Murphy's report, which he had just read again for the second time, the report that had been delivered to his door late the night before, just hours before the scheduled competency hearing he had called for nine o'clock this Thursday morning. His great concern, that of taking an incompetent defendant to trial, had now been alleviated. Although part of him had hoped to avoid a trial, to insure that the poor, unfortunate woman received appropriate treatment for her obvious mental disorder, another part of him believed that justice had to be served and would be by conducting a trial and allowing twelve citizens to decide Melanie Wyatt's fate.

He had worried unnecessarily about Murphy's ability to

come through for him. Barret liked Murphy—that was clear to all who knew them—but the judge did not trust him, could not count on him to dig in his heels and take a stand, no matter how popular or unpopular it was. He perceived Murphy as being the kind of person who preferred to be liked by everyone, who did not tolerate very well being disliked, and who would rather couch his words in euphemisms and innuendos than come straight out and say what he meant, if only to avoid being offensive to anyone. And the report he had just read reflected that tendency in the psychologist.

He rubbed his eyes with his thumb and forefinger and sighed as though he were weary. Three pages of technical talk that sounded like it was lifted directly from the Psychiatric Diagnostic and Statistical Manual were bad enough, but wading through them was such a chore for the judge, who liked matters to be spelled out logically, arguments to be built upwards, step by logical step, so that the reasoning itself could be clearly observed. After all, the real beauty of the law was in its manifestly intelligent reasoning. There was nothing irrational about the law. But, for those pages to go nowhere, to travel no progressive road, was unforgivable. Damn! He hated how shrinks answered all his questions with both yes and no. He hated inconclusive responses. He hated professionals who sat on the fence because they did not want to get their shoes muddy.

However, this time Murphy had not totally failed him. In the end, the young psychologist had come through for him with flying colors. There was hope for the boy yet, the old jurist thought as he turned from the window and returned to his desk. He gazed down at the closed report and, without opening it, saw the very last paragraph of the very last page, which determined that Melanie Wyatt knew what was going on around her and was, therefore, competent to stand trial.

* * *

Doyle agreed to meet Phyllis for breakfast before going to court only because the woman had sounded so distressed on the telephone. She had no obligation to Melanie's friend and was somewhat annoyed that Phyllis thought she had the right to call and try to influence Doyle's professional decisions about her client's welfare. However, the woman had sounded so helpless, so alarmed, that Doyle took pity on her and agreed to try to put her mind at ease.

They sat together now, these two equally beautiful women, in a corner booth at Nibbler's on Wilshire, the brown-leathered, fully glassed around early morning watering hole for lawyers on their way to court, and stared at each other over half grapefruits, toasted nearly black English muffins, and black coffee.

Phyllis had blurted out her concern over Melanie's immediate future. "Don't you trust my judgment?" Doyle finally asked with a biting edge to her voice.

Phyllis wavered before speaking. "I think I do. Roger says you're the best."

"Roger's prejudiced." Doyle smiled slyly at her. "He's mad about me."

Phyllis stared at her peculiarly. "I don't think so," she said.

Doyle made a mental note that the woman lacked a sense of humor and that she would have to watch her words more carefully from now on.

"Look," she said, "what's your problem?"

Phyllis bit her lip. "I've seen Melanie," she said. "I've been with her in that room. I've tried to talk to her."

"Okay." Doyle nodded, then shrugged. "What's the point?"

"There are times when she says things that I don't un-

307

derstand, that just don't make sense. Sometimes I think she's talking to herself, but she isn't. She's talking to somebody I can't even see. Half the time I don't know what's going on. She's answering questions that I sure as hell haven't heard. And I know it's all in her head."

"So?"

"Explain it to me," Phyllis implored. "If she's mentally ill, why are you letting her go to trial? Isn't she protected from being tried and convicted while she's in a state like that? I mean, like cut off from reality?"

Doyle nodded. "First of all, if you have any questions about mental illness or your friend's state of mind, I suggest you're speaking to the wrong person. You want to talk to Dr. Murphy. He's the expert in that stuff. If you're asking whether or not the law protects your friend while she's like she is, as you say, the answer is absolutely not! No! Nyet! The law isn't going to protect one goddamned hair on her head."

Doyle watched Phyllis's face register an advanced degree of shocked surprise. She continued. "That's my job, sister. That's what I'm here for. The law expects me to protect my client. The law demands that I do it. And, in case you're really interested, I'm very good at it, if I do say so myself."

"I'm sorry," Phyllis said contritely.

"Look! You don't have to trust me. You don't have to like me. I can understand that. As a matter of fact, I get a lot of that. I've been getting that shit since I was a girl in law school. I'm black and I'm a woman, and if I insist on being in the law game, then I should be in entertainment law, right? Maybe in the music business, like working for Motown records or something. Representing black artists, doing contracts. But, for God's sake, what the hell am I doing in the courtroom, litigating, in the holy man's arena?" Then her face clouded over. "Jesus Christ! Where's it written that you have to have a penis if you're going to represent dope dealers and drive by murderers?"

"I didn't mean anything like that," Phyllis said.

"Well, what the hell did you mean?" Doyle's eyes flashed.

Phyllis rubbed her forehead with her fingertips. "I spoke to Paul—Dr. Murphy—and he told me about why Melanie should stand trial. I mean, he tried to explain it to me, but I just didn't understand it."

"Did he tell you that he thinks she's a wacko?"

"Yes." Phyllis nodded slowly.

"Then what's your problem?"

Phyllis leaned forward and her face appealed to Doyle. "If she's like that," she said, "why don't you get her declared incompetent so she won't have to stand trial?"

Doyle leaned back in the booth and smiled broadly at Phyllis. She shook her head as if in wonder. "So that's what this is all about? You want me to go to court this morning and ask to have your friend put away."

"No!" Phyllis was shocked.

"Yes!" Doyle flung back at her. "That's exactly what you want."

"But, if she can't defend herself? . . ."

"Bullshit!" Doyle snapped at her. "I'm there to defend her. And I don't want her declared incompetent and shipped off to Atascadero State for a few years as a mentally disturbed offender and then brought back to stand trial after she's cured, long after the fact, when all the evidence is gone and the witnesses are gone and everybody's totally convinced she did it, anyway."

"So what do you want?" Phyllis's lips trembled and Doyle knew the woman was on the edge of tears.

"Listen," Doyle said, "I want what's best for her. I want her found competent, just the way Dr. Murphy's report says, and I want her brought to trial and I want to defend her on the grounds that she was insane when she perpetrated the act . . ."

Phyllis gasped and threw her hands up to her throat.

"What's the matter with you? Did you think for one minute that she was innocent? What kind of naive pussy are you?" Doyle looked at the woman with disgust.

"She is innocent," Phyllis said. "I've always believed that."

"You bet she is!" Doyle grinned and nodded. "By reason of insanity, and don't you forget it."

Doyle dug out a hefty chunk of grapefruit, stuffed it in her mouth, sat back contentedly, and chewed while her eyes remained fixed on Phyllis's dismally distraught face.

Paul Murphy parked his car in the subterranean garage across the street and dodged through the early morning traffic to get to the courthouse. He stopped at the cigar stand just inside the front door, buying a morning newspaper and a Styrofoam cup of hot black coffee that tasted sour and old but which, he told himself, was better than nothing. He walked down the long, wide corridor, only sparsely occupied, until he found an unattended wooden bench where he could sit alone and avoid human contact.

He had arrived much too early for court—at least twenty minutes too early—and he was upset with himself about that. He knew that having the dead time in which to sit around and reflect was dangerous for the safety of his decision; too much contemplation could seriously disrupt his plan. For, once having made his decision, as difficult as it had been, he knew he could ill afford to mull it over further. What frightened him and forbade him from additional reflection was the recognition that further pondering could easily cause him to change his mind, take the easy way out, and reverse himself. It was at times like these—when he was ambivalent, caught between what was right and what was comfortable—that he suffered most from cold feet.

Traditionally, he was not a man who marched to the beat of a different drum, as they say. He usually thought of himself as a pretty conservative guy. He was not a joiner, nor was he a rebel. And, he was certainly not a protestor. But, most of all, he was not a great risk taker. He knew that Judge Barret recognized him for what he was and enjoyed teasing him about it. He was as aware as anyone that their little monthly game at lunch was the judge's way of pointing out to Paul, over and over again, that he was not a man who was willing to take risks. And the judge viewed that as a failing.

Well, he almost said out loud as he shrugged his shoulders to himself, he was certainly going to take one hell of a risk this morning.

He took a long swallow from the acidy coffee in his hand and grimaced at the dark bitterness it left in his mouth, as if the bad taste was a premonition, a warning of what was yet to come. He shuddered slightly as he steeled himself for the repercussions of his intended performance. He knew he was taking a risk now. He felt the flapping butterfly wings of anxiety in his stomach, beating against his insides. He felt the drops of sweat slipping down his sides under his shirt. He felt the moderate but insistent ache in the front of his head, just above his eyes.

He knew the judge would be upset with him. He fully expected to be reprimanded publicly and was convinced that he was prepared and able to handle that. It had happened before and he had always survived it. And he would survive this forthcoming attack, no matter how brutal, just as well.

Harriet Doyle, of course, would be outraged. Perhaps, he feared her most of all. Even more than Judge Barret. He had seen her in action, knew her reputation, and was very much afraid that she was an enemy who held onto a grudge for an eternity. He was afraid that once he betrayed her, he would never get the chance to make it up to her. She would never trust him again. Of that he was convinced.

But it was Phyllis's reaction that worried him the most. He was not afraid of her; there was nothing terrible she could do to him. But he had developed some deep feelings for her, perhaps even loved her, and dreaded losing her before having the chance to win her. There had even been a moment the night before, during his quiet contemplation, when he had seriously considered withdrawing from the case altogether in order to preserve his relationship with Phyllis. But recognizing that it was his old fear of taking risks that made that gesture seem so attractive, he discarded the thought very quickly. He would have to take his chances with Phyllis, as he would with all the others. His commitment, he continually reminded himself, was to his patient, to Melanie, to the real victim in this episode who, no matter what, needed him to be strong.

TWO

The bailiff looked up from the magazine he was reading when Harriet Doyle, the first principal in the day's proceedings to arrive, entered the courtroom. He smiled at her and waved a friendly greeting. He nudged the court reporter, who sat across him, and she turned from her paperwork to look at Doyle as well.

Doyle grinned at them and moved quickly to the long defense table facing the raised platform upon which the judge's bench stood. She opened her briefcase, pulled out a sheaf of documents, on top of which was Paul Murphy's report, placed predominantly, and grinned to herself as she thought that the matter at hand this morning was going to be so simple that none of the material she was hauling around, other than the blue-covered psychological report, would be needed. It is all for show, she told herself, and to establish a record.

The morning's proceedings promised to be truly a simple matter. One, two, three. No complications on the horizon. They all wanted the same result. The judge. The prosecution. The defense. Everyone involved in this case wanted the same ultimate conclusion. This simple competency hearing, which would open and close quickly, would find Melanie Wyatt competent to stand trial and order her to proceed to court. They would then get on with their speedy trial, win an acquittal, and propel Doyle's client into some therapeutic setting for treatment and eventually home where she belonged. Now! The object was to get this hearing over with and get on with the serious business, she told herself. She was ready.

She glanced over at the prosecution table where Bruce Taggert, the Assistant D.A., had suddenly appeared. The well-dressed Taggert, who looked more like a tennis professional than a District Attorney with his dark tan, sunbleached blond hair, and lean, trim body, looked over toward her and grinned brightly as he held up Murphy's report in the air. He threw her a thumbs-up sign and winked as if, as coconspirators, they had already won his case for him.

Go ahead and strut, Taggert, she whispered to herself. Little do you know. She had to control herself to keep from gloating openly. She had her key motion already prepared, thanks to Paul Murphy, in which she would alter Melanie's plea to not guilty by reason of insanity. Taggert would never believe it, but she was more anxious than the D.A.'s office to get the trial started. She knew, was completely confident, that she could beat the system on this one. She could make one hell of a case for poor, unhappy Melanie Wyatt, which would stand out like the Rock of Gibraltar. No jury could convict her after Doyle got done with them. And, in addition, she would use this very report which, on its surface, appeared so damaging, but which, underneath, clearly proved her point that Melanie was nowhere near being sane on the night of Denise Wyatt's death.

She turned at the sound of the door to the witness room being opened and saw Melanie being wheeled into the courtroom by a uniformed sheriff and a white-coated hospital orderly.

"Melanie?" Doyle said, rising to her feet and reaching out to the woman as she was wheeled up to the defense table.

"Yes?" Melanie said, turning her face in Doyle's direction.

"How are you?"

"I'm okay," she said.

"How about your eyes?"

"Much better," Melanie replied. She smiled weakly at the lawyer and squinted to see her better.

"Can you see me okay?"

"Yes." Melanie nodded. "I can see much better now." She wet her lips with the tip of her tongue. Her hair was brushed neatly back, and with a touch of makeup, applied most probably by a nurse, she appeared almost pretty again. "What's going on here?"

Doyle sat beside her and leaned her arm across Melanie's shoulders. "This is a simple hearing," she said, "to determine your competency to stand trial."

"What does that mean?" Melanie sounded frightened. "Are you trying to say I'm crazy?"

"It's the judge, Melanie." Doyle deftly avoided answering the question. "He asked for the hearing. That's why you've been seeing Dr. Murphy."

Melanie turned to her sharply. "I don't understand."

Phyllis entered through the doors at the rear and moved far forward to take a seat. Doyle glanced back at her, caught her short wave, and nodded recognition.

"That's his job." Doyle said to Melanie. "He evaluates people for the court."

"Oh," Melanie said. Doyle was sure she still did not fully understand that her competency, her ability to assist in her own defense, had been evaluated by the man she believed was there to help her. She studied Melanie's blank face, searching for some sign of comprehension, but found nothing. Melanie's thoughts had already deserted the issue and were elsewhere. Only God knew where.

The rear doors opened again and Paul Murphy entered. He gazed around the room, saw Phyllis sitting by herself, and elected to sit across the room from her. He took a seat in the rear of the small courtroom and stared indifferently up at the judge's bench.

Taggert turned in his chair and grinned at Murphy. He held up the report again and waved it slightly, as if it were a fan. He formed an O with his thumb and forefinger and threw the sign to Paul, who ignored the gesture.

As the door to Judge Barret's chambers opened, the bailiff stood. "All rise," his voice boomed through the room.

They all rose to their feet except for Melanie, who remained in her wheelchair, Doyle's hand lying on her shoulder, as the judge entered and made his way to the high-backed leather chair that stood behind his desk.

"Be seated," the bailiff announced, and everyone returned to their respective seats.

Judge Barret sat and glanced around the courtroom. "How are we?"

Taggert rose to his feet again. "Your Honor," he said, "I think everyone is here and the people are ready to proceed."

"Well," Barret said, "for the record, let's get everybody's name on."

Taggert nodded. He spoke loudly and clearly for the benefit of the court reporter. "Bruce Taggert, that's T-A-G-G-E-R-T, district attorney's office, Los Angeles County." Then he sat down again.

Doyle rose. "Harriet Doyle, for the defendant." She

paused for a moment, then spoke again. "Your Honor, the defendant, Melanie Wyatt, is also present."

The judge looked down at the reporter and spoke to her. "This is a hearing to examine the findings of psychiatric examination in the matter of the People of the State of California versus Melanie Wyatt." He looked up then. "Is the defendant ready, Ms. Doyle?"

"The defendant is ready, Your Honor," Doyle answered.

Taggert rose. "The People are ready, Your Honor."

Barret smiled and rubbed his palms together. "Look," he said, "we're not going to be strictly formal here. I'm going to allow a lot. But we need a record, so let's not let ourselves get carried away. At the same time, we won't need lots of objecting. Let's save the posturing and get this over with in a nice, orderly fashion."

Taggert, nodding to the judge and still grinning, read from his notes while clutching Murphy's report in his hand.

"Your Honor, the defendant, Melanie Wyatt, has been indicted in the County of Los Angeles for the felony of murder in the first degree. Following the preliminary hearing, the court, for reasons known to itself, requested the defendant be afforded a psychological evaluation to determine whether or not she possessed the capacity to stand trial on that felony indictment. I understand the results of that evaluation were submitted to the court and to the defense yesterday." Taggert held up the blue covered report. "And, as of this morning, both counsels are now in possession of that report."

He looked over at Doyle, who nodded her acquiescence to him.

Taggert continued. "The examining psychologist found that the defendant does have the capacity to stand trial and all the interested parties in this matter have been so informed."

He paused and gazed around the room. "Since the court ordered this hearing and since I have no objection to this report, and it appears that neither does counsel for the defense, I would like to stipulate as to its reliability."

Barret glanced over at Doyle. "You want to raise any objections?"

Doyle stood. "No, Your Honor. The defense is perfectly satisfied with Dr. Murphy's report."

Barret thought for a moment, then he looked up. "Well, I think that's terrific, but it seems kind of hasty to me. You two may be content, but I'd like to hear some testimony from the good doctor."

"Well, I'll call him if you want me to, Your Honor," Taggert said.

Doyle glanced up and shrugged at the judge. "He's not my witness, Your Honor."

Melanie leaned over and whispered to Doyle. "What's happening?" Her words could be heard throughout the courtroom.

"Everything's just fine," Doyle said. She smiled and patted Melanie's hand. "It's going just the way we want it."

Judge Barret cleared his throat. "Well then, for the record, why don't you call him, Mr. Taggert?"

"That's okay with me, Your Honor." Taggert turned to the courtroom and said too softly, "I'd like to call Dr. Paul Murphy to the stand."

The judge frowned. "Bailiff! Get Dr. Murphy up here."

The bailiff rose and boomed. "Dr. Paul Murphy!"

Paul rose to his feet in the rear of the room and started forward down the short center aisle. As he passed Phyllis, he glanced at her and saw the fear and concern in her eyes. He smiled briefly, hoped he looked reassuring, and walked on.

At the witness chair, the bailiff swore him in. "Do you

318

solemnly swear that the testimony you are about to give shall be the truth, the whole truth, and nothing but the truth?"

"I do," Paul stated.

"Be seated, please," the bailiff instructed.

Judge Barret turned in his chair and leaned slightly toward the witness, affording him his full attention.

Taggert walked toward him. "Now, Dr. Murphy," he said, "I'm going to ask you a few questions pertaining to this report." He held up Murphy's blue covered report.

"All right," Paul said, nodding.

Taggert addressed the judge. "Do we need his qualifications on the record, Your Honor?"

Barret waved it away. "Don't waste a lot of time with it."

Taggert nodded and continued. "Doctor, have you appeared before this court in the past?"

"Yes, sir."

"Several times?"

"Yes, sir," Paul said.

"How many times, approximately?"

Paul thought for a moment. "I'd say about eight times."

"Have you ever been seriously challenged?" Taggert asked.

"No, sir."

"All right!" Taggert turned his back to Murphy and glanced up at the judge, who nodded his approval. "Tell us about your examination of Melanie Wyatt."

Paul, in his most professional manner, spoke out loudly to the courtroom. "I started with the usual interview. I asked questions and noted the appropriateness of her answers in order to determine her mental status. I administered, in addition, a battery of acceptable tests, such as the M.M.P.I., the T.A.T., the Bender-Gestalt, and the Rorschach, all of which contributed to my understanding of her mental condition."

"Did you draw any conclusions from all of that as to her ability to stand trial?"

"Yes, sir," Paul said.

"Would you tell the court what conclusion you arrived at, Doctor?"

"Well, I used as my criterion the standard yardstick of her ability to assist in her own defense."

Taggert smiled. "And your findings are in this detailed report?" He lifted the blue file a few inches off the top of the prosecution table.

"Well, yes, sir."

"Can you tell us simply what you found?"

Paul squirmed in his chair. He observed Doyle looking up at him expectantly. Taggert was almost packing his briefcase, pushing files toward it. Paul gazed back at Phyllis and thought how hard he had fallen for her and what a mess he was about to make for her.

"I determined, Your Honor," he said, turning to the judge, "that Melanie Wyatt is incompetent to stand trial."

Doyle was instantly on her feet. "Objection!" she screamed. "That's not what his report says." She waved the report in the air.

Taggert appeared stunned. He looked like a man who had been kicked in the stomach. "I don't understand, Your Honor."

Paul continued as if he had not been interrupted. "It's clear to me that the patient is out of touch with reality. She does not understand what is happening to her and she cannot possibly aid in her own defense."

Melanie, twisted sideways in her wheelchair, screamed at Doyle. "What's he saying about me? Is he saying that I'm crazy? Oh, my God!" She burst into tears.

Doyle continued with her objection. "This is a travesty,

320

Your Honor. I have a written report right here in my hand. . . . The man's totally contradicted himself."

Taggert, having recovered, approached the bench, speaking loudly. "The People are going to need some time, Your Honor. This turn of events is a complete surprise. I'm going to need a recess."

Barret, unable to handle all the objections at one time, resorted to his gavel and brought the room under control. He turned to Murphy and glared at him. "Yesterday," he said, "you delivered to me a report which indicated the opposite of that to which you are now, presently, testifying."

"Yes, sir." Paul retained a calm exterior.

Angrily. "How do you explain that, sir? Is there something you've just recently learned? Have you acquired some new information since yesterday evening?"

"He can't explain it," Doyle screamed irately. "It's a setup. He must have planned it this way."

"This is ridiculous," Taggert added. "I think he should be held in contempt."

"Well, Dr. Murphy?" the judge asked. "I think if you've learned something new you should share it with us. After all, this court is still interested in the truth."

Murphy simply shrugged. "I was wrong," he said.

Doyle shouted. "You were wrong? What does that mean?" She approached the bench. "Your Honor, the defense has prepared on the belief that Melanie Wyatt would be found competent. That belief appears now," she glanced angrily at Murphy, "to be erroneous. I want to refute these findings and I'm going to need time."

"Your Honor," Taggert said, "this is totally inexcusable. I can't—"

The judge wheeled on him. "Don't you dare tell me what's excusable or inexcusable in my courtroom, Mr. Taggert. That would be far too presumptuous, and I'm not in the mood to be put upon by you. And, as for you Ms. Doyle, you continue to shout out of order and I'll hold you in contempt."

Doyle sat down grudgingly.

Barret returned his attention to Murphy. "What does it mean, precisely, when you say you were wrong?"

Paul shrugged again and looked up at the judge. "I went over all the information—the test data, my notes from my interviews with the defendant and others—and decided that I had made some hasty and inaccurate judgments. In all good conscience, I don't believe I can continue to abide by those judgments."

The judge pursed his lips and considered Paul Murphy. "Can you offer this court anything new? Any concrete evidence that could indicate a reasonableness to your change of opinion?"

Paul appeared helpless himself. "Only that it's now my opinion, Judge. I just don't believe she's competent."

Judge Barret nodded to Murphy. There was no longer any trace of anger on his face. Instead, his expression had grown into one of firm resolve. "Clearly," he said, "the court wants to afford the defendant the maximum latitude in this matter, in order to fully protect her rights. If its expert witness wishes to change his opinion, the court is—and should be—grateful. However, I'm going to recess this proceeding until two o'clock this afternoon." The judge rose and spoke to Murphy. "I'll see you in my chambers, Dr. Murphy. Now!" He strode toward his door. He stopped and suddenly turned. "I'll see you all in my chambers. Right now!"

Paul sat silently on the witness chair, unable to immediately move. Doyle glowered at him. It was not so much that he had changed his mind that bothered her, but that he had not kept her informed, that he had not given her the opportunity to argue with him privately before he did his damage. That, and the recognition that he had inexorably altered her plans. She would now have to fight two major battles—first, to prove Melanie's competency, and then to get her acquitted. The odds against either one happening were short. She wondered how astronomical the odds would be against winning both.

Taggert glanced over at Doyle and shook his head in despair. His dejected expression seemed to agree with her that they would be at war for a long time, a very long, expensive time.

"You can step down," the bailiff said to Murphy.

But Paul did not hear him. He was staring at Phyllis, who stood at the back of the room watching him. On her face was an expression of bewilderment, and he knew she was thinking about what he had just done. Had he betrayed her? He was sure she was thinking that he had.

"What the hell was that all about?" Barret stripped his black robe off his back and hung it on a coat rack. Murphy sat in a chair to the left of the judge's desk while Doyle sat in the one to the right, glaring at him. Taggert sat forward on the edge of the couch.

They were in the judge's chambers, a dull office painted beige and furnished as coldly as if it were temporary. The imitation leather chairs were old, faded, and mismatched. The judge sat behind a huge wooden desk, which was piled high with unattended blue covered briefs. Along the walls was a series of small Currier and Ives prints, all of which looked like old faded Christmas cards trapped in thin, chipped wooden frames.

"It's crazy!" Taggert shouted across the room at Murphy.

Judge Barret's head snapped around. "Please! Let's keep it down. If we get into a shouting match, nothing will be accomplished."

Doyle held her hands out in supplication. "I'd like to say something."

Barret nodded to her. "All right."

"I don't know what's going on here, but I want to say that it certainly isn't fair to the defendant. There are so many shadows on the evidence now—which is all circumstantial, by the way—that there has to be a serious doubt as to her guilt." She turned to Murphy and appealed to him. "Why drag this out any longer than it has to be? Why make a person stand trial twice? What a terrible ordeal for her to go though."

Taggert jumped up. "That's all nonsense, Your Honor. Mrs. Wyatt is guilty. That's why she should stand trial. She's as competent as you or I. All this stuff is merely an attempt to obstruct justice."

"I don't think," the judge said, "that anyone here wants to obstruct justice, Mr. Taggert."

"Then let's go to trial," Taggert said. "Lay it all out for the jury. If they think there's a reasonable doubt of her guilt, they'll let her go. I have no fear of that. But, the State believes she's guilty and wants the opportunity to put the system to the test."

"Well, what do you think, Doctor? Is Mrs. Wyatt competent to stand trial or not?" The judge's tight voice reflected his discomfort. "It's been five minutes since your last announcement. Perhaps you've changed you mind once again."

Paul glanced about him. He gazed at the other people in the room. He knew what Doyle wanted. She glared at him with hatred in her eyes. He knew that she wanted a guaranteed package of innocence by reason of insanity. She needed this trial as soon as she could get it. And it was what Judge Barret wanted, as well. But he was afraid to deliver that. He could not in good conscience allow Melanie Wyatt to go to trial on the chance that she might be acquitted on an insanity plea. What if she were found guilty? Who could predict a jury's decision? It was too chancy and he felt too encumbered. The weight of the supposedly simple determination the judge demanded of him pressed down on him. Yes, he told himself. He had a fear of being responsible. He did not want to decide her fate. But he did not want someone else to resolve Melanie Wyatt's fate on a whim, either. He swallowed.

"Your Honor," he said, "Mrs. Wyatt is, at best, on shaky footing mentally. I think it's cruel and vindictive to make a courtroom spectacle of her at a time like this, when she can barely defend herself. We may have to wait some time before she's able to stand trial. Why torture her by throwing her into a proceeding which she will not understand? The things that go on at a trial might scare the daylights out of her. On the other hand, she may not be aware of what's going on and she'll daydream her way through it. Does the State want justice or does the State want revenge? Judge, I don't know how much more definitive I can be. I only know I can't allow that woman to go to trial yet."

"I still say that's crazy!" Taggert shouted at Murphy. "I don't see any evidence of the kind of mental illness you're talking about."

The judge scowled at Murphy. "You don't have that kind of power, Dr. Murphy. You don't determine who goes to trial or when."

"Damn!" Doyle said. "You betrayed our trust."

"I didn't mean it that way."

He turned to her apologetically. "I just think we shouldn't make an obviously innocent person stand trial."

"Stop!" Judge Barret cut him short. "Dr. Murphy, I feel that you are about to do exactly what I have time and time again warned you not to do."

"Well, Your honor, it's hard not to," he said, "you're asking me to determine competency. I—"

The judge said, "I'm asking for an opinion."

Paul shrugged. "I have given you my opinion."

"That may be true. However, I want a simple one sentence answer to my question. No mitigating circumstances. No psychological mumbo jumbo. Just an answer. I'll do you a favor. I'll throw out your report and I'll disregard your testimony right now. Let's start fresh. Okay?"

Paul shrugged. He glanced over at Doyle and lifted his shoulders slightly, as if to apologize in advance. She glared at him coldly.

"If I had to, I'd say what I said out there. She's probably incompetent and can't stand trial."

The judge sighed. He sat back and turned his attention to Doyle, who was staring at Murphy in disbelief. "That's it, then."

"Your Honor, this is a joke," Doyle insisted. "Whatever he says is invalid now, after all this flip-flopping."

"Look! Maybe I'm wrong," Paul said. "But I don't know how else to express myself. I'm afraid to let Melanie Wyatt go to trial."

He turned to face Harriet Doyle again. "I know you're good, Doyle. But at best it's a coin toss. You can't predict what that jury will do. Nobody can. And I don't want to be responsible for Melanie Wyatt getting convicted because she went to trial before she was ready to help herself."

Judge Barret grimaced at him. "If that's what you believe, why didn't you just say do?"

Paul shrugged and looked away. "You lawyers want everything to be so neat. All the pieces have to fit. They have to make sense. But to me, that's not the case. Half the time I'm flying by the seat of my pants. Half of what I do is based on my own intuition. You always want me to be definite. I can't do that all the time. Oh, sure, sometimes, when it's a cut-and-dried matter, when anybody can look at the behavior and know it's not normal. But in a case like Melanie's, there's just no way to make sense of it to you. Her mental status just won't fit the rules."

"Well," the judge said, "I don't really object to you changing your mind, but I would appreciate an explanation." He shook his head. "I think you should take a few minutes and help us understand."

Paul leaned forward in his chair. He looked around at the three faces staring at him. He wondered how receptive they would be. He wondered if he had not bitten off more than anyone could chew. He swallowed his fear and plunged ahead.

"It's not only that I believe Melanie Wyatt hasn't the capacity to stand trial. I also don't believe that she has the capacity to commit the crime she's been accused of, either."

The judge started to protest. "Of course, that's none of your business." He shook his head despairingly.

Paul nodded. "I know that, Your Honor."

Barret glanced at Doyle. "You understand? We're going to need another competency hearing. You better get yourself some expert witnesses."

Doyle shrugged. "I understand," she said unhappily.

The judge turned back to Paul and halfheartedly motioned him to continue. "Go ahead!"

Paul knew that there was little he could say now that could correct the impression he had left of himself. He had seriously damaged his own credibility and he would have to make a spectacular appeal to overcome that. He leaned forward and spoke directly to the judge. "Your Honor, we all have certain taboos that stop us from doing specific things," he began, "rules that have been drilled into us as children. 'Don't cross the street without looking' is a typical one. On the other hand, some people have more permission than others to do certain things. For example, if a child grows up in an environment in which the important adults in his life solved their problems with, let's say, violence, then that child would learn to do the same and he would have more permission to solve his problems violently than someone who grew up in an environment that hated violence.''

He glanced over at Doyle, as if to insure that he had her full attention. "So, if a child grows up where conscious, planned aggression is acceptable and taught and practiced— you know, like an eye for an eye, or if Johnny hits you, hit him back, or when someone abuses you, it's perfectly okay for you to get revenge ... things like that—then you'd expect that child to be capable, as an adult, of manifesting that kind of behavior. He'd be able to plan his revenge, to carry out a plot, to be creative and devious in his punishment.''

"What's the point, Murphy?'' the judge asked impatiently.

"The point is that Melanie Wyatt isn't like that, Your Honor. She comes out of an environment which was foreign to that kind of acting out. On the contrary, her own husband, who's committed to doing her as much harm as he can, has stated that she's impulsive, that she doesn't think things out, that she acts quickly and impulsively. Because, he says, she's always been ambivalent and can't make up her mind. If she thinks about it, he says, she won't do it.''

The judge nodded. Doyle, very interested now, turned in her chair and studied Murphy as he talked.

Paul grew excited as he warmed to his subject. "And we're talking about a crime here that was very carefully executed, carried out over a lengthy period of time—at least ten minutes, fifteen minutes. Who knows how much longer? How long does it take to fill a tub, carefully drown an infant, empty the tub, and clean up? Certainly none of those can be called impulsive acts of passion."

"That's a nice theory, Doctor," Barret said. "But it's not evidence and not nearly enough to dismiss a case."

"I know that," Paul said. "I'm not making a plea for you to dismiss. That's Harriet's job. I've spent some hours with Mrs. Wyatt and I'm telling you what I believe I've learned about her."

Barret nodded thoughtfully. "Go on, Paul," he said.

Paul nodded. "Even more striking, I think, is the personality style of Mrs. Wyatt. She's not the most assertive person around. On the contrary, she's the kind of person who would act out her most aggressive feelings in the most passive way."

He smiled at the judge. "Judge, you were fifteen minutes late to court this morning. If we knew, you and I, that you really didn't want to be here, that you resented this hearing taking place and that you were angry at having to show up here, we might say that you showed your aggression, your anger, passively, by being late and making us wait for you."

Judge Barret smiled at Paul and nodded his head. "That's not the case," he said. "But I get your point."

Doyle chuckled softly under her breath at Murphy's audacity.

"Well, that's what Melanie Wyatt might do," Paul said. "She'd keep us waiting. Or she'd clam up and not talk. Or she'd play dumb and incompetent so we'd have to do things for her. She'd burn the roast. Scratch the car twice a year like clockwork. Lose her keys three times a week. And, if she got really angry enough—let's say at somebody like me, at some damned busybody who comes along and sticks his pointy nose into her private business, who keeps probing and probing and asking and asking and making her see things she doesn't want to see—why, she might just go blind."

He paused and waited for effect. He watched their faces for a moment, until he was sure they were all hooked, then said, "People like Melanie Wyatt aren't perpetrators. People like her are victims. They find mates who are willing to torture them. They pick husbands who rant and rave and beat them and cheat on them. They become martyrs and sacrifice themselves to their drunken, arrogant, cruel husbands. They swallow their anger. They lock it up inside and punish themselves with it. They rarely act out against an external enemy unless it's done passively—by lateness, for example, or procrastination, or just plain stubbornness, like writing the same wrong address on the same letter three or four times because you're angry and you don't want the letter delivered, anyway.

"These people don't devise and carry out complex plans of murder. If Melanie Wyatt wanted to punish her baby, she'd have locked the infant away in the crib and gone to sleep and not fed her or changed her for two days.

"But Melanie Wyatt didn't even do that, because she wasn't angry with her child. At most, she was angry with her husband and he didn't even want the child, so it seems that to get even with him all she had to do was shower affection on the child instead of on him. And that's exactly what she did do. She chose the child over him. She threw him out and kept her baby.

"Does the State want us to believe that she then turned around and did murder in total contradiction of everything she stands for?"

Paul stared at Doyle. "No way, Harriet!" he shouted.

"Can anyone believe that this woman, so terrified of her own anger, who carried her pain silently for ten years in a bad marriage, who suffered incredible guilt if she merely raised her voice, who suffered guilt when her husband beat her because she believed she provoked him to it merely by being there, planned and carried out the heinous deed of the slow and painful murder of her own helpless child?"

He then turned his eyes to the judge. "No way, Your Honor. No goddamned way!"

He stopped and looked about him. Judge Barret was smiling at him. Doyle walked over to him, put her arms around him, and hugged him affectionately. "I may have you deliver my summation for me, Doctor," she said, and placed a warm kiss on his cheek.

"Yes," Taggert said. "Very well said, Doctor. But, if I believed what you've just told us, I'd have no perpetrator, no accused, and no defendant. And that's just not possible."

"Paul, what are you getting at? What do you actually think?" Doyle asked.

"It doesn't matter what he thinks." Barret snapped as he turned to Paul. "You intend to continue seeing Mrs. Wyatt, don't you? You're not planning to leave matters this way?"

"No, sir. And I intend to see Officer Wyatt again. And the child, too."

"I hope you realize that I am not at all satisfied with your performance here."

Paul nodded. "I know that, Your Honor."

"I don't think anyone else in this room is, either." Barret glanced around the room, then returned to Murphy. "If you decide to continue to insist on Mrs. Wyatt's incompetence, I want a written report validating that opinion. I want it on the record. No more unsubstantiated opinions, Doctor. No more junior detective. Have I made myself perfectly clear?"

"You have," Paul said.

"Good!" He turned to the other members of their party. "I'm going to give you all a forty-eight hour continuance. You two do what you need to counteract what Dr. Murphy will submit." Then he turned to Murphy. "And you! I'm only giving you forty-eight hours, also. You stuck your neck out. Let's see what you can learn before I chop it off. Maybe you can do the court a service, after all."

The judge rose to his feet. "Monday morning at nine A.M. See you all in court."

THREE

"You think I could do something like that, Doctor? To my own kid? I loved that baby. How could I kill somebody I loved like that?"

The next morning Chris Wyatt, dressed in his police uniform, sat across from Dr. Paul Murphy in the brown leather patient's chair and crossed his legs carefully so as not to interfere with the perfect crease down his trousers. He stared at Murphy with wide opened eyes, an expression of innocence fixed upon his face.

Paul returned the stare. "I haven't accused you of anything, Officer Wyatt," Paul said, although his questions certainly could be heard, by some, as accusatory.

Chris shook his head and shifted his weight in the chair. He did not want to lose his temper. He wanted to maintain his composure more than anything. His instincts warned him that this doctor was not a friend, not nearly as objective as he pretended to be. "Yeah, sure," he said. "But I know what you're thinking." he snickered, and smiled at Murphy. "You're thinking I blew my cool, maybe, and killed my kid. Hell! Melanie's your patient. You want to help her. I can understand that okay. But not at my expense. You know what I mean? Get that idea right out of your head. I don't blow so easy."

Paul nodded and smiled. "Believe me," he said, "I have no personal interest in you whatsoever. I wanted to talk to you only to better understand your wife. Maybe the kind of relationship you had. Tell me about her."

"What about her?" Chris asked.

Paul tried to fix onto Chris Wyatt's eyes, which avoided contact with him. "You think she's capable of killing her child?"

Chris hesitated. He wanted to be very careful with this man. He did not trust shrinks and wanted to be very cautious not to appear too eager to disparage Melanie. "Well, she sure knows how to be bitchy," he said. "You know, when she doesn't get what she wants."

"What do you mean by bitchy?" Paul asked.

"You know," Chris said. He shrugged and smiled as if to say, all us men know what a bitchy woman is like. "She'd fly off the handle. You know, get real mean and nasty."

"Physical?"

"Well, yeah."

"To you?"

"Well, yeah," Chris said. "To me and to the kids."

Paul leaned forward slightly. "Did she ever beat the children?"

Chris moved uncomfortably and shifted his weight again. "Well, I've seen her hit Polly."

Paul pushed a little harder. "I was thinking of beating, as opposed to hitting."

Chris squirmed slightly. "Well, no. But that don't mean too much. Now, don't go making something big out of that. You know, we cops know a lot about that domestic stuff. On television they always show the father beating on the kids. It's always a cute little girl and a bad daddy. But let me tell you something. Every cop knows that nine out of ten times it's the mother. You know what I mean? Fathers hit a lot, but it's always the mother who kills."

Paul nodded thoughtfully. "I think I've heard that before," he said. "I think I heard it from Sgt. Collins."

"Any cop'll tell you that," Chris said.

"Yes," Paul said. "I bet they would."

Melanie met Phyllis during the morning visiting hour, in the dayroom/lounge where the ailing prisoners were allowed to go to read or watch television or meet with friends or relatives. It was a pleasant enough room, evenly surrounded by large barred windows that allowed huge beams of daylight to pass through them. On the various tables scattered about the room, chess boards and backgammon games waited to be utilized. Along one wall, a large magazine rack held tattered torn, abused newspapers and magazines from months back.

An orderly had wheeled Melanie in and left her beside Phyllis, who was seated on an ugly flowered green couch in a far corner. The two uniformed guards inside the room shifted their weight and turned slightly, so that they could both keep Melanie in their sight from different angles.

Melanie felt so naked, so observed. She was sure that everyone who looked at her could see directly into her, beyond her clothing, beyond her skin, deeply into her. They could observe the empty worthlessness that was hidden inside of her.

She pulled the lapels of her robe more tightly around her and held them closed. She imagined Phyllis's freshness, her uncontaminated beauty, which she could only see in her mind's eye, and felt a brush of envy sweep across her. With her return from the dark, hidden place had come a more

335

realistic sensibility, a more accurate evaluation of herself. She could understand, now, how she failed to compare favorably with her friend, how much inferior to Phyllis she truly was.

Slowly, tears of self-pity began to emerge in the corners of her eyes.

"What?" Phyllis asked. "What's the matter?"

Melanie twisted her face in disgust. "I'm so bad. So ugly," she said.

Phyllis took Melanie's hand in both of hers. "Mel, you're looking so much better. You don't know."

Melanie squinted at her friend. She wanted to believe. She wanted to believe so badly. After a moment, she said, "I feel better." She wiped the tears away with the back of her hand. "And I can see better, too. I can almost make out your features." She laughed and shook her head. "You're still just a blur, but at least I can see the blur."

"Well, it won't be long before you'll be criticizing how I put on my makeup."

Melanie grew sad again. "I want to get out of here. I miss Polly so much. And nobody's telling me anything."

"There's nothing to tell, Mel," Phyllis lied.

Melanie frowned. "I know that's not true. I know that something terrible is happening. If you all leave it to my imagination, I don't know what I'll think." She dropped her face into her hands. "Dr. Murphy thinks I'm crazy, doesn't he?"

Phyllis shook her head, forgetting that her friend would not be able to see the gesture. "No. That's not true. He believes in you more than in anybody else. He's on your side."

Melanie turned away from her friend. She could not believe that Phyllis did not understand. Nothing would be solved until it was over, until she had been properly chastised. "If that were true, he'd let me go to trial. That's the best thing for me. Trial and punishment."

"Don't say that. That's a terrible thing to say."

"God!" she said to no one. "Why is it taking so long?"

"Don't give up," Phyllis said. "Paul Murphy is doing his best for you."

Melanie grew suspicious. "What do you mean? How?"

"He's trying to help you, Mel."

"How?" she screamed. "What's he doing?"

Phyllis, frightened now, spoke more softly. "He's trying to prove your innocence."

"That's stupid," she spat. "What's he doing?"

"He's interviewing Chris and Polly . . ."

"What?" Melanie screamed at her.

Phyllis pleaded, "He's doing everything he can. He's out there fighting for you."

She wheeled on Phyllis, sending her friend back on the couch. "Nobody's fighting for me! That's a lie! You're all against me." Her face twisted with rage. "Don't you think I know? You're all against me. All of you. Everyone."

"Oh, Mel," Phyllis wept.

"Where's my child?" Melanie shouted. "Why is he seeing my child? What does he want from her? Where's my Polly? Why isn't she here with me if you all care so much? Why?"

Phyllis cringed under the verbal attack.

Melanie glared at her viciously. "You stole her from me, didn't you? You're going to keep her for yourself, aren't you? I know you!" Melanie screamed hysterically. "You thief! Thief!" She began beating her fists on the arms of her wheelchair. "Thief! Thief!" She rocked her body back and forth until the chair almost tipped over, and one of the guards ran over and caught her. He held her down as she continued to scream at Phyllis. "Thief! Bitch!"

Phyllis, holding her breath as if afraid to ingest the contaminated air, backed out of the room and fled rapidly down the corridor. She did not stop running until she reached her car in the parking lot.

Chris was unable to sit quietly any longer. He had promised this doctor an hour of his time but had already been locked away with him for almost double that. Chris considered himself a pretty good interrogator, but sitting across from Paul Murphy, he knew that he was with a master, the unflappable Dr. Murphy. The man never blinked, took everything in his stride. What was worse, he never allowed any emotion to show on his face. He never let Chris know what he was thinking, how he was reacting to what he was hearing. That bothered Chris Wyatt. That bothered him very much. He liked to be in control. He liked to know what was happening, to be the force behind what was happening. He hated being on the wrong end of the questioning.

And the content of the questioning bothered him as well. At the beginning, he had thought he would enjoy releasing all his pent-up hatred for Melanie, but the more they talked about his past with her, the less he enjoyed slamming her. He could feel the joy slipping away from him. He could hear the cocky lilt filtering out of his voice the more he spoke. Finally, he could hear himself losing patience with the constant inquiry, could hear himself not believing what he was saying.

He rose from the chair and moved to the window. The little sunlight filtering in through the blinds hurt his eyes, and he turned away and stared at Murphy. He wanted to put his sunglasses on again but knew that Murphy would make an issue of them, would bust him on wanting to hide behind the colored glass.

"She got really bad," he said, "when she got pregnant with Denny." He put his hands on his hips and seemed to be challenging the doctor. "It was her own damned fault but she blamed me just the same. She screamed and yelled like I'd committed some terrible crime. Like I'd purposely made her pregnant to punish her. God! She got crazy. She should've seen you back then." He flung the statement at Murphy as though it were an insult.

Paul scribbled a short notation on his pad. "Why didn't she see someone then?" he asked in a flat, unemotional, nonjudgmental voice.

Chris laughed as though Murphy had said something truly funny. "If I even suggested it," he said, "she'd go nuts. One day we had the brawl to end all brawls just because I told her she could do better with Polly. I didn't dare suggest that she needed a shrink. God! She would've become a nuclear weapon."

Paul nodded slightly. "In what way could she have done better?"

Chris stared at Murphy for a long moment. He pressed his lips together and dipped his chin down toward his chest. He suddenly strode across the room and flung himself back into his chair.

"She could've loved her more," he said.

"Could she?"

Chris twisted over so that he was sitting on his hip. He threw one leg over the other and squinted at Murphy. He was swinging his leg now, and the high shine on his black regulation shoe caught and let go of the light in a kind of rhythm.

"You're damned straight," he said. "The one thing that Melanie lacks, really doesn't have too much of, is love. She never learned how to love. Oh, sure, she can take it if you're giving it away. But she sure as hell doesn't know how to give any. Shit! You could beg her from here to Mars and she wouldn't know how to love a man.''

"Did you ever tell her how you feel?" Paul asked.

"You bet I did," Chris exclaimed. "And, when I told her that, she went goddamned bananas. She called me every name in the book. Shit! I had to finally sit her down and tell her a thing or two.''

Paul stared at him. "Just what did you tell her?''

"Hell! It's in the police report. I mean, I told all this stuff to Collins when we talked about it.''

"Tell me.''

"Hell! I already went over it again and again.''

"Tell me once more," Paul insisted.

Chris shrugged and let the air out of his lungs in mock weariness. "I told her what I thought about mothers who hate their kids and treat them like shit and make them crazy trying to figure out how to get by. I even think I slapped her that time. I'm not sure. I don't remember all that well. But I remember I told her if she didn't shape up, I was going to leave her. I told her I'd take the kid and disappear if I had to, but that I would be going and to hell with her.'' He sat up and gazed directly into Murphy's eyes for a change. "That's when she told me she'd do it.''

"Do what?" Paul asked.

Chris nodded emphatically. He wet his lips and wiped the back of his hand across his mustache. "That's when she told me that if I left her, she'd kill the baby.''

That night, long after Paul had put his files away, poured himself a brandy, and put his feet up on his beveled glass coffee table, long after he had given up trying to locate Phyllis, who had never showed up at home, forcing Gladys to stay the night and frightening Polly half out of her wits, his private line rang. As he reached for the phone, certain it was Doyle on the line, just aching to lay into him some more, just waiting to call him some additional colorful names, he spilled his brandy on his trousers and whispered, "Shit," just as he lifted the receiver.

"What?" she said.

"Not you," he said hurriedly. "I spilled something."

"Oh," she said.

He grinned with relief. "Hey! Where the hell have you been? I've been trying to find you all evening."

Phyllis sighed deeply into the phone. "I was driving," she said. "I went up the coast, I don't know how far. Just been driving and thinking."

"You don't sound so hot," he said worriedly.

"I saw Melanie today," she said. She paused and he waited for her to continue. Finally, she sighed. "I'm still not over it."

"What happened?"

"I don't understand it myself," she said. "I don't know that woman. She looks like Melanie, but there's nothing left of the person I used to know."

"Tell me what happened."

"I was angry with you for saying in court that she's not competent. I thought you were betraying us. I'm so sorry. I really thought you had turned on us. But you were right. We were all wrong and you were right."

"Phyllis," he said soothingly, "calm down. Take it easy. Just tell me what happened."

He could hear Phyllis breathing deeply, trying to regain her composure. "She accused me of stealing her child from her. She accused me of stealing Polly. She was so angry. I've never seen her that angry." She sobbed. "She really is mentally ill, isn't she?"

"Listen," Paul said. "Why don't you come over here?"

"Why?"

He sighed. "I'd like to look at you while I tell you what I have to say."

"Is it that bad?" she said. "Go ahead. You don't have to be afraid."

"You're making it awful tough on me."

"Go ahead."

"Okay," Paul said. "There's no question that Melanie is a little paranoid and paranoia is an illness. But, in most cases, there is some truth, some reality in the basis for the paranoid fantasy."

"What are you saying, Paul? Are you telling me that I am really trying to steal her child?"

"Not the way you mean it," he said. "But haven't you thought about how nice it would be if Polly were your little girl? Haven't you kind of wished that it were so?"

There was a long silence, then she whispered. "Goddamn you, Murphy. Why do you have to be so goddamned wise?"

Paul said, "Those thoughts, those feelings, are perfectly normal. Not only do you love Polly, you also want to be a mother. That's instinctive."

"Oh, yeah?" she said.

"Yeah," he said.

When she spoke again, her voice was softer, happier. "Maybe I will come over for a while. I'll ask Gladys to give me another hour and maybe I'll come over. What do you think?"

"I think that's a terrific idea," he said. "We have a lot to talk about."

She chuckled. "I don't feel like talking."

FOUR

"You're eyes?" he asked.

"Much better," Melanie heard herself say.

"Can you see me?" He leaned forward, much closer to her.

"Yes," she said. "I can see you now. I can see the features on your face."

"Good!"

She wet her lips with her tongue and felt warm tears form in her eyes.

"Oh, thank God," she said. "I'm not crazy anymore."

He nodded soberly and she smiled at him, at the exaggerated seriousness of his expression.

"Thank you," she said in her most placating manner.

"Thank yourself," he said, fending off the manipulating false worship. "You're a very courageous woman."

It was the next day and they were in Paul's office now. He was so much more confident in his own surroundings. He knew that the work he wanted to do with Melanie would go much more easily, much more smoothly, in here, in this almost magic room, a cubicle filled with permission and protection, where Melanie could feel safe for the first time in so very long. He did not need to tell her. He could see her visibly relax as the tenseness in her facial muscles dissipated and her breathing became deeper and slower. She sensed that the prison ambience, to which she had grown so accustomed, had been left behind. She could feel the lack of penetrating observation. There was not the faintest hint of punishment in this room and she knew she was free to expose herself.

Melanie no longer required a wheelchair. She was now walking. Slowly, cautiously, for sure, but walking still. The guard who had brought her had left her seated in the same brown leather chair in which her husband had struggled the day before. That guard now waited outside with an abundance of *Psychology Today* back issues to peruse.

"You shouldn't underestimate your own strength," Paul said.

She smiled and turned her thoughts inward. She had never thought of herself as courageous. She had lived such a cowardly existence. She could not remember being unafraid, at least, not since childhood. As far as her adult life was concerned, fear was her most frequent emotion. She flashed on her meeting with Phyllis the day before and relived the terror that had come upon her when she believed her friend was taking her place in Polly's life. The unreasoning terror. Bizarre, distorted fear. A fear that made no sense at all, since if she were to be sent to prison, it would most certainly be Phyllis to whom she would want Polly entrusted.

"Maybe that's true. But I haven't been strong," she said. "I've been so afraid. All the time. So afraid."

He wanted her to talk about her fear. He wanted her to face it rather than to continue denying it. "Of what are you afraid, Melanie?"

She shook her head slowly. "Of him, I guess." She shuddered. "I guess he wanted it that way. He wanted to make a slave out of me."

"Who's him?"

"Chris. My husband."

Paul nodded his understanding. He was willing to begin with Chris, although he knew they would have to go much further. "How did he do that?"

She turned away and stared out the window at a pale blue sky and bits of buildings that stood up into it. She was exuberant that she could see them. They remained fuzzy, but she could see them. Two days ago, she thought, that seemed so impossible. I thought I would never see again. Today? Maybe I am strong.

"Melanie?" he said softly. "Tell me how Chris did that to you?"

She brought her eyes back to him. They were moist and red from crying, but clear and alive with a recent new understanding. She unblocked her thoughts and grappled with the memories.

"That first time, the first time he came home really drunk was about five years ago, I guess, when Polly was three. I was worried about him, you know, being on the streets at night. Not calling. He'd stayed out late before, so that part wasn't so terrible. But it was the not hearing, the not knowing. That was terrible.

"You know, when something is bad and you don't like it, how sometimes it stops bothering you as you get used to it. That's the way it was with him staying out late. I knew he was going drinking after every shift and I hated that, but I told myself he needed it. He needed to wind down at the end of the day and he couldn't do it at home. He needed the boys for that."

She looked down at her hands folded in her lap. She unclasped them, reversed them, then clasped them again.

"But this was the first time he'd come home really drunk. I still wasn't afraid of him yet, at that time. He hadn't ever hit me yet. I mean, I don't know what I would've done if he'd hit me back then. I mean, before I got used to the drinking. I don't know if I would've tolerated being hit before I was even used to the drunkenness. Because I think you have to give in, or lose out in little stages. I mean, piece by piece.

"Anyway, he made so much noise I came out, because I was afraid he'd wake the baby, and Polly used to be such a bad sleeper."

She suddenly grimaced and shut her eyes tightly. "He'd thrown up all over the living room carpet. There was a big pool of vomit and he was lying in it, with his face in it, and it was all over his clothes. In his hair. In his ears, even. He was almost covered with it.

"I'd never seen anything like that before. My father didn't even drink. I'd never seen anyone that drunk in my whole life. He looked up and saw me and reached out an arm to me, but I couldn't go near him. The sight of him and the smell of him made me sick." She shivered. "He asked me to help him."

She shuddered at the memory and looked around the room helplessly. "I told him I couldn't help him. I couldn't touch him all covered like that. He told me he was drunk and couldn't help himself, and he laughed as if it was funny."

"Paul nodded. "But it wasn't funny to you."

She laughed humorlessly. "Funny? I wanted to cry. I told him to shut the hell up. Polly was sleeping. He laughed harder and louder. He really thought it was all very funny. I wanted to cry. I don't know, to go crying to my mama, to get hugged and taken care of and not have to deal with that. But that wasn't possible, because all I'd get from them ... well, from daddy, would be I told you so."

"So, what did you do?" Paul asked.

Melanie straightened up in the chair. She brushed the hair back from her eyes with the palm of her hand. "I did my duty," she said proudly. "I picked him up, almost threw up myself, and dragged him into the bathroom and propped him up against the toilet bowl, with his head hanging over the open bowl. I got all his clothes off and threw them into the bathtub. I didn't know if they could be salvaged. I knew I was going to have a heck of a job scrubbing them. I got him stark naked and I washed him right there on the floor, with washcloths. I used about a dozen. But I couldn't lift him up to wash him. He was too heavy for that.

"I dragged him by the feet ... well, by the ankles really, on his back like a sack of potatoes, into the bedroom and got him into his pj's and put him to bed. You should've seen me getting him up onto the bed. It took me as long to do that as it did to do all the rest. He was out like a light. Snoring away as if it was nothing."

Paul leaned slightly forward. "Is that how you see a wife's duty?"

"Of course," she said, nodding her head emphatically. "Isn't it?"

He shrugged. "I don't know. Is it?" He needed her to see that she was hiding from her anger once again. He wanted her to recognize that she denied her feelings by giving value to duty and responsibility.

"You know it is. I had to clean up. Didn't I?"

"Did you?" Paul asked.

"Whose job is it, anyway? I did what I had to do. I went back and scrubbed the living room carpet. That took about an hour. But I got it pretty well cleaned up. It left a ring I never did get rid of, but I think that was from the soap I used. I mean, the place I scrubbed was probably cleaner than the rest of the carpet and that's what the ring is from. Didn't I have to do that?"

"You didn't have to," he said.

"No?"

"What made you think you had to?"

She started to laugh but stopped herself when he did not join her. "You're kidding," she said. "No. You're not, are you?"

"No. I'm not kidding," he said. "I want to know who made those rules. Who told you you had to?"

"You don't know anything," she said contemptuously. "What planet are you from?"

She slid down in her chair and a wave of disgust swept across her face. "You want to know who makes the rules? Who do you think?

"I don't know. You have to tell me."

"Okay," she said, "I'll tell you." And a sadistic grin crossed her face. "I was really cranky in the morning. See I didn't get much sleep the night before. And, when I finally did get to bed, he wouldn't let me sleep. He'd grunt and groan and toss all around, and it was impossible to settle down. So in the morning I was a real crank.

"He came into the kitchen for breakfast in the meanest mood and started snapping at me like I'd been the one who had been drunk and he'd been the one who'd cleaned me up and hadn't had any sleep. And, of course, like I said, I was cranky. I had Polly there refusing to eat her breakfast and the damned TV going full blast."

She covered her ears with her hands to show him. "So, I snapped back at him. He was standing over by the entrance to the kitchen, still in his pj's, and he looked awful and I said to him, 'Can't you see I'm busy with Polly? Why can't you wait your turn?' And he said his turn was any god-damned time he wanted it to be. And I said next time he

348

could clean up his own vomit. I guess I was still a little annoyed about the night before. Anyway, he took two big steps and he was right in front of me."

Melanie cringed in her chair and began to weep. Her voice became infantile and high-pitched. "And he had his fist back, and I scrunched down and he punched me on the top of my head. Believe me, I saw stars. I was down on my knees and my head was reeling, and I could hear Polly screaming off somewhere. And then a door slammed and I couldn't hear Polly anymore, and he lifted me up and slammed me against the wall and held me there, hanging like a piece of meat."

She wiped her eyes with her fists and stared at him. "You think that didn't let me know my place? It sure taught me who makes the rules in this world."

"Is that when you left him?" Paul asked.

She stared at him in disbelief for a long time. "No," she said softly, as if ashamed.

"After that he picked me up and kissed me and held me and was sweet to me for a long time. When he was like that, cuddly and loving, I could forgive him anything."

Paul nodded. "So when he told you he was sorry and asked to be forgiven, you would take him back."

"That's right," she said. "And, a week later, he'd do it all over again." She threw her head back and laughed. "That was like the college education I'd never really had. After a couple of times like that, I got an A in domestic relations 101."

She laughed until the tears drenched her face.

Phyllis brought Polly back to Paul's office that same Saturday morning, just after the guard had led Melanie out and driven her back to the prison ward.

They had arranged for the session with Polly the night before, while they had been together at his apartment. It was the first time they had made love, and it had been a hurried, shy, clumsy affair, but loving and warm nevertheless. Afterwards, when they lay in each other's arms, they both knew that there was much more to what they felt for each other than a physical attraction. The passion was there, yes, but there was so much more.

He explained to her why he needed to see Polly again. He told her how important it was to him to verify what had been told him by both Melanie and Chris. Not that it was important to know which one was lying. They probably both lied. All patients lied. It did not matter, since it was the process that occupied the therapist's interest, not the content of the stories being told. He had visited with Polly perfunctorily two days before the hearing, a brief fifteen-minute conversation to determine the effect of the family tragedy upon the child. What he needed now was to learn more about how the family functioned, how it malfunctioned as a unit.

They had agreed that Phyllis would not wait for Polly, that she would return after an hour or so and fetch the little girl before Melanie was brought back for her afternoon session.

She spoke briefly to Paul when he met them in the waiting room, took his hand, and squeezed it gently, enjoying the return pressure she felt from him, then delivered Polly, with an informal introduction, into his hands and left.

Paul reached out to the little girl and she took his hand in hers.

"Hello, Polly," he said.

She smiled up at him. "Hello, Dr. Murphy."

"It's good to see you again. Let's go into my room and we can visit."

"Okay," she said.

Inside the room, Polly stopped and looked around as if appraising the place for the first time, as if her previous visit had never taken place. She hesitated before choosing a direction. Finally, without Paul's prodding, for he wanted her to feel free to go wherever and do whatever she wished, she settled down on the end of the long leather couch and let her feet dangle over the edge.

He sat in his customary chair and crossed his legs. He looked at her and she smiled very properly at him. All in all, she was very, very proper in her pink dress, black Mary Janes, pink socks turned down on top, and her adult demeanor. She sat upright, head held up and hands folded neatly in her lap.

"Are you comfortable, there?" he asked.

"Yes, thank you," she said. She ran her fingers along the leather arm of the couch. "I like this seat."

"Do you know why I've asked to see you?"

She nodded. "Yes."

"Why do you think?"

"Aunt Phyllis told me," she said, "if I come here, I'll be helping Mommy come home."

"Do you want your mommy to come home?"

"Oh, yes."

"How about your daddy?"

"Oh, yes. Daddy, too." She gazed off and pursed her lips while she thought. "Will you bring them home, Dr. Murphy?"

"I'll try," he said. "But it's not up to me, Polly."

She cocked her head to one side and gazed at him. "So why did I come here?"

"Well," he said, "you can talk to me. Tell me things that bother you if you want to. And, later, I'll bring out some toys and we'll play together."

She watched him and thought about what he was saying.

"People come here all the time," he said, "to tell me how they feel about things. They tell me things they can't tell other people because they know I can keep a secret. And then they feel better after telling me."

"How do they feel better?" she asked.

"I think they feel lighter," he said. "When people have troubles, they feel heavy, and when they tell their troubles to someone, it's like sharing the load."

"What are troubles?" the little girl asked.

He thought for an instant. "Things that worry you," he said.

She shook her head. "I don't understand."

"That's okay."

"That's a grown-up thing. I don't know it."

"What's that, Polly?"

"What you said," she said.

"Why do you say that?"

" 'Cause when I tell someone things that worry me, something bad always happens. Every time I tell, Mommy and Daddy fight. The best thing to do is never tell. I'll never tell again." She looked at him expectantly. "Are you angry?"

"No," he said. "Should I be?"

She shrugged. "I'm not going to tell you anything!"

FIVE

After some time, when it was obvious that Polly had meant what she had said and had no intention of talking to him, he rose and went to the closet, pulling out a huge cardboard box filled to the brim with toys and gadgets of all kinds. He stationed the box on the floor in the middle of the room, being careful not to set it between the two of them where it might be viewed as a barrier, but off to one side where they could both observe it easily. Then he returned to his chair and sat quietly.

All the while, Polly had watched him surreptitiously with great suspicion, but when he turned to her, she had quickly shifted her eyes away toward a far wall as if disinterested. Now, she remained motionless. She focused her attention at a distant point far away from the big receptacle. Periodically, however, she would glance over at Paul and her eyes would yearn to sneak over to the box. But she resisted the temptation, jerking her eyes away swiftly and flinging them back to that distant spot instead.

Finally, she yawned and stretched in a kind of feline gesture and moved her legs against the leather of the couch. "I'm tired of sitting," she said.

He studied her conspicuous avoidance. "Would you like to walk around?" he asked.

She did not respond to him but, after a moment, slid forward till her feet were on the floor and pushed herself upright. She surveyed him cautiously, as if anticipating an impending reprimand. Instead, he smiled at her warmly and nodded his approval. She glanced away fleetingly and took a step away from the couch, a step toward the wall that was farthest from the box.

Paul observed her as she ambled slowly, running her hand along the panelled wall. Her fingernails clicked on each of the joints in the wood. She moved past the door and travelled the second wall all the way to the large windows, which looked out onto the street below. The blinds were closed, and she pulled two strips apart and peeked outside.

She backed slowly away from what she saw, taking very small steps until she bumped into the box and was surprised to have stumbled on it. She turned and looked up at Paul, who was watching her with mild interest. Without raising her hand, she pointed one finger at the box.

"I almost fell," she said, and giggled at her own clumsiness.

He could feel the child's ambivalence as it pulled at her. She wanted so desperately to get her hands into that mysterious container and yet she wanted, equally desperately, to avoid compromising herself with him. She had established her position in their relationship and she would stubbornly hold out no matter what.

"If you want to look into the box," he said kindly, "you may."

She studied his face as if she could read his intentions upon it. He was careful to disclose nothing. He would not gesture. He would not smile. He would not send her any message with his body language. He would give her no excuse to bolt from that box of toys. He bit down hard on his back teeth and controlled his facial muscles with an iron will.

Finally, she dropped to her knees and opened the loose flaps on top of the box. Her mouth fell open when she looked in. She reached a hand inside and touched its inhabitants.

She whispered in awe, "A ball. A doll. Another ball. Crayons. A man doll." She enumerated the items as she rummaged about, pushing some of them aside to better see the others beneath.

"Paints. A car. A truck. Soldiers. A horse." She named off the toys as she touched them carefully, fondling them cautiously with her fingers so as not to allow any to fall out of the box.

He trusted that her desire to remain aloof was deserting her and he decided to press his advantage. "You can take them out if you want," he said.

"Oh, no," she said, as if shocked at his suggestion. "They belong here."

"Well," he said, "Whatever you want. If you want to take them out, you can always put them back later."

She thought for a moment then, hesitantly, reached into the box and began removing the items slowly, reluctantly, placing them in careful order on the carpeted floor. She lingeringly and quite meticulously arranged them into categories: balls all together, cars with cars, dolls with dolls. When she had emptied the carton and all the toys were appropriately organized, she raised her beaming face to him.

"Now they all go back," she said to Paul. She dropped her eyes. "I have to leave soon," she explained to the playthings.

She deposited the balls back into the box, then the soldiers and the cars and the tractor and the blocks, until she had nearly filled the box again and all that remained on the carpet were four of the human dolls. Then she sat back on her legs and stared at the four lonely figures.

She pointed her finger at them. "That's a family," she said to no one in particular.

"Whose family is it?" Paul asked as insignificantly as he could.

"It's just a family. There's a daddy and a mommy and a big sister and a little sister," Polly said.

"Sounds like your family," he said nonchalantly.

She looked at him for a long time, screwed up her mouth, and studied him as if she were reading his thoughts. She turned back to the box, rummaged about, and found a bathing beauty. She laid it down with the others. "That's Aunt Phyllis," she said.

"Now is it your family?"

"No," she said.

"It looks like your family," he said.

"No, it doesn't!"

She reached over, grabbed the male doll by the legs, and flung it against the far wall. She clutched the female and flung it in the other direction. She picked up the baby doll and positioned it on the floor behind her, out of sight. Then she pointed to the two dolls remaining and, in a most serious tone, said, "That's my family."

Polly laughed loudly as she held the daddy doll over the mommy doll and pounded him down on her. Rather than continue to squat, she was sitting on the floor now and had placed the mommy doll on her back on the carpet in front of her and was holding the daddy doll suspended over her, lying on top of her, bouncing up and down on her.

Paul had innocently slid off his chair and was now sitting

on the floor across from her, as if the two of them were playing together, as if he were not an outsider to her fantasy.

"The daddy is making a baby on the mommy," she said gleefully, and she hammered the daddy doll down harder and harder on the other. "This is how you make a baby," she said. She dropped both dolls and turned to look over at him.

"How do you know that?" he said, sounding childlike himself.

"I saw," she said, and put her forefinger up to her pursed lips, warning him not to speak of the secret.

"What did you see?" he whispered.

"I saw my daddy jumping on my mommy and they were making a baby. That's how you make babies." She giggled and slapped her small hand over her mouth.

"When did you see?" he asked like a coconspirator.

"In the night," she said. "I heard them. Making babies is noisy." She nodded to him and grew serious. "I went down to see and I looked in the bedroom." She picked up the mommy doll and held it tenderly. "Mommy was crying. He was hurting her. But he told me."

"Who told you?"

"My daddy told me."

"What did he tell you?"

"He told me he wasn't hurting her. He was making babies." She looked behind her as if insuring privacy. "Daddy was angry at me."

"Why?"

"Because I looked. He told me not to look. He told me if I look, I'll go blind. If I'm a bad girl, I'll go blind, too." She nodded. "And God will hurt my arm again." She dangled her left arm out away from her body as if it were broken and useless.

"How does God hurt your arm?" he asked.

357

"He punishes me. Yes," she said, nodding forcefully, "God hurts my arm and Daddy takes me to the hospital to get it fixed. But God only hurts my arm when I'm a bad girl."

"Who told you that God hurts your arm?"

"Daddy told me," she said firmly. "In the car. He told me. 'Cause I'm a bad girl, and so God hurt my arm. He told me."

"Is that true? Are you a bad girl?"

She looked at him quite seriously and said, "Daddy doesn't lie. Daddy's a policeman. He never lies." She lowered her voice. "Mommy lies. He told me. Mommy lies a lot and that's why God punishes her so much."

"How does God punish your mommy?"

"He gives her black eyes." She giggled and covered her mouth with her hand again. "And he makes her ugly. Makes her face all puffy. Makes her sick so she stays in bed all day." She leaned forward and whispered to him. "And he gives bad mommies the curse."

"The what?" he asked.

She thought for a moment. "The curse," she said.

"What's that?" he asked.

"I don't know," she whispered.

She thought for a moment then, looking philosophical, said, "Mommy and Daddy fight a lot because of God."

"Because of God?" he asked.

"Yes," she said.

"Why because of God?"

" 'Cause mommy lies a lot and God punishes her and gives her bad babies, and bad babies make you fight a lot."

She turned from him, picked up the mommy doll, and raised it high. With her other hand, she shoved the baby doll up between the mommy doll's legs and under the dress.

She screeched with laughter. "Mommy has a bad baby in her tummy."

She threw the mommy doll across the room, wiped her hands on the skirt of her dress, and jumped to her feet.

"I have to go now," she said. And before he could say a word or rise to his feet, she was out the door and into the reception area, where she found Phyllis sitting and waiting.

That afternoon, when Melanie was returned to Murphy's office, she sensed a change in him. She was feeling so much better, she told him, since the morning session. She was feeling lighter, less burdened. Maybe there was something to this therapy stuff, she said. Maybe it did help, after all, to talk about the stuff that people usually keep locked inside.

He told her he agreed with that and was glad she was deriving some benefit from their time together.

She stared at him strangely, as if seeing him for the first time.

"What's wrong?" he asked.

She tilted her head to the side. "There's something different about you," she said. "You seem to be in a bad mood."

"I assure you I'm not," he said. He was not surprised at her perceptiveness. Her episode had stripped away the need for most of the social amenities, and she was seeing and hearing the world around her much more clearly than she had ever seen or heard it before.

"It just seems that way, then." She took her eyes away from him and let him know that if he was not going to expose himself to her, she might not continue to expose herself to him.

"You're angry with me," he said.

"No," she said without looking at him. "I'm just not in the mood to talk."

He watched her depriving him and was reminded of her daughter, who had used the same technique to demonstrate her pique. Of course, he told himself, it made sense that they would both be deprivers. The child had to learn it somewhere. Where better than in the home? The cycle of deprivation, he told himself. An old rule. Deprivers produce deprivers who produce deprivers who produce deprivers and so on, till the end of time. How to break the cycle; that would be the problem of the therapist who eventually received Melanie as a patient.

He sighed. "You think I'm holding out on you."

"No," she said. "I think you found out something terrible about me and you don't like me anymore."

"Why would you think that?" he asked.

She turned to him then and there was fear in her eyes. "That's the first thing that ever comes into my mind," she said. "When someone doesn't seem just right to me, I always think they're hating me because I must've done something terrible."

He nodded. "You're so used to feeling guilty, it's second nature to you now."

"It's been that way all my life," Melanie said. "As far back as I can remember, I was feeling guilty." She turned and sat sideways in the deep chair. Her legs were crossed and her foot dangled loosely.

"What about, mostly?"

She hesitated. "I guess about being so bad."

"Were you bad?" he asked.

"Oh, sure," she said. "I was very bad when I was a girl."

"In what ways were you bad?"

She laughed nervously. "I wouldn't eat. I used to make

my mother crazy at the dinner table. I'd shut my mouth tight and refuse to open it. I just wouldn't eat."

"Why was that? Do you remember?"

"I don't know," she said. She looked off and tried to think. "I hated her cooking, I think. I remember that I would eat certain things, but I wouldn't eat others."

"Do you remember how you made the distinction?"

"Let's see." She put the tip of her finger in her mouth and bit down gently on it. "I wouldn't eat lamb, I remember that. And I wouldn't eat salad. I hated fresh vegetables."

She dropped her eyes to her hands clasped in her lap. "Those are the things my father loved most. No, that's not true. He hated lamb, too. No. Those are the things he tried hardest to get me to eat. He used to beg me till he got red in the face. After a while, he'd lose patience and get angry and give up on me. Then he'd send me away from the table, to my room or something, and I remember feeling victorious, like I had won something. Anyway, the harder he tried, the more obstinate I became." Some tears fell onto her hands clasped in her lap. "See? I told you I was bad."

The roots of the passive-aggressive style, Paul thought, lie very deep. Melanie, as a very young child, had learned the power of passive resistance. She had learned how easily she could frustrate her parents with the simple unwillingness to comply. And she had learned how gratifying it was to observe others being frustrated and having no recourse. That was power! Melanie knew it then. And her present helplessness proved that she still knew it.

"How else were you bad?" he asked.

She thought for a moment. "There were so many ways. I don't know. It feels to me like I was always being scolded." She hesitated and corrected herself. "Not scolded. More like corrected. As though I was wrong so often and had to be corrected. That's what it was. I wasn't able to do things right. Or, I purposely did them wrong. Maybe that's why I remember being bad. I can remember in grade school how angry my parents got when the teachers sent notes home about my homework. They would scream and yell as if it were the end of the world."

"What about your homework?"

She laughed. "Oh, I was a forgetful kid, I guess. And I was always losing it, misplacing it, or something. I don't know. I just couldn't keep track of it." She laughed again. "And, boy, did I get scolded."

"Who did the scolding?" he asked.

"Oh, Daddy did," she said. "Daddy was the boss. He did the punishing and he did the disciplining." She grew nostalgic. "He had a way of scolding you that was devastating. He could just look at you disapprovingly and you would wilt. No doubt about it. Daddy was the big cheese."

"What did your mother do while you were being corrected?"

She laughed and then suddenly grew serious. "She cheered him on. I can see it like it was yesterday. I'm sitting at the table. My mouth is pressed tightly shut. Tears are rolling down my face. My father's scolding me, really tearing into me and threatening me. He's going to send me to bed without any supper every night for a week. And Mother is saying, 'Yes, that's good, good for her. She deserves it, give it to her.' "

Melanie stopped and looked up at the ceiling. Her face was contorted with rage. "Oh, Mother," she screamed, "you took such pleasure out of me being punished." She dropped her eyes to Murphy's face and locked her eyes onto his. "She loved to see him punish me. I loved him so much. I don't understand it. My mother was only happy when he wasn't loving me back. She'd get this big grin on her face and just have the best old time watching him reject me."

She turned and laid her cheek against the leather back of the chair. Slowly at first, she started to cry. Then, as the pain took greater hold of her, she wept more deeply. Her sobs racked her body and tears flooded down her face.

When Paul had calmed her, had risked touching her, and had held her as though she were an infant, letting her cry upon his shoulder, Melanie accepted the cup of hot tea he offered her and, holding it cupped in both hands, stared at him gratefully. She sipped at the hot liquid gently, just touching the tea to her lips and pulling the cup away quickly before scalding herself.

They talked about how accustomed she had become as a child to being wrong, to needing correction or instruction. They talked about how that training established for her the belief that she could not survive on her own, that there were just too many obstacles in life for an inadequate person like herself to overcome.

She was able to unite that insight with the recognition that if her husband had not already been a corrector when she found him, she quickly would have aided him in becoming one. She began to see how she created herself in the image of a victim for him, presented herself to him to be victimized, to be sacrificed for his own gratification.

She sighed and shook her head at Murphy as she recalled the twists and turns their marriage had taken.

"He started bringing home thin little paper books about the sexual revolution," she said. "He thought I was repressed sexually and he wanted to liberate me. He said to me that I was sexually uptight and that made me a boring partner. He said he wanted me to be free and wild and experiment with him." She laughed at the indignity of it.

"I said I didn't want to do that. Then he was insistent. And he was very persuasive when he wanted to be.

"He said it wasn't so much that I didn't know anything about sex as it was my attitude. He said I had an unhealthy attitude about sex. At first, I didn't know what he meant by that. I thought maybe he thought that I looked at sex like it was dirty. But that's not true. That was never true. I never think of sex as dirty. But that wasn't what he meant, either. He meant that I think that sex is for having babies, and if you're not trying to have a baby, you shouldn't be doing it. That's what he meant about my attitude. So I said to him, 'That's not true.' and he said so how come I don't want to do it with him so often. And I said that he didn't understand, that I can't turn it on and off like a faucet. Just because he wants it at that moment doesn't mean that I can want it at the same moment. So he said, 'Bullshit.' If I had a healthy attitude toward sex, I'd want it just as much as he wants it and we'd be doing it all the time."

"How did you feel about all of that?" Paul asked.

She scowled. "I felt like shit. But that was nothing. That was only the beginning. Pretty soon, he started finding new ways to do it. Not new ways, I don't mean new ways. I mean new positions. I guess they weren't so new, either, but they were new to me. He had me bending over the back of a chair. Had me sitting on him, then sideways sitting on him. Then, like almost upside down. Oh, all kinds of ways. I'm too embarrassed to tell about them all—even to you and you're my doctor—so you can imagine how raunchy they got. I don't know, maybe I do have an unhealthy attitude about sex. I don't know anymore." She shook her head resignedly.

"All of a sudden, he gets it into his head that what our sex life needs is pain." She nodded at Murphy and grinned at the silliness of it. "He must've picked that up in the

364

locker room. It's so goddamned macho, it sounds like something his drunken buddies would talk about."

She leaned back and folded her arms across her chest. "He says, all of a sudden, that pain is exciting. He says he wants to tie me up and do pain to me. He says not a lot of pain. Just a little pain. Not enough to draw blood or anything, he says. 'But enough to make it real exciting. I said, 'Are you crazy? How can pain be exciting?' He looks at me like I'm stupid and he says he doesn't know why either, it just is. And he's looking at me like I'm stupid.

"And I said to him, 'How come pain is exciting to you if I'm feeling it? Why don't you hurt yourself if you're into pain so much? Why do you have to hurt me?' I said. You know what he said?"

She paused and waited for Murphy to reply. When he nodded, she continued. "You'll never believe it. He said pain turns him on only when someone like me who's not into it is feeling it. Then it turns him on. It's nothing if the person feeling it is into it. Then it's masochism. Then it's sick. Can you believe that? How stupid he thought I was?"

Paul spoke softly. "Did you do it?"

She turned her face away from him. She bit her lip and resisted the tears that arose in her eyes. She nodded her acquiescence. "I kept giving in to him because I wanted to keep some peace in the house. I began to really worry about Polly, because she'd be hearing all this anger from him. He'd want me to strip right after dinner, and I'd tell him there was a time and place and what if Polly walked into the bedroom in the middle. And he'd start to scream, 'Fuck the kid, fuck the goddamned kid. Why does everything in my life have to revolve around that goddamned kid?' "

She shook her head sadly. "If we didn't have the kid, he'd say, we could be living the life of Riley. So I was really worried about Polly. I didn't want her to hear all that and think that she was unwanted, because that's not true. She wasn't unwanted. I always wanted her.

"But I stopped being so accommodating after a while. A little before I got pregnant with Denny. We had a big fight and I figured that's it. I don't have to take so much. There are limits. I don't know. Even I had my limits.

"He had a new idea one night. But he was smart this time. He didn't tell me the idea in advance. He waited to spring it on me at a time when I couldn't do anything about it.

"He'd been sweet to me most of the evening. You know, fixed me a cola while we were watching TV and talked to me like he thought I was really interested, told me about his day. He never did that, so I should've guessed that it was a special occasion. When we got into bed, he was very loving, very sweet. He held me for a long time and talked to me and he rubbed my hair and did those little romantic things that I like. And pretty soon I was ready. Boy, was I ready."

Melanie had wrapped her arms around herself and was rocking slowly back and forth. "I was thinking if he'd do it this way all the time, we'd have a great sex life. I hadn't been that ready in a long time.

"I pulled him on top of me and usually he'd argue about the position, but he didn't say a word. He got inside me and he was terrific. He was ready and he'd waited for me to be ready and it was perfect. He moved just right for me. Long and slow. It was loving like people, not violent like animals. I thought to myself, Tonight is my night, this is my night, tonight's for me."

She suddenly stopped rocking. And her voice escalated until she began to sound as she had just a few days before, when he had first met her. "And, all of a sudden, he stopped and he pulled himself out. I said, 'What's wrong? Don't stop,' I said. 'What's wrong?' And he jumped up and sat on my chest. Oh God, it's hard to tell you about this. God, I'm so ashamed. He sat on my chest and finished all over my face, on my mouth, in my nose, even in my eyes.

"I screamed at him, 'How could you do that?' I was so angry I could kill. And I screamed, 'How could you do that?' And he sàid it was wonderful. It was the best sex he'd ever had, he said. And I said it was disgusting. He laughed at me and told me about my unhealthy attitude. I said, 'Fuck my attitude! That was degrading and humiliating.' "

She stopped and lowered her voice. "And he said, 'Of course. That's the whole point.' "

Paul had planned to take Phyllis to a fine restaurant for dinner that night, but after spending a full day with the agonies of Melanie and Polly, he was not up to it. He felt somewhat guilty but had no trouble begging off after explaining his weariness to her. She agreed that they should go directly to his place instead, where together they cut up a fresh salad and he made some garlic toast and opened a bottle of Chianti.

He needed an easy evening, he told her. To reaffirm those traditional values that he used to believe in so fervently, he revealed. He needed to spend time with her that could not be considered hard work. He did not want to watch his manners, or be polite, or eat correctly. He could not handle the restaurant dating scene. He wanted to let it all down and be unguarded with someone, and he could not think of anyone he was more willing to trust at this time than her. She used that vulnerable moment to tell him that she loved him, really loved him, and wanted them to be defenseless with each other.

She compelled him to sit back after dinner and, moving around behind him, gently rubbed his temples. He closed his eyes and relaxed under her soothing, loving fingers as they massaged his anxiety away, as they permitted his body to shed the stiffness of his discomfort and experience the physical sensations her touch was provoking. Soon, he reached up, took hold of her arm, and moved her around in front of him again. He pulled her down onto his lap and kissed her with a sad kind of desperation.

"Loving you is so simple," he whispered to her. "Why is it that so many of us make it complicated? Is it because we don't trust things that are easy? Maybe we can't tolerate uncomplicated love because it doesn't hurt enough? Is that what our parents did to us? Did they teach us not to trust unconditional loving? Always to be suspicious? Expect the devious? Damn! What a world Melanie lived in."

Phyllis put her fingers to his lips and tried to stop him. "No more," she said. "Let's put it away for tonight. Let's just take care of each other."

She unbuttoned her blouse and slipped his hand in to rest on her breast. "I like it when you hold my breast," she said.

He leaned over and kissed her gently. He felt her quickened breath against his cheek. He rose and lifted her up in his arms. She felt weightless as he carried her into the bedroom, where they made love while she talked to him. As they moved together, felt each other rise and lower to each other's rhythms, mixed their anguished breath as their mouths searched each other's out, she spoke to him. She told him about her love for him, the intensity of her feeling for him, the bewildered hunger that drove her toward him.

When it was over they lay together, in each other's arms, and stroked each other's bodies with small, gentle motions of their fingertips. He lay silently, enjoying the texture of her, and perceived himself as so incredibly lucky to be there with her. And yet he felt so terribly anguished for Chris and Melanie, who had allowed themselves to lose by resolving to discover remnants of their faded intimacy only in the act of inflicting grief and misery upon each other.

SIX

In the morning, Sunday morning, in his office once again, feeling the pressure to conclude sitting across from Melanie, he marvelled at how refreshed she looked. His own weariness had not deserted him, had lingered on, so much so that he had had to crawl out of bed and had been barely successful in dragging himself into the shower upon waking. Shaving, at best a distasteful task on most days, had been an excessively difficult chore this morning. He had dressed lethargically and had driven indifferently into work, miserably accompanied by a dark, inexplicable dread rather than an excited anticipation.

Surely, in the years of his scrupulous listening, Paul had heard tales of horror equal to, and in some cases much worse than, Melanie's. Surely, as a trained, objective attender, he was adequately guarded against the kind of effect he was experiencing now, the discouraged lethargy that weakened his spirit. But it was not Melanie's legend that impacted upon him so treacherously, however; it was something much more rooted in his own internal experience. It was the doubt that had begun to prey upon his mind, the unbending belief in her innocence that had suddenly begun to falter, the awareness that the Wyatt family had charged full speed toward the kind of tragedy that had taken the infant's life. All this jolted Paul, leaving him so devoid of energy.

Melanie, however, appeared bright and clean and charged with stamina, as if the mantle of her illness had been lifted from her shoulders in one swift motion by some unseen hand, as if their sessions together had siphoned off much of her melancholy and left tiny glimmers of hopefulness in its stead.

He could not help but observe that as weary as he felt, that was how chipper she appeared. Ironically, they were both bearing the effects of their work together simultaneously and in equal proportion, almost as if Melanie were transferring her depression to Paul and drawing from him energy and joy. He chided himself that he was allowing his fantasies to borrow too much from Oscar Wilde, that there was no actual resemblance between them and the portrait of Dorian Grey.

She had shed her hospital robe and sat comfortably now in only the thin cotton prison dress, similar to the one she had worn when he had first seen her. Her cracked and chipped nails had been filed somewhat and were less rough and jagged. Her hair, combed back tightly and pinned into a ponytail, shone brightly and demonstrated the effects of long brushing. He could finally discern fragments of her former beauty.

She had entered the room eagerly, anxious to commence, impatient to engage him once again. Without waiting for his lead, she plunged into remembrances of her childhood. Animatedly, like a bird newly winging, her hand fluttered as she spoke, her eyes sprinted about, her breath was short and rapid with the excitement of epiphanous discovery. She dredged to the surface certain matters she had long ago put to rest, matters she had embedded deep within herself like little sickly bullets lodged too closely to essential organs to be probed for and removed.

"It was a whirlwind," she said, her eyes flashing with the titillation of the memory. "We met that last year in high school and fell in love, and no one, not anybody, was going to tell us we couldn't make it. We knew we could."

"When you say *anybody,* you mean your parents tried to stop you?" Paul asked.

"Oh, boy, did they ever! My father!" She wagged her head and her ponytail flapped. "But it didn't matter. Our minds were made up. Even my friend Phyllis tried to stop us. You know, usually, friends back you up on things like that. But Phyllis just hated Chris. She thought he was the worst dork. We almost stopped being friends over that, but finally she was my maid of honor, anyway."

"You started to say something about your father," he reminded her.

She paused and thought. "Oh, yeah! He never let me forget it. It was the worst damned thing in his life, he always said afterwards. He had big hopes for me, he used to tell me. You could've fooled me. He never told me about any big plans till after it was too late. College, a career, he used to say. But I don't remember him pushing me to school. I always thought he didn't care. But marrying Chris was like putting a knife into his heart, he used to say. He'd make this sad, down-turned face, like it really pained him, and he'd say I had robbed him of his last few good years."

She laughed and shook her head. "My father had the neatest way of making you feel lower than a bug. He was really good at it."

"Well, let's see," Paul said. "He was opposed to your marriage, but you did it anyway?"

"Yes."

"That was pretty assertive, wasn't it?"

"I used to think so," she said. "But I know better now. I was just being rebellious, like with dinner. The more Daddy said don't, the more I said I will."

"You wanted to hurt him," he said.

"Oh, yes. I wanted to hurt him like he hurt me."

"How did he hurt you?"

"He couldn't love me. That's how he hurt me. He didn't know how to love me. He thought telling me what to do was loving me. Fixing me all the time was loving me. Criticizing me all the time was loving me."

A vibrant stream of vigorous energy passed through her, causing her to shudder slightly as if a sudden cold wind had touched her skin.

"So you wanted to hurt him back?"

"You bet I did!"

"Marrying Chris did it, didn't it?"

"Oh, yes!" she said adamantly.

Paul paused and softened his voice, his eyes. "What else did marrying Chris do?"

She smiled at him and flipped one limp-wristed hand in the air. "It got me out of the house, if that's what you mean. I really wanted that. I can't tell you how much."

"Yes. That, too. What else?" he asked.

She stared at him and a slow, superior grin spread across her face. Then she said. "Of course. I know what you're getting at."

"Oh? What's that?" he challenged.

She laughed softly and blinked at him. Without him realizing it, she had slipped into a seductive posture and she seemed to be flirting with him now. "I can read your mind, Doctor."

"Oh?"

"Certainly." She wet her lips with the tip of her tongue. "You want me to say that marrying Chris got me punished

373

as well. You want to get me to admit that I'm self-destructive."

"Are you?"

"That's what you want me to say," she said coyly.

"Is it?" he asked. "How do you know that?"

She threw her head back and laughed, but her voice contained no sincerity. "I told you. I can read your mind."

"I doubt that," he said.

"I know exactly what you're thinking," she said. "I told you. I can read your thoughts."

Melanie's blind projection of the devastating fear of her own self-destructiveness made it safe for her, he knew, to talk about. As long as she could attribute her most frightening feelings to him, she could observe those feelings at least somewhat without admitting that they had any significant claim on her. He did not want to remove that safety factor. He did not want to remove the sense of permission, of protection, that beaming her feelings onto him lent her, but he did want to edge her toward recognizing her own terror and allowing herself to feel it without repercussions.

"Perhaps what you think you're reading," he said, "are your own thoughts which you're attributing to me."

She laughed loudly, gleefully, clapped her hands, and wagged an accusatory finger at him. "See. I told you I can read your mind. I knew you were going to say that."

Just as instantaneously as she had swung up, Melanie's mood crashed and she turned depressed and despondent. She insisted that she was not self-destructive, that under no circumstances could she be blamed for the direction of her life. She persisted in blaming her husband Chris and rattled off a litany of offenses, which sounded as though it had been memorized meticulously over the years.

"Then there was the time he raped me," she recounted. "Well, I think of it now as a rape. At the time, I thought it wasn't rape because I believed he had the right to my body. I used to really believe that. Can you imagine? I guess that's the way I was brought up, to believe that way. Now, today, he wouldn't get away with it."

"Wouldn't he?" Paul challenged her. "What would you do about it?"

"What would I do?" she asked. "I'd call the police and file charges against him. Today, wife abuse is a crime, isn't it?"

Paul nodded. "Technically, it's been a crime for a long time."

"But I still think that maybe I brought it on myself. I know, in my head, that that's not true. But in my heart I feel like I punished him too much and brought it all on myself. Maybe I shouldn't have refused him for so long. I'll bet it was six months that I didn't let him touch me. I pushed him away every time. Sometimes, I went into the other room and slept on the couch. I must've had two periods a month for those six months." She laughed at herself. "And I had more headaches than a hotel full of boxers."

Quickly, the laughter faded from her lips as she recalled the details of what she referred to as her rape. She slipped down in the chair so that the back of her head rested on the leather seat and her legs reached far out onto the floor.

Chris Wyatt had come home late again, although sober, that night. She had searched for some sign of drunkenness about him, smelling him, his breath, his clothing, and was surprised that no alcohol odor could be detected. She sensed some different aroma about him, however. Something. It was indistinct and difficult for her to distinguish. But it was something. Something unpleasant to her. He watched her sniff around him and grinned down at her.

When he saw that she was content he had not been drinking, he went to the refrigerator and popped open a can of Coke. He eyed her from the kitchen, then strutted, like a stalking cat, past her to Polly's room, where he thrust his head in the door and whispered a silly hello to the child.

She heard Polly squeal with delight when he entered her room and closed the door behind him. She knew he would sit on the edge of the bed and tell her fairy tales and bedtime stories, all of which starred cops and robbers rather than rabbits and wolves. That was one of his favorite things to do with her, to translate ancient tales into modern terms, into streetwise terms. Hunters wore uniforms and wise men were all detectives and anything that moved on wheels was a black and white.

Melanie could hear them laughing together through the bedroom door and she grew envious. She was jealous of him whenever he decided to give Polly a modicum of time. She gave the child all her time and all her energy, and yet when he came home and gave Polly ten minutes, the child was so grateful she could not get over it for days.

Melanie undressed quickly and threw on a pair of heavy flannel pajamas, thinking that there was nothing sexy about flannel pajamas and she would not give him the wrong idea if she played it safe and stayed as unsexy as she could. Somehow, she still believed that she was the culprit who was seducing him, turning him on and driving him mad with passion, so that he became cruel to her because of her leading him on. She could hear him saying things to her like, "If you're not willing to sell, don't advertise the goods," and, "If you don't want it, don't strut it around."

By the time he entered their bedroom, she was in bed with the covers pulled all the way up and tucked under her chin. He moved to the side of the bed and stood over her, looking down at her while she pretended to be asleep, a huge malicious grin on his face.

"Move over!" he demanded.

She kept her eyes shut tightly and did not respond.

"Move your ass!" he said. "I'm coming to bed and I don't want to walk around."

Without a word, Melanie slid over to the far side of the bed, her eyes still pressed tightly shut. She could hear Chris moving around the room as he pulled his clothes off. She could hear the articles of clothing hitting the floor as he dropped them, one by one, where he stood.

When he was naked, he walked around to the far side of the bed and crawled over her, moving very slowly and leaning all his weight on her, and then she smelled it. Then, without his clothing guarding it, she recognized the odor. She smelled its rich pungency and was repelled by it. The smell of a woman, of a woman's fluids all over him as if he had smeared himself with her juices, wafted off him and filled her nostrils. The smell of someone else's sexuality insulted her. He stunk from the wetness of her.

"Get out of my bed, you pig," she said to him, pulling her legs up and cringing back against the headboard.

Chris laughed at her. He laid back naked, exposed, and laughed at her. He knew that he stunk from a woman, and all the while that he was stinking from her, he was enjoying Melanie's excruciating discomfort, her aching realization that he was acquiring his corporeal satisfactions elsewhere. As much as she despised him, everything about him, she desperately wanted him longing for her. For some reason, it infuriated her that he could lust after other women. She dreaded his sexual advances, abhorred his wandering fingers primitively exploring between her legs, but still required his celibacy, his abstinence, his bitter chastity.

Losing control of herself, she sat up and pounded on him.

She beat on him, with diminutive fists, as hard as she could and screamed hysterically at him. "Get out of my bed, you bastard," she shouted. "You filthy animal!" She attempted to scratch at his eyes but he blocked her intended blows. "Ugh! I hate you, you piece of garbage."

He merely laughed at her. "You don't know what's good," he said. "You might as well bronze it for all the good it's going to do you." He grabbed the fleshy part of her thigh, inside her leg, and pinched a handful of it between his fingers, squeezing it and kneading it like a loaf of raw dough.

She cried out in pain. "God! That hurts."

"Of course, it does," he said, and grinned at her. "Can't you take a joke?"

"Get the hell out of here," she moaned. "You make me sick."

He scrutinized her and all traces of his smile disappeared. Without another word, he pulled her legs down and flattened her out on the bed. He climbed up on her and straddled her as though her abdomen were a saddle, pressing his knees to her arms to pin them down tightly so that she could not swing at him, struggle, or break away from him. Then, he commenced to slap her repeatedly, using his hand like a paintbrush, swinging in broad, wide strokes, right to left, catching each cheek as his hand brush swept by, again and again, until she was dizzy from the pain and constant motion. When he sensed that any idea of resisting further had departed from her, he stopped, perspiration dripping from his face, and reached over and pulled her mouth open.

"Taste her!" he demanded viciously. He endeavored to stuff his bulging, pulsating penis into her mouth. "Taste her!" he continued to shout at her. And Melanie, paralyzed from the neck down, able to move only her head, dodged him, flinging her head from side to side and bouncing her cheeks off the tear-stained pillow. All the while, Chris continued to demand and press upon her and stuff himself up against her face, her lips, her teeth.

"Come on and taste her, you bitch."

Suddenly, she stopped struggling, abandoned the battle, and gazed up at his ferocious face. "I'll bite it off, you son of a bitch."

Something in her voice warned Chris. He stopped moving also and, wet penis in his fist, considered her, cocked his head, and studied her, as if endeavoring to decide if she meant it, if she really would bite it off. What he saw in her eyes helped him decide not to take the chance. Instead, he flipped her over on her stomach and jammed himself into her.

The pain he caused her was excruciating, but she was hating him so much at the moment that it actually felt good. She remembered in fine detail the lectures he used to deliver to her about people who were into pain, and for a brief moment, like the quick cut of a scalpel, she understood what he had been trying to tell her.

She turned her face away from Murphy and chewed at her lower lip. "That was the night," she said.

"What night?" Paul asked.

"The night I got pregnant with Denny."

Melanie became impatient with Paul immediately after that, as if she regretted her disclosure, lamented the exposure of one of her darkest and sorest memories. Paul would have interpreted for her that what she labelled as impatience was in essence anger, but he was hoping she would make that connection by herself. He knew that if he were to point it out to her, she would merely deny it in her usual fashion and then, being on guard against his watchfulness, would alter her behavior accordingly and he would lose the advantage, the foothold he had gained into her unconscious. But when he pressed her on the matter of concern for Polly's welfare, she almost exploded at him.

"That's a dumb question," Melanie snapped, getting closer to real anger than she had before. "Of course, I was afraid for her. I was terrified for her. I'd lie awake nights agonizing over what to do about her."

"But you didn't do anything to protect her," Paul said, just a touch of accusation in his voice.

"Of course, I did!" she said.

He challenged her. "What did you do?"

She became sarcastic. "When? I mean, which time? You can't just ask a question like that." She sneered at him, shifted in her chair, then sobered. "I was scared for her for most of her life."

"At the beginning?" he asked. "What about at the beginning?"

She smiled humorlessly. "At the beginning I made a joke of it. Tried to laugh it off."

"Did that work for you?"

She stared at him, then dropped her eyes. "No," she whispered.

"What?"

"I said no!"

"Oh!"

"Then I started getting in between the two of them, sort of using myself as a buffer. She was very little then, so it didn't matter. She was only a baby and didn't understand what was going on, anyway."

"All right!" he said. "But what happened when she got older?"

"Then it got worse." She nodded. "When he'd go at her, she couldn't understand what he wanted from her. I started arguing with him on her behalf, but he didn't give a damn what I'd say. He'd go on torturing her, teasing her until she'd burst out into tears, and then he'd laugh at her. When she'd start crying like that sometimes, I'd beg him to stop."

"Did he?"

"No."

"Did it get worse?"

"Yes." Her eyes snapped to his face. "How did you know that?" She hesitated and gazed at him appreciatively. "Every time I came to her defense, he'd do it more. He'd pour it on and get more vicious and more cruel. After a while, I realized that he was doing it to both of us at the same time that way."

Paul nodded. "You say that after a while you realized what he was doing. What did you do after this realization?" he asked.

A look of bitterness crossed her face. "After the first time he hurt her or before?"

"You tell me," he said.

"After he started hurting her, I realized she was in real danger. I told her to be an exceptionally good girl when she was around him. I told her to do everything he said. Not to argue with him. To be respectful and courteous and never, never contradict him. I told her never to say no to him."

"Did she do all that?"

"Yes."

"Did it help?"

"No."

"Why not?"

She laughed. "He didn't need her to participate for him to be cruel. He knew she loved him and he used that to hurt her. Even if she said yes to everything, he'd find reasons to punish her. He was always criticizing her. There was no way she could please him."

"Does that sound familiar?"

"What do you mean?"

"Does that sound like someone else you know?"

"You mean me and my father?"

"Yes," he said.

"No," she said. "You don't understand. I was bad. I deserved to be punished. Polly was never bad. She never deserved it. That's a big difference. The two aren't alike at all. And, besides, my mother let it happen. She enjoyed it. I didn't let it happen." She stared at him wide-eyed. "Did I?"

"You tried to stop it," he said.

"Yes."

"By telling her to be good."

"Yes."

"But that didn't work."

"No."

"What else did you do?"

She shook her head. "Nothing."

"Why not?"

"I knew I was going to leave him."

"When?"

"Eventually."

"But you had another baby with him," he said.

"That's true."

"You feared for your first child, but you had another, anyway," he said. "Why did you do that?"

"What could I do?" she asked helplessly.

"An abortion?"

"No!"

"Why not?"

"Just, no!"

"Religious beliefs?"

She laughed. "No."

"Then why not?"

382

"I—I don't know." She became agitated and began to chew at one of her poorly filed nails.

Though his voice remained soft, low, his comments struck her like deadly arrows. "You wanted the child," he said.

She nodded. "Yes."

"So badly you'd subject it to his treatment?" he asked.

"I wanted the child."

"After seeing what Polly went through, you wanted the child?"

She turned away from him. "No," she said softly.

"No, what?"

"No. I didn't want the child." She spoke below a whisper.

"I can't hear you," he said.

"I said," she shouted, "no. I didn't want the child, goddamn you!"

"Then why did you have it?"

"Because he didn't want it."

Her eyes were riveted on him and slowly the tears came. Soon she was weeping deeply, sobs racking her body. She reached out her hand to him and he took it. Neither of them left the chair but their fingers remained fastened together for a long time.

When she finally looked up again, he noted that she seemed relieved, her face having softened. She took a deep breath and smiled weakly at him. He rose then, moved to his desk, and brought her a box of tissues. She nodded her thanks and wiped the remaining tears from her cheeks.

"We can break now," he said. "Get some lunch. Take a rest."

She shook her head. "Not yet. I want to get it out. It's like half in and half out. I want to get it all out."

He understood. "Okay."

She resumed haltingly. "One day he came home in the middle of the day, while Polly was at school, and surprised

383

me. I was in my third or fourth month by then, I don't remember which. That whole period of time is fuzzy in my memory. It was a hard pregnancy. There wasn't any real joy in it. I thought I wanted the baby but I knew he didn't, and I kind of half dreaded bringing her into a world where she wasn't really wanted. I can't think of anything worse to do to a child.

"We had a big fight that afternoon, the biggest we'd ever had. Over the baby. He still wanted me to have an abortion. By this time it was too late, of course. Too dangerous, and I wouldn't hear of it. But he'd found a guy, he said, who was supposed to be terrific and he could do it. This guy, he said, told him that all that shit about third month or fourth month being too late was Catholic propaganda, bullshit from the right-to-life weirdos, and he could do it for us with no problem at all.

"I didn't even want to discuss it. I told him it wasn't his life his friend was putting in danger. It was mine, and I wasn't about to do it. He said, the fuck I wasn't. I told him it was my body and I would say who touched it and who didn't. And I certainly had the right to say who'd cut it, didn't I? 'What if you started bleeding,' he said, 'what would you do then?' 'But I'm not bleeding,' I said, 'so I don't care about that.' And I told him I don't want to play 'what if' with him. All I wanted was to protect my baby and myself. He got really angry then. 'What about me?' he started screaming. 'Don't I count?' He called me a selfish bitch, always thinking about myself first, never thinking about him. Just me and my goddamned kids.

"He came after me with his fists, but I ducked and ran out of the room and locked myself in the bathroom. I was very afraid of him by that time. He'd hit me plenty and he'd done some real damage to Polly. You know about that. With the hospital and all. In Nevada. He was banging away at the door and screaming for me to let him in. When that didn't work, he promised to be good to me, told me he was sorry and promised that he wouldn't hurt me. I heard him crying on the other side of the door and I felt so guilty. I don't know why. I just did."

Her eyes pleaded with Murphy to understand. "He could beat on me and my children and torture us and humiliate us, but if I made him sad, I felt like I was being the most terrible human being on the face of the earth." She shrugged her shoulders and looked like a lost child.

"I felt so bad. I came out of the bathroom thinking I'd make it up to him and he was waiting for me with another idea. He grabbed me and threw me on the floor. He had a metal coat hanger in one hand and with the other he pulled my skirt up and over my head. All I could see in my mind was that metal hanger being shoved up me, sticking into my baby, killing it, maybe killing me. That's all I could see.

"I started screaming. I never screamed like that in my life. I know half the neighborhood heard me. I was screaming my head off. He got scared and he let me up. I don't know why he did that. He could've hit me, knocked me out, he could've killed me if he wanted to. But he didn't. He let me up. I got up and he was standing there in front of me, shushing me, telling me to stop screaming, holding his hands out to me, begging me to keep quiet. I think he would've promised me anything then. But I didn't want anything from him. I hated him so much. I reached back and kicked him in the groin, and when I ran out of the house he was rolling on the floor, groaning and holding his balls with both hands."

"Is that when you separated?" Paul asked.

"Yes," she said. "I took Polly and we stayed at Phyllis's place that night. And the next day, while he was at work, I packed up all his stuff. I don't mean I packed it neatly. I

385

was too angry for that. I picked it up and stuffed it into things and threw it all our on the lawn. The front of the house was covered with his clothing, his golf clubs, his tennis racket, all his stuff."

"You were taking a big risk. You had made an important decision."

"Yes," she said, "and I meant to stick by it."

"Were you frightened?" Paul asked.

She laughed. "Was I? I knew who I was dealing with."

"What did he do? Did he retaliate?"

"Oh, when he came home he had a fit. He saw all that stuff on the front lawn and he went crazy. But I'd known he'd do that, so I had my friend Phyllis over to stay with me and give me protection. He wouldn't do anything to me while a stranger was around to be a witness. And he knew how Phyllis hated him for the way he treated me. She'd love to be a witness against him in court. He knew that.

"He begged for a while, just like he'd used to, promised everything he could think of to get back in, but I'd had it with him. By that time, I knew I had to get rid of him for my own survival. I wouldn't listen to him. I shut my ears. I knew he was cursing me after a while, but I covered my ears.

"The last thing I remember about him is his standing out on the lawn in the middle of the night screaming to me on the inside that if it weren't for that goddamned baby in my belly everything would be all right between us, that all I wanted out of life was to bring babies into the world to be between us, to make us grow further and further apart. It was awful. He said that baby ought to die in my stomach, that I deserved that, that it was the perfect death for me, on the operating table, trying to save a dying baby and sacrificing the mother at the same time."

She clasped her hands in front of her, in her lap, and faced Paul with a calm but angry exterior. It was the first time he had seen a relatively normal person surfacing through her malfunctioning exterior.

"I never saw him again," she said. "I talked to him on the telephone a few times, but I got sick every time I heard his voice. The thought of his touch made my flesh crawl, so how could I ever take him back? Just the memory of the suffering he caused me and my children was enough for me to push him out of my mind and consider him dead and buried. Actually, that's close to what I did. I think I lived the life of a widow from then on. It was a choice, you see. In my mind I had to make the choice. Either he was dead, or I was."

She unclasped her hands and held them out supplicatingly, as if to indicate that her story was over. There was a finality about her. She seemed to have run out of words suddenly. Her eyes were bright and strong, but clearly there was nothing further she wanted to say on that subject.

Paul remained seated, thoughtful and contemplative, for a long time after Melanie had left to be returned to her hospital cell.

During his break, Paul called Doyle at home. He waited on the line for several rings while Doyle debated whether or not to take his call. Finally, she lifted the receiver. "Doyle!" she snapped.

"Hi," he said. He felt apologetic.

"Hi," she answered.

"I guess I owe you one," he said.

"One?" she said. "Are you kidding? I can't count how many you owe me."

"I did what I thought was right," he said. "That's what you told me to do, isn't it?"

There was a long silence on the phone. "All right!" she

finally said. "I'll buy that, no matter how misguided I think you are." Her voice softened. "How's it coming?"

"She's really opened up a lot," he said. "Actually, it's like floodgates. She can't stop."

"Well, that's good, isn't it? It'll help her feel better about herself, won't it?"

"I hope so," Paul said.

"I'm dying to ask if you've learned anything new," she said, "but I don't know if I want to give you the satisfaction."

"Look, Doyle, I know I disappointed you," he said, "but we both still have the same goal in mind. What I did, I did for Melanie Wyatt. I bought myself some more time, which I really needed. And so did Melanie, for that matter."

Doyle relaxed and withdrew some of the hardness from her voice. "Okay, Doc," she said, "truce."

"Thanks."

"Don't mention it."

"Thanks, anyway."

She laughed. "Now, I can ask."

He laughed with her. "I thought you never would."

"So, I'm asking," she said.

Paul grew serious. "I think you should reconsider the husband. I think of the two or three people involved in this case, he's the most likely candidate."

"What do you mean?" Doyle asked.

"He's certainly capable. The guy presents a deep-seated hostility that borders on rage. He's seething inside. If anyone in that family could kill, he's the one. He's hair trigger. Sure, he's a good actor and seems to be broken up over the loss of his kid, but most psychopaths are good actors. They can charm your pants off, sell you the Brooklyn Bridge if they want. But underneath, there is no conscience, no feelings of remorse, ever."

Doyle, pensive, hesitated before responding, then said, "He's a hard sell, Doc. I've been over him with a fine-tooth comb. He's not clean, but there's no evidence at all tying him to the crime. Your suspicion just isn't enough." She sighed deeply. "The real problem is Melanie. And I know where you're coming from, Doc. I like her, too. But, when you get right down to it, to the very bottom of it, we both know, don't we, that she's the one? We both know that, don't we, Doc?"

"I don't want to believe that," he said.

"I know."

"Doyle, if you only knew what I know about her. If you could hear the kind of life she had with him, you would understand."

"I do understand. I'm not faulting you. I wish we could pull it off."

"Isn't there anything we can do?" he asked.

Doyle sat back and raised her shoeless feet to the top of her desk. "You know there is."

"What?"

"Give me grounds. Give me an insanity plea," she said.

He was silent for a long moment. When he finally spoke, his voice was rough with emotion. "You know, Doyle, if she did it—and I'm not totally prepared to admit to that yet—there's only one reason, only one motivation she could have had." Doyle pushed an unlit cigarette into her mouth and waited and listened. "If she believed that she was saving her child from a life of pain and misery, if she was convinced that she couldn't adequately protect the child from Chris's abuses, then she might've acted out."

"But he was out of the house," Doyle said.

"That wouldn't matter," Paul replied. "If, in her troubled mind, she was convinced that he could get at them, that he would be able to continue to torture them, including the new child, whom he hated passionately, she could somehow perceive that ending the life earlier would, in reality, be saving the infant. She could've thought of it as a service. She could've been rescuing her baby. She could've done that, Doyle. She could've twisted it all around."

"That would be pretty crazy, wouldn't it?" Doyle asked.

"That might be more than enough crazy, Doyle," he said.

Doyle sighed, "But how do I get her to say that, Doc?"

"I don't know," Paul said sadly. "Maybe she'll do it on her own. Maybe she'll offer it by herself."

"When are you seeing her again?" Doyle asked.

Paul glanced at his watch. "I'm seeing Polly again in half an hour. Maybe I'll see Melanie after that."

"Will you call me later?"

He nodded.

"Doc," she asked, "will you call me after?"

"Yes," he said.

"No matter what?"

"No matter what," he said, and he was troubled that somehow he had lost Melanie—and himself—to the reality of the system.

SEVEN

He left Polly alone in the reception area for a moment and took Phyllis into his office first. As soon as the door had closed, Paul took her in his arms and held her close to him. He pressed his cheek to her hair, closed his eyes, and leaned his chin on her shoulder.

"What's the matter?" she whispered.

"I need some TLC," he said. "It's been a tough day."

She stroked the back of his neck with her cool fingers. "You want to tell me about it?"

"I can't," he said. "I want to, but I can't."

"Because you don't want me to know about Melanie?"

He shook his head. "Because I don't want you to know about me."

She pulled away from him. "I know everything there is to know about you, my love," she said. "There is nothing I could find out that could change how I feel about you."

He smiled at her. "I know that."

"I hope so," she said.

However, he thought, he could alter how he felt about himself. The manipulation he intended to perpetrate upon

Melanie weighed on him heavily, represented a compromise he would not have believed he was capable of fashioning.

"You said to me once," he said, "that Melanie had changed, that she wasn't the Melanie you had known since you were girls."

She nodded. "That's right."

"That night," he said, "she could've been the Melanie you don't know, couldn't she? She could've been the new Melanie you don't recognize. That's the one who might be capable of drowning her baby."

An instant of fear crossed Phyllis's face. "What are you telling me? Are you saying that you now believe she did it?"

"I don't know," he said agonizingly. "I don't know what I believe. Maybe I'm trying too desperately to find some way out for her. Maybe I want to rescue her too much."

Phyllis moved back close to him. She reached up and held his face lovingly between her two hands. "Don't," she said. "Don't rescue her. Don't find her a way out. Just do what you're supposed to do. Do it the best you can, and what happens will happen. No matter what that is, I will never hold it against you. I will never think that you could've done something for my friend and didn't." She kissed him lightly. "I would rather know that you abided by your principles. I love you and respect you, and you don't have to do anything special for me to keep it that way."

She kissed him passionately then, hungrily, and after she had gone and he was in the treatment room alone with Polly, it took him several minutes before he could get the feel and smell of her out of his mind.

Polly, seated on the floor again, the family of dolls spread out between her legs, laughed loudly as she held the daddy doll over the mommy doll as she had once before and hammered him down on her even more violently. She had lowered the mommy doll on her back again and was holding the daddy on top of her, lying flat on her, grinding away on her.

"The daddy is making another baby," she said, and brought the daddy doll down harder on the other. "It's the way you make a baby."

"You told me that before, Polly," he said.

She smiled and wrinkled up her nose. "I know," she said.

Paul was struck by how closely the child was recreating the earlier game, recreating that earlier experience. He was intrigued by the obvious fact that Polly wanted to share with him her attitudes about the relationship between her mother and her father, her perception of to what degree violence played a part in intimate relationships.

"You want to tell me about it again?"

She nodded. "My daddy jumps on my mommy and they make babies. I saw them in the night."

Continuing to grind the dolls together, she spoke more to them than to Paul. "Yes," she said, "in the night." She spoke through tightly clenched teeth, a redness appearing on her pale skin, a blush as if ashamed, as if enraged. "I heard them. Making babies. Mommy crying. Daddy blowing, like a big fish. Crying. Crying. All the time, making babies."

Polly brought the embracing dolls to her face and rubbed them tenderly against her flushed cheeks as if to cool her fevered countenance, as if to enlist in their exclusive loving party.

"Don't cry, Mommy," she cooed. "Don't cry, little Mommy. Daddy doesn't mean to hurt you. He's giving you another baby. He doesn't mean to hurt you." She separated the mommy doll and cradled it lovingly. "Don't cry, Mommy. He's not hurting you. He told me."

"Your daddy told you, Polly?" Paul whispered.

"Yes," she said, not looking at him. "My daddy told me."

"He told you he wasn't hurting your mommy?"

She nodded. "He told me he wasn't hurting her. He was making a baby." She glanced behind her to insure not being overheard. "Damn baby," she said.

"Why do you say that, Polly?" Paul asked.

"That's what babies are. Babies are damned." She glared at Paul. "Damn! Damn! Damn!" she said repeatedly.

"You're angry at the baby?" Paul asked.

Polly seemed to ignore him. After a long moment of silence, during which she lowered the entwined dolls to her lap, she spoke softly. "Daddy was angry at me."

"Why?"

"Because I saw." She glanced at him angrily. "I told you. I looked. I wasn't supposed to look. I could go blind if I was a bad girl." She smiled at the two dolls, and her fingers prodded and poked them with a vengeance. "And God will hurt Mommy again."

"How does God hurt your mommy, Polly?" he asked.

"God punishes her and gives her bad babies, and bad babies make you sick. Bad babies spoil everything."

She turned furious eyes to him, picked up the mommy doll, and held it high. With her free hand, she rammed the baby doll up between the mommy doll's legs and under her dress in another reproduction of her mother's pregnancy.

Polly slapped down with her open hand onto the pregnant mommy doll. "Bad baby," she said as she spanked the doll's stomach. "Bad baby."

She stood the daddy doll up, walked him over to the reclining mommy doll, and had him kick her in the stomach again and again. "Bad baby," she said in a deep daddy voice. "Bad baby."

"Daddy wants to kill the bad baby," she said to Paul.

"What does that mean, Polly? To kill?"

"Daddy wants to make the bad baby go away."

"How does he do that?"

"He puts bad baby in the trunk of his car, and when he drives away, bad baby goes, too."

"Is that killing?" he asked carefully, startled by the direction she was taking.

"Yes," she said.

"Did you see Daddy do that?" he asked. He wondered if the child could be the witness they had all wished for.

"No."

"What did you see?" he asked urgently.

"See? Here?" Polly asked, and she lifted the mommy doll. "Mommy loves the bad baby. Mommy won't let Daddy take the bad baby in the car."

"Why do you call her bad baby?"

" 'Cause Daddy said. Mommy lied and God gave Mommy a bad baby in her stomach."

"Was Denny a bad baby?"

"Denny's a bad baby," she said, nodding vigorously.

"What makes her bad?" he asked.

"God made her bad to punish Mommy."

She picked up the mommy doll, and taking the arm into her fingers, she bent it to stroke the doll's stomach. "Good baby," she cooed. "Good baby."

"The bad baby is now a good baby," he said.

"Yes," she said.

"How can that be?"

She looked at him with wonder. "She's both," she said.

"How?"

She thought and then her eyes lighted. "She's Daddy's bad baby and Mommy's good baby."

"I see," he said.

"Daddy wants to take her away and Mommy wants to keep her." She looked over at him and her face wore a worried expression. "Mommy loves the good baby so much. Mommy hugs the good baby. Mommy kisses the good baby.

395

Mommy wants to keep the good baby and won't let Daddy take her away."

"What does Polly want?" he asked.

She looked down at the floor. She raised the mommy doll in one hand and the daddy doll in the other, and brought them together face to face. She put their mouths together and wrapped their arms around each other. She pulled the baby doll out from under the skirt and dropped it at her side. Then she turned and looked up at Paul Murphy.

"You want the family together again?" he asked.

She looked back at the dolls and then up at him again. She seemed confused. She reached for the baby doll and then withdrew her hand. She dropped the embracing mommy and daddy dolls onto the floor and moved back from them.

Suddenly, she reached out and gathered up all three dolls into her open hands. She threw all three dolls high into the air, letting them each fall in a different part of the room, and wiped her hands on her skirt. Almost immediately she was on her feet, dashing about the room retrieving the thrown dolls. "I'm sorry," she said to herself. "I'm sorry. I'm sorry."

She returned to her spot on the floor and arranged the dolls all around her. The mommy doll lay to the left of her and the daddy doll to the right of her. Between her knees and in front of her she set the baby doll and a new doll, pulled from the toy box, which she named the Polly doll.

Paul sat forward anxiously in his chair. Was it possible, he wondered excitedly, that the child had been awake that night? Was it possible that she had seen what happened? Could she have watched it all happen? Could she have actually observed the murderer ridding the Wyatt family of the bad baby? She claimed to know nothing. But that would be her conscious mind expressing itself, he thought. Was she informing him, through her play, that she knew everything, that she knew exactly what had happened because she had seen it?

He regarded her carefully as she ritualistically moved the dolls about, trying to create working relationships. She grew more and more frustrated as it did not seem to work for her. The mommy doll and the baby doll left the Polly doll out, and the Polly doll and the daddy doll left the mommy doll out. The combination she resisted the greatest was all four dolls together, as if she understood that Denny was never coming back. When she put the mommy doll and the daddy doll and the Polly doll together she seemed happy, but that also seemed to challenge her understanding of her own reality and she soon grew sad.

As she moved the dolls around on the floor, she became more agitated. She looked to Paul for some kind of help, but he was helpless himself. She turned and looked back at the couch, as if longing to turn time back and be sitting there again free of this worrisome problem. Paul wished he could assist her. He wanted to guide her back to that night, to help her articulate what she had seen that night, to help her break loose of her bonds of duty and fear and guilt and allow her to pour out her terrifying recollections.

He could feel the frustration emanating from the child. Imbedded deeply in Polly was the need to please her father, to win him back into the family, to insure that she was a good girl by not betraying him. Paul grew even more excited as he imagined what visions the child could describe, as he visualized the child's experience rising to the surface and rescuing her mother from prison. Guiltily, he felt some sense of pleasure at the flashing thought of Chris Wyatt receiving what he so much deserved.

Paul wanted to urge her on. "Go on, Polly," he said. "Show me."

She gazed up at Paul and her petrified doe eyes pleaded

with him. Her little hands pulled unconsciously at the front of her dress, tugging at the dainty pink material.

Finally, she climbed to her knees, her eyes continuing to plead with him. For what? he wondered. Clearly, she was afraid to continue. Did she want him to stop her? She reached out and brought the baby doll up to her face. She stared at it for a long time, then began to ravenously bite and chew on it. She bit its limbs, its arms and legs, and she bit its buttocks. She chewed on her empty mouth, grinding her back teeth ferociously as if she were consuming the doll's flesh, and swallowed noisily to complete the pantomime.

She jumped to her feet and rushed to his desk. She pulled the brown plastic wastebasket out from behind it and dragged it into the middle of the room. She stood over it, looking down into it. She wet her lips with her tongue in the same fashion that her mother constantly did and rubbed her stomach gently with her free hand. With the other hand, she dropped the baby doll headfirst into the waste basket. She raised it up, holding it by its feet, and plunged it in several times. Again and again, almost as if washing it, as if drowning it. Then she turned and, hiking up the skirt of her dress, sat on the wastebasket as if it were a toilet into which she was passing the digested remains of the baby doll.

Ceremoniously, she stood, smoothed the front of her dress, and walked back to the couch, climbing up and sitting back as she had earlier. She straightened her skirt, pulled it over her knees and, clasping her hands in her lap, looked up at him and smiled.

Stunned, Paul had watched the performance, had experienced his own epiphany, and now his mind raced like a rocket. Suddenly, what was so dark and secret and hidden seemed so clear and obvious. Polly had wanted the family together again, and in order to do that, she would have to rid the family of Denny, the bad baby who her father did not want and had left the house, Polly believed, to escape. On the other hand, she wanted her mother's love as well and was envious of the increasing attention Denny got from her mother and knew how her mother would suffer without Denny.

What she needed to do, Paul finally realized, was to capture the essence of Denny and keep it and yet rid the family of the person of Denny that was a disrupting influence. In the child's mind, that was done by putting Denny—the quality of Denny—into herself by symbolically eating her, and then eliminating the person of Denny by defecating her out again and flushing her down the toilet. The toilet. She had drowned Denny in the toilet bowl headfirst, held by the ankles. No need to dry the body. No need to fill a tub. Nothing to cover up. Nothing to hide.

EIGHT

A week later, after the murder charge had been dropped and Melanie had been released, Phyllis brought her to Paul's office that last time. Phyllis remained in the car. She did not want to come up, did not want to be part of this last meeting. Paul was grateful to her for that. He, too, wanted the time for just him and Melanie. He knew that what he and Melanie had discovered together, in this perfectly protected, permissive room, might be lost without some sense of closure, some movement toward health that Melanie could carry away with her, with which to start over somewhere with someone, perhaps a dedicated therapist.

It had taken several days for Melanie to recover from the announcement that Polly had freed her. Being released from custody and returning home to the silent house afforded her little pleasure when she thought of Polly—frightened, alone, isolated in the Youth Authority facility. And, though Phyllis stayed with her, functioning for the mother much as she had for the child, Melanie remained detached, apart, remote.

When she could finally lift herself somewhat from her intense depression, she agreed to meet with Murphy once again. Actually, though she feared him—or feared what she suspected was his power over her—she anxiously anticipated the confrontational encounter. Her ambivalence toward him, that indistinct mixture of love and hate uniquely felt for the therapist, was the most intense feeling she could identify. The rest of her seemed so dead, so cold and wasted.

At first, Paul refused to talk about Polly. He, rather, wanted Melanie to scrutinize her own behavior. He wanted her to understand what role she had actually played in the overture to the Wyatt family tragedy. He wanted to break through the wall of passive incompetence she had erected to protect herself from the daily consequences of living.

"Surely," he said to her, "you could see how her father was affecting Polly. How could you not see that he was damaging your child?"

"That's easy for you to say," Melanie defended herself. "You have the benefit of hindsight. I wasn't looking for anything, so how could I spot it?"

"How about her teachers?" he asked. "Didn't they see that she was getting depressed or something?"

"Well, yes. That's true. Her teachers told me that she was withdrawing a lot in class. They called her reticent."

"What did you think of that?"

"That was earlier, before Denny was born. I thought she was reacting to me being pregnant."

"Well, that's a problem, isn't it?"

"Yes. I guess so," she said.

"Did you think it would just go away?"

"I don't know what I thought. I thought she'd outgrow it. I thought it was like a stage and she'd grow right through it." Once again, she shrugged helplessly.

"Anything else about school?" he asked.

She looked away. "Yes."

"What?"

"Her grades."

401

"They went down?" he asked.

"Yes."

"Had she been a good student?"

"Oh, yes."

"What happened?"

"She started to fail. In everything. She forgot how to add two numbers."

"What did Chris say about that?"

"He had a field day," she said. "He badgered her constantly about it."

"Did that help?"

"No."

"What happened?"

"Her work got worse. She stopped doing her homework. Started losing her papers." Melanie gasped. "Like I used to do."

"Yet you say you didn't notice any change in her," he said.

"I didn't!" she protested. "At home she was exactly the same. She was joyful and happy. She never gave us any problems. I told you."

"How did she handle her father's abuse?"

"The same."

"The same?"

She thought for a moment. "Well, actually it got better."

"What did?"

"Chris got better with her. Now that I think about it, it was better for her at home."

"To what do you attribute that?"

"I don't know. But now that I think back, I remember that she acted much more loving toward him during that period. And he was less critical of her. He scolded her about her schoolwork, but the rest stopped. The meaningless ridicule, I mean." She seemed to drift off into her private thoughts for a moment. "There was another change in Polly," she said. "I must've noticed it because I remember it now. But I didn't do anything about it."

"What was that?" he asked.

"He stopped attacking Polly, but he started attacking me more. He wanted me to give up the baby. He was angry that I wouldn't. He criticized me all the time. He scolded me and attacked me without a rest."

"What was the change in Polly?"

She put her hand up to her throat and her eyes grew sad. "She started taking his side." She could barely get the words out. "I remember her smiling face while he was cursing me. My God! It was like my mother. Polly was enjoying Chris devastating me. She was with him against me. She turned on me, her own mother."

"Why do you think she did that?"

"She wanted to cuddle up to him. We were on opposite sides and she chose him."

"Why do you think she did that?"

"Playing it safe?" she guessed.

"Why would she do that?"

She stared at him and the anger drifted from her face. "Because I told her to," she said. "That's what I taught her to do, isn't it?"

"Is it?"

"Yes. I trained her just like I was trained." She looked away and grew pensive. Paul allowed her the time and space to think about what she had just said.

Finally, he said, "What about her attitude toward the baby?"

"What do you mean?" Melanie asked.

"Did she love the baby?"

"Yes!" Melanie snapped. "No," she said almost immediately. "It wasn't love. It was more like curiosity."

403

"Did she play with her?"

"Yes. Like a child plays with a doll. Not like two children play together."

"Of course," he said. "The baby was too small."

"And she talked to her like Denny was a doll."

"What do you mean?"

She hesitated, then put her thoughts together. "She gave Denny different identities. One time she'd talk to her as if she were Denny. Another time she'd talk to her as if she were me. I think I'm saying that right. It's hard. Sometimes I'd overhear her playing house with Denny while she was asleep. I thought it was so cute. She'd talk to the baby and tell her all the gossip of the day."

"What kind of gossip?"

"Oh, things that'd happened to her at school. Things in the house."

"Chris was gone by then?"

"Yes. She'd talk about him, too. She'd tell the baby, 'I talked to Daddy today.' Things like that."

"Did that worry you?"

"No."

"Was Polly angry about her father being gone?"

"Yes."

"Was she angry with the baby?"

"I don't think so," she said.

"What reason did she think Chris had for leaving?"

She laughed. "It didn't matter what I'd tell her. She heard us fighting all the time. She knew we didn't get along."

"You hadn't gotten along for a long time," he said.

"That's true."

"So how did you explain his leaving?"

"I didn't."

"You left it to her imagination?" he asked.

"No," she said. "I got my friend Phyllis to do it."

404

"What did your friend tell her?"

"She explained about divorce, that sometimes people get tired of living together and want to make a change, you know. She told her that it didn't mean they didn't love the children. It just meant that they didn't love each other anymore."

"Do you think Polly believed her?"

"I don't see why not."

"Polly could hear what you were fighting about, couldn't she?"

"Yes. I guess so."

"What do you think she heard?"

"You mean fighting about having the baby?"

"Is that what she heard?"

"Yes."

"You see," he said. "All married people fight over their kids once in a while. The kids hear that. They know that. Don't you think?"

"Yes," she said.

"What else did she know?"

She stared at him. "She knew that her father was a drunk. She knew he hurt her three different times. She knew that I threw him out. She saw that. She knew that I was miserable. She saw me cry enough." She stopped and looked off.

"What else?"

"She knew her father didn't want that baby. I heard her once tell the baby that Daddy didn't want her." She turned back to him. "Do you think that she wanted the baby gone to please her daddy? To get him back?"

"What do you think?"

Her shoulders sagged and she looked pitiful. "I think I almost aborted myself half a dozen times just to appease him. Each time I managed to stop myself at the last minute.

But something inside me compels me to appease men. It's like that's the story of my life and I can't change it."

"You can," he said.

"I have to."

"You will," he said.

"Oh, God," she said. "Just let me save Polly."

"You first have to save yourself," he said.

She stiffened and gazed at him with anger in her eyes, but she knew he was right. Suddenly, she relaxed and said, "I suspected it was Polly right off, you know, but I wasn't sure. I knew for certain when my lawyer told me that there were human bite marks on the body. I knew it then because Chris used to bite Polly like that out of love. He'd say, "You're so delicious I could eat you up." When my lawyer told me, I knew for sure. What I didn't understand was why. But the bites helped with that, too. Her love was all mixed up with her rage. Just like mine."

"If you knew all that, why did you confess?" he asked.

She pondered his question for a moment. "Well, I wasn't going to let this world take both of my children, was I? I mean, what kind of mother would that make me?"

Then she smiled at him. "And then you came into it and I really hated you. Another man to push me and shove me and make me do things I didn't want to do. I knew you were dangerous. You could make me tell the truth. I know all about you shrinks. You get into a person's head and figure things out. I didn't want you to expose me and I knew you would. I felt that you cared about me and because of that you'd want to save me and you could do it, but if you saved me, I'd have to sacrifice my little girl. That was a bad place you put me."

"I didn't mean to do that," Paul said.

"You know, I've thought about this. I think it was you and what I was afraid you could do that made me crazy. I don't remember thinking that at the time, but I thought it afterwards, when I started seeing a little again. I kept thinking, If I'm crazy, he'll work on me but he won't trust anything I say. I don't know if that was a crazy thought or if that was a smart thought that made me become crazy. You know what I mean?"

He nodded. "Yes, Melanie. I know exactly what you mean."

"Anyway, I'm glad about you. I shouldn't have been afraid of you, because you wouldn't hurt me. You couldn't hurt me, anyway. Chris really couldn't hurt me, either, except that I let him. I guess I'm my own worst enemy. I guess I was raised that way. And I can see how I passed that on to Polly. Poor Polly. I have a lot to make up for, don't I? But I'll do it. I have faith in myself. Wherever we end up, I know one thing for sure. It can't be as bad as where we just came from.

"And I'm grateful to you, really. I don't hate you anymore. I won't ever forget you, I'm pretty sure of that. I'm even positive that we'll see each other again. Sometime. Don't you think so? I'm sure of it."

EPILOGUE

Paul Murphy pressed his nose up against the huge window and for an instant felt an odd mixture of childhood excitement and adult pride surge through him. The nurse, on the other side of the glass, her nose and mouth covered with a filtering mask, lifted the tiny infant out of the crib and held her up, cradled in her caring arms, for display to the new father.

Paul examined his daughter, as much as he could see of her, seeking some facial resemblance to his wife, but the tiny face offered no clues as to whose genes would be dominant in this child of their creation. He studied her thin, wispy vulnerability, her soft, uncoordinated fragility, and chuckled to himself, under his breath, at the thought of being able to care for such a gentle, susceptible entity.

For one of the few times in the past five years, since the last time he had seen her, his thoughts flashed to Melanie Wyatt and her children, and the smile of pleasure faded from his lips as if the recollection of that experience could somehow taint his newly born child. The memory did, however, suddenly remind him of the dangers of parenting that lay ahead for him and for Phyllis.

Standing in the hospital hallway, staring at his first child, he recalled that last day in Judge Barret's chamber when Doyle had faced Taggert, the irate D.A., and Barret the jurist, who had just told her that the State would not buy that an eight-year-old child could do her little sister in like that.

Doyle had stood before them, nostrils flaring like an enraged bull preparing to charge. With her hands on her hips, almost begging for a fight, she had leaned over the judicial desk and had unwaveringly argued her position.

She had pointed a charged finger at Taggert. "The reason the prosecutor won't buy my story, Judge, is because he represents our society and our society has a vested interest in putting Melanie Wyatt in prison. Otherwise, we'd have to admit that her little girl did something terrible to her baby sister, and God forbid we do that. But the idea that she's emotionally able can't be questioned anymore. Kids kill other kids all the time all over the world. Most of the time by accident. But many times on purpose. You don't like to hear that, Judge, do you?"

Barret had frowned. He had glanced over at Paul Murphy and shook his head in disbelief.

"But it's true," Doyle had said. "It's frighteningly true. But it's in society's interest to protect the belief that kids can't premeditate, at least not consciously. That's why every incident that hits the papers is called an accident. Hell, we want to believe that most people are basically good, and if we're not good when we're children . . . when, then? It's only after we've been corrupted by the environment that we go bad, right?"

She had turned her attention to Taggert and had flung the question at him. "Right?" she had repeated.

Taggert had shrugged. He was not about to get into a philosophical argument with her when she was on a roll. He felt comfortable that the judge would take care of that for him.

"That's an important idea for us," Doyle had continued. "Without it, we might give up trying to better ourselves and our world. As long as we believe that we're not basically destructive, we can be less pessimistic about our future, we can continue to struggle to be better.

"Every time a child makes a murderous attempt on the life of a sibling it escapes the attention of doctors, and teachers, and mental health professionals who believe that the kid had no intention of killing. At least, that's what we all want to believe.

"Your Honor, we've all been taught that children are our greatest asset and they have to be nurtured, and we all agree with that, but the extreme of that is that they can do no wrong. And that's a fallacy. And they want us to believe in the fallacy, because they also believe that the kinds of crime, of murder, committed in a society tell us what kind of society we have. And only a corrupt society, we believe, can produce tiny assassins. The idea that a small child can take another life is so foreign to our concept of the innocence of youth that we want to reject it. We have trouble recognizing angry, violent feelings in children, and by denying that they have these feelings, we adults can avoid recognizing those very uncomfortable feelings in ourselves.

"The fact is that crimes committed by children provoke a sense of horror in our adult world and we reject the idea. Even crusty old broads like me, we have trouble, because the idea of murder in general causes anxiety in me and an unconscious withdrawal from the subject. We won't even keep records of murders committed by children."

Judge Barret had cleared his throat. "That's all very interesting, Counselor, but I don't see how any of it applies here."

Doyle had pleaded. "Your Honor, what I'm saying is that there are enough shadows on the evidence now, all of which is circumstantial, anyway, to make us rethink what we heard at the preliminary hearing. Don't make an obviously innocent person stand trial. What a terrible ordeal for a person to go through, and especially terrible when it's unjustified. The only crime Melanie Wyatt committed was to confess to a crime she didn't commit. The idea that our children's behavior reflects on us was so ingrained in her that she was afraid to acknowledge her daughter injured her baby. She knew the truth but was unwilling to tell it. She was willing to allow herself to be convicted because she couldn't acknowledge, publicly or privately, that her child had committed the ultimate offense against society. God! Give her some credit! If there's anyone truly guilty of a crime here, it's our society, for contributing to the kind of conditioning that can produce a Melanie Wyatt, millions of Melanie Wyatts, all willingly participating as subservient, second-class citizens. Jesus, passing it on to their children."

Barret, obviously moved, had turned to Taggert questioningly. The district attorney had gazed back at him. "You know," he had said, "this is going to be a very tough case to prosecute." He had smiled weakly at the judge. "Besides, if they throw the kid situation into the defense, it's going to make all the papers and it'll become scandalous and we'll be damaging that little girl's life."

Doyle had nodded enthusiastically. "There are no winners here, Your Honor. It's a no-win situation. Let's give everybody a break."

"I have no desire to prosecute Melanie Wyatt at this time, Your Honor," Taggert had said.

"All right," Barret had said thoughtfully. "Let me think about it for a while and I'll tell you what I'm going to do."

A week later, Judge Barret submitted his recommendation, which set Melanie Wyatt free and allowed her to relocate to Florida with her child. But Paul had always tended to believe it had been Doyle's mystic persuasiveness that had motivated Taggert to drop the charges and the judge to free them both. And Doyle had always maintained it had been Paul's inappropriate testimony at the competency hearing that had bought them all the time they needed for the truth to surface. In addition, she had given Paul full credit for being the best detective on the case, a thought she had announced in Barret's presence and which had caused the judge to scowl at Paul and pout unhappily.

Doyle went on to negotiate a release for Polly, with the stipulation that the child would enter into psychiatric treatment, preferably in another state. Clearly, the California courts had no desire to try an eight-year-old girl for murder, anyway.

And Doyle, who had friends there, arranged living quarters in southern Florida for Melanie and Polly, got Melanie a job, found a therapist for Polly, and even advanced them some money to get started. They moved to Florida almost immediately after Polly's release. Melanie did not even bother to sell the house. On Doyle's insistence, she left that chore for Phyllis, who sold it rather rapidly and split the proceeds in two, giving half to Chris and sending half off to Melanie in Florida. It did not really matter. There was not that much left after legal fees and taxes and what all.

A few months later, at about the same time that the Wyatt divorce became final, rumors and gossip about his behavior became so exaggerated and caused him so much shame and embarrassment that Christopher Wyatt sought out therapy with Paul Murphy. Paul, believing he could not be effective with Chris because of their previous experience together, referred him to a colleague who, after a short time, con-

413

fessed to Paul that Wyatt had never hooked into therapy and had eventually just drifted away.

Paul had met him only one more time after that. It was in the hallway in the courthouse. They had seen each other approaching from separate directions and both had wanted to avoid the other, but they were trapped by walls without an exit. They stopped and shook hands awkwardly and talked for a moment. Paul tried to avoid the subject of Melanie and the case, but it seemed inevitable that Chris would get into it.

"You know," he finally said to Paul, "there's no way a kid of mine could do something like that to her little sister if she'd had a normal mother. I don't know how I lived with her so long and didn't see how crazy she was." He looked at Paul and smiled weakly. "I guess it's true." He shook his head. "Love is blind."

About a year later, Paul learned that Chris had left the city police and moved up north, where he joined the Highway Patrol. Paul heard that Chris had achieved a high station in the state police, had soon married again, and was expecting another child.

Doyle and Paul lost touch for a while, though they could have become close friends, perhaps even too close, he sometimes thought, when he remembered how sexy she was. Doyle seemed to drift out of the practice of criminal law and everyone who knew her agreed it was a terrible loss, both to the system and to the community. She rarely came out into the social scene except for some very special event—and it had to be very special. The rumor even circulated that she had begun to drink too much. But Paul never believed that. She did appear at Paul's wedding, though, after a two year absence. She even wore a tight black backless evening gown, which accentuated her magnificent body as it had rarely been exhibited before.

Paul had hugged her affectionately when she arrived and she, with both hands holding his face still, kissed him full on the lips. He marveled at the ambiguity of her; the sexy, exciting lady who could argue one minute like a British Parliamentarian and the next like a career sailor.

At about the same time, Paul heard that Melanie had gone back to school, to the University of Florida, and that Polly was doing very well in a special school for disturbed children. The therapist Doyle had found for her down there seemed to relate extremely well to Polly and the child was responding positively to treatment. He heard that Melanie was majoring in Psychology, with the ambition to become a marriage and family counselor herself. Paul liked that idea and moved about feeling very proud and self-satisfied for a couple of days.

Judge Barret continued to invite Paul to lunch in the judge's dining room once a month and the psychologist invariably found himself at Barret's table. However, three years after the disposition of the Wyatt case, the old judge suffered a mild heart attack and stepped down from the bench. It was not long after that that he was replaced by a younger man, a more aggressive man who demanded, as jurists do, definitive, precise responses to questions of nebulous human behavior. Barret was pretty well forgotten.

Paul managed to remember him, though, and arranged a regular chess game with him, at his home, every Tuesday afternoon just before dinner. They would play chess and argue about the unfortunate imprecision of the science/art of psychology. Sometimes, the new Mrs. Murphy would join them after the game and the four of them, the Murphys and the Barrets, would have dinner together.

Finally, just a year ago, Phyllis and Paul figured they knew enough about life to make good parents and they planned their own family. They signed a secret contract with each other, stating that they would not require perfection from each other, that they had permission to be angry with each other when it was appropriate, and that neither one was compelled to please the other all of the time. They developed a very open relationship in which there were no secrets, in which they were always honest with each other, in which lying was forbidden and quite unnecessary.

Staring at his infant daughter, Paul thought that the only secret he had never shared with Phyllis was that no matter how she dressed, no matter how much clothing was draped over her, no matter how bundled up she might be, he always envisioned her as a bathing beauty in a two-piece bikini, just the way Polly, sitting on his office floor cradling the almost-naked doll, had identified her.